The Glassblower

Morgan True Blum

The Glassblower

Dear Reader,

As silly as this may seem I would like to take a moment to issue a safety warning concerning some information in this book. The following story features a popular urban myth from my home town colloquially known as the Goat Man, or the Pope Lick Monster. Over the years several people have attempted to climb atop the Pope Lick trestle in search of the Goat Man, endangering their lives. The issue is serious enough that the Norfolk Southern Railroad felt the need to release a statement after a local movie was made about the legend in 1988. Unfortunately, that has not stopped thrill-seekers from traversing the bridge, and in 2016 a young mother died after being hit by an oncoming train. I therefore implore you, reader, to please not be tempted to explore the trestle after reading *The Glassblower*. It is not worth it, and you're not going to get to Voiler by jumping off of it, I promise.

Happy reading,
Morgan True Blum

The Glassblower

Prologue

It was Samael's long-held belief that the devil had it easy when it came to luring souls into eternal condemnation, for human beings constantly condemned themselves. Not only did this make the job easy, but it was also amusing. More often than not a man's virtue was the very vice which did him in. Even steel could be warped and perverted. Things given as a force for good were always so easy to corrupt. Conviction becomes wrath, chastity turns to pride, and love? Love was the most dangerous of them all. Love could make anything permissible. Ah, the beauty of human nature.

It was this very principle that came to mind when Samael searched through the box of paints excavated from Evangeline's studio, which had been lifted during the Land Lock when the kingdom was abandoned. At the time, searching through stolen boxes had seemed a hopeless endeavor. It was hardly the first time he'd scoured the artifacts in search of information about Evangeline's enchanted mirror. The former Queen of Ursa had crafted her looking glass thirty-five years ago. Its power had enabled the dying woman to preserve her soul in the manifestation of the Firebird. It was the Firebird that had brought her grandson, Pasha Chevalsky, to Voiler—the world where magic continued to thrive. Magic was, in a way, what Samael sought to cleanse Voiler of. Likewise it was now what Pasha was fighting most to protect.

With Pasha's arrival into Voiler, he could take back the throne Samael had stewarded all these years. Until the Firebird had appeared, Samael was sure the line of Northstars was dead. After all, he'd seen to it himself. It was he who had orchestrated the assassination of the King and the first seven princes. And in the end, it was he who had manipulated the youngest prince, Bruin, into breaking the alliance with Karkinos.

He should've known better than to believe the headlines all those years ago that Evangeline's infant daughter had died shortly after the mother. It was too convenient. And now Samael stood to lose everything. His power would reach only as far as his own miserable country of Draco. It would extend no more than their pitiful chain of horned mountains. That is, unless he stopped Pasha. Unless Samael found a flaw in the legality to prevent Pasha from ascending the throne, the kingdom of Ursa would slip from his grasp.

Unaccustomed to being outsmarted, Samael had collected an arsenal of unfavorable publicity to rely on. Yet he feared attacking Pasha's character wasn't enough.

The thought circulated through his mind as he stood amongst the crates of Evangeline's belongings in the library of Apophis Manor. His most trusted servant lingered nearby, as always.

"This may come as a surprise to you, Xylophis," Samael pressed his fingers to his chin, "but I actually prefer doing things legally. I'm certainly not above resorting to tools such as blackmail or bribery. But corruption often leaves a trail. We must present innocence," here he stopped to pour a decanter of fresh human blood into his wine glass, "even when there is none." He tipped it to his lips. "In the meantime we must also focus our efforts on collecting the shards of that bloody looking glass. Now that Staccato knows of the fragments' power, it's only a matter of time before the resistance figures out what it's for and starts looking for the pieces. It is imperative that we beat them to it."

"But, Your Majesty," began Xylophis, a hint of confusion in his voice, "if Evangeline really did manage to create the mirror Amnos, the looking glass spoken of legend, then shouldn't we have reason to fear it?"

Samael snickered and shook his head. "Oh, Xylophis, haven't you learned by now? There is very little in this world that is incorruptible. Where's your resourcefulness? When handled properly most anything can be used to one's advantage. Amnos is a weapon of great power. And what is more corruptible than power?"

He removed a box of paints from an old crate and blew the dust from the cover. It was useless. The boxes had been in his possession for ten years. During that time countless excavations had turned up absolutely nothing. They had one shard, but needed more information concerning the mirror. It had all been lost. Still, Samael pressed forward, removing the lid and rummaging through the calcified tubes of pigment with little expectation.

His nail snagged on a slip of material. He drew back in frustration. Samael's eyes traveled to the floor of the box in search of the thing which had caused the pain. Then he saw it. He saw it for the first time: an aged loop of ribbon cropping up from the seam where the bottom of the box met the side.

The lavender blue of his eyes illuminated. It was a false bottom. Breathless, he slid his finger through the loop of the ribbon and lifted the panel from the container. There, stuffed into the hidden space, was a worn leather diary. It didn't even have a lock. Samael flipped to a random page and, holding it up to the pale cylinder of lamplight, read to himself. As usual, Xylophis was insufferably restless.

"Your Majesty? What is it? Is it about the mirror?"

Samael ignored him as he continued to devour the entry. After he had crossed the halfway point he could hold back no longer. Arching his lovely neck, he parted his artistic lips and let out a delighted peal of laughter. Xylophis was impossible.

"Dear Cobra, I beg of you, what is it you've discovered?"

Samael held the diary lovingly to his chest. "Oh, Xylophis, I love it when people do my job for me!"

Chapter 1:
Paparazzi

Pasha Chevalsky rocked back on his heels as he watched the clerk count the *olaus* in her left hand while using her tentacles to bag his groceries, wipe down the cash register, and retrieve his receipt. Cecaelia mermaids were common in Cetus, he had been told, which explained why he had yet to see any beforehand. He was quite certain he would have remembered if he had encountered a mermaid with a lower-half resembling a cephalopod rather than a finned fish.

One by one the change dropped into the drawer with a metallic jingle. Pasha breathed a sigh of relief. He was still learning about the different types of currency in Voiler, and always grew nervous whenever he had to put his knowledge to practice. When she handed him his receipt, Pasha nearly tore the paper trying to free it from her suction-cup. Embarrassed, he thanked her, gathered up his things, and headed for the door.

The day was pleasantly swollen with yellow sunshine. It fell in golden ribbons across the wide, rippling canals of Ambergris Square. Like any other popular seaside town, Pasha could smell salty sand, fried food, burnt sugar, and sunscreen. On the nearest corner, a street vendor was popping pineapple-flavored kettle corn. Music either spun from restaurant Victrolas, or danced off the fingers of sylphs busking in the trees.

Somewhere down the block the bells of a trolley tolled, and the traffic cop would blow his whistle as motorcars passed on the most immaculate city streets Pasha had ever beheld. Down in the channels, mermaids swam in and out of the underwater shops.

Every inanimate object in this organic cityscape seemed to hum with life, from the onion-domed apartments suspended over the metropolis like beehives, to the moss-blanketed glass skyscrapers that twisted and bent like trees. Sometimes, if Pasha was quiet enough, he thought he could hear the buildings breathing, feel their lungs expanding, their bodies photosynthesizing.

The sun seemed to warm and open his bones when he stepped out onto the street. After spending the past six years in a drafty tenement apartment in New York City, the tropics were a welcome change. The humidity had buffed the chapped appearance from his lips and hands, and his wintery skin had now been sunburnt enough times to evolve into a ruddy tan. His mother said he looked handsome, but Pasha thought he wore it awkwardly.

When Pasha rounded the corner, his eyes were accosted by an unwelcome series of burning, white flashes and loud, metallic clicks. He stumbled against the sandstone wall in a daze, scraping his elbow on the rough brick. As he blinked away the stars, he became aware of a horde of reporters crowded around him. Questions fired at him one after the other.

"Mr. Chevalsky! Any word about the Cobra's trial for *The Rising Sun?*"

"Mr. Chevalsky, any thoughts about the Ecliptic Council's impending verdict for Cobra Samael's alleged involvement with the Battle of the Firebird?"

Pasha froze. In all the time he'd spent in Voiler, never had he been approached by a reporter—until now. What was he supposed to do? Should he say something? Surely not without Staccato or Sonata's consent. Camera flashes salvoed one after the other like fireworks. They pinched Pasha's eyes, causing him to sneeze.

"Mr. Chevalsky, is it true the photograph in *Good Morning New York* is really you? And if so, why were you running from the police?"

That last question might as well have been a gunshot. For a moment, Pasha forgot where he was. Was there really a photograph of him running from the police in an old newspaper from New York? And if so, how did it find its way to Voiler? He could think of only one thing to do. Ducking between two journalists, Pasha ran.

Questions bounced off his back like bullets. He wandered across the tracks of an oncoming streetcar. The bells banged in alarm. He staggered backwards and straight into the middle of advancing traffic. A motorcar squealed to a halt, blaring its horn. Pasha vaulted onto the hood, reached up and climbed onto the fire escape of a nearby office building. He could feel the unwanted attention of a dozen eyes as he breezed past the window.

From the rooftop, he sailed down a row of apartments and slid into a narrow alleyway. The passage was tight enough that he could climb down by shoving his feet and shoulders against the opposite walls. Outside, the street opened upon the high seawall lining the edge of the city. Pasha half entertained the thought of jumping into the water. Too bad he didn't know how to swim. Somewhere in the deep his mother and sister combed their hair, looked for shells, or whatever it was mermaids did. But it was unlikely they'd be anywhere outside the grounds of Tiaki, the Cetacean Palace where they had been staying. Sweating slightly, Pasha headed for the road which led back to the palace.

The pale yellow trees replaced the colorful structures of Ambergris Square. Soon the vein of paved road shrank to a dirt foot path, and the lush, tropical greenery of the Phoenix Islands spilled onto the soil in florid shadows. At the gate, Pasha was admitted onto the grounds by heavily muscled mermaid guards, and made his way to the guesthouses from there.

Outside, his cousin, Sonata, crossed the kitchen porch. Her large, round eyes, normally so dreamy and relaxed, were fixed tightly on a newspaper. Light danced on the surface of the jewel-studded adaptive legs she wore more like a fashion statement than equipment for amputees. Trailing behind her was Cello, her water-loving pet cat. As her eyes snagged on Pasha's frantic shape, she stopped and called out to him, holding up the front page.

"Please tell me this isn't you!"

The headline had upset her so much she didn't seem to notice Pasha's panicked sprinting. At the top of the stairs, he collapsed upon the deck with the grocery bags, red-faced and breathless. Sonata bent over him, her mass of curly, black walnut hair brushing the tip of his nose.

"My goodness," she exclaimed in her dignified accent, "whatever were you running from?"

The faintest trace of peach sun colored her beige shoulders. Pasha drew the back of his hand across his damp forehead.

"*Reportery ...*"

"What?"

Pasha took a deep breath, trying to keep his languages straight. "Reporters in Ambergris Square!"

Sonata frowned and covered her mouth in a distressed manner. "It wouldn't have anything to do with this, would it?"

She held the newspaper over Pasha's head. He scanned the headline.

"'Pasha Chevalsky's Secret Past. Is This the Future King of Ursa?'"

His eyes dropped to the black and white photograph below, taken from an old copy of *Good Morning New York*. It showed two police officers running up Fifth Avenue after a tall, skinny boy with a messy, duck-tail cowlick peeking out from an old newsboy cap. Pasha's mouth dropped in horror. The photograph showed very little of his face, certainly not enough to conclude it was Pasha. But it was him all the same. Hands shaking, he took the paper from Sonata and sat gaping at it.

"Where did they get ahold of this?"

"It was Samael who sold it to the papers. Said a friend of his from New York brought it to his attention."

"Did they say anything else?"

"Nothing of importance. So far it's all speculation. They don't appear to have any knowledge of your dealings with the Breadwinners, not so far anyway." Sighing, she straightened herself. "Very well, what did you tell them?"

Pasha propped himself up on his elbows. "Tell them? I didn't tell them anything! I ran!"

Sonata looked appalled. "You ran?"

"Well, what else was I supposed to do? They had me cornered!"

"You stick your head down, say 'no comment,' and press on! You really ran away to escape reporters?"

Weary of repeating himself, Pasha grew cocky.

"No, I ran all the way from Ambergris Square so the groceries would stay fresh!"

He threw himself back on the ground, his pores throbbing beneath a sticky sheen of burning sweat. Cello climbed on top of his chest and sniffed the bottom of his chin.

"I guess I've made a mess of everything now."

Sonata knelt down beside him and patted his head with maternal affection.

"One moment of bad publicity isn't going to destroy your entire career. It's time I taught you how to deal with the press. Meanwhile, stay out of the village. If you need anything from town let Pyro or me know, and we'll take care of it. That should probably go for your mother and sister as well."

As her comforting eyes swept over him, Pasha was reminded once more of his mother and her kind, gentle manners. Despite their different ethnicities, there was still a resemblance between them.

"Now you stay here and catch your breath. There are a few things I need to take care of before dinner." Smiling, she turned and disappeared down the stairs, Cello following after her.

From the wide, triangular bay windows of the kitchen, the familiar fragrance of butter and garlic simmering on a stovetop drew Pasha's attention. His eyes widened. He was supposed to be helping Faina prepare dinner! Groaning, he folded his arm over his eyes. In the midst of all the chaos he'd completely forgotten! Now he was dirty, and sweaty, and by no means in a state to be cooking. Before he could think of what to do, the candles on the picnic table sprayed into the sky like flamethrowers.

"And just where have you been?"

Pasha jumped to his feet. Faina stomped towards him in a pair of swishy beach slacks. There was a smudge of flour on the bridge of her prominent nose. Freckles fell in a starry lace over her rosy cheeks and shoulders and tangled themselves with the loose strands of raven hair wind-lashed about her face. As usual, her brown eyes sizzled and smarted with challenge, completely unaware her anger had sent the candles into hysterics.

Pasha threw up his arms, trying not to laugh as Faina pointed the end of a utensil in his face.

"This is how it ends, huh? Bumped off by a girl with a salad fork."

"That depends on how good your excuse is." Faina's mouth twisted as she took in his disheveled appearance for the first time. "And by the looks of it, you won't disappoint." She pushed aside his coarse, black bangs with the tip of her fork.

Pasha shrugged as though nothing were amiss.

"I was out getting the capers, remember?"

"Well, it's too late for the capers, I had to make it without."

"Will you spare me if I beg your forgiveness?"

"Oh no, don't you think you can go batting those big brown eyes at me, Pasha Chevalsky!"

Pasha dropped to one knee and laid a hand against his heart. "Please spare me, oh great queen of the kitchen! I know I deserve to be struck down by your almighty salad fork, but please have mercy on me!"

Faina snorted and cupped her hands over her freckly smile as she dissolved into giggles.

"Get up, you ham!" She gave him a playful shove, accidentally knocking him to the porch floor and sending them both into hysterics.

Pyro Anomaly wandered up the steps with a ruddy eyebrow cocked over his russet eyes.

"At it again, are we?"

He swept a calloused hand smirched with ash through his unkempt tangles of wild red hair. Generating a flame through his index finger, he lit a cigarette. The stairs creaked behind them as the enormous silhouette of Melodious Krüner lumbered onto the porch.

"Don't be so severe, *mein* friend. After all, 'there is a time to weep and a time to laugh.'" His bushy, mousy brown mustache flexed with a jovial smile, and he pushed out his blocky chin in a cheerful manner.

"Yeah, yeah, Reverend. For those two it's always time to laugh! It's funny, I used to think Russians were a stoic people until these two came along."

Faina whirled around with a knowing grin. "But we're also Americans."

Pasha snapped his long, clumsy fingers and nodded with approval. "Yeah, that's right! We're also Americans!"

Pyro looped his arm roughly around Faina's neck and tousled her hair with his fist.

"Alright, well, it's time for the Americans to get back in the kitchen and finish cooking dinner! There may be a time to weep and a time to laugh, but there's also a time to eat and that was fifteen minutes ago."

Ever since Pyro had been coaching Faina in her igneous abilities, the two had developed a chummy relationship and constantly teased each other. Faina laughed, chucking a fist at Pyro's brawny shoulder.

"Alright, alright! Hold your horses!"

Pasha made to follow Faina back into the kitchen, but she turned and stopped him with an admonishing shake of her finger.

"Oh no, you need to go wash up!"

"But I was supposed to help!"

The corners of her mouth tugged upwards. "It's alright, silly. I've got everything under control. You can give me your excuses later." She wrenched him around by the shoulders and waved him back towards his room. "Now shoo!"

Chapter 2:
Exonerated

When Pasha returned from showering, the setting had been laid out. Everyone was taking their place around the picnic table, including Pasha's mother and his little sister, Katya, who had come for dinner that evening, tempted by Faina's familiar recipe of *solyanka*.

Pasha pulled out a chair for his mother. Her heavily-lidded eyes beamed.

"My little gentleman."

Her chocolate brown hair, damp from the ocean, was twisted over one sunburnt shoulder in a thick, salty coil.

From beneath the tablecloth, Pasha could just make out his sister's sandy, sun-browned toes. Unlike Pasha and Lydia, Katya tanned beautifully without a single burn. The yellow undertones of her skin ripened to a gold as rich as her eyes and hair. He grabbed hold of her ankles and managed to drag her out from under the table.

"What do you think you're doing down there on the floor, *Rybka*?" Little fish.

"I was petting Mammoth."

As if on cue, Faina's gargantuan Caucasian mountain dog, or *ovcharka*, reared his damp nose and wagged his tail. Pasha tossed Katya into his arms with ease. Even at nearly ten years old, Katya was still small and light.

"You don't wanna have to wash up a second time, do you?"

Ignoring Pasha's question, Katya's eyes swelled, and he knew she was about to dive into a lengthy anecdote.

"Pasha, I used my healing powers to cure a paper cut today! I was just coming up from the beach when I …"

Pasha nodded as she prattled on and on. Katya had always been a talkative child, but with her powers advancing daily she'd become a regular chatterbox.

As soon as there was a break in her sentence, Pasha sat her in the chair next to his mother.

"That's great, *Katenka*. You're getting so strong."

Faina emerged from the kitchen, struggling to carry the heavy pot of stew to the table.

"Woah now, Faina." Pyro stood. "Let someone else do that."

Faina snorted. "That's awfully gentlemanly for you."

"Yeah, well, since Staccato's not here to move stuff with his mind there's no one to protect us from your clumsiness."

The moment Pyro had secured the pot, he turned and tripped over Mammoth's tail, sending the *solyanka* soaring into the air. With astounding reflexes, graceful Skelter sprang into action and caught the pot with both hands. Melodious unfolded his napkin.

"It is a blessing that we have Skelter in Staccato's absence then."

Pyro crossed his arms. "How do you know it wasn't me who caught the pot?"

Melodious raised a cynical eyebrow to such height you could almost see his pale, milky eyes for once.

"As I have said before, I may be blind but that does not mean I cannot see."

Skelter thrust his thumbs behind his braces with an air of triumph and bowed. His broad piano-key grin pinched the corners of his eyes which were as green as the inside of a kiwi.

Faina leaned against the porch railing and crossed her arms.

"Are you sure you're just an ordinary human with no magical powers?"

Skelter cocked his head slyly, causing his shower of dark curls to bounce against his olive skin. He'd grown them out somewhat during their stay in Cetus so his hair was styled more like the mermen. On particularly humid days he'd even taken to tying it in a bun.

Pasha's eyes fell upon an empty chair.

"Where's Sonata?"

Cicada, the esperite, now three months old—or still eighteen, depending on how one counted—drifted overhead. Her fine, blonde hair dangled behind her in a glowing cloud.

"Probably off somewhere arguing with Pyro."

"I'm right here, thank you!" snapped Pyro. "And you're about to get your hair in everyone's food."

It was just last December that Pasha had watched Cicada hatch from a Sycamore tree in Aquarius. It wasn't long before they figured out she was a genius, and since then her intellect had grown even sharper, her sentences quicker. Her thoughts came out in a wispy, alacritous blur.

Katya screwed up her eyes in contemplation. "She's getting close. I can feel her. She's angry about something."

Cicada wrenched her scowling baby face towards Pyro. "What did you do now?"

Pyro dropped his spoon. "Me?"

"Yes, you! Whenever Sonata is mad it's always your fault!"

"Both of you hush now," Melodious commanded, who always sounded far gentler than he looked. "We don't want Staccato to return to find everyone at each other's throats."

Pyro sniffed. "More like just my throat."

The floorboards gave a shudder as Sonata came stomping down the parapet, pinching a telegram between her fingers as though she would rip it to shreds.

"Well, look who's finally back!" declared Pyro. "What's up with you?"

Something in Pyro's cheery tone seemed to grate on Sonata's nerves. When she looked up, everyone at the table flinched.

Cicada flashed Pyro a look. "I knew it was your fault."

"I'll tell you what's up!" Sonata slammed the telegram down on the table. "It's official. Staccato sent me a copy of *The Daily Compass*'s featured story tomorrow. 'The Ecliptic Council Finds Cobra Samael Innocent.'"

Faina's spoon fell. "You're kidding."

"No, I'm afraid not." She read aloud. "'The presiding judge released the following statement to *The Daily Compass* on Wednesday: "We, the Ecliptic Council, have received no sufficient evidence proving His Majesty, Cobra Samael, ruler of the most honorable Constellation of the Dragon, had involvement in the 1925 New Year's Attack on the Phoenix Islands. We therefore conclude all charges against Cobra Samael should be dropped at once."' There is no justice."

Melodious cracked his ginormous knuckles like Christmas crackers and sighed.

"If you are looking for justice I would not count on the Ecliptic Council. The system has been broken for years."

"But how?" exclaimed Pasha. "I don't understand. The majority of the Council would have had to vote in favor of Samael's innocence."

Sonata twisted the telegram between her fingers until it was as tightly coiled as a unicorn horn.

"Well, it was close. We only lost by one vote. The representatives who voted in Samael's favor were Taurus, Libra, Capricorn, Gemini, Sagittarius, Virgo, and the United Federation of the Eridanus River Valley."

Steam poured from Pyro's nostrils. "Sagittarius? Are you kidding me? That's treason! King Thayer has been warring with the C.O.N. for years! I'll bet my last match that representative loses his job!"

Cicada burned with a vengeful white light. "Do you realize how large the populations of sylphs and esperites are in Virgo? They'll never stand for this!"

"Alright, hold on!" Sonata held up her hand. "That's not all. First, take into account the evidence. Regardless of the delegates' sentiments towards Samael, they could never honestly condemn him if there wasn't any evidence."

Pyro waved away his own cloud of smoke. "He's a bloody cannibal, and a proud one at that! What more evidence do you need?"

"I mean evidence specifically regarding the siege on the Phoenix Islands. Think about it, he had his face covered the entire time; the only eyewitnesses are Pasha and his mother. There are no photographs, and he has a solid alibi. The day the C.O.N. attacked Cetus, he gave a radio broadcast from Apophis Manor about Primal Instinct."

"But he was here!" sputtered Pasha. "We saw him! We talked to him!"

"I know, Pasha, I know. Obviously, the broadcast was prerecorded. But there are several citizens of Thuban who say they witnessed Samael wishing his people a Happy New Year from the balcony of the palace. Though I'm certain they were paid off."

"But what about the burns? When Samael caught the Firebird, he caught on fire. He would have to have sustained some kinda injury. Isn't that evidence?"

"Under normal circumstances, yes. But ophidians recover from external injuries ten times faster than the average human without the use of healing power. That's because ophidians shed their skin once a month. If the skin is damaged, they'll shed more frequently until the wound disappears."

Pasha threw up his shoulders in desperation. "Okay, so he doesn't have the injuries, but everyone knows Samael was after the Firebird. What about that?"

"I haven't told you the worst part yet. There was a confession."

A gasp circulated around the dinner table.

"A confession?" echoed Faina, her mouth full. "By who?"

"An ophidian named Geophis Vesper, a known member of the C.O.N.."

"So Samael has a martyr! Someone willing to take one for the team!"

"Precisely. Vesper took blame for the whole thing. He's sentenced to hang sometime in May."

Everyone fell into a dismal silence. After a moment or two had passed, Pyro propped his elbows on the table and pushed his plate away from him.

"Anything else new?"

"Staccato will be arriving back shortly. He says they've secured a date for the hearing. It's to be April second."

Pasha drew out a long sigh and leaned away from his food.

Sonata clicked her tongue. "Don't fret, Pasha. This first hearing is actually just for your mother. Yours is to immediately follow."

Lydia pivoted around, startled. "Me?"

"Yes, you see, you're technically first in line."

"But what about the bylaw? Staccato says Bruin made a bylaw that no female offspring of his can rule. The title has to pass to Pasha."

"Yes, they know that. But you're still the closest living relative of the former King. They want to make sure you're a true relation. I myself wasn't even aware of the formality. Staccato mentioned it in the telegram."

"And how do they plan to do that?" Lydia's hand fluttered to her chest. "Ask me questions? I was put in an orphanage when I was just an infant, raised by an adoptive father. I knew nothing of my background until just recently. I have nothing to tell them."

Pasha watched his mother with his head bent over his plate. When it came to discussing her upbringing, his mother was odd. She'd invented all sorts of fantastical details about her childhood when he and Katya were young. But the moment Katya was diagnosed with psychosis the stories came to an immediate end. If Pasha mentioned them at all, her entire body hardened and she'd shut down. Once she'd even lashed out at Pasha. Sonata put a comforting hand on Lydia's shoulder.

"Don't worry. It's like I said, it's only a formality. They're not going to interrogate you or anything."

Pasha raised an eyebrow. "Then why are they bothering her at all?"

"I know it's stressful, I know you both are very nervous, but I assure you there's nothing to worry about. Really, the person to ask is Staccato."

Everyone at the table sucked in their breath and watched Pasha to see how he would react.

"Of course!" He rolled his eyes. "In that case, I wouldn't count on any help!"

Staccato had proved to be just as bad as Lydia when it came to discussing his mother's background. The moment Pasha had begun asking questions, Staccato had gone through great lengths to avoid him. It was so comically obvious there was really no use in denying it, and Pasha could not quell his resentment.

"Look, I know Staccato has been a little busy lately," began Sonata, "but you can interrogate him all you want when he gets back. I'll see to it he has a talk with you, as well as your mother."

Pasha hunched his shoulders and struggled to focus on the plate of *solyanka* laid out before him. He rubbed the space between his eyebrows.

"How does an Ecliptic Council hearing work anyway?"

Pyro beckoned Sonata to her seat and pulled out her chair.

"Well, each country has a set of representatives that sit on the Council. They're appointed to be an extension of their nation's supreme government, standing in for a ruler on matters of international importance. That being said, the ruler may choose to represent the country themselves in certain matters of the court, especially if the trial directly affects them."

"And what do these representatives do during the hearing?"

"They're both jury and interviewer."

Pasha had just convinced himself to eat another spoonful, but this defeated his resolve at once. He set down his spoon.

"Interviewer?"

"Yes. When the trial begins you'll take the stand, and the council members will ask you a series of questions."

"For how long?"

"For as long as they want. In some cases the interview sessions have gone on for days."

Pasha slid his head into his hands and groaned. "I'm doomed, aren't I?"

Sonata reached across the table for Pasha's hand.

"Now, Pasha, really! I've had just about enough of your pessimism! The throne is your legal inheritance, and there is nothing Samael can say or do to alter that reality." She looked from Pasha to Lydia with an encouraging expression. "Now both of you relax and enjoy the dinner Faina worked so hard on."

Faina rolled her eyes. "Yes! Can we please change the subject before everyone loses their appetites?" She returned Pasha's spoon to his hand.

"Pasha!" Katya's voice was so loud with enthusiasm it made her brother jump. "If you can't stop worrying, I can calm you down! I can use my powers!" She leaned across the table for Pasha's hand. "All I have to do is touch you and—"

Ordinarily, Pasha would've met his sister's concern with tenderness and gratitude, but he was so tense, and so unused to the idea that Katya could manage his anxiety in any way, that he shrugged her off with an impatient huff.

"Katya, it's not that simple, okay? I know you're excited about your powers, but give it a rest!"

Pasha looked up just in time to see Katya drawing back with hurt in her eyes. He glanced back at his mother; she appeared to be too stunned by his outburst to scold him. Before he could smooth over the damage, Pyro wolfed down another mouthful and spoke between bites.

"You know, it's funny, I never expected Faina to be a good cook."

Faina hunkered down over her bowl and spoke in a low voice.

"Yeah, well, I got a lot of practice after I was kicked outta school."

"Ah, I've been there. What'd you get kicked out for? Setting something on fire?"

While Faina hesitated, Katya hopped up and down in her seat.

"Faina was expelled because she—"

Lydia swiftly pasted her hand over Katya's mouth. Pasha flashed his sister a look, and she scowled back at him with burning defiance. It was almost as though she had done it to get back at Pasha, even though it would've been Faina who suffered. Maybe he wasn't so sorry after all.

"Let's just say it was behavioral issues," mumbled Faina, "and leave it at that."

Perceiving the obvious tension, Sonata dabbed at her lips with a napkin and quickly changed the subject.

"So, Pasha. Have you given any thought as to what you'd like to toast your new reign with?"

Pasha chuckled. "Aren't you supposed to toast with champagne?"

"Not necessarily. I'd recommend a mermaid wine, a nice sparkling green harvested from the finest algae, aged fifteen leagues below sea level."

Pyro threw back a swig of his drink and wiped his mouth on his sleeve.

"I always thought mermaids favored *mer*lot."

Faina laughed so suddenly at his terrible pun she choked and had to cover her mouth with a napkin. Sonata tried to hide her smile, but it was plainly obvious as she bent her chin to her chest that she was amused.

"Perhaps if it was stored at the appropriate depth. And what about you, Pyro? What would you recommend?"

"My family always preferred beer. There's nothing like a good tankard of stout, after all." He stared at Pasha, as though expecting him to chime in.

The truth was, beer didn't appeal to Pasha; in fact, it rather turned his stomach. The ring at the Foxhole had always been ripe with the smell of sweaty men boiling the crowded air with their fermented beer breath. And the fact that Budweiser had advertised their drink as liquid bread leading up to Prohibition didn't exactly help.

"Didn't your family own a vineyard, Pasha?" asked Melodious. "I will bet you have a favorite vintage in mind."

His mother waved her hand and laughed. "He is only seventeen."

A smile appeared under the shadow of Melodious's mustache. "But you are Russian, are you not?"

"That is true."

Pasha's head sank to his chest. "Everything I know about wine I learned from bootlegging. The Red Army burnt down our vineyard when I was ten years old, and we were forced to leave."

Sonata leaned forward. "You mean you never had a drink of your family's famous wine?"

"Never."

The table went silent with pity. Pasha could not bring himself to look up. He was grateful when Pyro finally cleared his throat.

"Well, we'll help you pick out something special." His eyes swept around the table. "Won't we?"

Everyone twittered in agreement. Pasha managed to glance up from his dinner and slip Pyro a sincere smile of thanks. With his plate finished, Melodious stretched away from the table.

"Indeed! It shall be unforgettable, like a first kiss."

Pasha could have sworn he'd caught sight of two little devil horns sprouting from his sister's head as she looked up.

"Pasha likes to practice kissing on the back of his hand."

"What? No, I don't!" Pasha threw up his hands. His fingers curled into fists. It was all he could do to keep from leaping across the table and strangling Katya.

"It's true! When you were fourteen, Mama saw you kissing the back of your hand over and over!"

"That never happened!"

"Yes it did!"

"How do you know?"

"Because I'm a mermaid, and I know everything!"

"There's no way you could've found that out using your powers! Just because you're a mermaid doesn't mean you're a psychic! It means you can feel what other people are feeling!"

Pyro doubled over with laughter. "Well, did the practice pay off, Pasha?"

"No!" Pasha pinched his eyes closed, his cheeks burning hotter. "I mean, yes! I mean … That's not what I was doing!"

His mother laid a consoling hand across his. "It is nothing to be ashamed of, *Patulya*. If you're going to kiss someone, you want to do it right, after all."

"But that's not what happened!"

Katya pointed her finger straight at him. "It was right after Yuri Mishkin kissed Martha Geller, and all the boys were talking about it, and what you're supposed to do! Pasha was nervous all that week! I remember, because I could feel it! I bet he was afraid he didn't know how to do it right! And that's why he had to practice on his hand!"

Pasha slammed his fists on the table.

"That's not what happened!"

"Then what were you doing?"

Pasha bit his lip and glared off to the side. "I—I spilled vanilla on my hand and was sucking it off."

"Why did you have vanilla in your bedroom?"

"I didn't, I had just come from the kitchen! We were making cookies!"

Katya sighed and drew herself up with an air of self-importance. "You know, I can always tell when you're lying."

Pasha threw up his hands and began ranting in Ukrainian. Katya retaliated with equal volume. Lydia seized each of them by the wrist and squeezed. Pasha felt a rush of tranquility flush down his veins. His muscles involuntarily relaxed. He and Katya fell back in their chairs in profound silence. Lydia dusted off her hands.

"That is enough, both of you!"

Katya bowed her head and, flashing her eyes up towards Pasha, whispered, "I know who you're sweet on, Pasha."

Pasha glowered at her. "Mind your own business, Katerina!"

Chapter 3:

The Mourning Token

When Pasha arrived at the training field the following morning, he found his friends huddled into a giggling mass.

"What are you laughing about?"

Sonata's simper vanished. She smoothed the front of her pants and mustered an expression of sincerest sympathy.

"*Ahem*, good morning, Pasha! All ready for training? It looks like you are!"

Pasha narrowed his eyes suspiciously. "What's going on?"

Pyro was the first to break, chortling all the while. "You made the front page!"

He slapped the paper into Pasha's open hand and doubled over in laughter. Pasha felt his cheeks flush with an unbearable heat. There he was, standing outside the grocery, his head thrown back mid-sneeze. It was the worst picture he'd ever seen of himself.

"You have gotta be kidding me."

Pyro and Skelter collapsed over each other, choking and guffawing. Sonata bit her lip in apology.

"What happened exactly? Why are you making such a face?"

"It was the camera flash, it made me sneeze."

Pyro rolled up to a sitting position. "How can a camera flash make you sneeze?"

Faina wiped a laughter-induced tear from her eye.

"Pasha always sneezes if you shine a bright light in his face unexpectedly."

Pyro's eyes rolled to the heavens. "That's the silliest thing I've ever heard!"

"No, it's true! I'll prove it!"

She grabbed Cicada by the wrist and shoved the esperite's glowing hand into Pasha's eyes. Pasha's nose twisted. His muscles contracted. He struggled to fight it but it was no use. He wrenched his head back and sneezed. Pyro and Skelter staggered backwards in fascination.

"Blazes!" Pyro inched forward. "Do it again!"

Pasha tried to shield himself, but it was too late. Faina thrust Cicada forward a second time, a third time, a fourth time, until Pasha was nearly blinded from a sneezing fit. Sonata stepped between them.

"Alright, that's enough!"

Cicada shook her hand in disgust. "Yeah! I'm tired of being sneezed on!"

Sonata patted Pasha's shoulder. "Now don't be embarrassed. It's more common than you think. Staccato has the same problem, as well as our great-uncle Sharktooth."

"Isn't that the same mermaid uncle who also claimed to be allergic to water?" Pyro asserted with a wry smirk.

"That was Auntie Minnow."

Pasha rubbed a hand over his eyes, feeling absolutely humiliated.

"Aw, don't sweat it, Pasha," said Pyro getting to his feet. "It'll blow over, bad press always does. I should know! Why, when I was your age my parents couldn't keep me out of the headlines for anything."

"Why is that?"

Sonata gave an exasperated groan. "Don't ask."

Pyro brushed the dirt from his shoulders and looped his thumbs behind his braces.

"Oh, the usual stuff of youthful rebellion. Drinking, dueling, a few parties here and there. Not to mention all that media attention made me quite popular with the ladies."

Sonata rolled her eyes and unscrewed the cap off her canteen. "Your poor mother."

"Anyway, the point I'm trying to make is sometimes a little scandalous publicity can work in your favor." He propped his arm on the parallel bar and flashed Sonata a devious smile. "Everyone loves a bad boy, eh, Sonata?"

Without hesitating, she emptied the contents of her canteen in Pyro's face. Skelter scurried to his feet and clapped his hands together. Sonata jumped to attention.

"What's your idea, Skelter?"

Skelter flattened his hand and pretended to write on it as though it were a piece of paper. Sonata's eyebrows rose.

"Schedule an interview with a popular newspaper? Why, that's a wonderful idea! Don't you agree, Pasha?"

Pasha's chest sank. The last thing he wanted was more press. He tried to smile.

"Uh, yeah! Sure! You guys would know best." He coughed into the back of his hand. "But can't we talk about it later? I mean, we wouldn't wanna waste any training time!"

Pyro dusted his hands. "Pasha's right! There will be plenty of time for that later. Right now we've got more important things to do!"

Pyro had Pasha swinging from the low bar first thing. There was little Pasha needed to learn here, for he already had experience with gymnastics thanks to Faina's older brother, Leo. It was their tumbling skills that had enabled him and Faina to evade the police in New York City. But Pyro was not about to let them get out of practice. As Pasha balanced his hips against the bar, Sonata clapped her hands.

"My goodness! Before you know it we'll have him on the hoop!"

Pyro threw out his arms. "Oh no, Sonata, not the hoop!"

"What's wrong with the hoop?"

"You've seen the bruises that contraption causes! He'll be too black and blue to fight off any Primals. I hate it whenever you write that torchin' hoop into a show."

"Oh, now don't be so dramatic. It's a crowd pleaser."

"More like a wheel of torture!"

Faina leaned against the rail of the low bar. "Here they go again."

"Since when are you such a baby?" argued Sonata. "You're telling me you can take hit after hit when we're on a mission, but you can't handle a little bruising from the hoop?"

"It's *because* I'm taking hit after hit on missions that'd I prefer not to be incurring more bruises in between operations!"

Sighing, Pasha rolled forward and flipped off the bar. A peal of feminine giggles echoed over his shoulder. A group of mermaids were sunning themselves on the shoal outside the property line. They sat eyeing him with obvious seduction. Ignoring them, Pasha turned to Faina.

"So, what's Sonata been teaching you?"

But Faina didn't seem to be listening. She was gazing with intensity towards the bay.

"Thinking of going for a swim?"

Faina smiled back at him. "Maybe later."

She weaved beneath the high bar and folded her hands behind her back. Something about the way she was standing drew Pasha's eyes towards her hips. Her head tilted to the side, allowing her long ponytail to cascade over one shoulder.

"Do you think you could do that thingy from all the way up there?"

Her eyes drew a slow line to the tallest rod. It looked a little corroded. Parts of the metal flaked with red particles.

"I don't see why not. I've climbed things a lot taller than that. You've seen me."

Faina scooted him forward. "Well, maybe I wanna see you do it again."

Pasha didn't understand why Faina would want to see him work the high bar when he'd done far more impressive things back home.

He reached for the billet. "You do?"

Faina observed him with a half-smile and smoothed the ends of her hair. "Mhm."

Pasha's heart thudded. He wasn't about to tell her no. Pasha swung himself up and over the bar. The mermaids continued to watch him. One even clapped her hands and cheered.

"Do something else," Faina barked suddenly.

"Like what?"

"I don't know, improvise."

Pasha stared at her questioningly. She crossed one ankle over the other and smiled.

"Uh, alright. Yeah." Not sure what else to do, Pasha decided he would flip himself over. He made to swing back down. Meanwhile Pyro came sauntering towards them, his head still trained on Sonata. He did not see Pasha coming down overhead.

"Alright, back to busi—"

The bar buckled. Pasha felt the weight giving way. With a resounding snap the bar split in two. Pasha flew forward, propelling his legs straight into Pyro's groin. Pasha landed squarely on his back, the wind knocked out of his lungs. He stared up at the sky, afraid to look at the damage.

Meanwhile, Pyro had given a thin shriek and lay balled in a heap of inconsolable anguish at Pasha's feet. Pasha could hear the mermaids giggling at him from the shoal. Faina erupted into uncontrollable laughter.

When Pyro managed to bring his voice down to an appropriate octave, he curled up to face Pasha and Faina both.

"Penalty …" he wheezed.

Faina rolled her eyes. "Not again! That's the sixth time in the past three weeks!"

He pointed a finger at Faina. "I told you that bar was unstable!"

Pasha stitched his eyebrows together. Faina knew the high bar was unsafe? He whipped around to gape at her.

Faina shrugged in innocence. "I forgot!"

Pyro dusted his hands together. "Sure you did. Tomorrow, both of you, my cabin, penalty!"

Pasha drew back, his jaw hung open. "Me? What did I do?"

"Don't give me that. You expect me to believe Faina didn't warn you about that bar?"

"She didn't!"

"A likely story! You two are nothing but trouble when you're together!"

Faina raised her shoulders and heaved an aggravated sigh.

"Fine. What do we have to do this time?"

***

Friday morning, Pasha and Faina found themselves inside Pyro's chaotic quarters polishing weapons. To allow Pasha time for his punishment, Sonata had pushed back his economics lesson. Faina had finished her private instruction with Pyro that morning and had been unusually quiet since her arrival. As Pasha finished up one of Melodious's throwing knives, he flashed Faina a dirty look.

Faina raised an eyebrow. "You really think I made you fall on purpose, don't you?"

He threw down his rag. "Yes!"

"Pasha, how many times do I gotta tell you? I forgot the bar was broken."

"Come on, Faina, we're best friends! I'm well acquainted with your practical jokes, no matter how reckless they are."

With her back turned, Pasha saw her lower her head. "You didn't get hurt when you fell, did you?"

"Got the wind knocked out of me. But it could've been worse!" He paused as he noticed she was chewing on something. "What are you eating?"

Faina opened her mouth and cringed. Shaking her head, she gestured to her jaw.

"I'm not eating. Pyro is having me chew this Burning Bush Sap lately. He thinks he can train me into becoming a chief."

"You mean an igneous that can generate and manipulate fire even when wet?"

She nodded, unable to answer him. Pasha went on.

"And how exactly is that supposed to help?"

"Strengthens the jaw muscles, activates the ignition gland."

"The what?"

Faina massaged her mandible impatiently and spoke through her teeth. "Hasn't Sonata taught you about this yet?"

"No! You mean you have some kinda vestigial gland that allows you to breathe fire?"

"It's only vestigial if I can't get it to activate."

Pasha couldn't help but smirk. Faina caught him and slipped him a wry smile.

"Who needs school when you got the library?"

Pasha twisted his nose in grotesque fascination. "An oil burner with fuel!" He scooted closer across the floor. "Who'd of thunk it?"

Sensing his next question, Faina pointed to the front of her neck.

Pasha resisted the urge to poke. "It's in your throat?"

She nodded, tried to open her mouth, then winced. Pasha cocked an eyebrow.

"You gonna be alright?"

"It's just really sticky. You can only take a teaspoon at a time, otherwise your tongue will stick to the roof of your mouth, or your lips get stuck together."

"What does it taste like?"

"Kinda like spicy peppermint. It's not bad actually. Wanna try some?"

Pasha chuckled and shook his head. "I better not. Knowing you, you'll trick me into getting my mouth glued shut."

"Alright, give it a rest." She tapped the side of her mouth. "Although now that you mention it, it would be fun to fill a batch of truffles and slip it to Pyro."

"Why Pyro?"

"So we can catch him with his lips glued to Sonata!"

Pasha rolled his eyes. "Like Sonata would be caught dead kissing Pyro."

"I'm telling you, Pasha, Pyro and Sonata are madly in love!" She threw the back of her palm against her forehead and batted her eyes like a film star. "'Oh, Pyro, you irrational hothead!'" She turned and lowered her voice in an imitation of Pyro. "'Oh, Sonata, I love it when you call me an irrational hothead! Do it again!'" She continued back and forth. "'Let's run away together and start a family of fire-breathing mermaid babies!"

Pasha was clutching his sides with hysterical laughter. "You have one sick mind!"

She pinned her hands daintily on her knees and thrust her chest forward. "I like to think of it as creative."

Pasha smiled and shook his head. "Hand me something else, will you? I think I'm finished with Melodious's knives here."

Faina reached up over the table and, to Pasha's surprise, produced Staccato's stately silver staff. Pasha drew his brows together.

"He's back then?"

"Arrived last night. Still angry?"

Pasha snatched the staff and bit his lip in an unsuccessful attempt to keep from sneering.

"He's been avoiding me."

Faina's eyes glazed over as she sighed. "And what makes you think that again?"

"He won't answer any of my questions. The more I ask him, the more he tries to get away from me."

Faina set aside her work and, crossing her legs, leaned forward on her elbows.

"Why are you always so paranoid?"

Pasha drew back, offended. "How am I paranoid?"

"You're just like Katya. You always think you know what everyone's thinking and feeling."

He lowered his lids halfway. "Don't I?"

Faina opened her mouth to speak, then shut it. Pasha turned away, smiling with satisfaction as Faina groaned.

"What is it that you wanna know, anyway?"

"Well, for starters, I'd like to know why Staccato didn't tell me about Evangeline's mirror. I mean, it was the reason she went out to try and talk with Bruin in the first place. I wanna know why my mother was put in an orphanage in Siberia. If Staccato was one of the only people to know about her existence, he should know. And if all Polaris needed was a male heir to take back the throne, why didn't Staccato come for us when I was a baby? I could've spent my whole life training to become king! Now I'm cramming in all this information at the last minute. Not to mention we could've been spared the grief of the Revolution, and the War. I never would've had to become a Breadwinner. What was wrong with returning when I was five, ten, twelve? I mean, did we really have to suffer all that time?"

Pasha jerked the rag roughly over the staff and bore down on the handle with a vengeance. Faina steadied her eyes on him for some time.

"Staccato is probably just waiting until all this bunk with the Ecliptic Council is over. Maybe then he'll answer your questions. I'm sure it's all very complicated."

Pasha snorted dryly. "Yeah, it's complicated!" He squeezed his fingers against the smudges on the armillary sphere. "All very complica—agh!"

There was a crisp snapping sound as the end of the staff burst with a white light. Pasha and Faina flew to the ground with their heads covered. Pasha didn't remember opening his eyes, but when he did he was shocked to find himself staring down at a pair of bloody hands not his own. Pyro's cabin had disappeared. He was standing outside a smoking building on the grounds of Alfbern Hall. His mouth moved as he watched his feet back away. He was shouting in Staccato's voice.

"What have I done!? What have I done!?"

He had no idea what was going on and yet he could feel Staccato's overwhelming fear and panic.

Pasha blinked. He was staring at the opposite wall of Pyro's cabin, the wet rag at his side. It was as though nothing had happened. White vapors spun and dispersed across the room. He turned to Faina. She was bent low on her hands and knees, clutching her chest with one hand. Pasha swallowed.

"Are you alright?"

Faina jumped. Her eyes settled upon him.

"Yeah. I'm fine." Her eyes darted to the place where the staff lay. "But you might not be."

Pasha followed her gaze to the broken staff in the middle of the floor. The armillary sphere was cracked clean at the seam.

"I'm dead."

"You have *got* to learn to calm down."

Hands trembling, Pasha crawled forward to examine the staff. He reached out a finger. A wrinkle of violet energy pulsed across the circumference, causing Pasha to jump back. Faina leaned over his shoulder. She reached for a small, transparent box that had fallen out of the cracked armillary sphere.

"What's this?" She turned it over in her hands. It was made up of thin glass panels which ribboned lavender when the light struck at certain angles. The bezel was engraved with a tangle of honeysuckle and hazel vines. Inside was a lock of golden hair preserved on a bed of indigo silk. Pasha looked closer.

"It looks like a token of mourning or something. You know, like they used to do when our parents were growing up. Whenever a loved one died, the mourner preserved a lock of their hair."

"Papa used to keep one of those on the vanity. The hair was red, not auburn like Leo's, I mean bright red. He said it belonged to his grandmother."

"My father had one too." Pasha ran his thumb over the glass. "I wonder whose hair this is."

"Kinda looks like Katya's."

"A little bit."

"Maybe it's Staccato's hair, you know, before he went bald."

Pasha snorted. "You think Staccato was a blonde?"

"Maybe. One thing is for sure though, we better find a way to fix this fast unless we wanna end up scraping barnacles off the pier again."

"You're right. We better get Cici."

When Pasha returned with Cicada, she took up the staff and examined the armillary sphere.

"Easy fix. A small fracture to the core. Where's the nucleus?"

Pasha and Faina looked back at each other uncertainly. Cicada stared at them as though this were common knowledge.

"You know, the nucleus, the piece inside the core which connects the wielder to the staff?"

Faina held up the mourning token. "You don't mean this thing, do you?"

"That's it!"

"You mean to tell me that Staccato's staff is powered by a lock of hair?"

Cicada stopped and stared at her. "Well, yeah. Makes sense, doesn't it?"

"Uh, no!"

Cicada waved her hand and set about placing the nucleus back inside the core.

"In order for a miraculous's staff to work, it has to be fueled by something with emotional significance."

Faina's eyes glazed over. "It isn't his own hair, is it?"

"Of course not, Staccato has dark blonde hair."

"You mean 'had'?"

Cicada sat up straight. She studied Faina like the pieces of a puzzle. There was nothing more confusing to Cicada than other people's confusion.

"No, *has*. He shaves his head."

"How do you know that?"

"Haven't you noticed every few weeks he comes out of his cabin smelling like shaving cream? He's obviously not shaving his beard."

"But how do you know the color?"

"He'll have a few dark blonde hairs on his shirt collar. Well, blonde and gray."

Faina fell back in her chair, dumbfounded. "It's not even receding?"

"Nope. Watch him sometime, you'll see he gets little buds," she indicated to the front of her head, "all the way up here."

"Why would someone shave their head if they had a perfectly full head of hair?"

"Stylistic choice, I guess." She flipped her own hair over her shoulder. "Who knows why people do what they do."

Pasha stroked his chin as his eyes met Faina's. "Faina, you didn't … see anything after I broke the staff, did you?"

Cicada's eyes fluttered up from her work as she watched them. Faina nodded her head.

"You mean like a vision? Yes! It was horrible!"

"You saw Staccato with blood on his hands?"

Faina drew back, her eyes expanding. "Well, no. But …"

Before Faina could finish her thought, Cicada was interrupting them with an explanation.

"What you saw were Staccato's memories. A miraculous's staff contains at least one memory for every emotion. The memory depicts a time in the miraculous's life when the emotion was strongest. When the core broke open you were probably struck by one or two. What did you see?"

Pasha and Faina went silent. Pasha was the first to break.

"I … I saw Staccato … with blood on his hands. He was shouting, 'What have I done,' over and over. I don't know why."

Faina looked greatly disturbed by this bit of information. Cicada seemed mildly intrigued. Eager to change the subject, Pasha nodded to Faina.

"And you?"

Faina edged away with her hands folded in front of her.

"I saw … I think I saw Staccato trying to take his own life."

"What? How do you know?"

Faina opened her mouth to explain but shut it and shook her head.

"It—It just seems so personal." She sighed and rubbed the back of her neck. "He was in a dark room. I think he was younger, but it was hard to tell." She pinched the space between her eyebrows. "I can't go into the details, it's too much. Just trust me on this one."

Silence fell. When Pasha spoke he could hardly move himself to take his voice above a whisper.

"What could've made Staccato consider such a thing?"

"And what stopped him from following through?" Faina shut her eyes and leaned her head against the wall. "It felt like I was the one feeling it … terrible despair. Absolute hopelessness. And the loneliness, the loneliness was the worst of all."

Cicada's eyes narrowed as though she understood completely. "You must have been hit harder." She gestured to the cabinet. "Pasha, get me a bottle of ichor, will you?"

Unfortunately, Pyro's utility cabinet was as stuffed and as disorganized as Faina's.

"I can't find it," said Pasha, throwing up his arms.

Faina gasped as she looked out the window. "Well, shake a leg! It looks like Staccato just got up, and he's headed this way!"

"*Chort*," shoot, Pasha cursed, as he scrambled through Pyro's cabinet. Faina seized him by the shoulders and pulled him towards the door.

"Forget the ichor! I'll get the bottle from my room. You go out there and stall him!"

"Are you kidding? He doesn't wanna talk to me; he avoids me like the plague! One look at me, and he'll head for the hills!"

"That's what I'm counting on!"

And with that she shoved him onto the porch and slammed the door. Already Pasha could hear Staccato humming the same odd arrangement of scales to himself. He often did this when he thought no one was listening. At the sight of Pasha, Staccato stopped short on the stairs. His default expression of haughty impatience evaporated. For a moment he lost some of his characteristic composure.

"Oh. Hello, Pasha."

Pasha couldn't help but take pleasure in Staccato's look of cornered discomfort. "Looking for Pyro?"

"As a matter of fact, I was." Staccato forced an awkward smile. Clearing his throat, he eased back into his dignified pose.

"He's not here right now. Faina and I are polishing weapons. Pyro gave us another penalty." He jerked his thumb towards the cabin. "That's why we're here."

Staccato looked him over dryly. "Doesn't surprise me. My staff wouldn't happen to be in there, would it?"

"Faina's just finishing it up if you don't mind waiting a minute. It'd give me a chance to ask you some of those questions you promised you'd answer."

Staccato glared back at him with electric irritability. But Pasha wasn't backing down. He continued with sick pleasure.

"Ma's hearing is coming up, after all. It would be helpful to know some things about her upbringing, like why she was dumped at an orphanage in Lake Baikal."

Staccato turned towards the stairs. "That's quite alright, Pasha. I can come back later. I don't need my staff anyway."

Pasha pretended he hadn't heard him. "Why didn't you tell me about Evangeline's mirror?"

Staccato's sunken blue eyes burned behind his heavy lids with impatience.

"Really, Pasha, I can't talk right now. I must speak with Pyro."

"Well, if you just wait a minute, Faina will have your staff ready."

Staccato's broad shoulders stiffened. His graying beard seemed to prickle with agitation. The blue irises hardened to steel. An orange that had been sitting on the picnic table rocketed up from the fruit bowl, nearly hitting Pasha in the side of the head. It careened into Staccato's open palm. He scowled at Pasha over his shoulder.

"I don't need my staff."

Pasha gave an imperceptible nod of his head and receded against the door. Staccato turned and walked back towards the beach. Faina poked her head out the window.

"Wow. He looked mad. Nice job, Tom Thumb!" She beckoned him back inside. "I went out the back door to get the ichor." She gestured to Cicada who held out the staff. "Good as new."

Pasha's shoulders unwound from his ears.

"You're a life saver, Cici. Put it back on the table, and we'll try not to touch it again."

Cicada inclined her head. "Don't you want to take it to him now?"

Pasha shrugged and slumped to a seat at the table. "He said he doesn't need it. Didn't you see him make the orange fly off the table?"

Faina stroked her chin. "If he doesn't need a staff to use his powers, why does he carry one?"

They both stared at Cicada, but she must not have known the answer, for she remained silent.

Chapter 4:
Evangeline's Mirror

At suppertime, Pasha's mother surprised everyone with a dish of oysters she'd caught herself. It was not to Pasha's great astonishment, but certainly to his deepest insult, that Staccato did not show up.

Pasha had come to the conclusion that for some odd reason Staccato did not like his mother. Ever since she had arrived in Voiler, Staccato had avoided her as though her presence were infected. He even went so far as to take his meals in his room if Pasha's mother showed up for dinner. Pasha did not like anyone who disliked his mother, for he thought she was the kindest person in the world. And so his resentment towards Staccato deepened another shade.

When supper was finished, Staccato called everyone to assemble at the picnic table. He must have assumed Lydia had left after the meal, for he appeared quite at ease. His shoulders relaxed. He had his nose buried in a notebook, and, as usual, a cup of coffee in his hand. He didn't see Lydia emerging from the kitchen with a pair of shears.

Before Pasha could call out the two collided. The shears flew up and scratched a neat scrape across the back of Staccato's hand. His staff clattered to the floor with his half-empty mug.

Lydia pressed a concerned hand to her mouth and reached for Staccato's arm.

"Oh my! Forgive me, Mr. Nimbus, I did not see you there."

Pasha rolled his eyes as he watched Staccato draw back, ducking his head beneath her outstretched arm. He refused to look her in the eye. He shook his head and held his hand close to his chest.

"It's quite alright, Mrs. Chevalsky, my fault entirely."

But Lydia seized his hand, yanking him forward. "You poor man, look at what I have done! Let me heal that for you."

One might have though Staccato was a child receiving a shot the way he drew his eyebrows together.

"It's fine, really, I'm fine."

Lydia ignored him with a sweet smile. She traced her finger over the cut with a faint, pink light, until the fissure closed.

"Weren't you hungry? You did not come to dinner."

Staccato's reply was uttered in such a low tone that Pasha couldn't make out what he was saying. Whatever it was, it was a short answer. His mother withdrew her hand from his. The injury had healed.

Staccato stared with an empty expression at his hand. His long eyelashes shielded his bright, blue eyes.

"Thank you."

"It was nothing …" and then Pasha saw it. A thought had caught in the corner of his mother's eyes. She looked at Staccato as though seeing him in a whole new plane of reality.

"*Nadeyus', ya ne obidel tebya slishkom sil' no.*"

Pasha cocked his head. What was she doing? Staccato raised an uncomprehending eyebrow.

"I'm sorry?"

Lydia released the thought from her gaze and flashed him a self-admonishing smile.

"Silly me, I forget to speak English sometimes. I said I hope I did not hurt you too badly."

Pasha leaned cynically around the table for a better look at her. Forget to speak English? Mama had learned English at her father's knee. From what he understood, his mother couldn't even remember a time where she had not known English. She was definitely up to something.

Staccato shook his head and summoned his mug back into his grasp.

"No, not at all."

Before Staccato could stop her, Lydia retrieved the staff from beneath the table. As her hands enclosed around the object, she froze. Her eyes became unfocused and hazed. Pasha knew what was happening. Ever since Katya and his mother had discovered they were mermaids, their powers had been awakening. His mother had just discovered psychometry, the ability to read emotion attached to an object.

Pasha expected Staccato to snap at her, but to his surprise, Staccato remained calm. He quickly took the staff from her hands but was nonetheless polite. The trance broke. He coughed into his sleeve, pretending it hadn't happened.

"Thank you."

Embarrassed, his mother forced a smile and nodded her head. Staccato looked away and rose to his feet. Pasha watched his mother patter away down the stairs and disappear. What had she seen?

Staccato stood at the head of the table and cleared his throat, signaling for their attention.

Sonata propped her chin on her wrist and smiled.

"So, are you going to share your adventures in Libra?"

Staccato smirked at her. "That was the idea, yes. However, I believe you're all acquainted with any business I had at the Ecliptic Courts. At least I hope you are."

Pyro yawned and stretched. "What's this all about then? Please tell me we're going to see some action soon! It's been three months! I'm beginning to think all this training we've been putting Pasha and Faina through is pointless."

"I'm getting to that. I haven't just been in Libra. In fact, most recently I've been in Karkinos to visit with Javaid and Theo." Closing his eyes, he shook his head and corrected himself. "Former King Thessalos, that is."

Sonata waved her hand. "We all know who Uncle Theo is, Staccato." Thessalos was Javaid's older brother who had abdicated after the death of Evangeline, his youngest half-sister.

Staccato continued. "You see, after the Battle of the Firebird he wrote to me and asked me to meet him. He wanted to discuss some important information that he thought might affect, well, everything." Staccato paused to steel his jaw. Whatever it was he was about to share, he didn't seem happy about it. "I'm sure many of you recall how Evangeline's spirit was transformed into the Firebird."

Pyro scoffed. "Oh no, I totally forgot about the ghost lady who exploded out of a big, fiery peacock and slayed half the enemy with her weird, bright light of purity or whatever."

Faina leaned forward on her elbows. "It had something to do with the mirror, didn't it?"

Staccato stroked his beard. "Yes. Evangeline was an accomplished glassblower. Shortly before her death she attempted to recreate an ancient mirror from Voilerian legend, called Amnos. Amnos was said to have the power to fight off evil. She disclosed the information to Theo shortly before her death."

"And you," added Pasha.

He wasn't about to let Staccato get away with lying yet again. Staccato may have pretended not to know about the mirror, but Evangeline's ghost had insisted he did.

"Well, I was Theo's advisor and closest friend." Staccato snapped the notebook with apparent vexation. "As I was saying, Evangeline told Theo about the mirror shortly before her death. Naturally, Theo became concerned. Evangeline had been diagnosed with puerperal psychosis. She had lost her grip on reality. And truth be told, she was showing symptoms of mania long before Mrs. Chevalsky was born. It wasn't until recently, when King Thayer, head of the rebel network, discovered the C.O.N. had been collecting the mirror shards that Theo began to wonder if Evangeline was right."

It was clear from the sharpness of his tone that, unlike Theo, Staccato did not think the mirror could be Amnos. But he went on all the same.

"At the very least the mirror is a powerful one, Amnos or not. We're not exactly sure what it does or why the C.O.N. has reason to fear it. Its only apparent power we know of so far is that it somehow transformed Evangeline's soul and put her into Moram Mortem, or delayed death. This was a power not even Evangeline had foreseen. And it's supposedly capable of far greater things."

Melodious leaned back in his chair. "Why has the C.O.N. been hiding the shards away if they believe it has the power to bring them harm? Why not destroy the shards?"

"Given the mirror's extraordinary capabilities it's rather difficult to destroy, though I'm sure they're searching for a way."

Pyro snorted. "Difficult to destroy? She bloody dropped the thing and it shattered!"

Staccato craned his neck, as though he found Pyro's deduction exhausting.

"It shattered into exactly seven fragments. One shard for each power. That's as breakable as it gets without special instruction, and evidently it does not render the mirror powerless. Anyway, our goal is to collect the fragments, reforge the mirror, and find out why the C.O.N. wants it. Javaid tells us we currently have two shards in our possession. It's up to us to find the other five. We have one lead already. It just so happens," here he turned to Pasha and Faina, "it's being kept in familiar territory. An ophidian known as Dr. Edom Cottonmouth has been an undercover mobster in the United States for the past twenty years. He primarily deals with artwork, selling forgeries and stealing genuine masterpieces for his own collection. He's said to be quite the enthusiast with a particular interest in glassworks. And of course, we know why.

"It is my belief that he is hiding the shard amongst his private collection. I'm sending Pasha, Faina, and Pyro to go back and retrieve the shard during Lydia's hearing. The rest of us are to remain in Voiler. Seeing as I'm a lawyer and former Ecliptic Council representative, and Sonata is a monarch and blood relative, we will be accompanying Mrs. Chevalsky to court. Cicada and Melodious are to search the migration records in the capitol for any leads on Faina's father. Skelter will stay here in Cetus to look after the horses and Katya, while Katya looks after Mammoth."

Faina held up a hand. "Where exactly in the United States?"

"Did I not say? Sorry, do excuse me." He pulled a map from his pocket, and whipped out a pair of spectacles. He narrowed his eyes on a location circled in red pen.

"A city in Kentucky." He squinted. "Louisville."

Pasha's mouth fell open. "Louisville? Louisville, Kentucky?"

"Yes, that's the one." Staccato folded his spectacles and stowed them on the collar of his shirt.

Pasha and Faina leapt up from their seats. "Hot dawg!" they cried out in unison. Pasha pumped his fist into the air and swept Faina into a spontaneous waltz, singing:

"In the town of Louisville

Lived a man they called Big Bad Bill …"

Pyro and Skelter exchanged baffled glances.

"What are they so excited about?"

Skelter shrugged.

Faina leaned over the table. "Are you kidding? Anyone who's anyone goes to Louisville these days!"

"Yeah," agreed Pasha. "Haven't you ever heard of the Kentucky Derby? The Run for the Roses?"

Pyro held a sidelong glance. "Um, no."

Sonata nudged his shoulder. "It's a horse race. Pasha's family bred thoroughbred racehorses, remember? So, naturally he would be very interested."

Faina tugged on Pasha's arm. "Don't forget all the baby horses! And the mountains, and the moonshine, and— oh! What is it? Pasha, how do you say mint juleps in English?"

Pasha stared at her long and hard before answering wryly. "Mint juleps."

Faina bit her lip with a self-deprecating smile. "That's not the first time that's happened—and oh! The Seelbach Hotel!"

Staccato looked down at his notebook once more. "Ah, yes. The Seelbach. I've already booked your rooms there. Seems Cottonmouth is a regular."

Faina's hands flew to her cheeks as though she were trying to keep her jaw from dropping on the table.

"Really? We get to stay at the Seelbach?" She threw her head back and laughed aloud. Taking Pasha's hands, she jumped in place. "We're staying at the Seelbach, Pasha! We're staying at the Seelbach!" She flopped to a seat, tripping over her legs like a newborn colt, missing the chair entirely and falling on the floor.

Pyro raised his eyebrows in alarm. "Blue blazes, Faina! Calm down!"

"Do you think we'll get to see F. Scott Fitzgerald? Or Al Capone?"

Pasha snickered and helped her back into her seat. "Let's hope we don't run into Capone."

Ignoring their excitable outburst, Staccato went on.

"You have a few weeks to prepare. In the meantime, Pyro, I want you to up their training. It's vital that they know how to defend themselves."

Cicada rocketed up from her seat. "Now, wait a second, how come I get stuck going to Libra? I want to go where the action is! Send me to Louisville!"

Staccato pressed his fingertips into the table, forcing himself to appear as delicate as possible.

"We can't send you to Louisville, Cicada, you'd stand out too much."

"What are you talking about? I can blend in just fine!"

Pyro threw back his head and snorted. "Even the flowers can't help but keep an eye on you!"

"It's not my fault I'm so radiant."

Staccato remained adamant. "It's too much of a risk for an operation that's meant to be undercover."

"Then teach me how to fit in! What is it I'm doing wrong?"

Pyro leaned back against the table and crossed his legs. "How's this for starters? Let's pretend we're in the Other and you and I have just met." He held out a hand. "Hello, my name is Sylvus Fairchild."

"Hello Sylvua, my name is … Sylvia."

Pasha did not know it at the time, but apparently the name Sylvus Fairchild was the Voilerian equivalent of John Doe.

"Pleasure to meet you, Sylvia, how old are you?"

"Three months." As soon as the words were out of Cicada's mouth she bit her lip. "I mean twenty-three years!"

Pyro slammed his hand on the table and chortled. "You can't tell people you're only three months old! They'll think you're crazy!"

"Alright, alright. What else?"

Pyro gestured to her lower half. "You'd have to break out your legs. None of this cloudy, tail thing you have going on."

"Fine."

And with that, the sparkling trail of fog took on the shape of two spindly legs with knobby ankles. She planted her long, thin, pigeon-toed feet on the wood floor of the deck. There was something unnatural about seeing her with her feet pinned to the ground, like a cloud tethered to the earth against its will. One might have expected her to be uncomfortable, pained even. But what stood out most was her unforeseen but impressive height. She stood around five feet and eleven inches.

Pyro, who was known for being undersized, rose to his feet in obvious irritation.

"Tongs and torches!" He circled around her. "She's a bloody giraffe!"

Cicada craned her head to get a better view of Pyro. "Wow, I knew you were on the short side, Pyro, but now that I'm on the ground you're a regular gnome."

Pyro's face turned so red Pasha expected his freckles to start popping like bacon grease.

"Gnome? Let me ask you something, Cicada, how's the weather up there?"

Cicada hocked back and spit on the top of Pyro's head.

"It's raining."

"Why you—"

Staccato scrambled to his feet. "Alright, Pyro, that's quite enough!"

Cicada tried to take a step backwards, but her knees buckled and she fell to the ground in a tangle of arms and legs. Faina and Sonata helped her to her feet.

"You could do with some practice," suggested Sonata. "But until you refine your technique, it's best if you remain here."

Chapter 5:
Staccato's Secret

After dinner, Pasha collected his assigned reading and headed down to Sonata's quarters for his economics lesson. As he was about to approach Sonata's door, he was startled by the sound of a muffled male sob.

"Now don't get yourself worked up." It sounded like Sonata was comforting someone.

The window was ajar, and Pasha could make out every syllable of noise. He peeked around the sill. Staccato sat on the edge of a chair, cradling his head in his hands and crying. Pasha took a step back. He was utterly astounded. Staccato, never one to give in to any emotional display, actually had tears streaming down his face. A sliver of embarrassment found its way into Pasha's chest. He edged away. He would never wish to pry on something so personal.

"Pasha knows you've been avoiding him," remarked Sonata.

At the mention of his name, Pasha dropped to his knees and ducked below the window. If it included his name, it had to be his personal business, too. Sonata continued.

"There's no point in pretending like you haven't been." There was a hint of scolding in her tone. "Why can't you tell them the truth?"

There was a wheezing noise as Staccato caught his breath and found the strength to speak again.

"If I told them now they would have to lie in front of the Ecliptic Court. That wouldn't be right. There's too much at stake. Pasha must take the throne. It's for the good of Voiler. Telling him the truth now could jeopardize his chance of becoming king in a number of ways. Can you imagine if word got out? The shame they would be exposed to! Not just Pasha, but Katya, and Lydia as well."

Hearing Staccato say his mother's first name, let alone mentioning her at all, startled Pasha. He strained his ears as Staccato went on.

"Poor Lydia. How terrible it would be for her."

"You forget how resilient she is. She's no stranger to scandal, you know. There was the whole circumstance of her marriage, then, of course, all that business about Pasha's premature birth. She's strong, wonderfully strong."

"Just because a person is strong doesn't mean they deserve to be put through the fire. She's been through enough."

"You'll tell them afterwards, won't you? When the hearing is over?"

Staccato drew a long sigh. "No."

"No?" Sonata sounded shocked. "Staccato, you can't keep this inside of you for the rest of your life! You won't be able to live with yourself!"

"I'll be less likely to live with myself if I expose them to my poison."

The vision of Staccato staring down at his bloodied hands revisited Pasha's mind. A chill ran over him. What had Staccato done that was so monstrous? Could he have killed someone? His heart beat faster. Could he have killed Evangeline?

"What does that even mean?" scoffed Sonata, tender but admonishing.

"You know what it means. These things, they have consequences. What Pasha and Lydia don't know won't hurt them. I don't want to cause anyone more pain."

"But that's so silly!"

"Sonata," his voice took on a new gravity. "You must promise not to breathe a word of this to Pasha, no matter how much he pushes you. Don't tell Lydia, don't tell Katya, don't even tell Faina! You must promise."

Pasha could feel the stare of pitiful agony radiating from Sonata's eyes. When she didn't answer, Staccato took a shallow breath.

"I know you don't agree."

"It's not fair to you or her, especially her."

"Sonata, please."

A long silence followed. Sonata surrendered. "I promise."

"That's a good girl." He kissed the top of her head.

Cello leapt onto the sill of the open window and looked down at Pasha. Pasha's eyes grew wide.

"No, Cello," he mouthed. But Cello wasn't listening; instead, he batted his paw at a stray piece of Pasha's hair.

"Cello, what are you doing?" giggled Sonata from the other side of the cabin.

Pasha rolled back from the window and flew to his feet. He made a dash for the beach. He couldn't show up at Sonata's after hearing such news. She'd feel his nerves, his anger, his confusion. She'd know he'd been listening in a heartbeat. He had to talk with Faina.

***

When Pasha found Faina, she was up to her freckled knees in frothy whitecaps. She threw back her head and laughed as Mammoth galloped through the surf. Nearby, Katya floated over the waves. Her golden scales were so strikingly beautiful it made the glistening sand seem gray. At the sight of Pasha, she curled her tail up over her head and beckoned.

"Come play with us, Pasha!"

Pasha smiled but shook his head.

"I thought you had lessons!" hollered Faina.

Pasha did not say anything but motioned for her to come closer. Faina patted the top of Mammoth's sopping head and made her way over.

"What's up, buttercup?" She bent forward and twisted the water from her salty hair. Perhaps it was nerves, but it took Pasha several tries before he managed to get his voice working in a lowered tone.

"It's a long story, but I was eavesdropping, and now I need to avoid Sonata before she finds out."

Faina threw back her damp hair where it clung to her shoulders in a pattern of wisps and curls.

"In that case, you better steer clear of Katya too. Let me grab my shoes. I'll tell her that you and I are going for a walk."

Pasha waited against a palm tree as Faina ran off to gather her belongings. His eyes followed the sprinkle of water running down her knees. She slipped an airy cover-up over her pink bathing suit, and slid her feet into a pair of sandals. As Pasha glanced back at his sister, he saw he wasn't the only one watching Faina. Two handsome mermen with glossy ponytails kept an eager eye on her from their canoe. Muscles burst beneath their tan skin. Pasha glanced down at his pale, skinny legs. His shoulders slumped forward.

He called to Faina impatiently. "Hurry up, before I get caught!"

"Alright, geez!" Faina staggered through the sand with her bag thrown over her shoulder. She didn't stop but grabbed Pasha's wrist and towed him down a lush, overgrown path.

"We can say we were doing our homework. Besides it's not like this is your usual time for economics, so it will be easy to say you forgot. Hopefully you can dodge Sonata until tomorrow. The longer you wait the harder it is for mermaids to detect a lie. Pyro taught me that."

"I bet he did." Pasha chuckled. "Where are we going anyway?"

"To the top of the bluff over the lagoon."

"In that case, why don't we take Harpagos and fly?"

"Oh, let's enjoy the walk. Besides, it will kill time."

***

The foliage thickened in crisp crescents of lush palms. Tropical birds stirred from their nests and hung their bodies like ornaments against the clouds. Smoldering calderas squatted along the island like guardian warriors.

After an arduous hike the breeze picked up, and Pasha could hear the falls stirring the bay beneath them. The colors of the atmosphere melted together in a vibrant band of sherbet and melon. It looked so sugary sweet, Pasha could've sworn he smelled the citrus.

Faina stopped behind his shoulder. "I told you it would be beautiful."

"I never doubted you."

They sat down near the cliffside.

"So," Faina scooted forward, "what was so juicy that you felt the need to head for the hills?"

Pasha explained to her everything he'd overheard. By the time he was finished, Faina was leaning forward with her elbow on her knees, stroking her bottom lip with her pinky finger.

All she could manage to get out was, "Wow."

Pasha lowered his chin and stared at her. "Well, what do you think it means?"

"It's hard to say."

"Faina, what if … . I mean, do you think …" He trailed off and rubbed the bridge of his nose.

"Well? Do I think what?"

Pasha let out a long exhale through his nose. His voice dropped to a whisper.

"Remember the vision I was hit with when Staccato's staff broke?"

"Pasha, you're not suggesting Staccato killed Evangeline, are you?"

Pasha flailed his arms and slammed a hand over Faina's mouth. "Shhh! Not so loud!"

Faina lowered her eyelids as she pried his hand from her lips. "What on earth would give you that idea?"

"Well, for starters, he was standing outside a building with smoke coming out of it on the grounds of Alfbern Hall. What if the building was a forge? Evangeline was impaled by the sword Sarmentum after tripping over an anvil!"

"So you think Staccato pushed her or something?"

"Well … maybe."

"Oh, come on, Pasha!"

"Well, what do you think? What else could he possibly have been referring to?"

"I don't know! One thing's for sure, though, I doubt it was as crazy as what you're suggesting." She reached forward and rested her hands on his shoulders. "Pasha, listen to me. You're stressed! Why don't you take a moment to lie down, shut your eyes, and relax."

Pasha stared into her eyes for a moment. He nodded his head.

"You're probably right." He eased himself onto his elbows and allowed his head to fall back between his shoulder blades.

"Probably? Honey, with my track record, it's best not to question me."

Below them the treetops, like dominoes, trembled in a perfect crescendo. A gust of wind rolled up through the valley and the first trace of evening breath kissed the backs of their necks. Pasha yawned and closed his eyes. Five seconds later, Faina was batting his arm.

"Look, we can see Mama Lydia from here."

Pasha sat up and followed her finger to the place Faina was pointing to. Out in the ocean, his mother was lain out on a low, flat rock, absorbing the sunbaked warmth as twilight descended around her. Her pink tail dangled into the water.

"I have to admit, Pasha," began Faina, "when I first came here and saw what the mermaids were wearing I wondered how your mother was gonna cope. But it looks like she's pretty much embraced it."

"What do you mean?"

"Well, the fashion is a little more daring here, isn't it? I mean, I guess it has to be for practical reasons, especially if you're a mermaid, and that's who everyone takes their fashion cues from. I mean, hardly anyone wears stockings here unless it's cold, and you know why? Because the mermaids never wear stockings. They spend too much time on the beach, it's impractical. They all wear Turkish pants, and sarongs with the slit up the thigh, and seashell tops, and well, look at your mother! She's out there right now in basically little more than a corset."

Pasha's eyes glazed over. "And your point is?"

"I just didn't expect her to transition so well. You know, with her having been a proper lady and all that. The Baroness of Balalchik. I thought it would be a culture shock."

Pasha leaned back and shook his head. "You forget, my mother is a bohemian. One thing you gotta understand about Ma is she was never really a great society lady or anything like that. I mean, yeah, she married into an aristocratic family, but it was a huge deal."

"You mean because your father joined the Israelites of the New Covenant around the time he married your mother?"

"Actually, that was before he met Ma. Baba and Dido didn't find out until later, then they blamed Ma."

"So your father converted to Messianic Judaism and married a Christian. That doesn't sound like that big a deal. I mean, not a huge one."

"That's because there was more to it than that. Even I have to admit what happened was pretty scandalous."

"Ooh, a scandal! Do tell!"

Pasha raised an incriminating eyebrow, and Faina sobered.

"I mean, a scandal? Your family? I …" She rolled her eyes. "Oh, you know I didn't mean anything by it, Pasha! Why do you always gotta be so touchy?"

Pasha sighed and folded his knees.

"Alright, well as you know, my mother grew up in Lake Baikal where she lived a pretty isolated childhood with her adopted father. Papa was born the Baron of Balalchik, famous not only for the family name, but for the wine produced on the estate. After my mother's father passed away, she moved to Crimea and got a job working on the vineyard. While my grandmother was busy trying to set Papa up with Lady this and Lady that, my father fell in love with my mother, the hired hand. You can imagine the shock and outrage."

Faina shook her head back and forth in amazement. "Wow, different faith, different upbringing, different station. How did your father convince your grandparents to let them marry?"

Pasha gave an awkward laugh. "Uh, well, he didn't. They eloped in the night. They were planning to run away together, start over as peasants. My grandparents managed to trace them back to an inn outside of Yalta. They would've disowned my father if it weren't for the fact that he was the only male heir to the Chevalsky family. You know how it is in Russia. Only men can inherit titles. So unless my grandparents wanted to lose the estate to a total stranger they pretty much had to give my father whatever he wanted, and he wanted Ma."

"How romantic!"

"Yeah, but it wasn't easy, even after they were married. Ma never had many friends. She won over Dido in the end but Baba always resented her. Half of society did. She was snubbed by almost everyone." His shoulders rolled forward as he stared at the ground. "It's funny how hateful people can be sometimes. They said some pretty nasty things about my mother. About me."

"You? What did you have to do with it?"

Pasha sank over his knees with a gloomy expression. "I know it's hard to imagine anything else that could make my parents' marriage more shocking, but Mama was barely seventeen when she wed Papa. And as soon as they were married, she was expecting."

Faina lowered her eyes. "I see."

"And it didn't exactly help that I was born nearly two months early."

"You never told me you were premature."

Pasha looked out over the darkening edge of the sky. "Yeah. Mama said it was a pretty close call. I was so tiny that not even my grandparents could deny I came too early. That didn't change anyone else's mind though. People still tried to say that my father compromised my mother out of wedlock, then married her out of charity. They said I was … well, you know. Someone even started a rumor that my mother had taken a lover and that I didn't belong to my father at all."

Faina's nose contorted. "Where did they get that idea?"

"I don't know. Something about a man always hanging around the village, watching her."

Faina squeezed Pasha's arm and leaned her head on his shoulder, not saying anything.

"Ma was pretty lonely. Thing is, I think she would've been lonely even if that never happened. She's always been different, artsy, you know? Riding horses bareback astride, talking about things a lady would never mention, refusing to hire a nanny."

"What's so wrong about that?"

"Rich people don't raise their own children, not really. They hire a governess to do all the dirty work and only see their children at tea time. At least until they're old enough to wipe their noses. Thankfully, I didn't have that experience." Pasha lay back and stretched in the final pulses of warm sunset. "My parents spent all their time loving us. At least I still have one of them."

Faina looked down at him with a fond smile and pinned her hair behind her ear. "You sound like the Darling family."

"I suppose we do." Pasha smirked. "I guess that makes you Peter Pan."

They sat in silence, mingling their unspoken memories of what life used to be when their lost loved ones breathed the air they breathed, when they themselves were small enough to be picked up and held.

Chapter 6:

Portrait of a Young Miraculous

Panels of white sunshine hatched the floor of the library through the windows. Sonata had assigned Pasha and Faina a history report. They were each free to choose from any period in Voiler's history they liked. Pasha tended to favor mermaid history, which was idyllic and cultural. Faina had yet to channel her interests into one avenue and sat amongst a fortress of half-read volumes in the corner.

Presently Pasha had a book about Pescatarians, a reformation group in the 1600s that opposed intermarriage between mermaids and non-mermaids. The moment he looked up from the page his eye was drawn to a book about Voilerian wildlife. Thoughts of dragons and leviathans circled his mind. He set aside the Pescatarians and grabbed the volume from the shelf.

It felt as though he couldn't flip through fast enough. He stopped and froze as he came upon a black and white photograph of a wooly mammoth spanning across two pages. Pasha nearly dropped it. His mouth fell open, and he resisted the urge to laugh aloud. Spying Faina bent over a book of Voilerian dog breeds, he tiptoed behind her chair and slapped the open book in front of her.

"Feast your eyes on this!"

Faina jumped in alarm. "Pasha! You nearly …" As her eyes registered to what she was looking at, she trailed off. She made a noise that was something between a laugh and a gasp, and hopped up and down in her seat. "Is it real?"

Pasha pinned his chin on her shoulder as he turned the page to the description.

"You bet it is! 'Of the countless animal species hunted to extinction in the Other, it is estimated that at least three quarters of those species still exist in Voiler today, the majority of which are thriving. Take, for example, one of Ursa's most notable fauna, the wooly mammoth.'"

Faina shook her hands and squealed. "Pasha, I can't take it! It's too exciting!"

"I know, I know!" He went on. "'Ursa has the largest wooly mammoth population in all Voiler, with an estimated five hundred offspring born every year. They are most commonly found in the regions of the Boötes Mountains, but have recently been migrated as close as the Twilight Wood just outside of Polaris's more urban settlements.'" Here Pasha paused thoughtfully. "That's strange. Why would wooly mammoths come so close to civilization?"

"Perhaps if species are less likely to be hunted here, they have less reason to fear humans."

"Still, they need space don't they? And grass, and trees, or whatever it is they eat. They're not going to find much of that near the city."

Faina squinted her eyes and leaned in closer to the book. "Maybe it says why somewhere …"

Pasha continued to read. "'This strange phenomenon of encroaching on human settlements began in 1887, after King Bruin Northstar took the throne following the death of both parents, and seven older brothers. Bruin was said to have suffered from grief-induced insanity which supposedly affected his ability to rule and led to poor decision making. The deforestation of several acres in Polaris to build a sacrificial altar for Primals in the Twilight Wood is believed to be what inspired this unusual behavior in the wooly mammoth population.'"

"I wonder how much of that was Samael's idea," remarked Faina gloomily.

"Staccato did say it was his influence with my grandfather that led Ursa to its ruin."

A sparkling glare was thrown in their eyes as Sonata appeared around a bookcase donning an extra sparkly pair of prosthetic legs.

"There you are, Pasha! Might I have a word with you?"

Something in the way she was biting her lip told Pasha she had news he might not be happy to receive. He followed her to a secluded area. She stood staring at him, fiddling with her hands, and forcing a smile. Pasha eyed her with caution.

"What is it you wanna talk about?"

"Remember Skelter's idea about you doing an interview with a popular newspaper? Well, I've talked to *The Daily Compass* … "

Pasha felt his lungs tighten. "You want me to do a newspaper interview?"

"A newspaper interview?" She threw back her head and scoffed. "Of course not! That would be silly! Why would you think that?"

Pasha's shoulders deflated as he placed a hand against his rapidly beating heart.

"You had me scared for a minute."

"It would be a live radio broadcast."

"What? Live? On the radio?" He clutched at his throat. "*Nyet*! No! No, no! Sonata, I can't do a live interview! I'll humiliate myself! Didn't you see me on the front page of *The Rising Sun*? I looked like an absolute idiot!"

"That was an unfortunate accident. You were ambushed. This would be set up privately in a studio with professionals."

Pasha thrust his hands into his pockets and stomped past the performing arts section. "No!"

"Now, Pasha, really! This is what we've been working for! All those speaking lessons, all the study, all the elocution, this shouldn't be news to you!"

Pasha stopped. "I know."

"Then what's the problem?"

He turned and faced her. "I don't wanna make a fool outta myself."

Sonata crossed her arms, but her eyes radiated an understanding.

"Well, I hate to break it to you, Pasha, but if you're going to be king you're going to have to risk making a fool out of yourself a lot."

Pasha fixed his gaze on the fraying spine of a book. The title was so worn it was barely legible.

"I know it's something I have to do. I get that. I just don't know how I'm gonna do it."

"All they want to know is who you are. What kind of king would you be? Show them your heart. Show them the things that matter to you, what you're passionate about, what you want to change. There will be people who try to stop you, people who call you names. But there will also be hundreds who hear your voice and say, 'we're saved!'" She squeezed his shoulder. "Pasha, if there is one thing I have learned in my life about being brave, it's that if you face your fears once you'll be brave enough to face them again."

Pasha pinched his eyes closed. "How long do I have to prepare?"

"The interview is scheduled for March twenty-seventh at eleven o'clock, so about three weeks."

He drew a capitulating inhale. "I suppose that's plenty of time."

"I can give you a break on that report if you like."

Pasha shook his head with a half-smile. "Nah, that's alright. I like studying."

Sonata patted his back. "Let me know if you need any help. Try to keep me informed of what you're planning."

"I will."

Sonata departed with a friendly wave, and Pasha returned to Faina amongst her tower of books. At the sight of Pasha, Faina craned back in her chair, her long tangle of hair grazing the lower rung.

"What was that about?"

"I get to do a live radio interview with *The Daily Compass* in a couple of weeks."

"Gosh, are you nervous?'

"What do you think?" He tugged on a lock of her hair, and sat on the tabletop. He grabbed a book at random and cracked it open across his knee. After a moment of unusual silence, he glanced up to find Faina staring at the wall in contemplation. He snapped his fingers at the end of her nose.

"What's eating you?"

"Pasha, I've been thinking about something lately …"

He shoved a hand under his chin. "Yeah?"

"Well, you know how Samael found that newspaper with your picture on the front page? The one where you were running from the police?"

"Yeah. What about it?"

"If Samael managed to get ahold of that newspaper, can you imagine what else he's dug up on you? I mean, it wouldn't exactly be difficult to find out about your involvement with the Breadwinners. All he'd have to do is send someone asking around the Lower East Side. And if Samael knows about all that, you can guarantee he is gonna try to use it against you."

Pasha was silent as he let the information slip into his brain and root long enough to cause a slight throb between his eyes. Faina was right. His hands grew cold with fear. Next thing he knew he was tangling his fingers through his hair.

"Aw geez! Faina, what am I gonna do? If anyone finds out about the Breadwinners they'll never let me be king!" He buried his head in his hands. "How could I have been so stupid? All of this has been one gigantic waste of time!"

Faina seized him by the wrists and forced him to look at her. "Wait. Stop and think for a second. So far nothing has happened; nobody's said anything."

Pasha wriggled loose and paced back and forth in front of the window.

"No doubt Samael's waiting for the trial so I can publicly humiliate myself! Have a nice roasting in front of an international court of law! A public execution!"

"Pasha!" Faina yanked on his shirttail and pulled him into the open chair beside her. "Will you stop and listen to me?"

Astonished, Pasha nodded his head and stared at her wide-eyed.

"Alright." She pinned a curl behind her ear. "If there's anything the public likes more than a scandal, it's a redemption story, a comeback from a troubled, tragic past."

Pasha groaned but Faina ignored him.

"Listen! I know what I am talking about here. What if you were just honest with the press from the beginning? What if you went in and willingly told your story?"

"You think I should just waltz in there and say 'Hi, I'm Pasha! I'm a wanted bootlegger, a former accomplice to organized crime, and I wanna be your king!'"

Faina had to bite her lip to keep from laughing.

"Not like that, you silly ham. Look, everyone has a story. People don't just do things without reason. You joined the Breadwinners so your mother wouldn't have to work in that awful speakeasy with all those creeps. There was no sinister motive; it was purely noble. You sacrificed yourself for your mother. If you don't tell the truth and instead let Samael tell your story, it's gonna look like you were trying to hide something. But if you're honest from the beginning it'll look like you have nothing to be ashamed of, and you don't! If anything, you know what it's like to be poor. You know what it's like to do desperate things to support your family in hard times. That makes you relatable."

Pasha sat up straighter. "You know, Faina, I think you've got something there!"

"Of course I do!"

"The more I think about it, the more brilliant it is!" He took her by the shoulders. "Faina, you're a genius!"

Faina batted her eyes in an exaggerated manner. "I know, darling, I know. Beauty and brains, I'm the whole package!" She reached for a book across the table. "Now, forget your troubles and get a load of this!"

She opened a book titled *Karkinos: The Marble Kingdom*. She flipped to a page and turned it around for Pasha to see. There was a mischievous glint in her grin. Centered on the page was a black and white photograph of a striking young man with a familiar haughty expression. Elegance and refinement overflowed from his high, sharp cheekbones. He had one pomp, bushy eyebrow raised over his heavy-lidded eyes. Pasha's mouth fell open in bewilderment.

"Is that who I think it is?"

"It is! It's Staccato!"

Pasha had to cover his mouth to keep from laughing too loud. "How old is he there?"

"Eighteen, right after he snagged the job as Theo's advisor."

Pasha ran his eyes over the smug expression on the clean-shaven face. Faina clicked her tongue, unable to take her eyes off the photograph.

"He certainly was a dish!"

Pasha glanced off to the side. "Yeah, I guess …"

"Would you look at those cheekbones? He could have been in pictures!"

Pasha scoffed. "I don't know about that."

"I mean, what a sheik!"

Pasha shoved back from the table. "Okay, let's not get carried away here, Faina!"

He squinted his eyes. Even in black and white it was easy to discern the sun-bleached highlights in Staccato's hair. Pasha's coarse black bangs fell over one eye. He hastened to brush them aside. His chest deflated.

Faina tapped the page. "It seems strange to see Staccato with hair."

"Ha! A pompadour! And that collar! Looks like he was just as stiff then as he is now."

"Well, he must have loosened up after his first few months, because in the rest of the pictures he's a lot more casual."

"There's more?"

He flipped through at least a dozen photographs of young Staccato on the job. As his career progressed he appeared more and more natural, just as Faina had said. The stiff collar disappeared. He wore open shirt fronts. His pant legs became rolled up, exposing bare feet, and the relaxed style seemed to lend itself further to his natural good looks.

Pasha scratched at his chin. "I guess it would be pretty hard to keep up with the mermaids in dinner jackets and spats, don't you?"

Faina did not answer right away, she was too engaged with a photograph of young Staccato diving shirtless off the edge of a precipice.

"Faina! Stop flirting with the photograph!"

"I am not flirting with the photograph! I'm just trying to figure out who he reminds me of!"

"Yeah, right! You would flirt with a statue if you thought it was good looking!"

Faina turned and faced him with a maddeningly coy smirk. "My, my, I had no idea you were so jealous. However did you survive leaving me behind in New York?"

Pasha's cheeks cooked to a nice even red. "You make people uncomfortable when you do that, is all. How would you feel if I sat here making eyes at all the mermaid pictures?" He pointed to a beauty with wavy hair. "You'd feel pretty awkward, wouldn't you?"

"I'll say, since that's your great-aunt."

Pasha raised an eyebrow, then scanned the caption.

```
"Princess Estella Soter, Daughter of Queen
                 Atergatis."
```

Pasha drew back in horror while Faina dissolved into laughter.

"Forget I mentioned it," he murmured.

As Pasha returned his attention to the book, his eyes ran across a familiar face. It belonged to a tall, impressive merman with deep soulful eyes and a tranquil expression.

"There's Uncle Javaid, Sonata's father."

Pasha had met Javaid last December at the Christmas Ball in Pisces. It was easy to pick him out for he bore a striking resemblance to Sonata. In the picture, he and Staccato sat side by side in a keelboat. Javaid was holding a large flounder over his head. Staccato was doubled over with laughter.

"If that's Javaid," said Faina, reaching over to point to another figure, "this must be Theo."

It was as though Michelangelo's *David* had come to life. Theo was the embodiment of the classical ideal, with his high-bridged nose and chiseled face. An unchallenged authority rested in his eyes that was impossible to disrespect. Pasha thrust his lip out, impressed.

"He looks like a king."

They turned the page to a picture of all four Soters sitting together on a rock with their tails dangling in the ocean. Evangeline laughed as Javaid dragged Staccato into the picture.

"They were all pretty chummy," observed Faina.

"Staccato always said Javaid and Theo were his best friends."

Pasha's eyes swam through the pictures, desperately searching for some sort of clue as to what Staccato's big secret was. He ran his finger across Evangeline's face. Again he thought about the vision of Staccato with bloodstained hands.

Faina closed the book with an impish grin. "What do you say, Tom Thumb? Shall we take it back to camp?"

"I think that's an excellent idea, Hunca Munca."

***

Pasha and Faina arrived back at camp in no time. Staccato sat at the picnic table buried in notebooks and papers, finishing off his fourth cup of coffee. Behind him Skelter and Pyro were having fun beating each other up. Before anyone noticed Pasha and Faina, Pyro slammed Skelter to the table, causing a stack of papers to fall over. Staccato ripped off his spectacles and turned on the pair like lightning.

"If either of you touch this table one more time while I'm working I will personally throw you over the railing!"

Staccato could be as intimidating as thunder. But to Pyro and Skelter he was nothing more than rain against a windowpane. Pyro laughed and shoved Staccato's head.

"You'll have to catch us first."

They scrambled over the table like two cats, papers flying everywhere. Sonata appeared in the doorway of the kitchen. Her mouth fell open in horror, and she almost dropped her pitcher of lemonade.

"What have I told you boys? No roughhousing on the table!"

Pyro and Skelter froze. Skelter had Pyro by the scruff of the hair, and Pyro was yanking back Skelter's mouth like a fishhook.

Pyro rolled his eyes. "Yes, Mother!"

Skelter nodded his curly head.

"You said it, Skelter! Foiled again, by the pair of prudes. You two are no fun!"

Sonata swatted Staccato's shoulder with a dishtowel. "Why didn't you stop them?"

"Ow! They don't listen to me!"

"Then you should've come to me!"

Pyro rolled off the edge of the table and rubbed at his lower back. "That's right, Staccato, why didn't you go off and tattle?"

Staccato flashed Pyro a look. His eyes bore imploringly into Sonata's. "See?"

Sonata clicked her tongue and poured him a glass of lemonade.

"Poor Staccato." She kissed the top of her godfather's head. "Don't pay them any mind."

Skelter threw up his hands in a mockingly affectionate gesture while Pyro grumbled.

"Teacher's pet …"

As Sonata was retreating into the kitchen, Skelter held out his glass like a thirsty three-year-old. He indicated to the pitcher of lemonade with puppy dog eyes. Sonata swept her nose into the air.

"You may have some lemonade when you learn to conduct yourself with more propriety."

And with no more to be said, she sauntered back into the kitchen, leaving Skelter pouting with his elbows bowed on the table. As Sonata exited, Melodious passed her in the opposite direction, carrying a glass himself.

"At it again, are they?" he chuckled.

Staccato rolled his eyes. "Again would imply they that they stopped in the first place."

Melodious sat down at the table and placed the glass discreetly next to Skelter's elbow.

"Don't let her catch you."

Skelter smiled and signed his gratitude to Staccato who had no choice but to translate due to Melodious's blindness.

"He says thank you."

Having been satisfactorily requited with renewed peace, Staccato drew himself up and took notice of Pasha and Faina for the first time.

"Well, look who's back from the library!" His eyes traveled to the book in Faina's arm. "What have you got there, Faina? More Dickens?"

Staccato seemed to have taken a particular liking to Faina for some odd reason, a fact Pasha resented, fearing it might persuade his best friend to take up with the enemy. But then it wasn't unusual for Faina to win over the most unlikely of people, especially those of a melancholy disposition. Pasha himself was a testament to that.

"Not this time." With great ceremony, Faina held open the page with the picture of Staccato diving off the precipice, bare-chested and handsome.

Staccato's face fell in horror. His cheeks colored by rapid degrees.

"Oh, stars! Where did you dig that up?"

Skelter and Pyro practically tripped over each other to see the picture. Pyro took one look and fell back on his haunches with rambunctious guffawing. Hasty to satisfy his curiosity, Skelter pushed him aside. He doubled over with such intensity that it was difficult for him to laugh quietly. Grabbing the book, Pyro lay back on the table and held it over his head, wonderfully entertained.

"This is great! I've never been able to picture you with hair before! What color is that? Is that blonde? Were you a blonde?"

Staccato straightened himself with dignity. "It was hazel."

This brought on a whole new barrage of cackling. All this riotous noise lured Sonata out of the kitchen. She stared, utterly perplexed by the hysterical heap that had gathered on the porch.

"What have they done now?"

Tears running down his face, Pyro tried to point to Staccato. "Hazel … Hazel, he says!"

Sonata rolled her eyes and grabbed the book from Skelter. Her hard expression melted to sentimentality.

"Oh, look at that! Look how handsome you and Papa are!"

Pyro slapped Melodious between the shoulders. "Wish you could see it, Mel."

Melodious smiled appreciatively, but didn't appear to feel at much of a loss. Sonata came upon a photograph of the spring solstice festival where the group was piled into a spacious, canopied rowboat.

Pyro leaned over her. "Look at all those mermaids eyeing Staccato!" He gave his superior a playful punch on the shoulder. "Somebody had a finned fan club!"

Staccato looked away, trying to cover his smile, a remnant of pride hidden in his expression. Curious, Skelter pointed to a photograph of Staccato riding along the shore on a penny-farthing.

"Why the bicycle?" Staccato repeated. "Well, as you can imagine I was rather at a disadvantage whenever Theo traveled through the water. I may have been an excellent swimmer, but I couldn't be in the water all the time. The penny-farthing, however, helped me to keep pace while staying dry."

Melodious propped his elbow on the table and stroked his mustache. "Penny-farthings, I remember those. Used to startle me whenever I felt one breeze by on the sidewalk."

"Did you ever fall over?" asked Pasha, who would've been quite intimidated to ride from such a height.

"Only a handful of times, but you get the hang of it eventually."

A cool and loving hand lighted on Pasha's shoulder. He turned to find his mother fresh from the ocean, her wet hair tied into a long braid.

"What are you up to, my darlings?"

She gave Pasha and Faina each an affectionate kiss. As she leaned forward to peek at the book, Pyro leapt up and chucked it into the branches of an enormous tree. Faina stared at him as though he had just gotten up to dance the polka.

"What was that for?"

"I saw a mosquito."

"Where? In Australia?"

"My hand slipped!"

Pasha rolled his eyes. "It was nothing, Ma. Just some old pictures of Staccato when he worked for King Thessalos."

Faina crossed her arms and huffed. "I guess now Skelter will have to try and get it back."

Skelter rose, but Sonata jerked him into his seat by his belt loop.

"Or Staccato could summon it with his—" Before Pasha could finish, Pyro snatched up Staccato's staff and pitched that over the railing too.

Faina threw up her arms. "Did Skelter give you a concussion or something?"

Pyro sputtered as though Faina were being absurd. "What? Staccato could use the exercise!"

Pasha chuckled and crossed his arms over his chest. "According to him he doesn't need his staff to—"

"Exercise?" Staccato pushed back from the table, his nostrils flared. "You just wait until I fetch my staff," he stormed off down the stairs, "I'll show you an exercise … of my power, that is!"

Pyro threw his head back and chortled. "Yeah, yeah, go on, old man!"

Pasha cocked his head. What were they all up to? He glanced back at Skelter, who appeared just as confused as he was, then to Melodious who was happily whittling away at a block of wood with a pocket knife, and seemed the least affected of all present. Pasha was pulled from his thoughts as Lydia ran a finger over the curl at the nape of his neck.

"*Patulya*, don't forget to lay out the trundle for your sister tonight. It is supposed to storm, and you know how I feel about sleeping in the ocean when there is lightning."

"But you're a mermaid," observed Faina. "Aren't you safe from getting electrocuted as long as you have a tail?"

"I know it sounds silly but I just can't shake the fear of being in the water when there is lightning. Old habits, I suppose."

Chapter 7:
Bedtime Stories

That night, Lydia sat before the vanity running a brush through her thick blanket of long hair. Pasha knelt down beside her and pinned his chin upon her knee.

"So, Ma, what was all that about the other day with Staccato's staff?" For added effect he made sure to paste on a papery grin. No stranger to her son's clever yet well-intentioned wiles, Lydia eyed him with suspicion.

"What are you talking about?"

Pasha thrust out his lower lip and groaned. "Ma, I know you saw something, a premonition or whatever!"

With a clever smile she rose from the bench and patted his head.

"A premonition is when you sense something in the future. Psychometry gives you an indication of the object's past."

"Sure, whatever you say. But what did you see?" He scuttled to his feet and pursued her to the kitchen where she poured a cup of milk out for Katya.

"Pasha, I can't tell you what I saw, that would be an abuse of my powers and an invasion of Mr. Nimbus's privacy."

"What's the big deal? Katya abuses her powers and invades everyone's privacy all the time!"

At this remark, Katya, who had been reclining in the trundle, craned her head back and stuck her tongue out at her brother. Pasha ignored her.

"Please, Mama, it's just me! You can tell me, can't you?"

Lydia laid the cup of milk on the floor beside Katya's head.

"That depends, why do you want to know?" She pulled back the fluffy covers next to Katya and indicated for Pasha to lay down.

Knitting his hands behind his back, Pasha twisted the ball of his foot into the floor.

"Well, you see, I kinda, maybe, sorta overheard a conversation between Staccato and Sonata after dinner."

Lydia straightened herself with authority and propped her hands on her hips.

"Pasha Chevalsky, were you eavesdropping on a private conversation?"

Pasha flopped to his knees on the mattress next to his sister. "I wouldn't say that, exactly. Besides, I think you may wanna hear what I have to say."

Katya bounced to an upright position and clapped her hands together. "I wanna know! I wanna know!"

Pasha roped his arm around Katya's neck and pinned her against his side. "Who wants to play caterpillar?"

Katya struggled to lift her hand. "Me!"

Pasha picked her up and dumped her onto the comforter. He tucked the blanket around her and rolled her like a crepe until she was wrapped up like a cocoon. He bent his head over her.

"Is it tight enough?"

Katya smiled, and the compression of the blankets smushed her cheeks together.

"What?"

"I said, is it tight enough?"

"I can't hear you."

Pasha flashed her a smug smile and lay down, propping his head against his sister as though she were a bolster.

"It's tight enough."

Lydia sat at the edge of the bed and tried to suppress her smile of amusement.

"Alright, my little charmer, I'll bite."

Pasha regaled her with the conversation he'd heard outside Sonata's bungalow. He told her how Staccato had been crying over something he did, that he had been keeping some big secret which threatened to prevent Pasha from ascending the throne. When he had finished, Lydia stared at him with her brows knit together. She pressed a thoughtful hand against her mouth. Pasha laid his head on her knee and looked very much like a puppy begging for a treat.

"So are you gonna tell me what happened with the staff or not?"

Lydia sighed and ran her fingers through Pasha's bangs. "Nothing I think that would shed any light on your story."

Pasha's shoulders heaved with disappointment. Before he could sink any farther his mother tilted up his chin and looked him in the eye.

"If I tell you what I sensed, will you promise not to tell anyone?"

There was an honest sobriety in the way Pasha nodded his head. "I promise."

"And you promise you won't use it against Staccato to bully him into answering your questions?"

"Ma, you know I would never do that!"

Lydia pushed her hair away from her face. "I know, I know, but I have to make sure all the same." And giving way to a labored sigh she fell once more to sitting with her eyes closed, combing trancelike through Pasha's hair.

"Guilt, and a terrible sense of grief."

Pasha felt his heart sink like a stone inside his chest. "F—For who?"

A crease formed upon her brow as she pinched her eyes harder.

"I couldn't tell you the nature of the relationship. Perhaps a mother? A daughter? I don't know."

"They were female?" Pasha flinched as a shiver ran down his spine.

"I suppose they could have been male, maybe a father or son. I don't know why I said that."

"It's your intuition."

She peeked open one eye, a smile tugging at the corner of her lips. "You think?"

"That's how it works, right? You said there was grief, so the person must be dead." He steeled himself for the next question. "Could you tell how they died?"

"It is hard to say." Her eyes focused on Pasha. "Darling, what is wrong? Something has frightened you, I can tell."

Pasha ducked his head and pinched the space between his eyes. He quickly began spilling the details of the vision he'd seen when he broke Staccato's staff.

"Ma, what if Staccato killed Evangeline? What if it was her blood on his hands?"

Lydia took one look at her son and burst into laughter.

"Now, *Patulya*, sweetheart, that is truly ridiculous!"

"I'm serious, Mama! Think about it!"

Lydia cupped his face with both hands. "You are letting your worries get the best of you, my son." She pressed her lips against his forehead and giggled. "Pasha, Evangeline said it herself. It was Bruin who killed her, not Staccato. If she believed Staccato to be a dangerous or false man she would have warned us to stay away from him."

"I guess you're right." He rubbed his eyes and yawned, laying his forehead against his folded palms. A thought struck him.

"Mama, what if you're not really Bruin's daughter? What if that's the secret?"

"Pasha, enough, darling, you must stop! You will worry yourself to death! Besides, that would be an awfully serious thing to lie about."

"Well, it would have to be serious if it jeopardized my chance at the throne. Besides, what about your adoptive father? The one who taught you English? What if he was your real father?"

Lydia rubbed her face with the heels of her hands. Laying back on the pillows, she immersed herself into another bout of deep thought. When she didn't answer him, Pasha peeked his head over the bed.

"You said he adopted you when you were an infant. What if that was a lie? What if you were never in an orphanage? Mama?"

Lydia bit at the sides of her fingers. Pasha softened.

"I know you don't like to talk about it."

Lydia lay quietly for a moment with her forehead drawn together. "It hurts to remember."

"Because he died?"

There was a faint but unmistakable pain in her expression as she fiddled with the wedding ring on the chain around her neck. She nodded. Pasha climbed onto the bed and lay down beside her.

"How much of what you used to tell us was true? When we were little, you said you lived in a cottage in an enchanted rose hedge like Sleeping Beauty."

Lydia scoffed, but Pasha knew her well enough to know when she was hiding something.

"I always thought you were making stuff up to entertain Katya and me, but … it really happened, didn't it?"

Lydia rolled her head to one side and curled into herself.

"Ma, you're not crazy. Look where we are! It's entirely possible that all that really happened! You don't have to be afraid anymore! Katya was never delusional and you're not either. No one is going to take us away from you. Why do you doubt yourself?"

When she still didn't answer, Pasha sighed worriedly, and laid his hand on her shoulder.

"I know you really loved him, Mama. Tell me again, what was he like?"

All at once Lydia came back to life, laying her hand upon his. "My father was wonderful, Pasha. He spoiled me, really." A smile was tucked at the corner of her mouth. "He would call me 'Lydie,' or 'Lydie-bird.' Whenever he came home from a long trip he would pick me up and carry me everywhere, even when I was too big. He did it just so he could hold me in his arms. When he had to leave again I would cry myself to sleep. I hated it when he was away. I would lie in bed all day just so I could dream about him. I missed him that much."

"Why was he always away? What was he doing on those long trips?"

Her eyes lowered, dilating like a drop of ink from an overfull pen.

"I don't know. He never would tell me about his work, but he always came back banged up, scarred, and bloodied. When I was thirteen, he came home with a broken leg. After that, he retired, and stopped taking those long trips. He was only thirty-three at the time, but we never seemed to be in want of money."

"Could he have been a soldier?"

"Why would he keep that a secret?"

Pasha glowed with intrigue. "Maybe he was a spy!"

"For who? The Tsar?" She scoffed. "You know he used to tell me stories about my mother."

"Evangeline?"

Lydia nodded.

"He knew her?"

She fidgeted with the ribbon on the collar of her nightgown.

"And he couldn't have been lying. He told me she was a glassblower, that she had long, golden hair, and golden eyes. We now know all that is true. I know how that sounds, but Pasha, Bruin had to be my father, my mother's spirit said he was."

"What if she was lying?"

"Can spirits lie? I mean, if my soul were about to be put to rest, I am not sure I would feel comfortable lying."

Pasha looked very grave as he sat up. "Mama, why would your father know about Evangeline if he adopted you from an orphanage? That doesn't add up."

Katya kicked her feet in a most impatient manner.

"Can I come out now?"

Lydia laughed and patted Pasha's shoulder.

"You better let her out."

Pasha knelt down beside his bundle of a sister, took hold of the blanket's edge and gave it a solid yank. Out tumbled Katya, kicking her legs and giggling in an absurdly comical manner. Pasha and his mother exchanged amused glances. He cast the white sheets over Katya like a fresh, clean parachute. Pasha didn't know how he would fall asleep that night with all the questions whirring inside his brain. He could only find peace by promising himself one thing: that he would find the answers, no matter what.

Chapter 8:
Making Dreams

Pasha had little trouble sleeping through a storm. Something about the concussion of thunder pushed him further into a state of blissful unconsciousness. He chalked it up to six years living in the Lower East Side. New York could make a heavy sleeper out of anyone. But screaming was different than thunder.

When Pasha opened his eyes, his mother was thrashing violently. Sweat poured from the crook of her elbow. The line of her jaw tightened as she ground her teeth together. Arching her back, she let out a bloodcurdling scream. Pasha was on his feet, grabbing her wrists, and shaking her.

"Ma, wake up! It's just a dream!"

Katya clawed her way onto the bed and put her hands on her mother's cheeks.

"Mama, you're having a nightmare!"

With a deafening slam, the front door, which had been locked, blew open with such force Pasha thought it might fly from the hinges. They each let out a cry. A bright light poured in their eyes, causing Pasha to sneeze. Staccato was standing in the doorway, drenched in rain. He was clenching his staff as though preparing to run it through someone's skull. Pasha breathed a sigh of relief.

"It's just a nightmare! Nothing out of the ordinary."

Staccato deflated. Staggering, he put out his staff to steady himself. For a moment Pasha feared he might collapse. Lydia looked about wildly. Pasha squeezed her hand.

"It's okay, Ma."

Lydia pressed her palm to her forehead. As the tears squeezed from her eyes, Faina appeared behind Staccato.

"Mama Lydia?"

Pasha flipped on the lamp. "Nightmare."

Faina swept her way into the kitchen as though it were all very routine, which it was.

"I'll get some water."

Pyro poked his head around the door frame.

"Someone having a nightmare?"

Having gained some composure, Lydia sat up, embarrassed. She brushed her hair over her shoulder.

"Forgive me, I did not mean to wake everyone."

Pyro tossed his head back and sputtered. "Ha! Are you kidding?

Congratulations! You're only a member when you've woken everyone in the middle of the night screaming."

Lydia screwed up her eyes with a nervous smile. She whispered to Pasha, "Is he joking?"

"Nope. For fun, we keep a tally of who screamed the most in a month. Whoever wins gets the bear."

"The bear?"

"A stuffed bear. It's kind of a joke." He threw up his shoulders. "It was Sonata's idea. Pyro won last month."

With unabashed pride the igneous elbowed his way into the lamp light.

"Actually, I currently hold the all-time record."

Faina wiped the excess water from the side of the glass.

"Everyone's done it. Well, everyone except Cicada. She hasn't been traumatized yet."

"But if you really need the bear," joked Pyro in good-natured humor, "I may be willing to give it up for a night or two."

Faina giggled behind her hand. "Yeah, after all, Pyro has his stuffed dragon, Torchy …"

"I do not!" He smoothed his shirt front, and laid a hearty slap between Staccato's shoulders "Don't worry, Mrs. Chevalsky, Staccato here will fix you right up."

Lydia looked around to Staccato who was standing with his head bowed outside the circle of light. Faina slipped the glass of water into Lydia's hand.

"Staccato can create dreams. So whenever one of us wakes up in a fit, he makes sure we don't have any more nightmares."

Pyro gave a yawn and stretched his arms over his head.

"Yeah, pretty nifty power when you're a rough sleeper." He headed for the door. "Well, now that that's settled I think we better leave you to it." He whistled for Faina as though she were a faithful collie pup. "Come along, Beastie, you got training in the morning. Back to bed for you."

Lydia gave Faina a grateful kiss on the cheek. When at last they had gone, Pasha trained his eyes on Staccato, tense with anticipation as he turned to Lydia.

"You'll have to fall asleep first."

Lydia drew up against the pillows, her cheeks red.

"Really, you don't have to do this. I am sure you are very tired. I will be fine."

Staccato shook his head, his eyes riveted to the floorboards. "It's quite alright."

Anxious to have everything settled, Pasha nodded to the armchair in front of the hearth.

"Please, sit down."

"Thank you." Just as Staccato was about to lower himself into the chair, Katya glided towards him in a blur of blonde bed head.

"You don't have to sit in the dark, silly."

Katya scooted the chair to the bedside and, seizing him by the hand, towed him towards the seat. Staccato appeared intimidated by her well-intentioned willfulness, and he struggled to look her in the eye. With no argument to support his hesitation, he sat in the chair and scooted back so that he was situated behind Lydia's head. Katya dropped to her knees with a cheerful grin.

"That's not so bad, is it?"

She said this with such simplicity that she brought a faint smile to Staccato's lips. He shook his head, and returned his attention to Lydia.

"Mrs. Chevalsky, I realize this may be a somewhat personal question, but it helps to know what you were dreaming about."

"My husband's death."

"Ah, yes. I imagine that was very traumatic for you." Staccato laid aside his staff and rubbed his hands together. "I'll need you to try and fall asleep. If there's anything that would make you more comfortable, for example, I can step out of the room if you like …"

"I can help her fall asleep!" volunteered Katya.

Pasha helped her onto the bed. Katya stretched out her hand towards their mother's neck. A golden light fell from her fingertips. Lydia's eyes grew heavy. Smiling, she kissed the top of Katya's wrist.

"Thank you, princess."

Her gaze lingered on Katya until at last she shut her eyes. Her head dropped back, and her breathing became steady. She had one hand up by her head and the other lying across her stomach.

"She's asleep," said Pasha.

Katya hid her face behind her arm and struggled not to yawn. Pasha gave a sly smirk.

"I saw that." He scooted her back towards the trundle. "Go back to bed, *Rybka*."

With her knuckles still buried into her eyes, Katya slid into the pallet. She curled up under the sheets with her fist beneath her chin.

Already Staccato was rolling a ball of light in his hand like clay. He smoothed his thumb over an edge, rubbing out some discrepancy only he could see. Now and then he gave it a flick with his finger. The glow guttered like a bulb.

When at last the dream was ready, he extended his hand over Lydia's brow, hovering so he did not come into contact with her. It looked as though he were holding the sunrise upside down, and his mother's face was the last trace of midnight sky.

When the orb touched her forehead, it broke apart into a shower of glimmering particles. They sank away into her skin and faded. For a moment, a faint smile appeared on her lips. She turned her head on the pillow, happily contented.

When Pasha looked back at Staccato, he was shocked. His expression was weighed down with suffering. While Pasha's mother glowed with joy, Staccato had turned ashen and gray.

"Are you okay?"

Staccato gave a start, then, putting on a weak smile, nodded his head.

"Yes, I'm fine."

"Does it hurt?"

Staccato surveyed him as though he didn't understand, then, catching on, gave a slight scoff.

"No, of course not. I enjoy it, actually. It's nice to feel like you helped someone."

"You looked upset for a moment."

Staccato gave way to a long exhale and rubbed his eyes with the heels of his hands.

"I'm tired, Pasha. That's all. A lot of travel, you know."

His attention returned to Lydia, and Pasha supposed that he meant to keep an eye on her to make sure the dream stuck. He didn't know why, but Pasha no longer believed Staccato disliked his mother.

"Did you enjoy seeing Theo?"

For the second time, Staccato drew a labored sigh and leaned his elbow on the arm of the chair.

"He's slightly better. As I've said before, the death of Evangeline all but destroyed him, hardened him into a different person. He rarely comes up to the surface, even now that the Land Lock is broken."

"Is that bad for mermaids? Being in the water too long, I mean."

"Every bit as bad as staying out of the water, if you can believe it.

Mermaids have two forms for a reason. They need both water and air to survive. Not to mention the darkness. It can damage their eyesight."

Pasha watched his mother roll to her side. "I'm sorry you're upset about Theo." He was irritated with himself for saying it, but it was true. "You said you discussed a lot about Evangeline while you were there. Did he say anything about Evangeline showing up as a mermaid in the grotto?"

He was referring, of course, to Evangeline's mysterious appearance back in December when she had helped him find a way to break the Land Lock Curse. Though they had since discovered the Firebird to be Evangeline's spirit in a state of limbo known as Moram Mortem, no one had figured out how she had managed to escape her Firebird form. Little was known about the phenomenon, but up until that point it was generally believed souls in Moram Mortem could not return to their original state until their soul was freed by the fulfillment of a catalyst. After a brief reinstatement with their human appearance the soul would then go on to rest permanently.

"I'm afraid not," Staccato admitted, seemingly as disappointed as Pasha by the lack of information. "Honestly, I sometimes think it will be a miracle if we ever figure it out."

"Maybe that's all it was to begin with: a miracle."

Staccato appeared surprised. "Well, you certainly have come a long way since arriving in Voiler, haven't you? You wouldn't have said that when I first met you."

Pasha shrugged. "I'm just my old self again, is all. I wasn't always cynical." The silence which followed burned brightly on him like an overheated spotlight and he was eager to change the subject. "You were pretty close to the Soters, weren't you?"

Staccato smirked. "They were such a nice family, the four of them together like that. And Theo and Javaid's mother, Queen Timpani, she was quite nice too. So they say, anyway. She was Calliope's aunt, you know. Quite a resemblance between them."

"And Evangeline and Estella's mother?"

Staccato made a face. "I'm sorry to have to tell you this, Pasha, but your great-grandmother, Atergatis, was ghastly, may she rot in—" He stopped.

Staccato glanced up at Pasha. His eyes dropped to Katya, who was fast asleep. He never finished his thought. Instead, he reached his hand over Katya's sleeping form and showered her in a golden rain of sparkles. The shadow of a smile eclipsed her mouth.

"Not too much," Pasha warned. "She laughs in her sleep. She's done it since she was a baby."

Staccato turned with an amused smile. "She laughs?"

"Yeah." Pasha snickered. "And I don't mean just giggling. She really laughs, until she wakes herself up. It's pretty funny, actually. But she hasn't done it in a while, not that I know of anyway."

Staccato grinned and regarded the little girl with curiosity.

"She's a happy little thing, isn't she?"

Pasha hadn't expected Staccato to derive such delight from the idea. He was genuinely charmed. Pasha traced a wrinkle in the sheets with his toe.

"Yeah, she's all sunshine."

His smile fell. He felt frustrated for talking and laughing with Staccato. It made him forget how irritated he was, how maddening Staccato's secrets and strange behavior were. Staccato suppressed a yawn, and rose from his chair.

"They should be fine now. Get some rest, Pasha."

Pasha looked down at the floorboards. "Thanks for helping my mom."

Staccato nodded his head. He took one last look at Lydia and left the bungalow.

Chapter 9:

The Paper En Vogue

As Pasha was leaving the cabin for breakfast, Katya chased him down the parapet.

"So, when are you and Mama gonna tell me about the big secret?"

Pasha ground to a halt and swiveled around. "What big secret?"

"I'm not stupid, you know."

Pasha reached down and scuffled her tangle of curls.

"Of course you're not! Why would you say something like that?"

"Because you won't stop lying to me!"

Pasha smoothed back his hair. A long sigh escaped his lips.

"Fine. I was sharing a secret with Mama last night. Does that make you feel better?"

"No. Tell me what it is."

Pasha arched his back as though he would curse the skies. "Katya, I can't tell you what it is!"

"Why not?"

"Because you're too little!" He turned his back on her and walked away.

The planks trembled as she stamped her foot. "What you really mean is too crazy!"

Pasha's hands shook up around his head. "What are you talking about?"

But Katya didn't answer, she simply lowered her head. Her gilded eyes stretched. The sun was glinting through them like a prism. Her entire body tensed.

"What are you doing?" Pasha regarded her with a raised eyebrow.

"Finding out what you're hiding!"

The corner of his mouth tugged upwards. Before he could stop himself he doubled over in laughter.

"Well, I didn't think you were crazy before but I might now!"

Katya let out an angry growl and launched herself at his knees, slapping and shoving without discrimination.

"Woah! Woah!" Pasha placed his palm on her forehead and pushed her back. "Katya, calm down!"

Katya tore away from him, her shoulders heaving. "You'll be sorry, Pasha!" And with that she ran back into the cabin.

Rolling his eyes, Pasha headed towards the picnic table outside the kitchen, where he found Pyro sitting with one elbow propped on the table reading the newspaper, while Faina lay out on the surface trying with all her might to get it to move.

"Tired yet?" Pyro asked her in a bored manner.

Faina flipped onto her back and tried to pry his arm over with both hands.

"Nope! Not one bit!" But the strain of her voice betrayed her.

Pyro scoffed. "If you say so."

A mischievous light dawned in Faina's eyes. Rolling onto her stomach, she leaned forward and bit Pyro's knuckles. Pyro jumped back, throwing his newspaper into the air.

"Blazes, Faina!"

Faina rocketed onto her feet, throwing her head back and laughing maniacally.

"I win! I win!"

"Alright, you ferocious little beast, get down from the table before Staccato spots you."

"I got her," Pasha shouted, running up to the table and throwing Faina over his shoulder.

Footsteps echoed from within the kitchen, and Staccato appeared in the doorway looking tired and agitated. He took one look at Pasha and Faina and nearly dropped his coffee.

"Not so close to the railing! You two are going to break your necks!"

Typical, Pasha thought. Pyro and Skelter could be jousting from tree limbs and Staccato wouldn't bat an eye, but as soon as Pasha and Faina did anything it was always, "Get down this instant! You'll break your necks! You'll put your eye out! Get out of that suitcase before you suffocate!"

As Pasha was about to apologize, he noticed something hanging around Staccato's neck for the first time. It was a necklace with a small filigree box carved from a shell, no bigger than a fingernail. A turquoise clasp, so minuscule it was hardly noticeable, indicated the charm's ability to be open and shut, very much like a locket. It may have been a tiny trinket, but it was still too flashy for Staccato to have been wearing as a fashion statement. Pasha squinted his eyes. What could be inside of it?

Staccato must have noticed Pasha looking, for he immediately tucked it away into his shirt collar, safely out of sight. Before Pasha could stare any longer, Lydia flowed up behind Staccato, as smoothly and as quietly as water.

"Go for his knees, Faina. Gets him every time."

Staccato jumped, not having noticed her arrival.

"*Nyet!*" Pasha exclaimed. "Why would you tell her that?"

He tried to lean away from Faina as she reached for his knees, but she was too quick. In seconds Pasha lay on the ground. They rolled with laughter. Lydia patted Staccato's shoulder.

"They are sturdy children, Mr. Nimbus. With everything they have endured I am lucky they still laugh at all. Children shouldn't be made to grow up too fast. I should know."

Pasha watched curiously as Staccato stared at her with his mouth open. He'd never seen him so unhinged. Perhaps he was afraid she was mad at him for fussing at her kids. Lydia didn't seem to notice. She only smiled and turned towards the kitchen.

"I think I will go pour myself some coffee."

Melodious ceased playing his accordion and sniffed at the air.

"Alright, you two, enough horseplay for now. You better go wash up. Something tells me breakfast is about to be served."

And Melodious was right. After they had gone and rinsed their hands, Sonata laid out plates of biscuits with blushing slices of cured salmon. Katya was sitting at the table now, calmer than before. Pasha and Faina practically tripped over each other to reach the table first, their mouths watering. Pyro wrinkled his nose.

"What is it with you all and fish? Not you, Sonata, I get that. But Katya, you're too young to like …" Pyro plucked a jiggly sliver between his fingers, "whatever this is."

Before Katya could answer, Sonata cut in.

"She's a mermaid too, you know. And it's quite good if you would actually try it." She brushed a stray hair from his forehead. "Hold still!"

Pyro fidgeted as Sonata set him right. Once she was finished, she topped off his coffee, all the while combing her fingers through his hair. Pyro didn't even seem to notice. Everyone stopped to stare at them. As Sonata became aware of the attention, she jumped back as though Pyro's head had burnt her fingers.

"Must you wear your hair like a wild man all the time? You look like you were sucked up in a tornado!"

Pyro's lips fell slack as he eyed the faces around the table.

"I'll wear my hair however I want, thank you!"

Sonata swept up her nose and swaggered back to the kitchen, Pyro storming after her. A wry smile tugged at the corner of Staccato's mouth.

"Where are you going, Pyro?"

Pyro swiveled around with his eyebrows raised. "I—I'm going to get something that isn't mermaid food!" His eye twitched. "What does it look like I'm doing?"

As Lydia passed him, she pressed a hand over her knowing smile. Skelter lowered his newspaper to shake his head and sign to Pasha.

"What do you mean, they're fine?" Cicada wiped her mouth on her arm and swallowed. "You just wait, one of these days we're going to find Pyro lying in a shallow pool of salt water, dead!"

Melodious snickered. "You've given this some thought, haven't you?"

Skelter made a talking motion with his hand.

"Exactly," agreed Staccato. "Don't pay them any attention, they're all a lot of talk."

Cicada shriveled up her nose. "I am so confused."

Staccato gave a long sigh and dragged his hand across his forehead. "Cicada, after breakfast I need you to go down to the library."

Cicada leaned forward as though anticipating a very important assignment. "Okay, go on."

"Check out every book you can find by Jane Austen."

"Okay. Then what?"

"Read all of them by next Tuesday."

Cicada gave a faithful salute. "You got it, boss!"

Moments later, Pyro and Sonata emerged from the kitchen, Pyro's hair appearing wilder than before. They sat at the breakfast table in silence. Sonata folded her napkin in her lap and tried to behave as though nothing had happened.

"So, Pasha, have you told everyone about your upcoming interview with *The Daily Compass*?"

There was a gagging noise as Pyro choked. He almost spat his coffee in Melodious's face.

"*The Daily Compass*? You didn't!"

"Why? What's wrong with *The Daily Compass*?"

"You might as well just run another picture of him sneezing into the camera! Nobody in fashionable circles reads *The Daily Compass* anymore, not after siding against Draco back in 'twenty-one!"

"You read it."

"Do I look like a fashionable bloke?" He pointed a finger at Cicada. "Don't answer that. The point is, they've lost their respectability."

Sonata pursed her lips. "Oh, you mean for printing the truth and standing up for what is good and decent in our world?"

"I'm not saying they deserved it. Hellfire! You know I stand behind everything they report! But why not something more en vogue, like *The Morning Star*?"

"*The Morning Star*? That would be like feeding him to the lions!"

Finally Pasha got down his bite of food and was able to ask, "What are you two talking about?"

As Sonata sighed and rubbed her temples, Melodious set aside his fork to explain.

"In Voiler, the largest major international news outlets are *The Daily Compass,* which originated in Ursa, and *The Morning Star,* in Capricorn."

Pasha shrugged. "Makes sense. The most powerful countries have the most powerful news outlets. Karkinos excluded, of course."

"Well, Karkinos and Ursa are—I mean, *were*, a joint rule," noted Staccato, "but that's beside the point."

"After Draco gained representation on the Ecliptic Council," continued Melodious, "*The Daily Compass* received criticism for printing bad publicity related to Samael and the C.O.N."

"And as you know, Primal Instinct has enjoyed quite a success amongst the young and fashionable. Many of Samael's supporters rebelled against *The Daily Compass*, accusing them of slanderous and unfair rhetoric."

Sonata sniffed. "When in fact it was factual and just! All they wanted was to silence the truth so they could go on doing whatever pleased them without any opposition from the press."

"Anyway, *The Morning Star* is what's currently du jour."

Pyro set down his coffee. "Which is exactly why you should've set up Pasha's interview with them."

Too weary of arguing to raise her voice, Sonata rolled her neck with fatigue.

"Be realistic, Pyro."

"It may seem logical to have Pasha interview with the more popular news journal," began Cicada, "but think about it. *The Morning Star* worships Samael, and right now Pasha is a threat to his administration. If Pasha is restored as king, Samael will lose possession of Ursa's land. Draco's resources will diminish. They'll be left with almost nothing."

"But aren't they surrounded by rivers?" said Pasha "That should give them an edge on trade and plenty of fish, and since it's freshwater they wouldn't have to compete with the mermaids."

"Unfortunately, the rivers which encircle Draco are quite treacherous, bad enough that it makes navigation difficult. And the environment is too harsh to accommodate much wildlife. Then, of course, they're flanked by Karkinos on the south side. Samael would have to be a complete imbecile to try and encroach on those waters. And it's too cold and rocky to farm."

"If Draco once had an empire that spanned across all Voiler, how did they end up with such a pitiful plot of land?"

Pyro bit into a piece of bacon. "It was part of the Treaty."

"What treaty?"

"The Treaty of Zubeneschamali—'Chamali, for short. You know, the settlement that ended the Liberty Wars, the war that set Voiler free from Draco's tyranny centuries ago. They were to be 'chained to their miserable rock,' those were the words they used. Scorpius to the upper east, Sagittarius to the north, Ursa and Karkinos to the south, always to be kept in check. It was the treaty that prevented Draco from obtaining Ursa when Bruin was killed."

"What do you mean?"

"After Bruin broke the alliance with Karkinos he replaced Draco as Ursa's steward kingdom. After he died the Ecliptic Council decided it was a violation of the treaty. They gave the stewardship to Karkinos. It wasn't until the Land Lock that Samael took the reins." He lifted an eyebrow. "Honestly, Sonata, what are you teaching them in those history lessons?"

Sonata threw back her shoulders. "We just finished the Glorious Vision of St. Amberjack. They're not due to learn about the Liberty Wars for another two weeks."

Staccato gagged on his food, and had to stand to stop the choking.

"You just now finished the Glorious Vision of St. Amberjack?"

"Well, it's a very extensive subject—"

"It's an extraneous subject that hardly requires mentioning! We don't have time to dally over minor details."

Sonata scooted her teacup with one finger until it was situated in front of her.

"Well, we did start from the beginning. It takes time to catch up to present affairs."

"At the rate you're going present affairs will be ancient history! That's it, after breakfast see me in my quarters, I want to go over the curriculum."

But Pasha was not about to let them drift off subject.

"But all that stuff about the Liberty Wars, that was centuries ago, wasn't it?"

Cicada tore off the end of a strawberry. "Which is exactly why people are beginning to let up on Draco."

"When the Ecliptic Council denied Draco the stewardship of Ursa, Samael accused the Council of hanging on to ancient prejudices," explained Sonata.

Pyro dug his knife into his toast. "Said they were intolerant of his culture. That Draco had been a victim of international discrimination."

"Which is somewhat reasonable." Cicada stroked her chin. "I mean, a lot of our impressions of Draco are based on crimes committed hundreds of years ago."

Pyro snorted. "Trouble is, they're still being committed! Draconians are no less evil now than they were back then. If anything they're more violent. I should know, I dealt with them on a regular basis back when I worked for the Saighdeoir!"

"What's the Saighdeoir?" interrupted Faina.

"Special task force in the Sagittarian military. Do a lot of rebel work and bounty hunting. Now, as I was saying, Draconians are the most violent barbarians that ever did draw breath. Look at the C.O.N.! And who are they to accuse everyone of hanging on to ancient prejudices when they're slaughtering Fay! Sure they got a raw deal in the Liberty Wars, but it's not as if they didn't earn it."

As Pyro's rant ended, Sonata slipped an extra piece of bacon onto his plate when he wasn't looking.

"*The Morning Star* does not wish to report on the atrocities carried out by the C.O.N., the child sacrifice, dumping petrol into the mermaid kingdoms, setting colonies of sylphs on fire. Instead they glorify Samael and try to dig up dirt on the Fay. You can be sure *The Morning Star* would do nothing but twist your words until they had painted a picture of an ignorant, scheming upstart after Samael's position."

"And do not be surprised when they do go after you, interview or not," warned Melodious. "As Sonata said, Pasha is an opposition to Samael, and you can be sure *The Morning Star* will work to bring you down."

Pasha cracked his knuckles. "Slander I can deal with. If *The Daily Compass* is as fair as you say they are, then the only thing I'm worried about is doing it right."

Skelter pumped his fist into the air.

"That's the spirit!" exclaimed Pyro. "Now hurry up and finish your breakfast. We've got a lot of training to fit in."

At the mention of training, Lydia looked down and cleared her throat.

"Why must he have this combat training again, Mr. Anomaly?"

Pasha lowered his head as he whispered reassuringly to his mother. "Ma, everything is fine."

But Lydia ignored him. "Shouldn't he be focusing all his efforts on ascending the throne? Why does he need to be fighting? It isn't as if you are planning to send him off on some dangerous mission again, correct? I mean, had I known chasing the Firebird was going to turn into warfare I never would have let him go."

Pyro wrung his hands.

"Well, he's going to need to know how to defend himself while he's on his tr—"

Before Pyro could mention Kentucky, Pasha rammed the toe of his boot into Pyro's shin.

"It's not that I'm expecting to fight, Ma, it's just preparation. You never know what's gonna happen. I mean, the C.O.N. attacked us two months ago. Don't you want me to be able to defend myself if it happens again?"

Lydia scrutinized him in silence for a moment. At last, she straightened and sighed.

"You are right, I suppose."

Pasha would have to tell her sooner or later, but the last thing he wanted was a row over the breakfast table. It would be better to wait until the afternoon once things had quieted down, and they could speak in private, perhaps during a walk on the beach. Mama could never be upset when she was at the beach.

Chapter 10:
A Mother's Wrath

Unfortunately, Pasha had miscalculated the odds of invoking his mother's wrath. Apparently there was no time in which she was less likely to react to the news of his upcoming mission with anything less than volcanic fury.

Pasha dove between the slamming door and the threshold of his cabin as he called after his mother.

"Ma! Wait! Can we just talk about this for a second?"

But Lydia wasn't listening. She marched tightlipped down the stairs towards the door of Staccato's cabin.

"Staccato Nimbus!"

Pasha jumped. There was a sound like a heavy stack of books falling to the floor, followed by hurried footsteps. Staccato opened the door a fraction, half concealing himself behind the wood.

"Yes, Mrs. Chevalsky?"

"What do you think you are doing sending my children off on dangerous missions to tangle with thugs and ophidians?"

Staccato's mouth opened and closed several times, unable to get the words out.

"And what are you doing hiding behind that door?" she snapped. "If you have the nerve to send my children out like soldiers without consulting me, you better have the decency to come out here and face me like a gentleman!"

Staccato hesitated with his fingers pressing into the frame. He soon gave in and shut the door behind him. He kept his head bowed to his chest and would not look up at her.

"Do forgive me, Mrs. Chevalsky, but I wasn't planning on sending your youngest, only Pasha."

"Don't you give me that, you know I mean Faina, as well! We barely escaped New York with our lives, and now you want to send them off on some rendezvous with a C.O.N. member masquerading as an art racketeer? I will not have it! They are not going!"

"Again, my apologies, Mrs. Chevalsky, but I believe that issue lies with your son, not me."

Lydia stomped her foot as she edged closer. She had Staccato up against the door.

"I am their guardian! They are both just children."

"There is no law in Voiler, or America for that matter, stopping them from making their own decisions. Were Pasha under the employment of, let's say, an advertisement company, and you didn't approve, there would be nothing you could do about it, except threaten to kick him out of the house. Pasha and Faina may be under your legal guardianship, but there is nothing suggesting that they are currently dependent on your care. So as much as I sympathize with your plight, I'm afraid there is nothing you can do about it."

Pasha daren't even breathe. Staccato had completely blindsided her, and coldly, too. With no remaining argument to make, Pasha was worried that his mother might slap Staccato. Instead, she edged away from him, her lip trembling.

"You are sending my children headlong into danger! You are sending them after demons—creatures who drink blood, and eat human flesh! Creatures that want my son dead!" She bent her head forward, tears spilling down her cheeks.

Staccato's eyes grew wide, he fumbled clumsily as he removed his handkerchief from his pocket.

"Oh, now, please don't cry, Mrs.—"

But Lydia swatted him away.

"*Vy ne ponimayete, kakovo eto-poteryat' rebenka!*" You don't understand what it like to lose a child!

In a moment of exasperation, Staccato looked her directly in the eye.

"*Ya ponimayu.*"

The moment the Russian phrase tripped from Staccato's tongue, Pasha's mother fell back in silence. It was a habit she and Pasha shared, going off on rants in their native language, thinking no one else could understand. But not only had Staccato understood every word, he had answered her back.

Pasha was less surprised. He had known for quite some time that Staccato spoke Russian. He had learned it from his aunt, who happened to be the Chevalsky's neighbor in the Lower East Side: Poppy Potemkin. And that wasn't all. Much like Pasha, Staccato had a penchant for language, and spoke as many as five different tongues.

Staccato coughed into his sleeve. "I do understand," he repeated, as though saying it in English would make her forget he had just said it in Russian. "I never had any children of my own, but I can only imagine what that must be like."

Pasha watched his mother with a careful eye. She seemed to be only half listening.

Staccato went on. "Sometimes we have to let go of our children for their best interest."

"And sending them into danger is in their best interest?"

"They won't be alone. Mr. Anomaly will be accompanying them, and he is more than capable of protecting them from harm. Pasha and Faina are lending their time to a worthy cause. They're trying to make the world a better place. You should be proud of them."

There was nothing left for his mother to say. As her soporific eyes welled up with tears once more, Staccato's face contorted with horrible, wracking guilt. It reminded Pasha of Scrooge when he realized he was the dead man laying upon the bed. And seeing Staccato now, gaping at his mother with such sorrow, such apology, made Pasha reconsider everything he thought he knew about the man.

Lydia ripped away from Staccato's door, and stormed away in tears.

Chapter 11:
Pyro and the Power Drill

"Opa!" Pasha's heart fluttered as Harpagos gamboled across the final obstacle in their path. He ramped on his hind legs and beat his silvery wings like the ghost of a hummingbird. Pasha's hair was completely wild and windblown. His bangs fell over his forehead like heavy leaves on a branch. Sweat ran beneath his chin and down his lower back, soaking through his riding clothes. It felt exhilarating.

Up ahead, the caravan was parked beneath the muscular shade of a live oak. Its yellow paint popped against the black soil of the volcanic valley. Skelter was lain out on his belly in the back of the wagon, poking a screwdriver into something Pasha could not see. Nearby, Pyro ran a tape measure over Faina's hands while Sonata scribbled down the increments in a notebook.

Pasha slowed Harpagos to a trot and stretched in the breeze, letting the cool air breathe through the close-fitting fabric of his shirt. When he opened his eyes, Faina was staring at him. For a split second their attention met, then Faina's gaze quickly dashed towards the treetops. Curious as to what they were doing, Pasha decided to make his way over.

"You guys sure look busy."

Pyro threw the tape measure over his shoulder. "Well, if it isn't the Ukrainian cowboy! Been flying around the island, have we?"

"Just stretching the wings." Pasha gave Harpagos an affectionate pat. The pegasus snorted and reached back to nip at Pasha's bangs.

Faina ran her eyes over his boots and trousers. "I see you have riding clothes now."

Pasha glanced off to the side and reached back to scratch between his shoulder blades.

"Oh, yeah. Ma didn't like that I kept ruining all my nice shirts." He gave a short laugh. "And look." He indicated to the steel rings attached to his chaps where he was clipped into the saddle. "Now I don't have to worry about any more spills."

Faina ran her eyes over him a second time.

"They suit you."

Pasha felt as though the muscles in his mouth had been taken over, as he couldn't get rid of his goofy grin.

"You think so?"

Pyro groaned. "Faina, will you stop fidgeting?"

"What are you guys doing anyway?" Pasha asked.

"Glad you asked!"

He whistled to Skelter, who took a large book laying by his elbow and chucked it into Pyro's hands.

"So, I was thinking about what we might need for our mission, and until we can train Faina to generate her own fire I thought she might benefit from one of these."

He opened the book and pointed to a picture of a strange device which fitted over the thumb, middle, and index finger of the wearer's hand. Pasha scratched his chin.

"It's a lighter."

"Exactly! Discreet, convenient, and always on hand." He elbowed Sonata. "Get it? Always on hand?"

Sonata rolled her eyes, but Pyro caught her hidden smile.

"Anyway, all she has to do to generate fire is move her fingers like this." He brought his thumb and middle finger together. "The two strikers rub together to create a spark." He jerked his hand towards the other side of the wagon. "Cici's doing the handiwork."

"Very impressive!" Pasha extolled. "But isn't it a little conspicuous?"

Pyro gestured towards Skelter who smiled and waved.

"That's where ol' Skelly comes in. The way fashion's headed these days, it'll be easy to make it look like a trendy statement rather than a weapon. Skelter's job is to make it look stylish. Originally, Sonata was supposed to take care of that, but she broke the last one!"

Sonata threw up her hands. "Oh, as if you could've done any better! Skelter's the least clumsy out of all of us, you should have asked him in the first place."

Pasha unhooked himself and dismounted, allowing Harpagos to wander towards the patch of grass beneath the tree.

"But won't you be with us? Couldn't you generate the fire and Faina manipulate it?"

Faina's eyes glazed over. "The idea is for you and me to serve as the distraction while Pyro gets his hands dirty, since he's made sort of a name for himself. And he's not exactly a master at blending in."

Pyro swiveled around. "What are you talking about?"

"When you first introduced yourself, you called Canada 'Canadia,' and you had no idea alcohol had been made illegal in the United States."

"Oh, well, I know all about that now, don't I?"

Pyro shoved the book into Sonata's arms and resumed measuring

Faina's hand, while Pasha strayed over to the caravan to observe Skelter's work. The deafening whir of a power drill kicked on, causing them to jump.

The tape measure flew out of Pyro's hands, almost hitting Pasha. He pivoted around only to find Pyro with his head ducked low between his shoulders. Pasha's eyes scanned the horizon. It was as bright and as clear as he could've hoped, and yet he couldn't shake the feeling that an ominous storm had just rolled into the valley.

Sonata's voice was soft. "Pyro, calm down, everything is alright."

"Whose idea was it to give her a bloody power drill?"

"She needs it to construct Faina's lighter."

"She has a screwdriver! I told her if she was going to use that drill to do it in her room!"

Faina looked back at Pasha, her spritely eyes fizzled with concern. They had each sensed something was amiss. The drill fell abruptly silent, and their ears were left ringing.

"See now?" Sonata placed a hand on his arm. "She's stopped."

Pyro fidgeted. Even his freckles seemed to shrivel with tension. He was as frazzled as a spooked horse. Pyro stretched the tape over Faina's arm once more His fingers seemed unwilling to bend. The drill started up again. Pyro's hand flew up over the long pink scar marring his right arm. His nostrils flared. Pasha looked back at Skelter. He lowered his head, warning Pasha to prepare himself.

"It's just a power drill." Sonata placed her hand on Pyro's shoulder a third time but he shrugged her off. He dug his hands into his eye sockets, cringing as though he were in unbearable pain.

"I'm fine, Sonata!" The color of his complexion was approaching purple.

Skelter leapt to his feet as though any minute he might be expected to intervene. Pyro cupped his hand over his mouth.

"Will you stop that infernal racket?"

The power drill clicked off. Cicada poked her head around the wagon, completely oblivious to the tension feasting on the very oxygen they breathed. She smirked at Pyro in haughty defiance.

"Nope!" And with that she popped back out of sight. The noise started once again.

Sonata's mouth opened and closed in a plea the esperite never heard. Pyro cut around her, the outline of his muscles tight. Fearing another confrontation, Pasha tiptoed hurriedly behind Pyro while Skelter jogged ahead of him.

Pyro seared up behind Cicada and snatched the drill from her hand. Cicada snapped around. "Hey!"

But Pyro wasn't listening. He was stomping ghostlike towards the bay.

Sonata's voice quavered in volume. "Pyro? Pyro!"

Appalled, Cicada threw back her shoulders, preparing to charge. "Just what do you think you're doing?"

Faina snatched Cicada from behind, slammed a hand over her mouth, and wrestled her to the ground.

Once Pyro reached the edge, he chucked back his arm and hurled the power drill into the water. Cicada wriggled her head away from Faina.

"That's illegal, you know! Mermaids take that very seriously!"

Pasha joined Faina in slamming his hand over Cicada's mouth. Pyro pivoted on his heel and walked back to his cabin, sweat dripping down his temple.

Pasha knit his brows together. "What was that about?"

Sonata drew a long exhale and covered her face with her hands.

"It's … it's complicated." She squeezed her forehead. "I better go after him. Skelter, why don't you come along as well?"

Skelter was already hurrying to catch up with her. In moments they had disappeared beyond the path. Pasha shook his head.

"An explanation sure would've been nice."

Faina removed her hand from Cicada's mouth. "Someone's gonna have to fish that power drill out of the bay."

"I'll set Katya on it. It's too deep for you to go after."

Cicada sat up slower than usual. She hovered so low to the ground she was practically sitting on it.

"Cicada?" Faina's voice was slow and steady. "Are you alright?"

Cicada winced. Her lower lip pushed out. Just when they thought she might cry, she let out a wild animal cry of rage.

"I hate people!" She scrambled for something to throw. She took the book and tossed it into the air. "They don't make any sense! I hate them! I hate them! They're mean!" She took a screwdriver and hurled it. "And stupid!" She threw a pail of bolts. "And crazy!" Having run out of large objects to pitch, she screwed a bottle cap off a bottle and flipped it over her head. "And no matter how many books I read, I won't ever, ever, ever understand or be like them!"

Pasha grabbed her wrists. "Woah, woah, Cicada, calm down."

Her cheeks glowed hot with rage. "B—but—"

"I know how you feel. It's very frustrating." He took a deep breath, hoping she would follow his example. "Yeah, people can be complicated, and cruel, and confusing. But it's okay if you're different. You don't have to be like that. It's better if you aren't."

"But I have to be like them a little bit, don't I? Otherwise, I can't do things like go on undercover missions with you guys."

Faina shook her head and smiled. "Cici, if all you want is to go on undercover missions, you don't have to become like everyone else. You just gotta know how to pretend."

"Pretend?"

"All the world's a stage."

Cicada's tears dried and a light came into her eyes. "So, you're saying all I have to do is act like I know what I'm doing? Act like people?"

"It's actually kinda fun."

Pasha could see the wheels picking up steam in Cicada's brain. Her body rose a little higher off the ground.

"It's all just acting … It makes so much sense!" She zipped back and forth in a tizzy. "I have to rethink everything now!" She threw up her hands and ebbed with an enormous glow. "I'm so excited! I have to go read more!"

And with that, she rocketed into the trees in a brilliant, burning light. Pasha and Faina looked back at each other and laughed.

"She'll be fine," Faina reassured him.

"But what about Pyro?" Pasha dusted his hands on the knees of his trousers and exhaled. "Reminds me of Charlie Danziger."

"The guy in B4 who fought at the Somme?"

"Yeah. Aunt Poppy said it was Shell Shock. All kinds of things used to set him off: fireworks, engines backfiring … but I've never heard of anyone getting spooked by a power drill before."

"It has to do with his scar."

Pasha turned and gaped at her. "You knew how Pyro got his scar and you didn't tell me?"

"It's just kinda personal."

Pasha groaned and flopped back on the ground. "Okay, but is it really a secret?"

"Well, I guess not …" She cast her eyes thoughtfully towards the ground.

Frowning, Pasha folded his hands over his stomach and tried to appear interested in the clouds. If she really didn't feel comfortable sharing with him, he didn't want to push her. He'd been nosey enough lately, after all.

"It's okay, Faina. If you don't think you should tell, I won't make you." He tapped his foot and smiled blissfully up at the sky. Faina stared down at him with a raised eyebrow.

"It's killing you, isn't it?"

Pasha threw up his hands in feigned innocence. "What? I said you didn't have to tell me!"

"Uh-huh, sure." She lowered herself onto her stomach, her feet pointing in the opposite direction of Pasha's.

"Do you remember the article you read last Christmas about the 1902 Sheritan Hostage Crisis? And how Pyro and his sister were taken captive?" She wound a blade of grass around her finger.

"Yeah."

"Well, do you remember what it said about the C.O.N. torturing Fay to reveal their true names so they could tattoo it on their arm?"

Pasha closed his eyes and exhaled, annoyed that he hadn't pieced it together before.

"They branded him, didn't they?"

Faina cast her eyes down and nodded.

"But—but he was only … what? Nine years old?"

Faina pulled her hand away, snapping the sod in two. "And his sister was only six. They were water tortured, Pasha. They were children, and the C.O.N. forced their heads under water to get them to talk." She drew a sharp breath through her nose.

Pasha winced. "So the drill …"

"It reminds him of the tattoo gun." Faina stole a timid glance at him from beneath her eyelashes. "When something bad has happened, it's little things like that that stay with you, I guess. For Pyro it's the sound of a power drill. For Charlie Danziger, it's fireworks. For me, it's having stopped up ears."

She didn't have to explain what dreadful memory stopped up ears brought back for her. Pasha knew. They had both been nearby when the cart full of dynamite exploded in the Financial District killing her brother. They were fortunate they themselves hadn't been caught in the eruption, but the noise had left them with ringing ears, and had temporarily made Faina deaf on one side.

"For you, it's having something trickle down your back," she continued.

Pasha's shoulders tightened as though the lash of Klokov's whip were about to strike his back again. They'd discovered this association one summer when Faina had slipped ice down his back as a joke. The shock of a fluid trail trickling down his spine was so like the sensation of blood pooling over his numbing skin, he had nearly had a full-blown panic attack.

"But, I still don't understand. How did he get the burn scar?"

"He was so ashamed of his name being tattooed on his arm that he burnt it out himself." Faina cringed as the words came out of her mouth. "Can you imagine a little boy trying to burn his own flesh off?"

Pasha took up her hand and gave it a comforting squeeze. He could feel the conversation sucking her back into another wave of grief. Only a couple months had passed since the murder of Anya and her Uncle Matvei, and it didn't take much for her to retreat into herself these days.

Chapter 12:
Staccato the Liar

Sunday was Katya's birthday. With Faina's help, Pasha baked her a cake and decorated the picnic table with pink paper flowers. Flour, sugar, and icing splotched the kitchen counters in sweet-smelling smears. With nearly everyone seated at the table outside, Pasha quickly set about rinsing off the dishes.

As he turned on the faucet, he caught a glimpse through the window of Staccato coming up the walk. Pasha sniffed with a condescending glower.

"Well, well! Look who showed up!"

Faina glanced out the window and rolled her eyes. When she didn't answer Pasha, he went on.

"I bet he doesn't know Ma is here. Watch, as soon as he sees Katya he'll turn right back around!"

Faina crossed her arms and sighed. "You're reading way too much into this. Staccato's just awkward. He's not avoiding your mother."

"Well, things really oughta be awkward now, since she bit his head off."

Faina deposited the frosting knife into the sink.

"Staccato's like a cat. He's unpredictable."

Pasha jumped back, startled as Cello leapt atop the counter. Pasha and Faina watched dumbfounded as he waded into the half-filled sink as though it were a hot spring. Pasha threw back his head and laughed as he fished the feline out of the water.

"He's certainly more catlike than Cello is!"

Katya raced past the window in a tizzy of excitement. Pasha looked up just in time to see her trip on her shoelace and go flying across the porch. Her cheek struck the floor with an audible slap. Water splashed over the counter as Pasha dropped the dishes he was cleaning and bolted outside to check on her.

"Katya! Are you …" He trailed off as he rounded the corner, stumbling back several paces.

Staccato was beside Katya on his knees, waiting on her with the tenderest gentility. He pressed his fingers softly against her cheek.

"It doesn't hurt when I touch it?"

Katya shook her head. "No."

"You're sure you're alright, darling?"

Pasha narrowed his eyes. At this point it seemed useless to try and understand Staccato. He was put off by Pasha's mother and yet he couldn't resist being drawn to Katya. Katya stared up at him with kind, friendly eyes.

"I'm fine. It didn't hurt."

Staccato smiled. "Well, that's a relief. You wouldn't want any bumps or bruises on your birthday. Let's see, you're ten years old today, aren't you?"

Katya nodded and giggled into her hands. "How old are you?"

Pasha was just about to step forward and remind her of her manners, but Staccato answered her as calmly as if she had asked about the weather.

"I'll be fifty-five on the twenty-third of next month. Now if I'm fifty-five and you're ten, how much older does that make me than you?"

Katya screwed up her eyes in concentration. "Forty … forty-five?"

Staccato smiled and squeezed her hand. "Excellent. Forty-five years. Can you imagine being that old?"

"It doesn't seem that old to me."

Staccato laughed. "You're too kind."

Seeing that Katya was going to be okay, Pasha edged away and returned to the kitchen.

"What's the matter with you?" said Faina. "You look like you've seen Mammoth walking on two legs."

Pasha shrugged as he gathered up the dishes and cutlery. "Maybe I did."

***

Everyone was in high spirits as they ate, but then it is difficult to be melancholy when there is cake. When everyone had had their fill, the conversation fell to Pasha's interview.

"So, I think I've finally decided what I'm gonna tell *The Daily Compass*," announced Pasha, pushing back his plate.

Sonata's eyes stretched open. "Have you now?"

"If I'm gonna be king, I think it's important that I be honest and forthright with my people from the start, so … I've decided I wanna talk about my former involvement with the Breadwinners."

Staccato froze. Pyro choked. His mother's shoulders heaved with a noiseless sigh. He wished he could suck his words back in like spaghetti. Lydia turned to Katya with a forced smile.

"Katya, darling, why don't we walk down to the beach and see if we can come across any more sand dollars?"

Sensing the mounting tension at the table, Katya took her mother's hand. As their footsteps died down the stairwell, Pasha sighed.

"I shouldn't have brought it up just then."

Staccato pressed his long fingers to the bridge of his nose and portioned his words out.

"Pasha, if this is your idea of a joke, I feel I must inform you at once it's not amusing."

Pasha's sneer of disdain was unavoidable.

"Of course it's not."

"You say that as though it were obvious."

"You say that like it's a bad thing."

Sonata's shoulders steeled as though preparing to take charge of a sinking ship. She forced a smile. Her eyes met Pasha's. He had her support.

"Let Pasha explain himself."

Staccato fidgeted. His lip twisted over his teeth. "What's to explain? He wants to spill his secrets to—"

Sonata turned on him with all the dignified authority of a queen.

"Let Pasha speak!"

Even the tide seemed to fall still. Pasha did not know how or why, but he was suddenly braver, bolder, less inhibited.

"After Samael dug up that picture of me running from the police, I realized it wouldn't be difficult for him to find out the whole story. And if Samael knows about my past, we can be sure he's planning to use it against me. As I said, I'd like to be an honest ruler. I did what I had to to keep my family out of poverty, to keep my mother from having to work a dangerous job she hated. It was survival. When we fled Russia, we didn't realize how difficult things would be.

"Sonata asked me what kind of king I'd be. I'd be a king who knows what it's like to be desperate, who's no stranger to struggle. The things Ursa is experiencing right now, I've been there. Think about the women being forced to seek employment as *saignants*. They get paid to let ophidians drink their blood. That's no different than my mother having to dress like a showgirl and serve illegal alcohol in a speakeasy! No one should have to go through that. I want my people to know I'm someone who feels their pain."

Sonata beamed with pride. "Well said, Pasha!"

He looked around at the table. Skelter nodded his head in agreement. Melodious smiled his approval. Cicada glowed, and even Pyro seemed to have been convinced. Faina gave his hand a squeeze. As Sonata was about to clap her hands on his cheeks, Staccato erupted.

"No."

Pyro folded his hands and muttered over his shoulder, "Come on, Stacca—"

"No! Absolutely not! It's reckless, it's thoughtless, it's irresponsible!'

Before he knew it, Pasha was on his feet in a cold rage which astonished everyone.

"Telling the truth is irresponsible? You would think that! I've asked, pleaded, begged you for the truth for months now! Why didn't you tell me about the mirror? Why was my mother abandoned? If you knew I existed, why didn't you come back for us? I wouldn't even be in this situation if you had taken us back to Voiler when I was born! I would never have become a Breadwinner! We would never have been attacked by the Reds! My father wouldn't be dead!"

Staccato was stunned by Pasha's sudden explosion. His lips moved but he could find nothing to say.

"No answer?" Pasha scoffed. "I'm hardly surprised."

Staccato lowered his voice. "I realize I haven't exactly been forthcoming when it comes to your questions, but I can assure you there is nothing sinister going on here. I've kept nothing from you."

"Liar! I heard you! I heard you and Sonata! She begged you to tell me the truth about whatever it is you're hiding, and you refused!"

Sonata's mouth fell open in horror. She clutched her head as though the very thought brought her pain.

"That's why you skipped your lessons! I knew something was wrong! Pasha, you must forgive us!"

"You said if anyone found out it would threaten my claim to the throne." His eyes narrowed on Staccato. "You said what happened was your fault, something you did. Well, it seems we're both in a similar position, Staccato. Each of us has something in our past we'd rather not talk about, something we'd like to hide, something so big it could ruin my chances at saving Ursa. You do what you want with your secret, but I'm not gonna hide! I didn't suffer so I could live the rest of my life in shame. What purpose is there in that? I'd like to think I suffered so I can give someone else hope, so I can show them understanding. I'm not gonna lie. I'm gonna do what's right!" He shoved away from the table. His heels ground into the floor as he turned to Sonata. "I'm not mad at you."

He flashed Staccato a cold glare. With his emotions spilled across the table like marbles, he stormed back to his room.

The next morning Pasha skipped breakfast. He was too embarrassed to show his face. He retreated back to his room and curled back into his comforter, feeling absolutely wretched.

In his misery, Pasha fell back asleep. Someone knocked at the door.

"Pasha?" It was Sonata. "Pasha? Are you alright?"

He tried to smooth his hair back down. "Come in! It's unlocked!"

The door opened. Seeing Sonata had brought him a tray with coffee and one of Melodious's pastries, he hastened to help her.

"Aw, Sonata, you didn't have to do that."

"I had a feeling you might be starving yourself to save face. Looks as though I was correct."

"Well, I appreciate the gesture … and the accurate conclusion."

She patted his head and together they sat at the table.

"You needn't feel ashamed. Your reaction was understandable. A bit overdone, but understandable. You had clearly put a lot of thought into your decision, and it was nice to see you so confident, so convicted. It showed just how far you have come, which makes Staccato's response all the more disappointing."

Pasha sneered out the window. "Yeah, well, there's a lot of things I find disappointing about Staccato." He stopped himself, and looked down at the table. "Sorry. That was rude. I forgot he's your godfather."

She laid a hand on his arm. "It's alright, I understand. Yes, Staccato has been …withholding some information from you, but with good reason. It's easy to condemn Staccato when you don't know all the facts. His reaction to your proposal last night, although wrong, came from a desire to protect you. Staccato has done a lot for our family."

Pasha realized her use of the phrase "our family" was an attempt to drag him into some familial bond with Staccato. He didn't resent her for it, but that wasn't going to happen.

"I know it seems hard, Pasha, but trust me, if you knew why Staccato was keeping secrets you'd find it easier to forgive him."

"Then tell me the reason."

Sonata's shoulders tensed. She withdrew her hands into her lap and fiddled with a ring on her finger.

"I know you know what happened, Sonata. I know you know what he did. And I know you wish he would tell me, so why can't you?"

"Because it's not my secret to tell."

Pasha fell back against his chair, discouraged. But he couldn't be mad at Sonata. She was one of the nicest, most trustworthy people he had ever known, and it wasn't fair to put her in the middle.

"Can I still share my story with the press?"

Her eyes swelled with sincerity. "Of course you can. It's entirely your decision. No one can tell you what to do."

"But what do you think about it? Do you think it's a good idea?"

"Absolutely. You raised a good point when you mentioned the newspaper. If Samael managed to uncover that, we can be sure he knows a lot more."

Pasha sighed and folded his hands together. "Something else has been bothering me. If Samael does know about my past, why hasn't he released the information yet?"

Sonata gave a distant shrug. "Samael is very careful with his valuables. I'm convinced there is very little he does on impulse. He saves his best pieces for the right time. He had possession of the trident, Sea-Splitter, ever since the attack on Polaris, and yet nearly twenty-five years passed before he actually used it. Who knows how long Samael would be planning to hold on to that information. Yes, I believe your best choice is to come out with the truth. As long as it remains a secret it's a weapon Samael can use against you, but the truth—well, it's as the saying goes, I suppose—'The truth will set you free.'"

Chapter 13:
Coulter and Coulter

The radio station was a decidedly modern building fashioned from green glass with fan-shaped windows. When the motorcar stopped in front of the revolving doors, Pasha felt more out of his element than ever. Beside him, Sonata sat in prim contentedness waiting for the chauffeur to open the door. Pasha's reflection stared back at him from the sheen of his new leather oxfords. Beneath the brim of his smoky gray fedora he did not look like himself.

Faina elbowed him in the side. The door was open and Sonata had already exited. Pasha tipped his hat low over his eyes and scooted out into the sunlight. Bodyguards flanked him in a long wall of tridents. As his mother stepped out of the car, she reached up to preen Pasha's bangs for what felt like the billionth time. Hooking his arm through hers, the four made their way into the lobby.

An igneous with bobbed hair and slouchy slacks escorted them up the lift to the recording studio. The receptionist set them up in the green room. It was a wide, well-decorated space with sunken floors adjoining the sound booth. Bay windows with brass frames afforded them the ritziest views of the cityscape. Coffee and cookies had been set out for them on the coffee table, and a cup was poured for Lydia. Pasha watched as the fresh heat from the pot made an opaque cloud on the black lacquer.

"Mr. Coulter and Mr. Coulter will be with you shortly," the receptionist informed them in a posh dialect. Sonata thanked her, and the woman left the room. When the door closed, it dawned on Pasha that perhaps he should remember to breathe. Sonata patted his knee.

"Nervous?"

Pasha's dark eyes grew even wider, so they shined like the lacquered coffee table.

"Very."

Sonata clicked her tongue. "Too bad she didn't put out any tea. I don't imagine coffee would do much to calm you."

Pasha did not answer; instead, he turned his attention to Faina. Her face was hidden beneath a straw cloche. With her lace-gloved hands she fiddled with an embellishment on the hem of her skirt. Smirking in a coy manner, Pasha lifted the brim of her hat to peek at her eyes.

"You under there?"

Faina cocked a bushy eyebrow and smiled. Sonata eyed them for a moment, then rose and directed Lydia's attention to the window, pointing out the architecture of the city. Pasha let the hat drop back over Faina's eyes. He glanced down at a magazine on the coffee table. A well-known mermaid actress was posing on the cover in a promotion for her latest film.

"*The Bird and the Fish*," he read aloud. The mermaid film star was draped back in the arms of a seraph in a pose imitating the famous *Cupid and Psyche* statue. "Sounds like a love story. You know anything about it?"

"If I had to guess I'd say a mermaid falls in love with a seraph, and they struggle to make it work because they're from two different worlds."

"It's been awhile since we've been to the pictures."

Faina looked up at him. Pasha scooted closer.

"Tomorrow's your birthday. Maybe—"

"Hello, hello all!" The door swung open. Two smartly dressed men with pleasant faces bumbled into the room. The first was a short bulb of a man with apple cheeks so freckled and florid they reminded Pasha of two halves of a watermelon. His receding honey-colored hair was slicked into a slippery side part, and his eyes were shielded behind a fashionably tiny pair of coke-bottle glasses.

The second seemed to float behind the first like a friendly ghost in a tall, looming shadow. His eyes were heavy-lidded half-moons, closely set on either side of a long, protruding nose. He wore a sleepy, draped smile across his wide, thin mouth.

At the sight of Sonata resplendent in her wrap with the fluffy feather trim, the men removed their hats and bowed.

"Your Highness," burbled the first as he kissed her gloved hand. "So lovely to see you again, Princess Sonata."

"A pleasure as always, Mr. Coulter." She stretched out her hand to the second. "Mr. Coulter."

The shorter Mr. Coulter twiddled his fingers excitedly and looked round for Pasha.

"And where is His Majesty?"

Sonata drew Pasha forward and gestured to the first gentleman.

"Pasha, meet Mr. Horace Coulter," then to the second, "and Mr. Orville Coulter."

Horace flushed with excitement. "It is an honor to meet the true king at last!"

The brothers bowed in time holding their black derbies close to their chest. Pasha blushed and shook his head.

"Oh, you really don't have to …" But seeing as they weren't listening he trailed off and coughed into the back of his sleeve. "Uh, thank you.

It's a pleasure to meet both of you. Thank you for taking the time to interview me."

"Not at all, dear boy, not at all! I can't begin to tell you how delighted Orville and I were—weren't we Orville?—when Princess Sonata reached out to us with her request. Samael has been bad for business, very bad for business indeed! The sedition that man advocates! You have no idea!"

Pasha got the impression Horace was the more talkative of the two. He prattled on in his transatlantic accent hardly without pause. After introductions and a bit of polite conversation, he was escorted into the live room where a table was set up with two microphones.

Horace flourished his hands. "As I was saying, Your Majesty, Samael has all but destroyed our reputation after taking Ursa into his stewardship. These days Polaris is rife with manipulative, divisive, one-sided press masquerading as fair and objective! I'm sure you've heard all about *The Morning Star*! The editorial standards are abominable, I tell you, just abominable, Your Majesty."

"Mr. Coulter, you really don't have to keep calling me 'Your Majesty.' My first name will do just fine."

Horace stumbled back in alarm. "Your first name?"

"Please, I'd be much more comfortable if you did."

Horace gave a slow nod of his head, and relaxed a little. He pressed his fingertips together as though about to attempt something very daring and modern.

"Pavlo, then?"

"Pasha, actually."

Horace's eyebrows rose so severely they almost pushed back his hairline.

"Pasha? My, my, I do feel honored! You see, I read up on Slavic customs before you arrived. From what I understand, that's an awfully familiar name for someone of your upbringing."

Pasha tried not to laugh. He was referring to the fact that "Pasha" was the diminutive of his actual name.

"Uh, it's nothing really. Everyone calls me Pasha. It's sort of like how some people named William go by Bill."

"Interesting, so you'd rather everyone address you as Pasha?"

"I would. I don't like the idea of being formal and grand. It's not me."

Orville scribbled in his notebook. Horace stared at Pasha for a moment, then burst open like a firework.

"I love it! It's so new, so contemporary, so personal! Quick, Orville, turn on the recorder before we lose this glorious content!"

Pasha looked over his shoulder at his mother, Sonata, and Faina, all gathered around the glass window. He smirked. It was difficult not to like the Coulter brothers. As Horace waltzed to a seat in his swivel chair and adjusted his notes, he reached up to flip a switch on the microphone. A red light flickered on. He spun round in his chair and pressed a button on the intercom, which was wired to the control room where Orville was fitting a pair of large headphones over his ears.

"All set, Orville?"

Orville nodded his head and flashed Horace a thumbs up.

"Excellent!" He turned over his wrist to stare at his watch. "We're on in, five … four … three …"

The last two numbers were mouthed silently. The "On Air" sign lit the corner of the ceiling. Horace cracked his knuckles.

"Good evening, and thank you all for tuning in. This is Horace Coulter with *The Daily Compass*, and you're listening to the Blue Hour, when we present you with a feature interview, someone new and exciting every week to keep you abreast of the latest affairs of the day. Here with me today I have seventeen-year-old Pavlo Chevalsky, supposed heir to the throne of Ursa, whose legitimacy hearing with the Ecliptic Council is coming up in April of this year. Thank you for being here with us today, Mr. Chevalsky."

Pasha jumped to attention, nearly hitting his nose on the microphone.

"The pleasure is all mine, Mr. Coulter."

"Now, Mr. Chevalsky, you were just explaining to me before our interview started that you much prefer to be addressed as Pasha. Would you like to share with the listeners why it is you prefer the name Pasha?"

Pasha cleared his throat and, nodding his head, went on to repeat everything.

"I see. Now do you happen to know the meaning of your name? Is there some kind of significance there?"

Pasha's eyes glided to his mother at the window. "Uh …" She was mouthing something he couldn't make out. "Well, it's Ukrainian for Paul. As for its meaning …"

He narrowed his eyes on his mother's lips. Something with an "m" in it.

"Uh …"

Faina rolled her eyes, scribbled out the words on a napkin, and held it up to the window.

"Small and humble!" he blurted. "It means small and humble!'

"Wonderful! Wonderful! And might I say very appropriate from what I've heard about you. Now, Mr. Chevalsky, Pasha, I understand there's something you'd like to share with the public about your background. You have quite a story to tell. You've seen so much in your seventeen years of age."

"That's right, Mr. Coulter. Before I can even consider ascending the throne, I feel the people must know who I am truly and honestly."

"Let's start from the beginning. Where were you born?"

For the next several minutes, Pasha regaled the listeners about his home in Crimea, about the rise of communism, how the Bolsheviks came to power, and the day they attacked Pasha's family.

"My father tried to hide me in a winepress but the soldiers found me. Instead of taking me out of the wine press, they tried to crush me inside. I slipped out, and they took me prisoner with my parents. No one could find Katya, my sister. She had been asleep in the nursery." Immediately the feelings of panic and grief began to rise up in Pasha's throat. He quickly swallowed. "We thought she was dead. They'd set fire to the house."

Horace was leaning on the table with his mouth half open in shock. His forehead had gathered into a tight knot.

"After they had taken all of you prisoner, what did the Reds do?"

"They hanged my father."

"How old were you when this happened?"

"Ten."

Pasha felt the scratchy brush of the cypress tree as though it still swayed overhead. He could still feel his clothes, wet with wine, clinging to his skin in red patches. Inside he felt like Atlas, trying to push back an entire world of dark memory before it sank into his brain.

"But you and your mother escaped?"

Pasha nodded, forgetting to speak. Horace folded his hands and leaned forward again in astonishment.

"How?"

Pasha closed his eyes as he summoned the memory to the forefront of his mind.

"It can only be described as miraculous. To this day I still don't understand how it happened. A sort of mass hysteria broke out over the soldiers. It started with the sentry. He began tossing his head, like he had flies on him or something. Then he started waving his arms at things that weren't there. He dropped to the ground, screaming and pulling his hair. Everyone stopped to see what had happened.

"It started spreading. Soldiers everywhere were throwing themselves into uncontrollable fits. I'd never seen anything like it. While all that was happening my mother managed to free her hands. She secretly let me loose. The sentry had dropped his revolver on the ground. Mama took it and shot the executioner dead. One of the officers saw. He turned to shoot my mother but a stray bullet hit him in the chest. They were so crazy, they were shooting each other! With all the commotion we were able to get up and flee into the woods.

"We didn't know where to look for Katya. For all we knew she had died in the fire. We hadn't gone very far when we found her asleep in a ditch. My horse Harpagos was hitched to a tree nearby. I guess the army had tried to confiscate him, like most soldiers do. There was a bundle of belongings tied to his back. Probably stuff they meant to steal. There was money, expensive jewelry, but also clothes, my father's balalaika, and even a doll. Katya was covered in soot but she wasn't harmed. She couldn't remember how she'd escaped or how she'd ended up in the woods. It was almost as if everything had been preordained. And so, with Harpagos, we rode to a seaport and bought tickets to America."

He went on to recount his mother being laid off, and having to drop out of school.

"And how did you feel about having to discontinue your education?"

Pasha bit at his smirk. "It may sound funny to some people but I was heartbroken. I had good grades, and I got a lot of encouragement from my teachers."

"Tell me, Pasha, did you make any attempt to continue your studies after you were released from your education?"

Pasha replied that he had been determined to read all the books in the public library by the time he was fifteen. He had sworn to better himself. He promised he would be the next J.D. Rockefeller.

Horace waggled his eyebrows. "You had ambition!"

Pasha chuckled. "I got made fun of a lot."

"But in the end it wasn't enough, was it?"

"Our family became very desperate."

Pasha explained Prohibition to Horace, and described the riotous speakeasies that popped up overnight, as well as his mother's incident with the stalker.

"We couldn't go to the police; my mother was selling illegal alcohol. She could've been arrested herself. There was nothing to be done."

Horace set his elbows on the desk. "But you did something, didn't you, Pasha?"

Pasha sank his teeth into his lower lip. It was the moment of truth.

"I sought help from the Breadwinners. They were the good guys around the Lower East Side, the champions of women and children, protectors of the widowed and orphaned. They took in young immigrant men struggling to care for their family. I fit the bill perfectly. I asked to join."

"And were your pleas fulfilled?"

"They were. They took me on as a street fighter, one of the highest-paying positions for someone my age. But it wasn't that simple. I had to pass initiation."

Pasha went over the details of his three trials, ending with the flogging when Pasha was handcuffed to a post, lashed twenty times, and had salt water poured over his wounds.

"And your mother knew nothing about this?"

Pasha rubbed the back of his neck, trying to avoid glancing back at his mother.

"It wasn't long before she found out. I didn't plan on telling her, of course, but word gets around. By then I had already passed my initiation and there was nothing she could do about it. Once you're a Breadwinner you're a Breadwinner for life; desertion is punishable by death."

Horace shook his head in astonishment.

"So at twelve years old, you, Pasha Chevalsky, in an act of love and sacrifice, sold yourself to a street gang to support your family and protect your mother from a violent renegade?"

"Yes, sir. That's what happened."

Horace leaned back against the chair with a satisfied smile.

"My, my, Pasha Chevalsky! What a riveting story! You heard it here folks, right here on the Blue Hour with *The Daily Compass*! No doubt you good people tuned in today asking yourselves, who is Pasha Chevalsky? What kind of king would he be? And I believe today, Pasha, you have answered that question. Here is a young man who has been tried and tested, a man of noble blood who is no stranger to hard times. He's resilient, he's resourceful, self-sacrificing, and above all he is as his name says: humble. Folks, I give you Pasha Chevalsky: The People's King!"

***

When the motorcar pulled up to camp, everyone, save Staccato, came running down the stairs. Pyro dragged Pasha from the car.

"You did it, Pasha!"

Katya, who had been riding Pyro's shoulders, leapt down with a squeal and threw herself at Pasha's knees. Lydia slid from the passenger seat with a smile.

"Did he sound alright?"

"Are you kidding?" Pyro slapped his knee. "He was amazing!"

Cicada swirled around Pasha in a ribbon of diaphanous light.

"Perfectly executed, Pasha! You had them eating from the palm of your hand!"

Melodious grabbed him from behind and lifted him onto his shoulders.

"Well done, *mein* friend!"

Pasha winced as something shiny pelted his face. Skelter and Katya were tossing confetti at his head. Pasha shielded himself and laughed as Faina scrambled out the backseat.

"Wait for me! I wanna throw confetti at Pasha too!"

They laughed and cheered and played all the way up the steps. At the landing Melodious ground to a halt. Staccato stood with his arms crossed as though he had been waiting to see Pasha. Pasha's smile vanished.

Before he could try to escape, Melodious set him down in front of the miraculous. They stood face to face. There was a slight smile playing on Staccato's features as he looked Pasha over. Just when he thought Staccato was about to address him, he instead turned to his mother.

"You must be very proud, Mrs. Chevalsky."

Lydia placed a hand on Pasha's shoulder. "I am."

"As am I." Staccato looked Pasha in the eye. "You did what was right and what was honorable, and you did it superbly. I apologize for trying to discourage you and pressuring you to hide." He lifted an eyebrow jokingly. "I've never been more pleased that someone didn't listen to me."

Pyro slapped Pasha on the back. "That oughta make you feel good, Pasha. He's never said that to me!"

Staccato rolled his eyes and scoffed. "If I did you probably weren't listening."

Pasha was silent for a moment. Staccato had apologized for not supporting him with *The Daily Compass*, but he hadn't apologized for lying. Furthermore, he wasn't offering to share the truth. And yet peace was something Pasha longed to restore.

"It's okay," Pasha finally conceded. "I understand why you were scared. I mean, I was taking a huge risk."

"And it paid off." Staccato folded his hands behind his back. "You're very brave, Pasha. I hope you know that. Very brave indeed."

Chapter 14:
To Kiss and Tell

On the morning of Faina's birthday, Pasha dashed down the parapet towards the aroma of coffee in search of the birthday girl. From a distance he could see the rest of the company gathered at the table, but no sign of Faina. A giggling noise from below the porch drew his attention over the railing. Faina's coffee sat on the edge of the steps. She was crouched beside the hatched skirting watching a turtle who had taken residence there.

Already the morning sun was summoning the freckles from her skin like the heads of daisies. Pasha crept down the stairs, folding his large, clumsy hands behind his back. Quietly, he vaulted over the railing and snuck up behind Faina. As he was about to seize her shoulders, she jumped round to face him.

"Boo!"

Pasha fell back on his haunches with a gasp, nearly hitting his head on the bottom stair. Faina threw back her head and laughed with childish amusement. It was easy to envision her levitating into the air like Peter Pan.

"Nice try, Chevalsky, but you'd have to get up pretty early in the morning to catch me by surprise."

Pasha sat up and rubbed at his lower back. "To be fair, I did get up fifteen minutes earlier than usual."

"Evidently, that wasn't early enough."

"Alright, you pixie, lend me a hand."

Faina reached out her arm. With a sneaky smile Pasha seized her by the hand and jerked her down into the sand. The two dissolved into giggles as Pasha roped his arm around her neck.

"Happy birthday, Faina!"

Faina snickered and gave him a playful shove.

"You didn't really get up fifteen minutes early, did you?"

Pasha was was interrupted by a papery swat on the back of his head. Pyro's shadow craned over the bannister.

"*Oi*, Mr. King-to-Be, what are you and birthday girl rolling in the dirt for?" He cast the newspaper in a triangular sheet over Pasha's face. "You're front page news!"

Pasha stifled an irritated groan. Before he could tell Pyro they would join him in a minute, Faina plucked the paper from his head.

"Oh, this is wonderful, Pasha!"

Pyro snapped his braces. "They ain't got nothing but good things to say about you, mate."

But Pasha didn't really care; he was too preoccupied with procuring their privacy.

"Swell. We'll be up in a—"

"What about the other papers?" blurted Faina. "What did they have to say?"

Pyro jerked his thumb up the steps. "That's why you gotta come upstairs! Skelter went out this morning and bought a copy of every journal this side of the Ecliptic!"

Pyro dragged Pasha to his feet and led the two up the deck.

To say Pasha hastened through his breakfast would be an understatement. He was so anxious to give Faina her present he considered skipping his meal altogether. Fortunately for his stomach, he quickly dismissed the idea as ludicrous.

Everyone's voices fought to read the article they'd excavated aloud. The general consensus was Pasha was an unsung hero, a perfect underdog, a tried and true savior of justice. That isn't to say there weren't reviews of an unsavory nature, but no one bothered to bring those to the breakfast table.

With all the excitement over Pasha's triumph, he was never able to secure a moment alone with Faina to give her his present. By the time dinner rolled around, Pasha decided to abandon all pretenses. After Faina took her place at the table he walked up behind her and dropped something sparkly around her neck.

"Pasha, what are you—"

She looked down at the golden sunflower pendant resting against her chest. Her expression became as soft as butter. She twisted around in her seat and threw her arms around Pasha's waist.

"Oh, Pasha! It's beautiful! You know you didn't have to get me anything, right?"

"Doesn't mean I can't." He circled his arms around her and brought the pendant closer to her face. He pressed a latch hidden along the seam.

"It's a locket!"

As Pasha unfolded the hinges, numerous specks of yellow light danced along Faina's freckles.

"It was made by esperites." Pasha brushed a stray hair from her cheek. "The lights will never go out."

He held it closer so she could see the photograph inside. Faina pealed with glittery laughter.

Pyro leaned over his plate. "Well? What's it a picture of?"

"It's a picture from when we were kids. A photograph my brother took."

"I had to get it copied." Pasha gave a nervous chuckle. "I hope you don't mind that I had Katya swipe it from your trunk."

"Of course I don't mind!"

In the photograph, their cherub faces were crowded together, their sunburnt cheeks sticky with vanilla ice cream, their fingerprints pruned with the stain of cherry syrup. They clasped each other in one of those unapologetically loving embraces, the kind of hugs children give each other when they're too innocent to be embarrassed by affection.

Pasha felt Faina's fingers enclose around his. "I love it, Pasha!"

Before he could grow any more flustered, Pasha slunk back to his seat and resumed eating.

Cicada sank her fork into her mashed potatoes. "Do you guys ever miss New York?"

Pasha shrugged. "Parts of it. I miss the Chinese restaurant we used to visit all the time. I miss my friends. Don't miss being a Breadwinner, or living in a tenement."

"Do you think you'll ever go back and visit?"

"I'd like that very much now that I don't have to worry about the Breadwinners. I'd kinda like to go back and thank Roman for saving the girls' lives. He was the one who hooked Faina up with a getaway car while I was gone so they could escape the Bowery Butchers."

Faina turned bright pink. Pasha stopped cutting his meat.

"Faina, I think you've got a bit of a sunburn."

"Sunburn?" She smoothed her napkin over her lap. "Oh, yeah. You're probably right."

Katya stared at her like a cat about to corner a mouse.

"She isn't sunburnt, she's nervous."

Pasha scoffed. "Nervous? What are you talking about? Why would she be nervous?"

Faina's mouth opened but Katya cut her off.

"Because she's thinking about that kiss she gave Roman at the ferry terminal. Is that what you're thinking about, Faina?"

Pasha froze. Faina folded her hands in her lap and stared directly at Katya.

"I have no idea what you're talking about, Katya."

Lydia's head jerked up from the opposite end of the table. Her shoulders rolled forward like a stalking lioness.

"Katya!"

But Katya did not listen. "Don't you remember kissing Roman the night those men shot at us on the Bowery?"

Pasha's eyes bulged.

"You did what?"

The edge in his voice caused everyone at the table to cease their conversations. They turned and stared at Faina, who was now bright red.

"What are you talking about, Katya? I didn't kiss anybody at the ferry terminal."

"Yes, you did. I saw you. You kissed Roman in front of the ticket booth just before he left."

Lydia's eyes bore across the table like spotlights from a guard tower.

"Katerina …"

"But it was so romantic!"

"Katerina, *budet*!" Enough!

Pasha's head felt so heavy he thought it would pull him down over his plate.

"You kissed Roman?" A dozen eyes bore into him. He coughed and shook his head. "Uh, in front of my little sister?"

Faina craned low over the table, her eyes heavy as she stared up at Pasha.

"It was just a little peck." Her voice was low but her words were crammed on top of each other in a rush to escape her mouth. "It didn't mean anything." She made a move for Pasha's hand beneath the table, but he drew back.

"Really? Because according to Katya it was very romantic!"

"She's a ten-year-old little girl! Of course it would look that way to her! I kissed him like a relative, like I'd kiss my brother."

"You would kiss your brother on the mouth?"

"What? Ew! Of course not! Look, if I had thought there was anything inappropriate about what I did, I wouldn't have done it!"

Everyone's eyes darted between the pair as though it were an intense game of ping pong that for some reason they shouldn't have been watching. Pasha waxed scarlet.

"You don't see anything wrong with what you did? You can't think of one reason why you shouldn't have kissed Roman?"

Faina hesitated for a moment as though thinking it through. To Pasha's surprise, she sat a little taller.

"Well, no. Not exactly. If I had been walking out with someone that'd be one thing, but as I recall there was no such arrangement."

Pasha couldn't keep from raising his voice as he scowled at her in disbelief. "What do you mean there was no such arrangement?"

Faina's lips pressed together in a thin line. Her nostrils flared.

"Allow me to put it in terms you'll understand. Let's say I was selling pumpkins, and you wanted to buy some. Unless you say you want the pumpkins, I'm gonna sell them to somebody else!"

"I did want your pumpkins and you knew I wanted your pumpkins! In fact, I thought I had already bought your pumpkins!"

"If you wanted the pumpkins, then why did you leave them? You should have taken the pumpkins with you when you left!"

"I was coming back for them!"

"Well, sorry, but this pumpkin stand doesn't offer layaway!"

By now the table was dead silent. Everyone eyed the pair as though they'd downed a barrel of whiskey. Cicada couldn't stand it any longer.

"What on earth are you two talking about?"

Pasha ignored Cicada's question. "What kind of a sick person is Roman anyway? You're sixteen years old!"

Pyro grumbled into his glass. "That is a good point…"

Sonata smacked his arm. "Butt out!"

Faina ground her teeth together. "I'm seventeen, thank you."

Pasha was on his feet. "He's four years older than you! You're a minor! He's a filthy—"

"Pasha!" his mother finally shrieked. She indicated towards Katya and the present company. "Calm down!"

Faina held up her hands. "Well, let's not jump off the deep end here. We're not talking about a relationship, we're talking about a kiss! It was a simple peck of gratitude! Meaningless!"

"'Peck of gratitude'? Gratitude for what?"

"Gee, I don't know! Saving our lives? Getting us to the ferry terminal alive?"

"That's all it takes? Driving you to the ferry terminal?"

Everyone let out a horrified gasp, with the exception of Cicada who sat sucking the gravy from her spoon, oblivious to the implication.

"Pasha, that is …" Staccato fumbled for the proper words, "an incredibly rude thing to say!"

Faina pressed a hand against her chest. "What did you say?"

The lights on the candles poured over the tapers. The red wax melted so quickly it pooled onto the table like thick puddles of blood. Pyro jumped to attention and absorbed the flames with a wave of his hand. The reality of Pasha's words echoed back to him. His mouth opened and closed like a suffocating cod.

"I …"

Lydia flew up from her seat and grabbed hold of Pasha's ear. She dragged him back to the kitchen, away from their audience, and made him stand against the counter.

"I did not raise you to talk to a woman that way! Not to mention she is your best friend, and it is her birthday! Five minutes ago you were singing Roman's praises, now you are trying to pin him as some kind of pervert?"

Pasha crossed his arms and glowered like an idiot at the cabinets.

"I don't appreciate her kissing Roman in front of my little sister, and he's too old for her! It's inappropriate!"

Lydia rolled her eyes. "Don't give me that, Pavlo Chevalsky! I wasn't born yesterday!"

"But, Ma, she … she …" He trailed off.

At length, Lydia sighed.

"You left."

"I was coming back. She knew I was coming back. I did what I had to."

"And so did Faina."

Pasha stared at her in confused silence. Lydia clicked her tongue and ran a hand over her eyes.

"Pasha, Faina in all likelihood is never going to see Roman again. And it wasn't like Katya said it was; you know how your little sister likes to exaggerate."

Pasha's eyes widened. "You mean you saw—"

"I did." She held her chin high. "You have nothing to be upset over. It meant nothing. If it had meant something I would have felt it. Now I want you to apologize. You go have a talk with Faina, and I will go have a talk with Katya."

"Who is mad with power, by the way!"

Lydia threw her hands up and smacked the counter. "Did I not just say I would talk to her?"

Pasha backed down slightly. "Yes …"

"Okay then!" She pinched the bridge of her nose, and adjusted his collar. "What has gotten into you lately?" She cupped his cheek and brushed her thumb beneath his eye.

"What do you mean?" He tried to sound angry but it was impossible beneath her affectionate touch.

"Arguing with your sister, your outburst with Staccato, and now flying off the handle with Faina?" She brushed his bangs to the side.

Pasha snickered. "You bit Staccato's head off first, remember?"

She managed a weak smile. "This isn't like you, *Patulya*. You are always so calm, so gentle."

Pasha shut his eyes and expelled a long-held breath through his nose. He didn't have to answer. She already knew what he was feeling.

"You're stressed."

Pasha nodded and rubbed his eyes with both hands as she held his head against her shoulder.

"Well, don't let it get the best of you, my darling." She kissed his head. "You're too sweet for that." She ran a finger over his forehead. "Go patch things up with Faina and give that mind of yours a rest."

When they returned to the table, Faina was gone. Pasha ran back to Faina's cabin. He pounded on the door.

"Faina!"

But there was no answer. He jiggled the door handle, but it was locked. He pressed his ear against the door. Sobs echoed through the wood.

"Faina, come out and talk to me, please!"

He slumped against the wood with his forehead pinned to the knocker.

"Faina, I'm not leaving until you come out here and talk to me!"

The door flung open with such ferocity Pasha would have fallen face forward if Faina hadn't shoved him back.

"You're the meanest person I've ever met, Pavlo Chevalsky!"

Pasha was aghast. "Faina, please! I'm sorry!"

"You're nothing but a bully!"

"I know, I'm so sorry, Faina! Please let me make it up to you!"

"Make it up to me? I don't wanna have anything to do with you ever again! You stay away from me!"

She ripped the locket from around her head, shoved it into his hands and slammed the door.

Pasha was reeling. He stared down at the necklace. He let the locket drop to the doormat.

"Fine …" he half whispered. Pinching his eyes closed, he made his voice angry. "Fine then!"

And swiveling around, he marched himself back to his own cabin.

Chapter 15:
Pulling the Trigger

By morning Pasha's hurt feelings had calcified with a hard coating of anger and defense. The sting had burned all night until he forgot that it wasn't a part of him. He headed off for lessons at the shooting range, a creature of bitterness.

When he arrived, Faina was perched atop the fence, swinging her feet back and forth. Her lips perked up into a grin.

"Pasha!"

Pasha felt as though every knob in his spine had become as stiff and unyielding as a stripped screw. It burned like a hot iron rod beneath his skin. Ignoring her, he plopped down on the bench and laced up his boots. The wood sank and squeaked as she sat beside him.

"I said hello, Pasha."

The light caught on something shiny around her neck. Pasha couldn't believe it; she was wearing the locket!

"What's the matter?"

She tried to scuff his hair, but Pasha leaned away. Faina's head bent a little between her shoulders. Before he could inflict any more damage, Pyro clapped his hands together.

"Alright, you two, enough horsing around. Time for target practice."

Pasha stood and approached Pyro as he held out the rifle.

"Pasha, you're the one who needs the most practice, so you're up first. Sonata and I will be watching from the sides." He shooed Pasha and Faina behind the booth.

Pasha waited until Pyro had taken his place next to Sonata several yards away, then he held up the rifle.

"You're holding it wrong," Faina corrected him in a matter-of-fact tone. She seated herself on the ledge to his right.

Pasha sighed and rolled his eyes. "I am not."

"Except you are."

"Mind your own business."

"Sorry for trying to prevent you from blowing your thumb off."

Pasha glanced down at his hands. She was right. With a long sigh he corrected his grip and squinted through the crosshairs.

Faina's hands dropped to her side with a thud.

"Why are you so angry with me?"

There was little emotion in Pasha's answer.

"I wasn't aware I felt anything towards you." Even he had to admit this was an overly sharp barb, but he wasn't sorry for long.

"Really?" She leaned to one side, thrusting her hip out as she did. "Not a thing, huh?"

His eyes instinctively zeroed in on her legs. Faina's lips twitched with a smug simper. Without answering, he turned back around and took aim at the target. But Faina refused to let it go.

"If that's true, there must be some other explanation as to why you're being a complete rhymes-with-grass."

Pasha craned his head back with a sarcastic smirk. "Very witty."

Faina bent her chin to her chest. "Your hair looks nice."

Pasha lowered the gun and shook his head, exasperated.

"I don't understand you! You always do this!"

"Do what?"

"Blow up in my face, then turn around and act like nothing ever happened!"

"You said you were sorry."

Pasha narrowed his eyes. "You never said *you* were sorry."

"Sorry for what? Kissing Roman?"

He turned his back on her.

"Faina, I couldn't care less who you kiss. Although I don't know why you'd kiss someone just for driving you to the ferry terminal."

"Maybe if you hadn't left us to fend for ourselves you could have driven us to the ferry terminal!"

Pasha was in danger of throwing down the gun as he turned to face her. His nostrils flared. His teeth clenched.

"I didn't have a choice!"

"You had that stupid mirror you used to call Aunt Poppy, but I didn't hear from you until you needed something from me! You promised you would come back for me, but it wasn't until I was lying half-dead in a warehouse that you even considered coming home!"

Pasha drew back, speechless. His eyes widened. He'd never thought of it that way before. Had she really felt he abandoned her? Pyro hollered from across the way.

"Pasha! What are you waiting for? Shoot already!"

Pasha clenched his jaw and lifted the rifle to eye level once more.

Faina heaved an impatient sigh. "You're still holding it wrong."

"I am not holding the gun wrong!"

"Yes, you are!" She pointed to his thumb. "You're gonna break your hand." She tugged at his elbow. Pasha pulled back.

"Will you leave me alone? I know what I'm doing!"

"Obviously not!" She batted his arm back down.

"Faina, let go!"

"No!"

The gun kicked off between them. A loud popping noise thundered through the air. A horrible pounding force jabbed against Pasha's hand. He dropped the firearm. Across the field, Sonata shrieked and jumped to her feet. Blood spattered the hem of her skirt. Pyro cried out and fell over, clutching his leg. Pasha held his throbbing hand to his chest as he and Faina froze in horror. Pyro rolled in the bloodstained grass.

"My foot!" A stream of curses, some familiar, and some Pasha and Faina had yet to hear, fountained from Pyro's mouth. Sonata flapped down beside him like a frightened bird. She struggled to hold him still so she could absorb the pain. The Two Bad Mice sank behind the booth.

Faina glared at Pasha. "What did you do?"

"Me?" Pasha pivoted his head towards her. "You're the one who grabbed me!"

"Gee, I wonder why! Let me see your hand, crybaby!"

She yanked his injured palm towards her. Pasha winced.

"Looks like you just bruised it."

They jumped as Sonata roared across the field. "Pasha! Faina! Come out here now!"

One at a time, their guilty faces peeked over the wall.

***

Faina had been right about Pasha's bruise. Sonata was able to repair him within minutes. Pyro, on the other hand, was not so lucky. An emergency caim was treating him inside his cabin. Meanwhile, Pasha and Faina sat outside and endured a public, thorough, lengthy, raging reprimand from Lydia and Staccato.

"I simply cannot conceive how you two could be so stupid," thundered Staccato with chilling savagery. They knew he could be intimidating, but this was achieving new levels. "You could have easily hit his chest, or his head, or his neck! You could have hit each other! You could have killed someone!"

It was difficult to say which was worse, Staccato's fury or Lydia's disappointment. Her eyes burned holes through their chests.

"Both of you know better than to act so irresponsibly! You should be ashamed of yourselves!"

"A gun is a dangerous weapon, and if you two can't show proper respect for its power, you can't be a part of this team!"

Lydia started to add something but stopped to glance curiously at Staccato from the corner of her eye.

Pasha gave an involuntary whimper. "I'm sorry it happened." He threw a glare at Faina. "But Faina grabbed me!"

Faina snapped her spine straight. "You were holding it wrong!"

Staccato held up his hand. "Faina, even if Pasha was holding it wrong, even if his hand was going to disintegrate into ash, you never, ever, *ever* grab someone who is holding a gun! That is common sense! I would've expected better from you! If Pasha insists on acting foolish, that's his prerogative. There's no questioning that both of you behaved irresponsibly, but Faina, what you did was by far much worse!"

Pasha sat a little taller. "You were showing off!"

"I was not showing off!" She pounded her fist on her knee. "I was trying to be nice but you wouldn't listen to me because you're still sore that I kissed Roman!"

Lydia threw up her hands in desperation. "You two are still going on about this?"

Staccato pinched the bridge of his nose. "Teenagers."

Pasha turned away from her. "Maybe I'm just sick of you bossing me around!"

"Will the both of you shut up already?"

Pyro sped out of his cabin in a wheelchair. He snatched them both by the shoulder and shoved their faces together.

"Hell's Bells, I'm this close to smacking the both of you! You have five seconds to kiss and make up before I lock both of you inside a trunk and leave you there to sort things out!"

Faina snorted. "What do you care?"

"Yeah!" Pasha bobbed his head. "You're always complaining about how much trouble we are when we're together!"

Pyro shot up his eyebrows. "Are you kidding? However pesky you two may be together, you're regular terrors when you're out of sorts, with a wake of collateral damage catastrophic enough to rival Armageddon! I've already been shot in the foot thanks to your little tiff. This goes on any longer, and I've no doubt the two of you will find a way to kill us all! Now I don't care who started it, or who said what, you all will put this argument to bed right now, or I'll have you scraping barnacles off the pier for the rest of your life!"

Faina tilted her head away with a haughty frown. "I don't think so!"

Pasha countered with an exceptionally arrogant sneer, which he had come to master over the years.

"Get over yourself, Faina."

Weary of the prolonged conflict, Sonata plowed forward.

"Alright, if you two aren't going to admit your feelings, I will! Faina won't apologize because she's spiteful. She won't resolve things until she's made sure Pasha's paid for his insult, that's why she threw the locket in his face. She thought it was just nasty enough to give Pasha a dose of his own medicine. Pasha won't apologize because his pride is hurt. He made himself vulnerable once and got his feelings hurt. He isn't about to do it again by pretending nothing happened. The truth is, both of you are sorry. Pasha is sorry for hurting Faina. He's afraid she'll never trust him again. Faina is sorry for making Pasha feel betrayed. Deep down, she's *terrified* he hates her. There. The empath has spoken. Or would you like me to go further?"

Pasha and Faina looked as though they were standing in front of a large audience in their underwear. Sonata had ripped their feelings out and put them on display. Slowly, their eyes found their way back to each other's poppy-colored faces.

Pasha's mouth barely parted as he spoke. "I didn't mean to make you feel abandoned!"

Faina stuck out her lower lip. "I didn't mean to hurt you."

"You can name a punishment for me if you want."

Faina coiled her arms around his neck. "No, you name one for me."

Staccato stabbed the ground with his staff. "I'll name one for both of you!"

Melodious put a finger to his lips. "Let them finish."

Pasha and Faina began spilling apologies left and right, hugging each other until their skin turned red.

Pyro rolled his eyes. "All the drama!"

"Come now, Pyro," teased Melodious. "Can you honestly say you were any different at their age?"

"Or one year ago for that matter," muttered Staccato.

Lydia sat back and chuckled. "It is just a phase, Mr. Anomaly. They will grow out of it eventually."

"Yes, well, that's all very touching," snapped Pyro, "but what are we going to do about the missing shard? I'm not much help if I can hardly walk."

Pasha craned his head. "Can't Sonata just heal you?"

It wasn't often Sonata was cross with Pasha, but she now stared down at him with dry annoyance.

"You broke the bone. It's going to take some time for him to fully recover."

Staccato massaged his forehead. "I'm afraid Sonata brings up an excellent point."

Melodious stepped forward. "Couldn't I go in Pyro's place?"

Pyro sputtered. "Are you kidding me? How many giant, legally blind Germans with near-radar capabilities do you think are walking around out there?"

Sonata shrugged. "He's right. Melodious is rather recognizable. If it weren't for the trial, I would go. I guess we could send Skelter."

At the mention of such an idea, Faina broke away from Pasha in alarm.

"Are you kidding? We could never take you or Skelter along with us, it's too dangerous there!"

Pyro leaned on his elbow, scrutinizing the both of them.

"What are you talking about?"

"They have Jim Crow laws in Kentucky! All of the south does!"

Staccato's expression grew pained as he furrowed his brow. "Faina is right. I looked into it for myself. I had hoped perhaps with Kentucky's proximity to the north the laws may be different, but it appears that isn't the case. You can't even share a waiting room at the train station."

Sonata and Skelter exchanged a look of ineffable hurt that only they could understand. Cicada hooked a strand of hair awkwardly behind her ear and shrugged.

"Well, what happens if they do break the law?"

Faina's eyes sobered. "They could be lynched."

Pyro's brows drew together. "Lynched? Why?"

Sonata groaned in exasperation. "Because we're not white! Honestly, Pyro, it was your foot that got injured, not your head!"

But Pyro wasn't catching on. "White? You mean like what Pasha was talking about on the radio with the White Army thing in Russia?"

Pasha gaped at him. "Pyro, *white,* like the color." As if saying it a second time would somehow get it through.

Sonata covered her eyes and growled. "Pyro, did you ever pay attention during Other-Worldly Studies? In the Other, they classify people by their skin color! They take pride in it! They kill each other over it! They give each other derogatory names!"

Melodious cleared his throat tactfully. "Parts of the United States have laws against black people and white people intermingling."

"What Pasha and Faina are trying to say is that if I showed up with them and did one little thing out of custom, violence is likely to ensue. Skelter might be able to get by a little easier than I would, but it's a risk nonetheless."

"Okay, hold on," Pasha interrupted. "I realize Voiler is years ahead of the Other in terms of progress, but surely the idea isn't that foreign to you, is it?"

Cicada scoffed. "Are you kidding? Voiler has its own set of identity issues. When people have wings, fins, and horns, who cares about skin color?"

"Right, well, the Other sure is one topsy-turvy place," muttered Pyro. "Guess Pasha and Faina will have to go it alone."

Their attention was drawn to the side as Cicada's light shrank. Her tail straightened into legs, and her feet descended towards the ground. Without explaining herself, she took out a pair of heels she'd hidden behind the kitchen door, and slipped them over her large feet. She wobbled with determination to the middle of the circle.

Everyone stared at her in confusion. Pyro looked her up and down as though her brain were floating outside of her head.

"What are you doing?"

Cicada pinched the baggy folds of her gauchos and made a clumsy attempt at a curtsy.

"Hello, my name is Cicada Sycamore. I'm eighteen years old."

Pyro arched his head back and groaned. Melodious swatted his arm discreetly.

"Be nice," he whispered.

Staccato rubbed a stressed hand over his eyes.

"Face it, Cicada," said Pyro. "You're not going."

Cicada stamped her foot and nearly knocked herself off balance. Before she could roar her defiance, Skelter signed.

"Why not?" repeated Pyro. "Because she'll blow their cover!"

Skelter pointed to Pyro and struck the side of his head with the heel of his hand.

"Yeah," agreed Cicada, "you're forgetting how smart I am! You always underestimate me!"

Pyro crossed his arms and leaned back in his wheelchair. "Look, I know it always seems like I'm giving Cicada a hard time, but it's for her own protection. She still has a lot to learn about the world."

Skelter made rapid movements.

"Yes, I know she learns at the speed of light."

Skelter continued on. When he was finished, Pyro nodded with stubborn eyes.

"Even if she has learned more about a variety of subjects than the rest of us have, she still doesn't know how to be inconspicuous."

Cicada shook her fist. "My mother sent me here to help you! If you don't use me, what am I good for?"

They looked to Staccato for the final word. At length he sighed.

"Cicada, you can help us by searching through the migration records at the Ecliptic Courts."

Cicada's light grew white hot, and everyone was forced to shield their eyes.

"Fine!" She rocketed into the trees and disappeared.

When the aftereffect of Cicada's impressive exit had worn off, Pasha dusted his hands and hooked his arm through Faina's. They crept to their feet.

"Well, now that that's settled, I think Faina and I will go involve ourselves in some sort of community service. You know, to better our character and become model citizens." He gave Faina a wink as they edged back towards the stairs. "Won't we, Faina?"

"Oh, yeah! Like planting a tree!"

"Or picking up trash!"

"Or helping old people cross the street!"

"Good idea! To the nursing home!"

Staccato summoned the chairs to slip back beneath them.

"Not so fast, you two," exclaimed Lydia.

Staccato examined the head of his staff, his eyes half-shut.

"We're far from finished."

Pasha and Faina exchanged apprehensive glances as the miraculous cut a slow circle around them. All the while he tapped the armillary sphere to his lips.

"Until your departure, you are each to remain in your rooms, only to come out for lessons or if otherwise summoned. You will take your meals there. During each day of your sequester you are to write no less than three hundred lines, the content of which will be decided. You will write one apology letter to Pyro, one to Sonata, and one to me. Every night you will wash the dishes by hand, and every morning you will run five laps around the camp. Twice a week you will polish the weapons, firearms excluded. You will have no music, no radio, and no pleasurable reading material until you leave for your trip."

Pasha and Faina gave little trouble in the way of accepting their consequences. Pyro rolled forward with zeal.

"Don't I get to assign a punishment, seeing as I'm the injured party?"

Staccato motioned him forward with a gallant wave of his hand. "By all means."

Pyro cracked his knuckles with a devious smile. "Alright, my little nuisances, ten laps around the guesthouses, go!"

Chapter 16:
Katya's Apology

On the first day of their punishment, Pasha lay on the floor and bounced a tennis ball against the wall. He was still sweating from laps, and his skin had only just begun to cool. There was a knock at the door.

"Who is it?"

A tiny voice whimpered from the other side. "It's me, Katya."

Pasha's mouth drew into a tight frown. "What do you want?"

"Can't I come in?"

Pasha sat up and hurled the tennis ball against the bedpost. It ricocheted with a loud thud and struck him between the eyes. Pasha fell back clutching his forehead.

"Fine! Whatever!"

The doorknob twisted. A small figure shadowed the threshold. Pasha rolled onto his stomach and lay face down on the rug, refusing to look at her. He felt her footsteps reverberate through the floor.

"I'm sorry for making you and Faina fight."

Pasha didn't say anything. He didn't move. Katya's knees popped as she knelt down beside him.

"My whole life, everyone thought my brain was sick because I knew things they didn't. You and Mama are always afraid I'm fragile. When it turned out I was an empath, I thought all that would stop."

Pasha sat up on his elbows. "Katya, the reason we don't tell you things isn't because we think you're crazy. It's because you won't stop blurting out everyone's private information. If you do that, no one's gonna trust you!"

Katya's shoulders drew inward. She stared down at the ground.

"I know that now. I thought I was trying to prove myself to everyone, but really I've just been showing off. I should never have told you Faina kissed Roman. I only did it to make you angry. When I felt your pain, I hated myself for what I did. And I hated that I hurt Faina. She didn't have anything to do with our fight."

Pasha shifted onto his back and pulled Katya into his arms. He kissed the side of her head.

"I never once thought you were crazy. Just imaginative. I forgive you."

Katya buried her face into his chest. "You probably wish one of Mama's other babies had survived instead of me."

Pasha's mouth fell open in shock. "Katerina Ruslanova Chevalsky!

How could you say such a thing?"

She sniffed, tears filling up her eyes. "Because I'm such a bad sister!"

Pasha cupped her face in his hands. "First of all, I wish all of Mama's babies had survived, including you! And if they had, I wouldn't love you any less! Don't you ever, ever think I would give you up for anything!"

"Even after what I did?"

"Katya, you're not a bad sister. You made a bad choice, is all. Empathy isn't empathy if you use it to hurt someone. You're a Fay, that means you have supernatural gifts. But if you don't use your talents for good, you might lose them."

Katya's head jerked up. Her eyes widened with horror.

"Is that true?"

Pasha nodded his head. "Just like liliths and furies get their powers from doing acts of evil, a Fay can lose their power if they use it to make trouble."

"How can I make sure I never use my powers to do bad?"

"Well, you could always practice. How about this? While I'm gone, try to think of a way you can use your powers to help someone rather than humiliate them. Find someone who is hurting and try to make them feel better. Is that a good idea?"

"That's a perfect idea! But when are you going to be gone? Did Staccato decide to let you go to Libra with Mama and Sonata?"

"No, silly, I'm going to Kentucky, remember?"

Katya's smile fell from her lips so suddenly Pasha half-expected to find it lying somewhere on the floor.

"Oh ... but Staccato said ... I thought ..."

Pasha sat up on his elbows. "What? What did Staccato say?"

"I heard Staccato say to Mama that he decided to cancel the trip after you shot Pyro in the foot."

Pasha's chest burned with disappointment. "Oh, you mean as punishment?"

"No, because it's too dangerous."

"Too dangerous? Staccato said we couldn't go because it was too dangerous?"

Katya appeared surprised by her brother's confusion. "Weren't you gonna steal something from those bad men who drink blood, and who cut off Sonata's legs?"

"Well, yeah, but it's not like I haven't faced them before. Heck, I took on Samael face to face!"

"He knocked you off Harpagos and threw Mama off a cliff," she reminded him, still regarding him with a baffled stare from the corner of her eye.

"But I've been training for this kinda stuff for almost six months now!"

At last Katya screwed up her eyes and shook her head. "Pasha, I thought you hated fighting. All you ever want to do is stay at home and read. Why is it so important for you to go to Kentucky?"

By now Pasha had gotten to his feet and was pacing the floor. He stopped with his back to his sister. How could he explain all this to Katya? It wasn't that he particularly wanted to go and face off with a bunch of ophidians, it was the fact that Staccato didn't trust him enough to get the job done. It just seemed like another way to control Pasha, to keep him in the dark.

"Katya, would you do me a favor and go tell Staccato I'd like a word with him please."

She smiled obligingly. "Of course!"

Shortly after, there was a sonorous knock on the door that could only have been made by the head of Staccato's staff. Pasha got up from the armchair and opened the door. Staccato was standing patiently on the other side of the threshold. The confident and almost defensive way he rested on his staff told Pasha that he had been expecting the conversation that was about to take place for some time.

Pasha invited him in and the two sat down in the armchairs before the empty hearth.

"I found out through Katya that you decided to cancel the mission to Louisville." Pasha had been carefully crafting this statement from the moment Katya left, arranging his words so that Staccato knew in no uncertain terms that he did not appreciate this information being passed down to him secondhand.

Staccato leaned cooly back in the armchair, not the least bit intimidated. "As a matter of fact, I did. You seem surprised."

"I am actually." He gripped both arms of the chair, trying to remain cool.

Staccato's cheek twitched as he tightened his jaw. "With no one available to chaperone you, you can hardly expect me to send the two of you off to tangle with an infamous C.O.N. member on your own."

"Why not? We've done it before."

The back of Pasha's neck had begun to sweat again from the excess of sunlight invading through the open window, cooking the floorboards, and boiling the moisture in the air.

Staccato rested his temple against one finger and crossed his leg as though it were all very tedious. "You aren't referring to the incident in Pisces, are you? If I remember correctly Faina almost lost her legs, and if it weren't for Pyro you very well could've been smothered by pythons."

"What about Fornax and everything that happened afterwards, we seemed to handle that pretty well, didn't we?"

Staccato met his gaze with tense frustration. At length he sighed and uncrossed his legs.

"Forgive me if I'm wrong, but it seems as though you're arguing for the sake of arguing. I would have thought you'd welcome an opportunity to stay at home and avoid danger."

Pasha's brows contracted involuntarily.

"What are you trying to say?"

"Oh, for goodness sakes! Just this once, could we please have a conversation without the assumption that everything I say has a double meaning?"

"Well, maybe if you were more forthcoming I wouldn't have to assume all the time!"

"What do you want from me?"

"I want to know why you don't trust Faina and me enough to let us go to Kentucky without a chaperone!"

Staccato blinked slowly in a mocking gesture. "Well, the incident with the gun certainly didn't help you any!" He loosened his cravat, exposing his dampened collar.

Pasha may have been angry but he was mature enough to accept that what had happened with the gun was wrong. He nodded his head respectfully.

"I understand, but I don't believe you solely based your decision on the incident with the gun."

"You're a mind reader now, are you?"

Pasha did not answer but stared him down, angrily clutching the arms of the chair. The velvet felt hot against his fingers, and was not at all comfortable. Staccato drew a deep inhale through his nose and sighed.

"The fact of the matter is, you and Faina are seventeen. You've only been exposed to magic for less than a year—"

"None of that seemed to matter when you wanted me to catch the Firebird!"

The look that flickered in Staccato's icy blue eyes conveyed to Pasha that he was doing everything within his power to keep from exploding over being interrupted. He folded his hands tightly.

"The Firebird was a necessity. As far as we knew at the time the fate of Voiler rested upon you catching the Firebird. The situation with Cottonmouth however, is different. Anyone can steal that shard—"

"If anyone can do it, why not me?"

"Will you please let me finish?"

Pasha fell instinctively silent, allowing Staccato to continue.

"I must say, I find it rather offensive that you would accuse me of not trusting you when I was willing to let you go under Pyro's supervision—an idea which your mother abhorred—and yet I fought your corner! You act as though everything I do is some sort of attack on your character! And honestly, I refuse to put up with it any longer!" He got up from the chair and made his way towards the exit. "You're not going!" And with that he slammed the door shut behind him.

Chapter 17:

The Compromise

Staccato ripped the cravat from his collar with all the passion of a disgusted sergeant tearing off his chevron before quitting the army.

"Why must it be so ungodly hot?" he mumbled as he shoved the cuffs of his sleeves halfway up his elbows. His eyes darted towards Pasha's window just in time to see him kick the corner of his trunk and fall back in the armchair. Staccato's nostrils flared.

"Boy thinks he has it all figured out." Staccato shook his head, and marched onwards. "Doesn't even know the half of it."

Staccato reached the picnic table on the porch in four pounding strides. It wasn't until after he slammed his staff on the table that he noticed Melodious sitting there with his Bible open. His hand ceased to move over the raised braille characters, and the corner of his mustache was flicked up so as to suggest the hint of a smirk. Staccato glared at Melodious the way an alpha wolf might glare at a subordinate daring to take a bite out of his kill.

"Amused, Melodious?"

Melodious smiled in a way that Staccato found maddening.

"It had grown a little too quiet for my taste. When one is blind one develops an appreciation for sound."

"And how about an appreciation for privacy?"

"When one wants privacy it is custom to speak at a low volume."

Staccato winced in annoyance. "You wouldn't happen to know of any other pronouns to use in place of 'one,' would you?" By now his sarcasm had sharpened to immeasurable degrees.

"If it bothers you so I am happy to replace it with another."

Staccato stared with contempt at the passive old reverend. At times, Melodious's inability to take offense could provoke a reaction from Staccato worse than if he had slapped him in the face. And yet, he always managed to win him over in the end. Melodious knit his sturdy fingers together and rested them on the table.

"If you should like to vent, I am 'all ears' as they say."

Staccato continued to glower at him for a moment longer, then at last rolled his eyes and let his staff rest against the table.

"That boy's suspicions are out of control! I can't even tie my shoe laces without him accusing me of harboring some ulterior motive! It's as though my very existence offends him!"

"And you don't believe you have done anything to arouse his suspicions?"

He tangled his arms across his chest like a child who had been caught disobeying his mother.

"Not really, no."

Melodious feigned surprise, which Staccato found rather patronizing. "No?"

"Now don't you start! There's a reason I'm the head of this expedition! Thayer appointed me as leader because I know what's best. I know what's best for this company, I know what's best for my colleagues, and I know what's best for him." He pointed a finger towards Pasha's door. "Any information I've withheld from Pasha has been for his own good!"

"Are you certain you are not overcomplicating matters?"

Everything inside Staccato froze. The flow of air halted halfway through his lungs. Cold, undiluted fear prevented any reply from rising to his lips. Melodious rubbed his hand over his eyes and shook his head.

"You don't have to share with me whatever it is you are trying to keep secret, Staccato. But it does little good for you to pretend like you don't have any at this point. I have no doubt your intentions are pure for withholding information from Pasha—"

"I refuse to discuss this." His words sped out from between his lips like a well-aimed dart, and was hardly above a whisper.

"Very well. In that case, it may behoove you to let Pasha and Faina venture to Louisville."

"What? Why?"

"To placate the boy, of course."

"And why on earth should I have to placate anyone? Let alone an overly suspicious seventeen-year-old in serious need of an attitude adjustment!"

"For your own peace of mind."

Staccato pressed his lips together in a thin line, and raised an eyebrow. "I'm surprised at you, Melodious."

"Why is that?"

"Didn't you have five children?"

"I did."

"Then you know that giving in to the demands of a child will spoil them. Furthermore, I didn't cancel their trip to punish Pasha and Faina, I cancelled it for their own protection! In no way are they equipped to take on a prolific C.O.N. member by themselves! Pasha and Faina haven't even known of Voiler's existence for a full year! You really expect me to send them off to Kentucky to carry out an elaborate heist with thugs and bootleggers?"

Melodious rubbed his hands together and chuckled. Staccato's nostrils flared.

"What's so funny?"

"The fact of the matter is, you are not asking them to do anything different from what they were already doing before you came along!"

His shoulders unwound slightly. "I suppose that's true."

Staccato tilted the chair on its back legs as he contemplated what Melodious had said. Pasha and Faina did have an abundance of experience when it came to dealing with thugs. And it was possible that Pasha's history with the Breadwinners might afford him some sort of clout with Cottonmouth's colleagues. Furthermore, Staccato thought it best for Pasha's nerves that he be absent for his mother's court date in the long-run. Indeed, it had been for this very reason that Staccato had scheduled the trip at such a time in the first place.

"You tell him."

He grabbed his staff and got up from his chair. Melodious shut his Bible once again.

"Tell him what?"

"That's he's going to Louisville."

Chapter 18:
The Subaquatic Railway

To get to the gateway which led to Louisville, Pasha and Faina had to be taken to Alrisha, an underwater city in Pisces, halfway between Sheritan and the Phoenix Islands. Each mermaid kingdom housed an underwater station with countless gateways to the Other. The quickest way to reach the station was by the Subaquatic Rail.

On the day of their departure, the company—with the exception of Skelter and Katya who would be staying behind in Cetus— made their way to the terminal in Ambergris Square. Pasha stared up at the low glass building with curiosity.

"So, if the Subaquatic Rail is the fastest way to travel in Voiler, why haven't we used it before?"

They passed through the revolving doors. Having already obtained their boarding passes, they bypassed the booth and headed down the long, dark ramp to the concourse.

"It was shut down during the Land Lock." Staccato's suitcase floated behind him. "It's owned and operated by the mermaids, after all."

"And it's all underwater?" Faina questioned in amazement.

Sonata turned and looked over her shoulder.

"In a way. The train itself travels through a transparent tunnel. That way there's no risk of hitting any mermaids or sea creatures. There are even special water entrances for the merfolk. You'll see in a minute."

As they exited the tunnel-like passage, their breath was whisked away in a moment of contrite awe. All about them was an endless expanse of blue ocean frontier fading away into clouded shadow. The walls of the enormous space were glass. It was like an underwater aquarium. Pasha gazed up at the elaborately domed ceiling shaped like a nautilus. Rippling fragments of water danced along the mosaic floors. Pasha felt as though he were inside a jewel box on a sunken ship.

The train was made of a coppery bronze material. Long bulbous windows swelled from the cars like symbiotic bubbles. The conductor stood outside on the platform. He was dressed in a shimmering sea green uniform tailored like a navy commander's with brass seashell buttons. Large copper goggles sat on the brim of his hat.

Sonata gestured to the archways at each end of the concourse. Mermaids came and went down the long passages.

"Those are the water entrances. Passengers gather into chambers a few at a time where they can metamorphose into human form. Then they come out the other side."

All about them people bustled with luggage and boarding passes like any other train station. Everyone in the terminal stopped and turned as the signal to come aboard was sounded. But instead of a shrill train horn, the sound was something more like a naval captain's whistle.

Pasha raised an eyebrow. "Is that us?"

Sonata smiled. "That's us."

The party made their way onto the train. They filed through the long hall of compartments until Staccato settled on a space far from the traffic of scurrying passengers. Melodious hoisted everyone's belongings into the bin as though arranging teacups. Once he was finished he joined Staccato and Cicada in the compartment across the aisle.

Pasha was surprised Cicada hadn't chosen to sit with Faina and him. Perhaps she didn't feel like talking to anyone. After all, she'd been sulking ever since Staccato had refused to let her go on the mission.

As they settled into their seats, Sonata helped Pyro from his wheelchair. He winced as Sonata propped up his leg.

"Ow, ow, ow!"

Sonata rolled her eyes and placed two fingers on the side of his neck.

"You're fine."

"Just like old times, isn't it, Sonny?" observed Pyro while everyone settled into their seats.

Pasha and Faina raised their heads. Sonata glared at Pyro and waved her hand.

"Twice Pyro has had his legs atrophied after being imprisoned in a water tank."

Faina looked alarmed. "You were imprisoned in a water tank?"

Pyro frowned and nodded his head. "We used to call it an 'igneous snare,' back when I was a member of the Saighdeoir. As you know, a full-blooded igneous becomes powerless when overly wet. So they chain you up and stick you in water up to your chin. Except for mermaids, humans can't handle being in water that long. It does stuff to you. ..." He drew his eyebrows together and rubbed the back of his head.

Sonata patted his arm. "Typically, after the victim has been released they don't have much use of their arms or legs for a while. Their strength becomes sapped."

Faina inclined her head. "And you took care of him?"

Sonata pursed her lips and sat up straight. "Well, I do know a thing or two about losing the use of one's legs. Not to mention I am the only member with healing capabilities."

The car gave a sudden jolt. Pasha, Lydia, and Faina fell back against their seats as the train shot down the long, copper tunnel.

Sonata crossed her ankles in a relaxed manner. "Here we go!"

Pasha clutched the armrest. The moment the darkness fell away, Faina batted his elbow for attention.

"Pasha, look!" She pointed out the window.

As the train made its way into the blue, the underwater metropolis of Cetus came into view. Glass towers of corkscrew buildings rose up from the seafloor. Their panes waxed with an opal sheen as the light rippled above. Grand archways and statues carved from paua, abalone, and alabaster littered the city. Crowds of mermaids with long, elaborate braids hustled along shops nestled in the reef. Presently, they passed an area resembling an underwater dog park where a young mermaid threw a ball to a sea lion. Pasha glanced over at Sonata.

"Is she playing fetch with a sea lion?"

Sonata looked out the window, threw back her head, and trilled with delight.

"Oh, how adorable! My mother's next-door neighbor used to keep a sea lion growing up. Bruno, she called him."

Faina snapped to attention. "You mean mermaids keep sea lions as pets?"

"Well, of course! Seals, sea lions, they're quite similar to dogs, really. Although mermaid pets usually live a more free-range lifestyle than animals like cats and dogs."

Pasha exchanged a knowing glance with his mother. "Imagine if Katya had a sea lion as a pet."

Lydia tittered and shook her head.

"I wouldn't if I were you," warned Pyro. "The stench is unbearable."

Sonata tossed her hair over her shoulder as Cello emerged from her purse.

"Oh, Pyro, you're exaggerating."

Pyro winced as Cello hopped onto the seat and used his injured leg as a bridge to Pyro's lap.

"I am not! Listen, stick to land animals." He stroked Cello's spine. "No sea lion could ever compare to our Cello here."

Faina's eyes glittered with wicked delight. "You mean Sonata's

Cello?"

"That's what I said." He pinched his eyes and shook his head. "That's what I meant."

Pasha nudged Faina with his elbow. At this point, Pyro and Sonata had caught on to Faina's suspicions. Before Faina could question them any more, Pyro reached for his newspaper.

"Oh, would you look at that! They've already run an article about Pasha and Mrs. Chevalsky's upcoming court dates."

Pasha groaned while Lydia leaned back against the seat and closed her eyes.

"Hold on now!" He threw out his hand. "It's not that bad. They've listed the representatives to act as jury for your case. Let's see, from Aquarius we have Deciduous Larch, he's an alright chap. Bit of a stick in the mud." He elbowed Sonata. "Get it? Stick in the … no? Okay then. Ahem. He's a sylph. Capricorn has Mega Cabral, well, she's not all that bad considering … and would you look at that! Representing Aries is Furnace Tine, Ol' Furny, now we're talking!"

Pasha blinked. "Who?"

"Furnace Tine! He's an old friend of the family."

"His name is Furnace?"

Pyro shrugged and bit his lip. "I know, bit traditional, isn't it? The Tines always were a little stiff. They could've at least spelled it F-E-R-N-I-S."

He returned his attention to the paper. Pasha stiffened as Pyro's lips wrinkled into a frown.

"What's wrong? What is it?"

"Remember how Sonata explained that sometimes rulers can step in to represent their own country in matters of personal interest?"

"Yeah …"

"Well, it looks like Samael will be stepping in for Enoch Adder."

Lydia gasped. "What?"

Pasha slid his head into his hands and groaned. "Well, it's not like we didn't see it coming."

Lydia braced the armrest. "I can't face that man again! He tried to have my son killed! He hurled me off a cliff!"

"You'll be fine, Ma." Pasha reached out for her hand. "He can't hurt you in front of all those people."

Sonata was quick to agree. "Pasha's right. You'll be absolutely safe once we reach Libra."

Lydia swallowed and tried to steady herself.

"Let me see that, Pyro." Sonata snatched up the newspaper. "From Pisces we have Mardel Delmar, oh, I know him!" Pasha could tell she was forcing a lightness into her voice. "He's an excellent merman, Pasha. Besides, you know anyone from Pisces is bound to support you."

"Isn't that the chap who courted your ma?" asked Pyro in a bored manner.

"Oh, that was a long time ago."

"Weren't they almost engaged or something?"

Sonata shrugged. "What does it matter? Papa managed to draw her attention in the end."

Pyro stretched his brows and sucked his teeth. "Well, I gotta hand it to your father, it's no easy feat snatching a mermaid who's committed herself to another man."

Sonata wheeled around, offended. "What do you mean?"

"I'm just saying, when it comes to love, mermaids are an aggressive set. Once they've set their eyes on a man they're regular bearcats."

"Excuse me?"

"It's true! Why do you think the Other has so many legends about mermaids luring sailors off to their death? They all want a snorkel in the seaweed!"

Pasha and Faina burst into uncontrollable laughter.

"They want a what?" Pasha wheezed.

Pyro grinned mischievously. Once he had an audience, there was no stopping him.

"What? You've never heard of a snorkel in the seaweed? Tangling tails? Fish kissing? Fishing with your—"

"Pyro!" Sonata was affronted.

She gestured to Lydia, but rather than be offended, Lydia appeared to be as entertained as Pasha and Faina. Pyro couldn't help but snicker as the adolescents fell to pieces.

"What? I'm just trying to educate them. Pasha, if you ever cross a mermaid who's hot to trot, prepare yourself, they can be downright aggressive, and they don't take no for an answer!"

Sonata shook her head at Pyro, clearly embarrassed while trying not to laugh at the same time.

"That's a complete overstatement."

At last, Pyro tossed his hands. "Alright. Maybe I'm exaggerating a bit."

"Thank you!"

Pyro threw Pasha and Faina a wink.

Within an hour or two the train was pulling into the copper tunnel of the terminal at Alrisha. Out on the concourse, Pasha and Faina said goodbye to Lydia. She buttoned the top of Pasha's jacket, then straightened Faina's tam. She stood back to take them in.

"Be careful."

Pasha gave her one last hug. "We will, *Mamochka*."

She took their left wrists and planted a kiss on the base of their palms. Immediately, Pasha felt his heart swell with all the warmth of her love.

"Pasha has his calling glass," Sonata reminded her, "so we should expect a call from them once they reach the Seelbach."

Staccato drew his eyebrows together and looked around. "Where on earth has Cicada got to?"

Pyro jerked his thumb towards a bookshop. Staccato nodded.

"I see. She does like her books lately. Can't say I begrudge her for that."

"Only so she can avoid talking," added Pyro. "She's still sore about you not letting her go with Pasha and Faina."

Staccato rolled his eyes. "She'll get over it. Ready Sonata?" Staccato placed each of his hands on Pasha and Faina's shoulders, and guided them towards the exit. "Come along, you two."

Chapter 19:
The Citescape

When the four exited the building they found themselves at the heart of an underwater city encased entirely in clear glass.

"Not all of the underwater districts are in the water," explained Sonata, fluffing her coat collar. "Many of the libraries and museums are preserved in air domes, for obvious reasons. We call them vivariums. I can only imagine how many of those books had gone moldy in the grotto Aunt Evangeline showed you, Pasha."

Pasha recalled the sneezing fit he had undergone the moment he had entered the chamber.

"A lot."

Staccato and Sonata led the way to a columned government building where mermaid guards flanked the entrance. Sonata held Staccato back by the arm. Her eyes flicked towards his neck. He stared back at her, confused.

"It's a government building." Her voice was hardly above a whisper. "You have to take it off for security purposes."

Her eyes widened as she caught Pasha and Faina staring. She forced a smile.

"Staccato's getting over a cold." She reached around his collar and removed the necklace with the filigree charm. "The shell has petrichor in it. Opens the lungs."

Pasha had completely forgotten about the necklace. Apparently, so had Staccato, judging by the look of self-admonishment on his face.

"And security won't let you wear it?" said Faina with a raised eyebrow.

Pasha could see from the way Sonata's forehead was gathering into a pucker that she was searching for an explanation. Before she could come up with a reply, Staccato tossed the charm into his pocket.

"C.O.N. members have been known to smuggle poison in them. Happened a few years back." He rolled his eyes dramatically and made his way towards the stairs. "Terrorists. Can't even take a breathing aid into a federal building now."

As they headed up the stairs, Faina leaned over Pasha's shoulder.

"I'm calling bull on that one."

"You said it."

As they passed beneath the archway, the guards held open the door. Inside, a radiant mermaid with an elaborately knotted headscarf sat meditating behind a desk with her eyes closed. Sonata cleared her throat. The mermaid peeked open an eye.

"We have an appointment to see the gateway station. Princess Sonata Soter and Sir Staccato Nimbus."

The mermaid repeated the names back in a dreamy state.

"Princess Sonata Soter and Sir Staccato Nimbus …"

Pasha and Faina exchanged baffled glances as they waited for her to go on. At last she nodded her head.

"Yes, yes. Queen Calliope is expecting you." With a languid arm she beckoned an attendant dressed in a flowing green sarong. "Will you please show Her Highness and guests to the Citescape?"

The attendant nodded and gestured for them to follow.

Pasha tilted his head towards Faina. "Wonder why they call it 'the Citescape.' Isn't that like a painting of a city?"

Faina shrugged. "You know Voiler, everything has a double meaning."

They were led down a series of long, spiraling staircases until they reached the basement. The attendant unlocked two enormous oak doors. At first, Pasha thought they had entered a gallery. Massive paintings, all at least six feet high, crowded the walls and the geometric maze of dividers.

The room itself was vast and overall dark. As a matter of fact, they couldn't make out how far the room went on, for the end was clouded in shadow. The brightest sources of light seemed to emanate from the paintings themselves, and varied depending on the subject. The attendant bowed and exited the premises, shutting the doors behind her as she went.

No sooner had she shut the door than a musical and languid voice echoed from behind a painting.

"*Bondias* again, my lovelies!"

Queen Calliope emerged from the shadows, her smile bright and welcoming as always. She was swathed in a train of bright pink chiffon which split up the leg. Her top was fashioned from an assortment of tropical flowers that matched her earrings. She'd grown out her hair since Pasha had last seen her, and now sported a short afro embellished with orange blossoms and jasmine flowers.

Sonata reached forward and grasped Calliope's hands, exchanging kisses on each cheek.

"Calliope, how lovely to see you again!"

Calliope repeated the ritual with Faina. She extended her hands simultaneously to Pasha and Staccato. They each bent low to kiss them. As Pasha straightened, she tilted his chin up.

"You're taller, *mon duls*," which was *fontrois* for "my sweet." "And handsomer."

Pasha aimed a bashful smile at the floor. "Thank you, Your Majesty."

Calliope's bangles clicked and rattled as she batted Staccato playfully with her wrist, startling him so much he almost stumbled backwards.

"As for you, you old devil, you're looking a little tired."

Staccato swayed awkwardly and fidgeted with his cravat. "Am I now?"

She swaggered away from him with an alluring glance over her shoulder.

"You are. But then, exhaustion always did suit you."

Pasha and Faina fought the urge to burst out laughing as Calliope drew them down the hall of paintings. While Staccato, Sonata, and Calliope chatted away, Pasha observed the countless works of art. They brushed past a painting of Paris. Pasha ground to a halt, his eyes wide open. The slightest trace of a silvery trail was traversing across the night sky: a shooting star. Pasha yanked Faina back by the shoulder.

"Did you see that?"

"See what?"

"There was a shooting star, just now! In the painting!"

"*Wi*, I am sure there was." Calliope pivoted in place. "The paintings reflect the time and season of their subject in accordance with the present. Even the constellations will alter themselves accordingly."

She gestured to a painting on the opposite wall where the sun had risen over Mount Fuji.

"As you can see, in Japan it is still early morning."

A wind stirred the branches of the cherry blossoms. Pasha could've sworn he smelled the fuchsia-colored trees. All of a sudden, Staccato sneezed so loud Calliope jumped with wide eyes.

"*Saloo, mon sher*," bless you, my dear.

Staccato sniffed. "*Gracease*," thank you.

"Boy, that cold must have really got you, eh Staccato?" Pasha shoved his hands into his pockets with a hint of sarcasm.

Staccato flashed him a subtle glower, but Calliope shook her head.

"A cold? Oh no, no, no, *mon sher*. Staccato has had a mold allergy since he was a child. He always gets like this when he is down in the vivariums." She gave Staccato a teasing smile. "Some son of a mermaid you are."

Sonata shook her head. "Actually, Calliope, Pasha is right. Staccato has been suffering from a cold."

Pasha watched the two closely. A meaningful look passed between them. Calliope gave a short nod.

"Ah, I see. Well, then, we better get you out of here soon before the damp makes it any worse. Let's see. The painting you are looking for lies here…"

They meandered past depictions of famous cities in the southern United States until they reached a painting with twin spires.

Calliope threw out her hand with dramatic presentation. "Louisville, Kentucky."

They stood before the painting admiring the grand architecture of the famous racing track. A cool breeze rippled across their foreheads.

"Smells like rain …" Faina's lips curled into a magical smile, "and butter frying!"

Staccato smirked. "No moonshine?"

But Pasha could smell horses, and leather, tobacco smoke, and bourbon. There was straw, and icy mountain air as crisp and as fresh as a glass of ice water.

"Now there are a few things you need to know." Calliope rubbed her hands together. "The image depicted in the painting does not reflect the location of the gateway itself, at least not in this case."

Faina knit her eyebrows together. "It doesn't open at Churchill Downs?"

"No. This gateway will put you beneath the train track of the Pope Lick Trestle in a town called Fisherville."

"But how will we get to the Seelbach?"

Calliope pulled a pair of keys from her pocket and looked over her shoulder at Staccato.

"Faina mentioned she could drive."

Pasha's eyes slid in a furtive arc towards his companion.

"She mentioned, did she?"

Staccato crossed his arms. "Well, she did drive your mother and sister to New Jersey."

"Straight off a dock!"

Faina's hands jumped to her hips. "That was intentional! Besides, that's not the only time I've driven a motorcar."

Pasha rolled his eyes. "Please, you aren't referring to the time we hauled that hooch from the Yale Club in your uncle's delivery van, are you?"

Faina threw up her shoulders. "We made it, didn't we?"

Sonata tried to hide her apprehension by ducking her chin into her collar.

"You don't have any experience driving, do you, Pasha?"

"I'm from New York. If we aren't walking, we're riding the subway. Faina thinks she's an expert because her brother used to make deliveries back when her uncle's grocery was a liquor store."

Staccato massaged his eyebrows and held up a hand. "Regardless, I have faith in Faina's abilities."

Pasha couldn't help but wonder what Faina had done to earn trust from such a skeptic, but he said no more, and chalked it up to her characteristic charm. Staccato handed them a map as Calliope placed the keys in Pasha's hands.

"You will find a Rolls Royce parked off to the side of the road. It should take you an hour to reach the Seelbach."

Pasha pushed out his lip in astonishment. "A Rolls Royce? How did you manage to get us a Rolls Royce all the way out in the country? Do people come here often?"

Calliope fiddled with her earrings. "A seraph came through just last week. Said he was headed for a town called Point Pleasant in West Virginia. Something about a bridge. As for the car, well, let's just say we have friends in high places."

Staccato chuckled. "Several stories high, as a matter of fact."

Sonata and Calliope giggled. Faina and Pasha exchanged confused looks. Staccato's laughter faded and he cleared his throat.

"You'll understand when you get there."

"Now listen carefully," Calliope portioned her words out with care. "What I am about to say is very important. When you are ready to return, the way to get back to Voiler is a leap of faith."

Pasha's stomach lurched. "Oh no, not another one of those."

Faina knitted her brows. "What? What's that?"

"You wouldn't remember, you were unconscious when we brought you back from the Other. Had to take the elevator ride from Hell somewhere up in the Bronx that opened up in Larame."

"Why didn't you just take the Grand Central Gateway?"

Calliope gave a penitent shrug. "The Grand Central Gateway hadn't serviced Larame until a month ago."

"So what horrifying act of bravery must we complete this time?" asked Pasha.

"You will have to climb to the top of the trestle and jump off the bridge."

Pasha winced. "Please tell me this bridge is two feet high."

Calliope fidgeted with the many rings on her fingers. "It is ninety."

Faina threw down her hands. "What?"

"Can't we just drive back to New York, and take the train in Soter Hall?" Pasha pleaded.

Sonata brushed forward to put a soothing hand on their shoulders.

"You'll be fine. The gate has never failed anyone before. You'll end up right back here, safe in the Citescape."

Pasha and Faina glanced at each other with uncertainty.

"I'm afraid you must hurry," concluded Staccato with a hasty look at the clock above the door. "Sonata and I have to be back at the station to catch our train to Libra."

Calliope reached forward and pulled a hidden lever on the wall. Steps emerged leading up to the picture frame. Palms sweating, Pasha and Faina stood on the top stair facing the artwork. It was nightfall.

"When you hear the chime, you may step through the painting."

Pasha and Faina waited, all the while squeezing each other's hands tighter and tighter. The sound of rustling leaves brushed their ears. A strong whirlwind peeled across their cheeks. There was a clicking noise at the top of the frame as a compartment opened like a cuckoo clock. A wooden miniature of a horse and jockey popped out on a spring, and the first notes of *My Old Kentucky Home* tolled. Together, Pasha and Faina stepped over the picture frame and disappeared.

Chapter 20:
The Pope Lick Trestle

Pasha and Faina huddled beneath a bridge. The breeze blustered and the bluegrass teased their ankles. When at last they found the courage to open their eyes, it took a moment for their vision to adjust to the darkness.

Faina put a hand over her lips. "We made it, Pasha!"

Pasha breathed a sigh of relief. A train horn blared in the distance as two deer came prancing out of the bushes and leapt over the creek. Far away, Pasha could make out a curvy horizon line of blue hills.

Faina meandered in a circle beneath a tall tree. "It's pretty here, isn't it?"

"From what I can tell."

She ran her hand along the trunk. "Makes you miss the country, doesn't it?"

But Pasha wasn't listening. There was something unsettling about the bridge that he couldn't place his finger on. He took the map from his coat pocket and unfolded it.

"I didn't even think to ask what time it is here." He brought the map closer to his face and squinted. "Ugh, it's too dark. I can't see where he marked the car."

"I have a flashlight." Faina sat on her knees and rummaged through her suitcase. "You were really after Staccato back there, weren't you? What do you think that necklace is really for?"

"It's not for curing coughs, that's for sure. Find that flashlight yet?"

"Not yet. I can't see where to look."

"Well, hurry up, it's kinda creepy here."

Faina giggled over her shoulder. "Creepy?"

"Yeah, don't you think?"

She paused to take in their surroundings a second time.

"Well, I didn't think that before, but now you've put the idea in my head!"

She pulled something oblong from within her pack. A light flickered on. She shined the flashlight across the map. Pasha traced his finger against the place Staccato had marked and followed the line to the car.

"What if it got stolen?" Faina suddenly exclaimed.

"Considering we have the keys, I'd say that's doubtful."

They made their way down an overgrown path, Faina swinging her suitcase all the while.

"So, what do you think Staccato meant by that joke? The whole 'friends in high places' thing. He said we'd understand once we arrived."

Pasha shrugged. "If you ask me, he has a weird sense of humor."

"Funny, it always struck me as being similar to yours."

"Me?" Pasha looked almost offended.

"Well, you've both got that dry, dark wit."

Pasha hunched his shoulders. "I am not like Staccato." He plodded ahead of her.

"You're touchy like Staccato. ..."

Pasha was about to make a retort when he thought he spied a pair of glowing eyes in the bushes. As he was turning around, they disappeared.

"Did you see that?"

"Probably just another deer."

"Whatever, let's find the car and get outta here."

As Faina shined the flashlight up ahead, the light reflected off something sleek and shiny. Pasha jingled the keys in his hand.

"That must be it."

They made their way onto the road, eager to get a better look at the ritzy vehicle. After a moment of oohing and awing, Pasha unlocked the passenger door and held it open for Faina. Faina flashed him a wry grin.

"What do you think you're doing? I'm the driver, remember?"

Pasha returned her smile and shrugged. "Well, it was worth a shot."

Tossing Faina the keys, he took their suitcases and threw them into the back. They climbed into their seats and shut the doors. Faina placed the flashlight in Pasha's lap and clutched the wheel.

"Alright, where are we headed?"

Pasha turned the map over in his hands. "Uh, looks like we're gonna head east, then take a turn on …"

The pair of glimmering eyes briefly resurfaced, this time in the rearview mirror. The train horn blared a second time. Pasha thought he heard a muffled giggling noise. He whipped round to Faina.

"Was that you?"

Faina shook her head, her fingertips pressed over her lips.

"So you heard it?"

Faina was too frightened for words. She nodded her head. Pasha was about to suggest they put the key in the ignition and drive off, when something banged on the hood of their car. Pasha and Faina grabbed hold of each other, screaming at the top of their lungs.

"What are you hollerin' for?" demanded an elderly voice from outside the car. A lantern shone through the windshield. Beyond the light they could make out the creased face of an old man. He was outfitted in a faded plaid shirt, and held a rake in his right hand. His bushy eyebrows dangled low over his chartreuse eyes like Spanish moss. In the dim light he appeared almost green.

"Doggone kids, comin' out here to park your fancy motorcars!"

Pasha cranked the window down. His expression smoothed over with a sense of disdainful tranquility.

"Did you just hit our car with a rake?"

"Well, I knocked twice! Thought you might be having some trouble with your motor."

Faina leaned over the passenger seat.

"Oh no, no motor trouble, thank you. We're visiting from out of town and stopped to check our map."

The man gave a jerk of his head.

"I see. You must've come down here to catch a glimpse of the Goat Man."

Pasha cocked his head. "The what?"

"You know, the Pope Lick Monster. Ever since they ran that article in *The Journal,* folks been traveling from all over to see if the legends are true."

"So what exactly is this legend?"

"They say an evil spirit with the body of a man and the head of a goat lives beneath that there trestle; a demon who lures souls onto the bridge to meet their oncoming doom."

"So a half-man, half-goat draws you up the trestle to get hit by a train?"

"Depends. If the train don't get you, they say the very sight of the monster will drive you to jump to your death."

As ridiculous as it sounded, Pasha couldn't help but feel a slight shiver crawl up his spine. Faina leaned over him and held out the map.

"I'm afraid we're not familiar with the Goat Man. But do you have the time? We have reservations at the Seelbach."

The man rubbed his curly beard with long, gnarled fingers that could have easily been tree branches.

"It's half past sunset. 'Bout eight o'clock. You'll want to take Taylorsville and head through the Highlands."

Faina smiled and handed the map back to Pasha. "Thank you, sir, we appreciate it very much. We'll be outta your hair now."

The farmer smiled, charmed. "My pleasure, ma'am. Take care

now."

"Same to you!" Faina turned the key in the ignition and the engine started up. The farmer drew back, still holding his lantern aloft. For a moment Pasha thought his eyes glowed.

"Ya'll be careful, and watch out for the Goat Man."

Faina gave a friendly wave. "Will do!"

As they took off up the road, Pasha hunched down in his seat, looking baffled. "What kinda backwood nonsense was that?"

Faina flexed her fingers on the steering wheel and giggled. "Scared, were you?"

Pasha tangled his arms across his chest. "No!"

"You did say it was creepy here."

"I wasn't the only one screaming, you know."

"I only started screaming because you started screaming. Roll up the window, will you? Those cicadas are deafening."

A faint light rose from the backseat. "You called?"

Faina squealed and slammed on the breaks, throwing Pasha against the dash. Unfazed by their reactions, Cicada floated over the front seat, beaming adventurously. Faina swiveled around.

"Cicada, what are you doing here?"

Pasha rubbed the side of his head. "Yeah, you scared us half to death!"

Cicada scoffed and threw her hands on her hips. "What do you think I'm doing? I've come to help!"

Pasha's eyes adjusted. Cicada had pinned her shining yellow hair into a castle bob at the nape of her neck. She wore a pale yellow drop-waist dress with a stylish coat and oversized hat. The effect was decidedly modern.

"Does Staccato know you're with us?"

Cicada clutched her sides and laughed. "Well, of course not!"

"Then how did you get here?"

"I've been hiding in Faina's purse this whole time." She shrank down in size and lifted the pocket of the handbag. "All I had to do was slip away when no one was looking."

Pasha narrowed his eyes. "So that was you giggling before that old hayseed showed up?"

Before Cicada could reply, the calling glass gave a pulse from inside Faina's clutch. Pasha reached into the back and held the mirror up to their faces.

"Hello?"

Cicada dimmed her light and ducked down to the floor. Staccato appeared in the glass, Pyro, Sonata, Melodious, and Lydia crowded behind him.

"You wouldn't by any chance happen to have a stowaway, would you?"

Frowning, Pasha tilted the mirror so they could see Cicada huddled behind the seat. Staccato jabbed a long, aristocratic finger at the glass.

"Cicada Sycamore, you come back here this instant, young lady!"

Cicada crossed her arms like a small child. "Make me!"

"If you don't turn around and come back right now, your mother will be hearing from me!"

Cicada folded her hands behind her back and leaned into the mirror.

"You're going to travel all the way to Aquarius just to tattle on me?"

Staccato stretched back, surprised by her cheek.

"I—I might just!"

Cicada blinked slowly. "Uh-huh, right."

"There are other ways to reach Mother Genesis, you know," whispered Pyro over Staccato's shoulder.

"Go ahead." Cicada's voice smarted with challenge. "Tell her. I'm only doing my job."

Pyro pushed forward. "Tell her you'll dock her pay!"

Cicada pretended to yawn. "Mother sends me an allowance anyway."

Pyro was ready to tear hair from his head. "For doing what?" Sonata slammed her hand over Pyro's mouth.

Staccato released a heavy exhale and turned to Pasha and Faina. "How far are you from the trestle?"

Pasha shrugged. "We haven't even left yet."

Staccato gritted his teeth at Cicada and furrowed his brow.

"I'm going to count to three, and if you're not out of that car and heading back to the bridge, I'll—"

Cicada placed her hands on her hips. "You'll what?"

"I'll—I'll write your mother!"

Plopping herself down in the seat, she squinted her eyes and blew a raspberry into the mirror. Pasha wrinkled his nose and wiped the glass with his sleeve. He watched as Staccato pinched his temples.

"Fine. Fine! Stay there! But you are to remain completely out of sight! Do you hear me?"

Cicada leaned against the door and appraised her cuticles. "Oh, I hear you."

"Good." He returned his attention to Pasha and Faina. "Let us know when you reach the Seelbach."

They said goodbye, and Staccato's face was replaced with Pasha's reflection. Cicada stretched her long legs across the backseat.

"So, let's take a look at this map here. I can't wait to see the lobby."

"Didn't you hear what Staccato said?" Pasha stared her down. "You're to stay completely out of sight."

"Yeah, not gonna happen."

As if to show she was capable of behaving like an ordinary human, she turned off her light. Pasha and Faina rubbed their eyes in the darkness and looked her over. Much to their surprise she appeared perfectly normal. She still possessed a faint glow, but it was just enough to add radiance to her appearance rather than make her seem otherworldly.

She scrambled into Faina's bag and took out a copy of James Lane Allen's *Flute and Violin and Other Kentucky Tales and Romances.*

"I've been studying up on southern United States literature."

Faina smacked her forehead. "I knew my purse felt heavier!"

"You don't have to worry about a thing." Cicada sat up straight and transformed her voice into a honeyed, southern drawl. "As far as anyone knows, I'm Cecelia 'Cici' Butler. My Granddaddy was a Breckinridge, and my Mama grew up raising cane, Hell, and thoroughbreds over in Lexington."

Pasha and Faina's jaws dropped as they exchanged fascinated glances. Cicada shrugged.

"All the world's a stage, honey."

At last, Pasha cleared his throat and held out a hand.

"Well, in that case, pleased to meet you, Miss Butler."

Chapter 21:
The Dragon in Seersucker

When Pasha, Faina, and Cicada pulled up in front of the Seelbach, Pasha heaved a sigh of relief.

"'Faina can drive!'" He staggered out of the passenger seat. "Faina can put her foot against the pedal and her hands on the steering wheel, but in no way does that mean she can drive!"

Faina tossed his hat out the door. "Aw, pipe down, Pasha! It's not like you could've done any better."

Pasha held open the door for Cicada and took her bags.

"You know how one-way streets work, don't you? They go one way!"

"Hey, that Ford pulled off to the side, didn't he? Besides, we're here. Let's just sit back and enjoy the rest of the evening."

A man on the sidewalk happened to notice Cicada as she was passing by, and took his cigarette out of his mouth to whistle at her.

"Nice legs!"

Without missing a beat, Cicada shouted back. "Thanks! They're attached to my butt!"

Pasha covered his eyes and groaned. "Cicada!"

Meanwhile Faina dissolved into a fit of laughter.

"Oops!" Cicada gritted her teeth in self-admonishment. "Sorry, I forgot the accent!" She opened her mouth to say it again, but Pasha slammed a hand over her lips.

"That's not a normal thing to say!"

"Why not? It's the truth! They are attached to my—"

Pasha cut her off with an exasperated groan. "I'm gonna go check us in; in the meantime, Faina, please explain to Cici how to behave."

"Seemed like a pretty good answer to me," muttered Faina.

Pasha tipped the valet, and together they passed beneath the hunter green carapace and through the double oak doors. Upon entering the lobby, Pasha, Faina, and Cicada each gasped in amazement. At the far end of the room was a grand carpeted staircase of celestial blue, flanked with gold bannisters. The place was lousy with polished marble. There were white marble floors, slate-colored marble pillars, and archways trimmed in golden marble strips.

Faina's jaw hung open. "Holy smokes!"

Their eyes followed the glamorous figures pacing back and forth on the gallery. Throbbing behind each shadow was the distant hum of jazz music, bubbly champagne-infused laughter, and clinking crystal.

Once Pasha had checked them in and a bellhop had taken their bags, the three gathered into the lift. As the operator pulled the lever, Faina had to clench Pasha's arm to keep from jumping.

"Can you believe it, Pasha? I've never seen anything so fancy in all my life!"

"Uh, you do know we've been the personal guests of two different rulers since December, right?"

"Okay, fine, I've never seen anything so fancy in the Other."

Pasha was surprised by how quickly Cicada caught her mistake. She cleared her throat.

"The other what?"

Pasha watched Faina's eye widen as she realized what she'd said. "I said that backwards. What I meant to say is that I've seen so many fancy things in other countries, but I have yet to see something so fancy in this country."

"We've rob—I mean, visited several houses on Fifth Avenue as well as the Yale Club."

Pasha glanced nervously from the elevator operator to the bellhop, but neither of them appeared to have been listening. Pasha resisted the urge to sigh. They'd hardly been in the hotel five minutes and already he and Faina had carelessly risked blowing their cover. Despite having been born and raised in the Other without any knowledge of Voiler's existence, Cicada was doing a better job of blending in than they were! Pasha steeled his jaw. He refused to mess this up. He would not give Staccato the satisfaction of being right. From now on he would be more careful.

"Alright, alright," Faina conceded. "I'm just really excited, okay? Don't ruin it for me!"

Her exuberance was infectious. Pasha couldn't help but smile. He kept thinking how pretty her black hair looked against her red tam.

A thought occurred to him. Maybe he should tell her. He leaned a little closer.

He was about to open his mouth when the doors of the lift opened, and standing in the middle of the hallway was a familiar bronze-haired twenty-something with sparkling blue eyes, a chiseled face, and dimples. A cigarette was pinched between his fingers.

"Faina?"

Pasha's mouth fell open. His eyes glazed over in contemptuous disbelief.

"You have got to be kidding me."

Faina lit up. "Roman?"

She raced into the hall to greet him. Cicada leaned over to whisper in Pasha's ear.

"I take it this is the guy you accused Faina of giving her pumpkins to?"

Pasha sighed. "This is the guy." They exited the elevator to catch up with Faina. Pasha turned to the bellhop, a boy who was probably not much older than he was.

"We can take the bags from here, thank you."

Pasha tipped the boy, and with a friendly smile the bellhop departed.

Roman held Faina at arm's length, looking her over like she was a cocktail on the rocks and he wanted nothing more than to drink her up through a straw.

"What's this, you've done something different with your hair!"

Pasha cringed as Roman reached up to brush a stray curl from her cheek. Faina demurred.

"Oh, just trying a new style," she patted the ringlets tucked against her forehead.

He chucked her under the chin. "Well, you look awfully cute."

Pasha cleared his throat, causing Roman to look up. A glimmer of recognition came into his eyes.

"Pasha Chevalsky! How long has it been?" He looked Pasha up and down. "You're all grown up now!"

Pasha forced a smile. "Yeah, I used to think you were tall."

Faina shot him a warning glance. Pasha's brusqueness seemed to have been lost on Roman, for he threw back his head and laughed.

"Yeah, can't say I quite measure up to your stature, pal." He punched Pasha on the arm. "You know when Faina here told me you were a street fighter for the Breadwinners, I almost didn't believe her."

Pasha gave a twitch. "You don't say?"

"Yeah, but then I had no idea you'd gotten so tall! I bet you had those other kids quaking, eh?"

Pasha narrowed his eyes. "I ranked fifth out of twenty-four."

Roman drew back and took a drag from his cigarette. "Golly! Look out, Jack Dempsey! So, what are you kids doing on this side of the Mason Dixon line?"

Faina pulled Cicada forward. "Just visiting an old friend."

Fluttering her eyelashes, Cicada held out her hand in a lofty manner for Roman to kiss.

"Cecelia Butler of the Lexington Butlers. Friends call me 'Cici.'"

Roman waggled his eyebrows. "Well, well, pleased to meet you, Miss Cici."

Faina went on. "We were actually hoping to meet with Dr. Edom Cottonmouth, the art racketeer."

Roman's eyebrows stretched up his forehead.

"Edom Cottonmouth? What do you want with him?"

Faina looked back at Pasha and wrinkled her nose up in a teasing smile.

"It's a long story. Here to talk business, you could say." She winked.

"Ah, I gotcha. Well, you're in luck. He's a regular down at the Rathskeller. Likes to play poker with Al Capone. He's here tonight as a matter of fact. Say, if you three aren't too bushed after your trip, how about you come join me down in the Rathskeller? See if we can't find an excuse to get you a little more acquainted."

As much as Pasha would've loved to avoid Roman, he couldn't forgo the opportunity.

"That'd be great."

"Swell! Come down around ten o'clock. Wear your Sunday best." And with a friendly nod he strolled back down the hall, and the three made their way to their adjoining suites.

***

When ten o'clock rolled around, Pasha, Faina, and Cicada made their way towards the basement where the Rathskeller was located. Pasha was dressed in the navy suit he'd worn to his interview with *The Daily Compass*. Faina and Cicada complemented each other nicely, Cicada in a satin dress of pale gold while Faina sported a rose-colored chiffon number.

When it came to grandeur the Rathskeller certainly did not disappoint. The subterranean ballroom was tiled in warm shades of terra-cotta and gold. The decor featured a symbols and heraldry borrowed from a variety of creeds, societies, and mythology with no real consistency.

As they made their way beneath the extravagant high vaulted ceilings, several heads with scallop patterns of marcel waves turned to stare.

Roman lifted a salutary glass from the bar and beckoned them over. He scanned Pasha's attire.

"You clean up nice, Chevalsky."

Roman himself was dapper in a satin tux.

"Thanks." Pasha pulled out a chair for Faina, but Roman cut across him. He took Faina's hand and twirled her in place.

"Don't you look stunning!" He drew her to a chair on his opposite side.

Cicada shrugged apologetically at Pasha and took the seat next to him. She seemed to have pieced together the situation by now. Maybe those Jane Austen books helped after all. Roman turned to the three guests.

"So, what's everyone drinking?"

Pasha slumped morbidly over the bar. "Coke." He jumped to attention as Cicada opened her mouth. He jerked his thumb towards her. "Also coke."

Faina leaned forward on her elbows and smiled. "Coke is fine."

Roman repeated the order to the man at the bar, ordered himself an old fashioned, then returned his attention to Faina.

"If you like coke, allow me to introduce you to something really nifty." He pulled back the collar of his jacket just enough to let the light glint off his silvery flask. "Ever had a bourbon and coke before?"

While Roman's back was turned, Pasha drew his eyebrows together and shook his head from side to side.

Faina glanced down at her hands. "Um …"

Pasha pointed to the back of his throat and made a gagging sign. He cut his fingers across his neck.

"No, I don't believe I have."

Roman's lips stretched into a slithery smile. "Trust me, you'd love it."

Pasha threw up his arms at Faina, who shrugged. Cicada turned to Pasha with her eyes squinted in confusion.

"Don't they have peony milk?"

"No, Cici, just drink your coke. You like coke, don't you?" Without waiting for her reply, he leaned back in his chair and addressed Roman. "So, you never told us what brought you down to Louisville."

"I'm assisting Mr. Burinsky on official Breadwinner business. Boss provides the tin lizzie, I provide the driving." He glanced around before leaning in closer to whisper. "We got a lead on the Sippenhafts."

Pasha's eyes grew wide. "Anastas?"

"Shhh! Not so loud. Back in January I went shooting with my cousin and a couple of Breadwinners."

"Shooting?"

"Yeah, there's a range up in Maplewood Klokov visits from time to time. Anyway, we got to talking and it turns out one of Klokov's associates in the horse racing business said a couple of Butchers had been hanging round the Downs."

"The Downs?"

"Churchill Downs."

Perhaps it was the delicate nature of the situation, but Pasha could've sworn there was a hint of condescension in Roman's voice.

"Anyway, the guy starts asking around, and it turns out Anastas and Vadim have been doing some outta town work for their boss. An excuse to get outta New York, you see."

Pasha's eyes glimmered with violent thrill. "And you're gonna kill him?"

Roman tapped his nose and grinned. "That's the idea."

When Pasha looked up, Faina had paled six shades and was staring up at him with pleading eyes. A smooth sliding sound turned their attention in the opposite direction as their drinks careened down the bar. Roman took his hands off the counter.

"Heads up!"

When his cup had ground to a halt, Pasha took a handful of peanuts from the bowl set between him and Roman and sprinkled them into his coke.

Cicada was intrigued. "Is it good like that?"

Pasha nodded as he took a sip. "Try it."

Pasha immediately regretted this suggestion as Cicada dug both hands into the bowl and dumped a cup's worth of peanuts into her drink. Roman stared at her awkwardly while she sipped loudly from her straw. At once Cicada's eyes widened, and she threw Pasha an enthusiastic thumbs up.

Roman glanced around to make sure no one was looking, then he topped off Faina's glass with the bourbon. Pasha eyed her warily.

"Go ahead," egged Roman. "Give it a try."

Faina stared for a moment at the cup, and Pasha could sense that she was secretly irritated. She scoffed.

"I didn't realize you were actually going to do it."

Roman waved his hand. "C'mon, you'll love it. I promise."

Faina smiled in a way that was tighter than usual, and raised the glass to her lips. She took a drink. Her eyes and nose instantly puckered.

She set the glass aside, sputtering and coughing. Roman patted her on the shoulder.

"It's a little strong." Her eyes watered.

"Pasha," Cicada tapped on Pasha's shoulder and indicated to a hulking figure seated at a table across the room. "Something tells me that's the man we're looking for."

"What makes you say that?"

She gestured to the back of his neck. "See behind his collar? His skin is peeling."

"He could have dry skin."

"But doesn't he give you a bit of an uneasy feeling? Just wait until he turns around."

Pasha trained his eyes on the figure at the card table, willing the stranger to show his face. As he turned his head, Pasha felt the old, familiar sensation of chilling discomfort. The features were too handsome, too symmetrical, and yet he was different from other ophidians. There was a ruggedness seldom present in the aristocratic facades of native Draconians. To top it all off, he was ginormous.

"Looks more like a fury than an ophidian to me."

Cicada set her drink aside. "That's because he's a Herculean."

"What does that mean?"

"Don't you know about the legend of Lake Hercules? It's said those who grow up drinking the water from the lake will be big and strong. Melodious is from Lake Hercules, remember? Only his family had to leave once Draco conquered Sagittarius for the territory."

Pasha nodded his head. "Is that really why Melodious is so huge? Because he's from Lake Hercules?"

"Yep. And it's no different for the ophidians. The ones from Lake Hercules have a sturdier look about them than their cousins in the capital. It's a harsher climate, so they're a lot less delicate."

"I'll say! He makes Samael look like a pansy!"

Cicada stifled a snort. "If you ask me, Samael already looks like a pansy."

Pasha was about to laugh when he was caught off guard by another round of Faina's coughing.

He flashed a look at Cicada. "I told her she'd hate it." He offered Faina his coke.

Faina smiled and raised a tempting eyebrow. "Does it have peanuts in it?"

"Would I drink it any other way?" Pasha winked.

As Faina reached for the cup, Roman waved Pasha away and tipped the glass of coke and bourbon to her lips as though he'd shove it down her throat.

"Nah, she'll get used to it after her third sip."

Faina grabbed the glass to keep it from spilling on her dress and flashed Roman a dirty look from the corner of her eye, but said nothing. Pasha was perplexed. It was unusual for Faina to hold back in such a manner. Regardless, Roman's behavior had rubbed Pasha the wrong way.

"She needs something on her throat." He pushed the glass forward.

"She's got something on her throat." Roman pushed it back.

"Yeah, and it's burning a hole through her esophagus." He slid it back.

Before Roman could offer another protest, Faina reached around and grabbed the glass.

"I need the salt and fizz. Thank you, Pasha."

Cicada folded her gloved hands over her lips and mumbled to Pasha. "We should find a way to talk to him."

"Something tells me we shouldn't disturb him in the middle of a game."

Cicada rubbed her chin. "What are they playing?"

"Looks like poker."

"You know how to play?"

"I do." He eyed her suspiciously. "But I'd rather not introduce myself to the dangerous criminal by taking his money in a game of cards."

"I think you're being a little overly cautious."

Before Pasha could answer, the band struck up. Faina clapped her hands together.

"*The Sugar Foot Stomp*! Oh, that's one of my favorites! Let's dance, Pasha! Please!"

Roman's nostril twisted over his lip as he eyed Pasha cynically. "You dance?"

Faina swatted Roman on the shoulder. "Of course he dances! Why wouldn't he dance?"

Roman tossed back his drink. "No offense, of course. You're just so quiet."

"Pasha and I used to dance all the time down at the Foxhole. He's a regular Oliver Twist. We would tango, Charleston, foxtrot, you name it!"

Roman smoothed a curl over his forehead. "Did you, now? Guess by then I'd moved up to the Bronx."

Pasha smirked and screwed up his eyes. "Yeah, you'd probably grown out of it just as we were hitting the scene. You're what? Five years older than us?"

Roman glared at Pasha, then forced a smile. "That's right, you're still just a kid."

He reached over and tousled Pasha's hair patronizingly. Pasha's cheeks flushed with rage, but before he could say anything Faina towed him to the dance floor.

"Come on, let's go!"

The moment they were out of earshot, Faina slammed her hands on Pasha's shoulder.

"Alright, what did you and Cicada find out?"

"We think we've spotted Cottonmouth playing cards at that table."

Faina peered over his shoulder. "You mean that big bruno with the cheaters?"

"That's the one."

"Can we get a closer look?"

"Anything you want!" He slipped his arm around her waist and, with the other, held up her hand. Together they danced their way towards the card table.

Pasha glared smugly back at Roman, who was still seated at the bar looking dumbfounded. But Cicada had disappeared. Pasha's face fell.

"Uh, Faina, where did Cicada go?"

He spun her back in so they faced each other. Faina craned her head towards the card table.

"That wouldn't be her sitting next to Cottonmouth, would it?"

Pasha nearly dropped her. "What?"

They hastened to the back for a better look. Sure enough, there she was, seated between Cottonmouth and some gangly man. She twirled a strand of yellow hair flirtatiously around the finger of her satin glove.

Faina squeezed his shoulders. "Pasha, they'll eat her alive!"

"She's putting down money!"

"What money? That better not be my money!"

Roman sidled up behind them. "Your friend says she's a real 'dabster' at cards, whatever that means."

Faina clenched her teeth. "Is she, now? I never knew!" She tugged on their wrists. "Well, what are we waiting for, fellas? Let's see what a dabster she is!"

As they approached the table, Pasha was offered a better glimpse of Cottonmouth. His hands were folded cooly beneath a masculine chin neatly trimmed with a black goatee that matched the long, thick ponytail slicked back at the nape of his neck. A pair of tortoiseshell pince-nez balanced on the bridge of his nose. And no amount of tailoring could have helped the unnatural appearance of his ballooning muscles being stuffed into his blue seersucker suit.

Overall he had the absurd look of a dragon trying to pass as a human by putting on a pair of spectacles and a suit. Yet as he held his Cuban cigar between his perfect teeth, Pasha could not deny Cottonmouth had the quality of a true southern gentleman.

At the sight of Pasha and Faina, Cicada seemed to ebb with a faint light.

"Gentlemen, Dr. Edom Cottonmouth," she crooned in an immaculate southern drawl, "allow me to introduce my two very good friends, Paul and Stefania Lapochkov. They're visiting Louisville on their honeymoon."

A bead of sweat trickled down the back of Pasha's neck. It had never occurred to him to use a fake name, and yet it would've been downright idiotic to give Cottonmouth his real name. Roman didn't so much as bat an eye. He was accustomed to these sorts of business exchanges, being an associate of a Breadwinner associate.

Cottonmouth ran a wary glance down Pasha's face and shoulders, then thrust his massive hand forward in greeting.

"Pleased to make your acquaintance, Mr. Lapochkov." His voice was flecked with front porches and lazy summer evenings. He kissed Faina's hand, and Pasha watched a slight tremor run down her shoulders. "Mrs. Lapochkov."

Cicada gestured to the man with the corbeled cheek bones and suspicious eyes.

"Mr. Bige Clay."

They exchanged greetings, and turned to the third opponent with thin lips and thick eyebrows.

"And Mr. Alton Letcher."

Pasha tried not to swallow as he shook the gangster's hand. Cottonmouth pulled out two chairs. Roman must have needed no invitation, for he casually pulled up a seat next to Clay.

Cottonmouth leaned away to blow his cigar smoke in the opposite direction.

"So, tell me, Mr. Lapochkov, are you a gamblin' man?"

Pasha forced a smile and tried his best to appear witty and at ease.

"You might say that." He fell back on his old Russian accent, drawing inspiration from his mother. "Unfortunately, cards aren't my sort of …" he turned to Faina. "*Kak ty skazhesh'*, darling?" How do you say?

Faina molded her voice to the same Slavic trill. "Cup of tea."

"Cup of tea!" He slapped his hand on the table. "That is the phrase!" He gestured to Cicada as she laid down a card. "I will leave that to Miss Butler, here."

Cicada wrinkled her nose playfully and returned her attention to the game. Cottonmouth twirled a strand of his ponytail around his finger.

"And what is your sin of preference?"

"I am a thoroughbred man, myself."

Cottonmouth raised his eyebrows. "Then you've come to the right place."

"That I have."

Letcher looked up from his fold. "I take it you'll be laying down some dough at the tracks this weekend, then?"

Pasha examined his shoelace in a bored manner. "Money is not a currency I would normally stake my luck on."

Clay chuckled coarsely. "If you ain't playing for cash, what else are you playing for?"

Faina leaned forward to pinch Pasha's cheek. "*Palushka* here prefers something more sophisticated than cash. Don't you, darling?" Apparently they'd had the same idea.

Pasha tickled beneath her chin. "Exactly, *solnishko*," sunshine.

Cottonmouth turned his head curiously. "Such as?"

"We're fond of artwork."

He raised his glass. "I see, a man of taste."

Pasha gestured to Faina. "My wife here has a particular interest in glassworks."

"My mother took me to Venice when I was just a girl to see how Murano glass was crafted. We hear you boast quite the collection when it comes to glassworks and ceramics, Dr. Cottonmouth."

"Indeed, you heard correctly. How long are you staying in Louisville?"

Pasha leaned back and put an arm around Faina, "As long as my little *kroshka's* heart desires." He cuddled his nose into her cheek. "Isn't that right, my princess?"

Roman was glowering at them both. Faina giggled and waved him away.

"Darling, you spoil me!"

Cottonmouth smiled amiably. "Well then, you simply must come by my abode and let me show you my collection. I've recently acquired a Mesopotamian piece I'm particularly fond of."

Faina made her eyes swell with enthusiasm. "Have you, now? Oh, well, that would be simply wonderful! How lovely of you, Dr. Cottonmouth! We Russians have heard tell of the famous hospitality of the American south, but I did not believe it until now."

"Tomorrow then? I live just over in the Highlands."

"Can we, darling?" pleaded Faina, thrusting her lower lip out to Pasha.

Pasha made an excellent show of mentally scanning through their schedule. He rubbed his chin and, with his free hand, played with a curl in Faina's hair.

"I don't know, sweetheart, weren't we planning to stroll along the riverfront tomorrow?"

"Oh, there will be plenty of time for that. Let us take Dr. Cottonmouth up on his invitation."

At last Pasha smiled. "Alright then, whatever makes you happy." He rubbed his nose against hers.

"Excellent!" Cottonmouth pulled a gold embossed card from his chest pocket and handed it to Pasha. On the back was an Algonquin seal with a serpent biting its own tail.

"That's my address. Around noon, shall we say? You'd be just in time for tea."

"It is a date, then."

"Oh, and do be sure to bring along this lovely creature." He reached across to graze his lips over the top of Cicada's wrist.

"Oh, do stop, Dr. Cottonmouth, I'm blushing like a peach."

***

By the time the trio made it back to the accommodations, it was late. Cicada had been unwilling to leave the card table, and Pasha and Faina didn't want to leave her unattended. As they pattered down the hall, Pasha stretched his arms over his head and yawned.

"Say, Cicada, where did you learn to play poker anyway?"

"*Pride and Prejudice.*"

Pasha stopped and turned to stare at her. "You're telling me you learned to play poker from a fluffy Victorian romance novel?"

Cicada tossed her hand. "Well, technically it was Commerce, but they're pretty much the same thing. It was actually very interesting. I noticed the boys at the other table had a game of *Vingt-un* going."

Pasha removed his room key from his pocket. "That was Black Jack."

"Same thing."

Cicada reached into her purse and handed Faina a thick wad of bills. Faina looked down at the money and cocked an eyebrow.

"What's this?"

"Your cut of the dough, of course!"

Faina balked at her. "You gambled with my money?"

"Relax, I was never in any danger of losing it."

Pasha turned the key in the lock. "Oh, really? And why is that?"

"Because I cheated, of course!"

Faina gasped. Pasha scrambled to retrieve the keys he had dropped on the floor.

"You cheated at cards with thugs?" He swung open the door and pulled her inside.

"Well, yeah, it was easy. It's all mathematical, you see—"

"Shhh," Faina hushed, hastily shutting the door behind them.

"I don't care how you did it!" Pasha was practically spitting. "Just don't do it again! I don't know what you've read about organized crime, but these are some of the most dangerous men in the country. Do you understand? If you cross them, they will kill you!"

Cicada narrowed her eyes. "What do you mean, don't do it again? How else are you going to get that shard off of Cottonmouth? I saw what you two were cooking up at the card table. You're going to try and get Cottonmouth to bet the shard in a game. You wouldn't leave something like that up to chance, now, would you?"

Pasha leaned back against the wall and massaged his forehead.

"That's the idea. But I haven't worked out all the details yet, okay? So until we know for sure what we're doing, no more cheating at cards!"

Cicada hunched her shoulders. "Fine." She glided back towards their adjoining door. Faina glanced worriedly at Pasha.

"Are you sure you can get Cottonmouth to take such a gamble?"

Pasha closed his eyes and sighed. "I don't know, but I'm gonna try."

Chapter 22:
The Hearing of Lydia Chevalsky

The interior of the courtroom was hive-like, and hexagonal in shape. It had a high domed ceiling and a series of stacked boxes similar to an amphitheater. At the top of the ceiling was a stained glass mosaic of a barn owl's face.

The floor level was rimmed with twelve chambers, each reserved for an Ecliptic kingdom. Behind those chambers, a foot or two higher, were cells of greater width for non-Ecliptic countries with significant demographics. There was a place for the officials of the Seraph Federation, and the United Societies of the Eridanis River Valley. Seven chambers belonged to the seven mermaid kingdoms, and finally, there was Draco's box.

As Lydia took her seat next to Staccato, she shivered under Samael's icy blue gaze. His head was pressed against the high-backed chair, while his hands rested on the plush, velvet arms. The gauzy sleeves of his ophidian robes draped to the floor. The veil of his crown was pulled back over his long chestnut hair, showcasing the startling comeliness of his face.

At the sight of Lydia he leaned forward. His eyes trained on her, demanding her to look at him. When Lydia could bear it no longer, she glanced up. Samael's perfect lips split into a delighted grin.

Out of nowhere, Staccato reached over and gave her hand a comforting squeeze. Lydia jumped back in surprise. Realizing what he'd done, Staccato stared down at her, mortified. He dropped her hand at once.

He'd hardly spoken to her after Pasha and Faina's departure. On the train he had sat in a separate compartment by himself. As soon as they'd arrived at the hotel, he had locked himself in his room. Her eyes glimpsed his collar. Hardly five minutes ago, she had watched him remove the tiny filigree pendant before entering the building and hand it to Sonata. Her gaze travelled his neck to his face. Instinctively, she blinked in surprise.

It was as though she had never seen him properly until now, for his features had a new distinction, and had even brightened. She tried to remember what his face had looked like before, and was horrified to realize she couldn't. It was almost as if Staccato's looks had been so ordinary they were immediately forgettable. That wasn't the case now. He had eyes the exact color of the lake she had grown up on. They were so bright, so comforting, that she did not want to look away. Something familiar stirred in the back of her head.

When Staccato caught her staring, Lydia turned her attention to the box below, where King Javaid and Queen Constanza sat. Like Samael, they too had elected to represent their country in person. They were an impressive couple, sitting proudly in their box. Javaid's royal blue robe was open at the chest, and the beads of Constanza's headdress cascaded against her tan forehead.

Lydia adored Constanza and Javaid. They were so kind, so loving, having wept when they were introduced to her last Christmas. Of course, Lydia understood why. Her mother was Javaid's little sister, and the couple hadn't seen her since she was a baby.

The large wooden doors pulled back. An official-looking seraph darkened the doorway with his broad gold wings.

"All rise for Judge Tyto Alba."

Lydia staggered clumsily to her feet between Staccato and Sonata. A woman with a heart-shaped face and a massive pair of feathery sienna wings glided to the high podium at the far end of the room. When she situated herself on her perch, she gestured for everyone to sit.

Chairs scraped the floor as the courtroom settled into place. The Judge cleared her throat.

"The Council is gathered today to decide whether or not Lydia Sylvia Davidovitch Chevalsky neé Kingsley is the legitimate offspring of King Bruin Halborn Northstar of Ursa and Queen Evangeline Ophelia Soter. The legitimacy of Mrs. Chevalsky's relation will determine whether or not her son is eligible to rule over Ursa." With a graceful sweep of her head, her large eyes fell upon Lydia in the box. "To begin, the Council would like to call Mrs. Chevalsky to the stand."

Lydia swallowed hard as she rose and made her way down the stairs. The heels of her shoes seemed to keep time with the heavy beat of her heart. She took her place at the stand in the center of the courtroom, and folded her hands in front of her. The Judge inclined her head.

"Your full name?"

Lydia tucked her chin to her chest. "Lydia Sylvia Davidovitch Chevalsky."

"Closer to the mic, dear."

She leaned forward and repeated her name.

"When were you born, Mrs. Chevalsky?"

"March twentieth, 1890."

"How old were you when your father, David Kingsley, adopted you from the orphanage in Lake Baikal?"

"Only a few months. At least, that is what he told me. I was still an infant."

The Judge peeled through an impressive sheath of papers.

"Mrs. Chevalsky, according to my notes you had a rather extraordinary childhood. Would you share with us what that experience was like?"

Lydia paused, taking a minute to unstick her tongue from the roof of her mouth. This was the moment she had dreaded above all else. She'd always had enough sense to keep the fantastic aspects of her childhood a secret from everyone. Everyone, that is, except her children.

In the beginning she'd seen no harm in it, painting bedtime stories of wild unicorns, enchanted music boxes, and kisses with healing powers. Then Katya was diagnosed with psychosis, and Lydia became convinced her daughter had inherited some kind of mental delusion from her. If anyone found out about the crazy stories she'd shared with her children, they might try to put her in an institution and take Pasha and Katya away from her. She never spoke of it again, not until now.

"When I was a girl," she paused and cleared her throat, "I lived inside a little cottage surrounded by a fifteen-foot-high rose hedge on all sides. The entrance was enchanted so that only those who knew the magic words could get in or out."

She chanced a wary glance around the courtroom, expecting everyone to break out into appalled laughter. But they did not. They remained listening as though it were all quite normal. The Judge nodded and smiled.

"I am sure I needn't remind you enchanted shrubberies are not an uncommon practice in the Other."

Feeling more comfortable than before, Lydia straightened and cleared her throat.

"I am aware, Your Honor."

"Can you tell us who was allowed in the hedge?"

"Well, there was Papa, Baba Yaga, Grandma Lucy, and myself of course. That was my family."

The Judge knit her hands below her chin. "Tell us about Baba Yaga. Who was she?"

"Baba Yaga was my father's aunt. An older woman who lived in a cottage outside the hedge. After my grandmother died, *Tetya*—that was what I called Baba Yaga—kept watch over me when Papa was away."

"Why was she called Baba Yaga? Did she have another name?"

"I never knew her to have any other name than Baba Yaga. People thought she was a witch, and well … she wasn't a witch, but she did have power. She could move things with her mind, and confuse people, and cast illusions, and a number of other things which I never really knew the extent of."

"And your father? Was he like your aunt? Could he move things with his mind?"

"He was, though I believe he held back in front of me. I don't know why. He would never tell me how he had obtained his powers."

The Judge paused, glanced momentarily back at her box, then resumed.

"Did your father carry a staff?"

Lydia kneaded her index finger on her left hand as she summoned the image of her father's fingers resting on the head of his cane.

"He had an ebony walking stick with a handle in the shape of a raven."

A few council members made note of this detail and took a moment to scribble it down on paper. For several minutes, Lydia regaled the Council with all sorts of details about her childhood. The story ended with her father's mysterious disappearance.

At length the Judge came to the end of her notes and gave Lydia leave to return to her box. No sooner had Lydia's heel struck the stair than a gavel was tapped softly behind her.

The Judge's eyes flicked towards Draco's box. "Cobra Samael?"

Samael looked down at Lydia with a sickeningly sweet smile.

"You mentioned your father was a friend of Evangeline's."

Lydia's head sagged. Already Samael was trying to steer the trial to his benefit, but Lydia would not condescend to lie. She returned to the podium.

"He was."

"And yet he said he picked you up from an orphanage when you were only a few months old."

Lydia nodded but did not speak.

"Did you ever think perhaps this man was your real father?"

"I did. Until recent events, I had always believed him to be my real father, even though he told me I was adopted."

"Did you ever express these beliefs to him?"

"Yes."

"How did he respond?"

"He would turn very stern and deny it."

"And how did that make you feel?"

Lydia tightened her shoulders and shifted uncomfortably. "It made me feel … forgive me, Your Majesty, but I fail to see how that question is relevant." She looked imploringly back at the Judge.

The Judge nodded. "There is no law saying you have to answer every question, Mrs. Chevalsky. You have a right to maintain your silence if you so wish."

"I do wish it."

Samael sat back, nonplussed by her refusal. When it was clear he had no further questions for Lydia, the Judge allowed her to return to her seat. His voice slipped over the microphone.

"Your Honor, I would like to present evidence I've gathered concerning Mrs. Chevalsky's parentage. I believe the court will find it quite significant."

The Judge conceded with a nod of her head. With his eyes narrowed on Lydia, Samael floated gracefully to his feet.

"Over the past few months, Sir Staccato Nimbus and Princess Sonata have claimed this woman is Evangeline's heir. I assure you, dear Judge, I do not dispute this claim—quite the contrary. But you see, this is not sufficient evidence to conclude that Mrs. Chevalsky is the rightful Princess of Ursa."

Sonata snapped her head towards the microphone. "Whatever do you mean, my dear Cobra?"

"Evangeline's sole claim upon Ursa was procured by marriage. You might even go so far as to say Evangeline's parentage borders on irrelevant. It was King Bruin who was born into the ownership of Ursa, and by his blood only can it be bequeathed to another. As much as I hate to stir up scandal, the fact of the matter is, Evangeline was not faithful to Bruin."

A sensational hum circulated throughout the court, growing louder with each round.

"I object!" Sonata rose to her feet. "How dare you! I assure you, Cobra, this is no place for vulgarity! This is a matter of international importance!"

"I agree, it is a matter of international importance. Thus it is imperative that we not shrink away from the truth in our sensitivities, but look boldly and objectively into the face of veracity itself, no matter how vulgar and tawdry the facts may be. The courtroom is a place of law, Your Highness. If you are unwilling to address the accuracy of this claim for fear of indelicacy, I suggest you involve yourself in other matters. I hear Lady Acquarone is in need of volunteers for her charity raffle, if you're interested."

A few of the council members laughed, encouraging the smugness in Samael's expression to grow. Sonata blushed crimson with rage, but she could not argue this point.

"And pray, what evidence have you of this tactless and presumptuous accusation?"

A grin unraveled across Samael's lips. "Plenty. In fact, not only do I boast sufficient evidence to support my claims, but it just so happens that the perpetrator himself is in this very courtroom." He pointed a finger at their box. "Evangeline's lover was none other than Sir Staccato Imperious Nimbus!"

Lydia's eyes stretched wide. Everyone swiveled around to stare at the miraculous. Staccato sat with his lips pressed together, his shoulders forced into a stiff posture of coolness. At length, he lifted his chin and spoke into the microphone.

"And what evidence do you have to base such a ridiculous claim on?"

Samael beamed and reached for something beneath his desk. He dropped an aged diary onto the surface. Staccato turned as pale as talcum powder. With great ceremony, Samael flipped open to the first entry. He turned to the Judge.

"May I?"

Dumbstruck, the Judge bobbed her head in compliance.

Samael cleared his throat. "*June twenty-first, 1888. ...*"

Chapter 23:

An Ambitious Upstart

The large painted doors of the Advisory Quarters in Alveare thundered open. Nineteen-year-old Staccato Nimbus skidded into the hallway of the north wing in his bare feet. In his haste, his leg suddenly slipped. He stumbled to catch himself before he fell off the walkway lining the wall, nearly falling into the water and crashing into the maid who was swimming up the corridor. The maid flailed backwards, startled, then placed a hand to her chest.

"Are you alright, Mr. Nimbus?"

Staccato stopped and held out his hand apologetically. "Forgive me, Phrygia, I didn't mean to frighten you. I'm quite alright."

The pearl comb that had been pinned in her hair began to float away. Staccato hastened to retrieve it and held it out to the girl.

"Just running a little late, is all."

Phrygia pursed her lips and raised a teasing eyebrow. "Well, don't you hurt yourself now. You'll be no help to His Majesty with a broken leg."

Staccato slicked his shiny, dark blonde hair back and took off down the hall.

"Don't worry about me, Phrygia! I'm nothing if not careful!"

It was not the most forgiving of days to sleep in, not that the King was particularly fussy about such things. It was the day before the annual water chariot races, the first event of the holiday of Summer Solstice. Theo would be eager to ensure everything was prepared for the celebration. Furthermore, Theo's youngest sister, Princess Evangeline, had just finished her final semester at Petitella School for Girls in Cassiopeia. The Princess would be returning home from school just in time for the revelry.

Though Staccato had worked at Alveare for at least six months now, he had yet to meet Theo's youngest sister, for she'd been away studying glassblowing. As far as he knew, she was exceptionally gifted in her craft. At the age of fifteen she'd made a name for herself creating ornate glass mirrors using some unheard-of technique. What that technique was, Staccato hadn't the slightest idea. He knew very little about glassblowing.

Staccato jumped across the water to the other side of the hallway, his foot narrowly missing Theo's pet sea turtle, Ulysses. As Staccato steadied himself, Ulysses swam to the side of the parapet and laid a ball at Staccato's feet.

"Not now, Ulysses, I've got work."

Ulysses gave a disappointed blink and sank back under the water in search of someone to play with.

Staccato had always found it odd that Theo doted upon his half-sisters, Evangeline and Estella. The circumstances of their birth weren't exactly favorable. Less than a year after Theo's mother, Queen Timpani of Pisces, had died, his father, King Nereus, remarried a wealthy, arrogant, tight-lipped mermaid from Cassiopeia.

Atergatis was a self-made woman. Born with nothing, she rose to fame by crafting cosmetics and selling them to high-profile women. Her products were considerably popular in Cassiopeia, where beauty was so virtuous it became a vice, and they were said to be quite effective—so effective, as a matter of fact, that they became one of the most expensive products on the market.

None of Nereus's children had any fondness for Atergatis, not even her own daughters. Estella had sprung from her union, shortly followed by Evangeline. With such a detestable excuse for a stepmother, Staccato would've understood if Theo and Javaid had despised their sisters. Instead they loved them as dearly as they loved each other.

"Estella and Evangeline didn't choose how they came into the world," Theo would often say.

Staccato didn't understand the love between siblings. He himself had only one bully of an older brother, and they seldom spoke. And yet, despite the perplexity of the Soter siblings' relationship, it was precisely what Staccato loved about them: they loved each other.

Staccato rolled back his sleeves and brushed the water droplets from his trousers. He made it to the dry stairwell and carried on towards the roof of the palace. Theo had mentioned the night before that he wanted to get a bird's eye view of the coral garden for First Feast. As Staccato stumbled out the door, the wind whipped a stray hair across his forehead. Scrambling to set it back in place, he looked around. No one was present except for a servant sweeping the leaves from the patio.

"Has the King arrived yet?" asked Staccato, trying not to appear concerned.

"On his way up." The young attendant gave Staccato an amused once-over. "Did you really think you were late, sir?"

Staccato straightened his shirtfront and smiled. "Late for being early."

The servant chuckled and continued his sweeping. Staccato rubbed his eyes and collapsed into a chair. He leaned forward with his elbows on the railing, propping his chin on his fist. He hoped the breeze might wake him up a bit. He swept his gaze over the dark mountains, admiring the rich summer foliage. In the distance, a whale was whipping its fins out of the frothing waves. As he followed the road to the thin line of beach below the hillside, he noticed a golden-haired girl paddling through the shallows near the east wing; a mermaid. Staccato found this odd. Rarely were any of the royal household up and about before he was, and she certainly wasn't a member of the staff.

He leaned in closer as she sank back against the waves, letting her hair fall away from her shells and spread in a golden fan around her. She had alluring almond eyes and a natural, ethereal quality baked into her features. Her lips were fashioned so she always had the hint of a smile at the corners of her mouth. She curled her fins upwards; Staccato could see she had shimmering gilded scales on her tail. As she sank below the water, Staccato's heart sank with her. She was a gorgeous drop of sunshine.

After a moment or two of heartache she burst up from the waves, throwing her hair back in a perfect arc where it smacked against bare, sun-browned shoulders.

Staccato waved the servant to his side and pointed to the attractive mermaid bathing in the shallows.

"Who is that?"

"That would be Princess Evangeline."

Staccato crept back an inch, trying to stave off the blush threatening to color his cheeks. He forced himself around, feigning disinterest.

"I see, uh … if you're done sweeping, would you mind checking if the King is on his way?"

"As you wish, sir."

Staccato waited until the attendant had shut the door, then he wrenched himself around just in time to see Evangeline scrambling out of the sea, the water clinging to her hips transforming into an airy, cotton sarong behind her. A maid helped her into her kimono. She was every bit as attractive in her human form: long-limbed and tan, almost bird-like. And there was something endearing and soft about the way her belly stuck out a bit.

The door opened, and Staccato turned to see the King striding towards him across the patio. The breeze combed through Theo's warm curls of soft brown hair. He was almost gold in complexion. He definitely looked the part of his title: chiseled, handsome, and powerful.

For a moment Staccato was afraid he had caught him admiring his sister. His heart pounded fearfully as Theo approached him. The King stopped short, put a finger to his chin, and, smiling mischievously, looked Staccato over.

"How many minutes did you beat me by?"

Staccato allowed himself to breathe. "Five at most."

Theo broke into laughter. "Honestly, Staccato, it'd do you well to relax a little more. You live life far too much by the book."

Staccato snickered. "How else would I have come so far? I came from nothing, I grew up with nothing, and yet here I am today. If life has taught me anything, Theo, it's that there's nothing so imperative to success as hard work, responsibility, and dedication. And no distractions, that's very important."

Theo scoffed. "That's exactly what you need, a nice distraction, preferably in the shape of a beautiful woman."

Staccato resisted the urge to glance back over the railing. "It takes a lot more than a pretty face to draw my attention. Besides, I hardly have time for such things."

Theo patted his shoulder. "You speak of love as though it is a choice."

"Are we talking about love? I thought I came up here to assist you with the preparations for the Summer Solstice Festival."

"Haven't you learned by now, Staccato? All we mermaids ever do is talk about love."

Staccato smirked. "I believe you're in danger of making a terrible generalization about your people. I might point out that you haven't any sweethearts to speak of."

Theo gave a good-natured shrug. "We all know why that is, don't we? Honestly, mermaid women and their obsession with two-leggeds! You'd think by now we mermen would be facing extinction."

Staccato nodded his head in an exaggerated fashion. "Yes, I'm sure that must be why." He smiled sarcastically.

"You just wait, Staccato, one of these days you're going to find yourself a girl that you'll break all the rules for."

Staccato threw back his head. "Ha! You're very droll, Theo. Speaking of mermaids falling for two-leggeds, it would seem Estella has found herself a nice situation." He gestured across the bay to Alfbern Hall, so close one could almost swim to it. "Engaged to the eldest Northstar, Prince Mathgemain, soon to be king over the most powerful kingdom in all Voiler! You like Mathgemain, don't you?"

"How could anyone disapprove of Mathgemain? He's brave, clever, and utterly devoted to my sister. I couldn't have found her a better suitor if I tried."

"I suppose you can't go wrong with a Northstar."

Theo's eyes glazed over with a dark humor. "Well, almost. You're forgetting Bruin."

Staccato grinned facetiously. "Silly me. Since he seldom comes out of hiding it's so easy to forget. Did you have to remind me?"

Theo smiled but said nothing. Staccato rubbed his chin.

"I don't understand. All the others are so pleasant and kind, and yet every time Bruin crosses my path he thinks up a new way to insult me."

"Did you catch his most recent exploit in the headlines?"

Staccato chuckled. "You mean how he and his friends got drunk, tied a soldier to the back of a live orrick and threw them both in the bay?" Which was no easy feat considering an orrick was, in simplest terms, a fourteen-foot-tall horned grizzly bear with shaggy fur like a yak.

Theo sighed and rocked back on his heels. "The head of the L.A.S.A. nearly lost her hand trying to untie them."

Staccato shook his head. "Why is Bruin so ghastly?"

"Mathgemain attributes his behavior to being the youngest."

"That's hardly an excuse."

"Out of eight, I mean. You know how the hold Ursine superstition goes. A monarch who bears seven consecutive sons will see his family name prosper, but an eighth son tempts fate. Apparently, Bruin was one too many."

"You don't mean to say his parents resent him for that?"

"More the opposite, really. Mathgemain says they spoil him out of pity. He says Bruin was never made to do anything growing up because they felt sorry for him. It wasn't as if Bruin was ever going to have a chance at the throne, so why bother? His parents decided they'd let him have it easy. He's been mollycoddled his whole life."

Such an explanation prompted Staccato to double over in laughter, leaving Theo baffled.

"What's so funny?"

"You mean to tell me all that dark, broody behavior, and he's just a little brat?" He wiped a laughter-induced tear from his eye and patted Theo on the back. "Well, I suppose that's the only drawback of having Estella marry into the Northstars: you'll be seeing a lot more of Bruin."

Theo managed a weak smile, but on the whole didn't seem to find the situation as amusing as Staccato.

"Yes, well, as if I didn't dislike him enough to begin with, the little devil's gone and taken a shine to Evangeline."

Staccato shrugged, as though it were nothing to be taken seriously. "What's to fear? It's not as if she'd be interested in keeping company with such a brute."

Theo let out a long sigh. "Evangeline is … kind. Too kind. When it comes to empathetic pursuits, her compassion trumps all other abilities, perhaps even inhibits. It clouds her judgement. She's easily manipulated. You should see her around her mother. Atergatis keeps a tight rein on Evangeline. It's too bad our grandmother is gone. After father died, she was always there to shield the four of us from Atergatis's influence. I'd hate to think what our childhoods would have been like had we only Atergatis to parent us."

"Yes, Queen Theodosia was a wise and benevolent woman. I do not doubt she would have kept Atergatis in check. But just because Evangeline is kind doesn't mean she'd tolerate someone who was so obviously rude. Does it?"

Theo sucked on his lower lip. "I don't believe Bruin is rude to her, at least not to her face. But I don't trust him enough to allow him into her company, that's for certain."

"Well, I'll be sure to keep an eye on him during the festivities."

Theo chuckled. "I'd appreciate that. If the job were left to me I'd be tempted to throw him out, and I can't indulge that. Bad for foreign relations, you know."

***

The colors of evening bled down the horizon like watercolors on a fresh canvas. Below it the bay was heavy with traffic. Countless boats were making their way towards Kyriakos Stadium, their flickering spheres of lantern light mirrored and distorted in the waves. As they drifted closer, each passenger would abandon their champagne and coquettish exploits to stare up in wonder at the arena.

Kyriakos Stadium itself was a feat of architectural majesty, rising up from the waves like an island of white granite. Mermaid statues with glowing eyes adorned every archway, marbled busts crowned Corinthian columns the size of redwoods. And any mermaid trading their fins for feet that night would find themselves walking on a mosaic path of bioluminescent shells that lit up beneath their toes.

Already the fragrances of Summer Solstice were climbing to the stars. Sticky, sweet notes of *bezofarouche*, fresh honeycomb cakes with pomegranate seeds, clung to noses. Crowns of aphrodisiac flowers were traded between doe-eyed lovers, and come midnight the ground would be so littered with shed petals they would diminish the glowing walkway.

Never a disappointment, the people bustling through the entrance were nothing short of a lavish spectacle. Snail-shaped bustles fanned out from behind every mermaid woman as they rose up out of the water or stepped from their gondolas. Fishnet shawls swathed bare shoulders, the fanciest of which were knit with precious pearls. As always, their skirts were fashioned in what had come to be known as "the mermaid cut,"—being shorter in the front to expose the legs and longer in the back to stay consistent with the times—but never to be confused with "the mermaid silhouette."

Even the servants had a special uniform reserved for these sorts of public appearances. Wreathes of lavender crowned the maids and matched their draped tunics, while the butlers and footmen donned liveries knit from garlands of ivy.

Staccato stood just outside the King's box, leaning against the archway. Shimmering drapes of chiffon stenciled with the royal crest billowed behind him in the breeze. The servants had been hurrying in and out setting up for the arrival of Theo's brother and sisters, who were to come later in their own private water carriage.

It was getting late. Guests poured in. Theo had excused himself to shake hands with Salmone Pesci, a renowned olive merchant and father of Constanza, the current object of Javaid's affections.

A large gold-burnished gondola drifted beneath the grand archway, weighted down by a procession of pompous, overly dressed figures with long, traipsing veils. It was Cobra Samael and his entourage. Staccato rolled his eyes.

"Splendid! What is he doing here?" He said this to no one in particular, but to his surprise one of the maids answered him from behind the drapery.

"You know Cobra Samael. He must keep up appearances. He's convinced himself that if he attends mermaid functions he'll appear less prejudiced. That way he can get away with all sorts of slander."

Staccato was intrigued. "I've never thought of it that way before."

"Makes perfect sense, doesn't it? He comes, indulges in a few cultural rituals so he can get his picture in the paper, then the next day he gives a speech at some university saying the Fay population has grown too large and needs to be monitored. Afterwards he'll turn it around on the rest of us.

Yesterday, Empress Tsunami of Scorpius called the Cobra an unnatural demon for permitting child sacrifice within his own country. And do you know what his response was? He invited her to discuss cultural differences over a freshly prepared *saignant*. When she refused he called her an intolerant chauvinist."

Staccato rubbed his chin. "I believe it was Senator Ione who said that, but I see your point."

There was a pause. Clearing her throat, the maid answered quite confidently.

"No, no, Mr. Nimbus, it was Empress Tsu."

Staccato thought it awfully forward for a maid to refer to the supreme ruler of Scorpius as Empress "Tsu," a rather familiar name.

"My dear girl, I assure you it was Senator Ione."

Before he knew it, a folded newspaper was thrust out from the curtains and placed in his hands.

"I have the article from *The Daily Compass* right here."

Staccato scanned over the headline. Sure enough, there it was, "*Cobra Samael Calls Empress Tsunami an Intolerant Chauvinist.*"

Staccato's eyebrows rose, impressed.

"Ah, I see. Well, the lawyer doth think he is wise. I commend you, Madame. You seem to take an avid interest in politics. May I ask what attracts you so?"

The girl tittered. "I would think it shameful for a person in my position not to be acquainted with the affairs of the day."

Staccato leaned against the archway with a wry smile. She obviously had a wonderful sense of humor, and he couldn't help but flirt a little.

"I wholeheartedly agree. It's important for people of every station to be acquainted with the affairs of the day. My family was rather poor, you see, and I wished to better myself by getting an education in law. Ambition is a fine quality."

For a moment Staccato thought he heard a fan sliding open as the girl struggled against a fit of giggles. Thinking he had impressed her, Staccato straightened his shoulders with pride. Finally, the girl composed herself.

"I see. You must be awfully clever."

Staccato wrung his hands with a bashful smile. "Oh, I don't know about that. ..."

"You're a wonderful asset to the King, you know."

Staccato bit his lip. "You think so?"

"Oh, yes. Theo's very fond of you."

Staccato's limbs went stiff. Theo, she had said, not King Thessalos, not His Majesty. A deep flush flooded over his cheeks as he found the courage to turn and face the girl he had been speaking to. He peeled back the curtain. A bright, smiling face stared back at him. A heavy coronet sank to one side on her mass of golden waves. It was Princess Evangeline.

"It's a pleasure to finally meet you, Mr. Nimbus."

Staccato's shoulders wrenched upwards. His mouth fell open in perfect mortification. She must have come in from the back without him noticing; she, the Princess, and he had mistaken her for a servant! He threw himself down on his knees.

"Your Highness, I beg your forgiveness! I mistook you for someone else. I'm afraid I'm not familiar with your voice!"

Evangeline giggled into her fan and shook her head at the humiliated mass kowtowing at her feet.

"My dear, Mr. Nimbus, what do you think you're doing?"

Staccato dared to open an eye. She was even more beautiful up close, he thought, as she stood near enough for him to fully appreciate the color of her eyes, which, like Theo's, were sparkling metallic gold. Dressed and dry, there was a flighty, windblown look to her clothes and hair that made her approachable, playful even. She had her hands placed comically on her hips and was staring down at him with a smile that scrunched up her eyes. Staccato looked utterly baffled.

"I, um …"

Evangeline's smile blossomed to its full beauty. Laughing, she bent down to hoist him back onto his feet.

"Tell me, do you call my sister 'Your Highness'?"

Staccato kept his head low beneath her gaze, a rather difficult accomplishment considering how much taller he was.

"No," he admitted shyly.

"Do you call Javaid 'His Highness'?"

Staccato bit back a smile. "Not to his face."

"And Theo, do you address him as 'Your Majesty'?"

"If I did he would laugh at me, and make fun of me for days without end."

She hooked her arm affectionately through his and led him to a seat in the box.

"Then you shan't address me with such titles either. You may call me Evangeline. You are brother to my brothers, blood to my blood, the dearest of friends to my family, and so it shall be with us."

Staccato felt the color of his cheeks deepen. "Your Highness is very kind."

"Ah-ah," she corrected him. "Give it another try, Mr. Nimbus."

Staccato smirked. "Only if you agree to call me Staccato and not Mr. Nimbus."

A smile pinched Evangeline's eyes so they sparkled with warmth. "Very well then, I think that's only fair."

At that moment, Estella bustled into the box with Theo in tow. In contrast to her sister, Estella was elegant, polished, and, like her eldest brother, there was something about her which commanded respect from all types of people. Staccato thought she would make an excellent queen. However, she always gave the impression that she was holding something back. Sometimes it was an opinion, sometimes a comeback, but Staccato got the feeling it was a sort of passion. He could see it in the way her lips twitched during heated dinner conversations, in the caged look that some- times came into her eyes, and the tenseness of her posture whenever her mother was present.

"Ah, there you are, Evangeline!" Estella smoothed her auburn locks over her shoulders. "It appears you've finally met Staccato."

Staccato clenched his jaw as Evangeline opened her mouth to speak.

"Oh, yes. Staccato has been such a gentleman. When he saw I was all alone he insisted on keeping me company until you returned."

She turned and winked at him. Theo smiled, and, dropping his voice, leaned over Staccato's shoulder.

"Well done, my friend."

As Staccato turned to face him, he noticed for the first time that Theo had a small purple petal tucked behind his ear.

"That's a lovely hair ornament you have there, by the way," he teased.

"What?" Theo raked his fingers through his curls, and, finding the flower, let out a hearty laugh. "That explains the look the Count of Al-Safik was giving me."

"Sure you weren't sporting a lover's garland?"

"If I were, is it likely I would have taken it off?"

"It would be if you were keeping it a secret," Staccato laughed. "Have you seen the Northstars yet?"

Theo plucked an oyster from a tray and held it to his lips. "We've just come from their box. They're over on the far side."

"Is Bruin with them?"

Evangeline was too engaged with Estella to have overheard Staccato and Theo. Theo nodded, trying to mask his amusement as he handed Staccato his binoculars.

"He grew a beard."

They sniggered as Staccato looked through the lenses and rooted out Bruin from amongst his brothers. They were all similar, with their dark hair and heavy features, but Bruin stood out by his sulking disposition. He was broad-shouldered, broody, and aloof. He kept to the back of the box and eyed the passing women from the shadows.

Staccato scoffed. "Shouldn't he be sulking around a heath somewhere?"

Theo snorted, causing them both to laugh until Estella sobered them with a look.

"What kind of trouble are you two stirring up now?"

She swatted at Theo's shoulder with her fan and pointed to Javaid. The youngest Soter brother was lingering in the Pesci's box, trying to draw Constanza's attention away from her paramour, Mardel Delmar.

"Theo, go help Javaid before he makes a fool of himself in front of that poor girl."

Evangeline craned her head back. "Oh, let him be, Estella. He's a man in love."

"Yes, with another man's intended!"

Theo and Evangeline couldn't help but laugh.

"Oh, Estella," Evangeline whined, "don't you ever break the rules?"

Estella couldn't seem to shake off her worry. Another of those caged stares was growing in her eyes, and Staccato couldn't help but feel sorry for her.

"It's not that I don't want to break the rules, but you know how it is; if one of us steps out of line, we all suffer! Can you imagine what Mother would do if Javaid's little flirtations got in the papers? We wouldn't be able to go out for ages!"

Evangeline clicked her tongue affectionately and kissed her sister's cheek.

"Poor Estella, always putting everyone else's needs ahead of her own!"

"Nonsense, Estella isn't half as selfless as you make her out to be," said Theo playfully, keeping his hands behind his back.

"Oh?" Estella placed her hands on her hips. "And what makes you say that?"

With boyish pride, Theo removed a copy of *Teeth and Daggers: Everything You Need to Know before Visiting the Isle of Monmoss Marta* from behind his back.

"Planning a trip anytime soon?"

Evangeline jumped up and down with delight. "Estella broke the rules! Good for you, darling!"

Estella's eyes swam with alarm as she jumped and snatched the book from Theo's hands.

"Maybe I am! What is it to you?"

Theo shrugged. "Just wondering why it's okay for you to have a bit of fun but not Javaid."

She wiped an invisible speck of dust from the cover. "The difference is in a couple of months I'm going to be free of mother, and Mathgemain and I will be able to go wherever our hearts desire. Javaid has no such end in sight yet, and neither does Evangeline. You know how it is, collective punishment."

"Javaid is twenty-one years old, and Atergatis is not his mother. Therefore he has no obligation to put up with her."

Estella lowered her voice. "Collective punishment." She darted her eyes towards Evangeline.

Theo drew a long, thoughtful glance towards his youngest sister, then lost all sense of humor.

"Alright, I'll see what I can do." And with that, Theo departed from the box like a thunderous cloud.

While Theo was exiting, Phrygia brushed past him and bowed to Estella.

"Your mother wishes you and Princess Evangeline to come and greet the Earl of Kochab."

Estella smoothed the ruffles of her blue skirt and beckoned Evangeline forward.

"Thank you, Phrygia, we'll be along shortly."

Evangeline placed a hand on Staccato's shoulder. Staccato felt his chest throb.

"Excuse us for a minute, Staccato."

Staccato nodded, watching her hair flow behind her as she descended the stairs. They hadn't been gone long when a pale hand drew back the sheer curtain. A handsome but hairy gentleman bobbed his head in. At the sight of Staccato his face fell.

"Oh, it's you."

Staccato sneered as Bruin made his way into the box without invitation.

"Good evening, Your Highness. The Soters have stepped out for a spell, but they should return in a moment."

Bruin pasted himself against the far wall and helped himself to a shrimp from the bar.

"I'll wait here then."

Staccato would have loved to tell him he could not wait there and could kindly leave, but he knew better.

"Fall off your penny-farthing lately?" He did not wait for Staccato to answer but snickered derisively. "You're quite the spectacle, you know, traipsing after Theo in that contraption. The first time we saw it, Mother thought the Cirque De Fay was in town."

Staccato had to grind his teeth together to keep from mouthing off. "To answer your question, no, I have not had any falls recently." He smoothed back his hair and assumed a dry manner. "I do hope you aren't bored already. I understand you're not easily amused."

"It's true, I'm not a fan of these shallow, bourgeois diversions."

Staccato took a deep breath to avoid saying what was truly on his mind. "Come now, you needn't have a penchant for competitive sports to enjoy Summer Solstice. I daresay the food is enough to keep one entertained. The *bezofarouche* are especially good this year."

Bruin twisted the end of his nose and looked disdainfully upon the platter of immaculately glazed, hexagon-shaped cakes. "I'm afraid I'm not overly fond of insect by-products."

At this remark, Staccato could help himself no longer. "Shouldn't you be lamenting to a raven about a dead lover somewhere?"

"No need for hostility, Staccato. People might think there's a little of your father in you after all."

The silverware on the table trembled. Bruin glanced from the cutlery to Staccato and smiled.

"I knew you were an ambitious upstart, Staccato, but I had no idea you had such a temper. I'll remove myself for your sake." He lingered at the curtain. "Do tell Evangeline I dropped by. I've been admiring the neckline of her dress since I arrived."

Staccato swept dangerously forward. "I'm not sure if you're aware of this, but I happen to have the authority to throw you out, and the power to do so without assistance or disturbance. What's more, something tells me your brothers would be quite understanding should I choose to exercise that right."

"My brothers, yes; however, Mother and Father might not be so forgiving. And it is Father's head who bears the crown and all."

Without another word, he left.

Chapter 24:

Cottonmouth's Manor

"Faina, why couldn't you let me drive this time?" Pasha whined as they ambled towards Edgehill Road.

"Have you ever driven a motorcar before?"

"Well, no, but—"

"That would be why."

Cicada leaned forward between the two front seats. "Can't I try?"

Pasha threw back his head and scoffed. "Definitely not. And don't get all huffy about it either. You've been a huge help so far, Cici. But a motorcar isn't something to mess around with."

Faina glanced back at Cicada in the rearview mirror. "Which is why I'm driving and not Pasha."

Cicada sighed and resigned herself to watching the pink dogwoods pass outside the window.

Faina flexed her hands on the wheel. "So how do we plan to get Cottonmouth to bet the shard? We can't expect him to risk something so precious on a whim."

Pasha shook his head. "No, we need something enticing. Something to show him we mean business."

They each in turn glanced back at the esperite, who shrugged her shoulders.

"What are you looking at me for?"

Pasha smirked. "You're the one with all the brilliant ideas so far."

Cicada drew herself up and patted the ends of her castle bob. "Oh!"

"Hey, hey!" Pasha threw up his hand as she emanated a faint light. "Watch the glow, remember?"

Cicada quickly shut off her light. "Sorry."

"Is it this one?" asked Faina, craning her head out the window.

Nestled amongst the sunny Victorian mansions at the top of a hill was a spacious plantation-style home covered in ivy and encircled by a white porch. It was every bit as beautiful as the other residences, and plentiful in luxury. Yet there was an unexplainable eeriness to it all, felt rather than observed. It seemed natural that a ghost might wander past the freshly painted black shutters. The three exchanged knowing glances.

Pasha and Cicada recited in unison, "That's the one."

They pulled up the ponderous driveway. The car ambled past the manicured verdure and dangling bougainvillea towards the manor. Goosebumps crept up Pasha's arms.

"I think it's safe to say if we're offered any wine, we shouldn't drink it."

Up ahead, Cottonmouth was waiting for them on the steps of the front porch holding a tobacco pipe in his hand.

Cicada flexed her lip. "He seems strangely friendly for an undercover ophidian."

"Maybe the South has rubbed off on him," suggested Faina.

"Or he's playing into the part."

"You think he suspects us?"

"Not necessarily, but I don't believe he's inviting us over to his house purely out of the kindness of his heart."

A morbid thought occurred to Pasha. "Do you think he wants to eat us?"

Faina clenched the steering wheel tighter. "Is it too late to turn around?"

"Relax!" Cicada placed a hand behind their headrests. "If anything happens just remember you're armed, you're trained, and you have me to get you out of a tight spot."

Pasha heaved a sigh. "If you say so."

They parked on the far side of the fountain. Rubbing his hands together, Cottonmouth rushed down the stairs to help them out of the car.

"Mr. and Mrs. Lapochkov! What a pleasure it is to see you again!"

"What are our names again?" hissed Pasha through gritted teeth.

"You're Paul and Stefania Lapochkov, and I'm Cecelia 'Cici' Butler."

Cottonmouth opened the passenger door and drew back, surprised to find Pasha rather than Faina. Pasha tipped his fedora and chuckled.

"My wife is the more experienced driver."

Cottonmouth reached around to kiss Faina's hand as she exited the driver's side.

"I see, a genuine woman of modernity."

Faina pursed her lips in a sophisticated manner and tossed her hair.

"My husband likes to tease me and call me a flapper."

Pasha chucked her under the chin. "What can I say? She is my little spitfire."

Cicada extended her leg audaciously from the back seat and stretched a hand towards Cottonmouth.

"I do declare, Doctor, you're as handsome as a month of Sundays."

"Well, well, if it isn't Miss Butler! Look at those rosy cheeks! Why, if I were a butterfly I'd sip the nectar right out of those dimples!"

Pasha and Faina shivered in unison.

Taking Cicada's hand, he drew them towards the entrance. "If you folks'll follow me I'll give you the grand tour."

The decor of Cottonmouth's humble abode was sparse but selective. On the whole, every detail fell under the category of antique, artifact, or specimen. There were imported divans, Persian rugs, and Ming vases. Apothecary jars of various oddities were placed strategically throughout the house. Cottonmouth's own personal monogram with the Algonquin seal could be found everywhere.

"I'm certain by now you've noticed my recurring theme of serpents." He stood back to admire the family crest mosaicked into the floor of the parlor. Faina was the first to respond.

"Naturally. A cottonmouth is a type of snake, is it not?"

Cottonmouth turned with studious, dignified eyes, and crossed towards her.

"It is a type of water moccasin." He puffed on his pipe and gestured once more to the design. "My mother was Cherokee. Spent her childhood on the hillsides of Pine Mountain in the Appalachians. Did you know the Cherokee are taught to honor the serpent? So convicted are they of its divinity that it is considered sinful to murder or offend one."

Faina squeezed an unconvincing smile from her lips. "I did not know that, how interesting."

"I'm afraid you're not alone in your incomprehension, Mrs. Lapochkov. Very few have been exposed to the innumerable benefits of snakes. For example, they're marvelous for keeping out rats and other vermin."

He led them to the door of his wine cellar, and hesitated with his hand on the knob.

"Before I lead you to the cellar, I feel compelled to warn you I employ snakes as a means of preserving my valuables." He removed a walking stick from an umbrella stand in the corner. Taking a match from his pocket, he lit a sconce on the wall and lifted it from its mount.

Pasha fumbled with his pockets. "Y—you mean you keep snakes free range in your basement?"

Cottonmouth smiled as though discussing a hobby as mundane as beekeeping.

"Never fear, they shan't bother us any." And opening the door, he started down the passage, taking the time to strike each stair with the end of his rod. "Stereo hearing," he explained over his shoulder. "They do not like the vibrations in the earth, find it disruptive. They're sensitive creatures, delicate constitutions and all."

Cicada shrieked as she almost came into contact with a slithering adder on the stair. Cottonmouth chuckled.

"Don't you fret, Miss Butler, he's more afraid of you than you are of him."

Cicada tried to repress the expression of disgust in her tone. "Is that so?"

Faina scrutinized the creature with an inquisitive tilt of her head. "They're poisonous." Her accent had thinned from the distraction. Cottonmouth didn't seem to notice.

"An excellent observation, Mrs. Lapochkov. What gave it away?"

"The shape of the head."

"Ah, yes. Head shape is an excellent way to identify serpents." As Cottonmouth shined the torch along the bottom stair, his face lit up with rapture. "Well, what do we have here? Henri, you old devil!"

He allowed a particularly large timber rattlesnake to wind its way up the staff. Pasha, Faina, and Cicada sloped instinctively backwards as Henri was brought to eye level.

"I've had Henri since he was just an egg, found him 'neath the shed after the thaw last spring." He indicated to the sides of Henri's face. "Look at those fine cheekbones. Yes, sir, there's venom in those mandibles, no doubt about that." Giving his staff a shake, he let the beast slither off down the railing. "No doubt about that."

The three took baby steps as they entered the high-vaulted chamber. The space shared more resemblance with a Parisian catacomb than a cellar. A series of dark passages led in several different directions. Pasha's mind struggled to guess at their various purposes. As they meandered through the wine racks, they were horrified to discover snakes nesting amongst the bottles.

"Many of these I ferment myself, right here in the cellar." Cottonmouth pointed to one of the halls. "I have my own winepress, you see. Since Prohibition began I've managed to collect a small fortune selling to gangsters like Capone." He ran his fingers tantalizingly over a brand or two before hauling an aged bottle from the shelf. "Here's a brand you might be familiar with, Mr. Lapochkov."

As he blew the thin sheet of dust from the label, Pasha felt as though his heart might stop. He clutched Faina's shoulder. No words came to his lips.

"You have a Chevalsky?" Faina said for him.

Cottonmouth waggled his eyebrows and matched the gesture with a wry smile.

"I have several. This particular vintage is from 1908. A sparkling wine, one of the limited editions. Only two hundred produced in all."

Pasha's chest ached. Whenever a Chevalsky was born, his family would release a limited edition sparkling wine to celebrate the occasion. The bottle in Cottonmouth's hands was from 1908. Pasha's heart sank. It was his birth year, his vintage. He found himself thinking of Katya.

"You wouldn't happen to have a 1915 Limited, would you?"

"As a matter of fact, I do. You're a fan, I take it?"

Faina squeezed his hand. "It was all his father ever drank when Paul was a boy. Didn't you always say how your father used to smell of tobacco and Chevalsky wine, darling?"

Pasha gave a slight nod.

"Yes, they don't make them like these anymore. Out in the open anyway." Cottonmouth gave Pasha a hearty slap on the side of his arm and ushered them down one of the corridors. "This is where I keep my wine-press," he chattered on. "Have the grapes imported from Napa Valley."

Just as he was about to open the door to the winery, a second room caught Pasha's eye. He halted, wide-eyed in the middle of the passage.

Cottonmouth crept up behind him. "I see you've discovered my laboratory."

He opened the door wider and invited them inside. It looked like a dungeon for torture, or at the very least where Dr. Frankenstein birthed his famous monster. The far wall was stuffed with shelves from floor to high-ceiling. Containers one might assume to be more wine concoctions crowded the racks. They knew better.

Numerous leather-bound copies of anatomy books sat stacked on tabletops and desks. There were cadavers, microscopes, bell jars, and charts. Metal cupboards had been pushed back into the crawl spaces, concealing who knows what in their locked drawers.

But the most frightening furnishing of all was the old hospital bed. Its casters had rusted. The series of buckles lay stiff on the thin mattress. Nearby sat a rolling cart of various surgical instruments.

Cottonmouth pulled at his beard. "I'm an amateur phlebotomist."

"You study blood?" Faina translated.

"Something I dabble at. Are you familiar with the studies of Canadian Lieutenant Lawrence Bruce Robertson?"

Pasha fingered the pulse at the base of his throat. "The man who performed blood transfusions during the war?"

"Thanks to Mr. Robertson's innovative research, doctors in London are now opening clinics where they preserve vitals in a system they call 'blood banking.'"

With her fingers steepled together at her lips, Cicada wheeled around.

"And as a man of medicine, you take interest?"

"I take an avid interest, Miss Butler. Over the years I've tried to persuade the Board of Health to allow me to open such a clinic right here in Louisville, but I am repeatedly rebuffed. Much like the resourcefulness of the bootlegger, I have taken to harvesting and storing my own samples, should an emergency ever occur."

"How ever do you manage to find donors?" inquired Faina, resisting the urge to bite her nails.

"There is a wealth of volunteers to be found amongst progressive reform groups. But when they run in short supply, Mr. Letcher usually manages to find me a connection."

Pasha shivered. At length, Cottonmouth clapped his hands together, causing the trio to jump.

"Enough of this morbidity. We must strive to be considerate of the ladies' sensitivities. After all, ya'll came here for the artwork, did you not?"

They hastened out the door and followed Cottonmouth to the room where he housed his private art collection. The gallery provided a more forgiving environment for works of art and was much drier than the rest of the cellar. The sconce was not needed here, so Cottonmouth deposited it on a mount outside the door.

The lights flickered on. Pasha was so impressed by the beauty of the collection he actually managed to enjoy himself for a moment. Statues of marbled colors were annealed into horse heads, flowers, and abstract deco designs. Suncatchers and chimes trickled in teardrop silhouettes from the beams. Light panels shone through the frames of stained glass, causing rainbow refractions to stencil the floor. Many had been imported from Europe, and some were old enough to earn the status of relics.

Faina pointed upwards. They all three tilted back to find their faces reflected back at them. The ceiling was covered with Venetian mirrors. Some were whole artful pieces, others just fragments.

"My mirror collection." Cottonmouth's voice was oozing with pride.

"My, my!" Faina pressed her hands together. "You really do boast quite the treasury."

Pasha swatted at Cicada's arm. When the esperite brought her sharp eyes to his gaze, he mouthed as quietly as possible.

"Which one?"

She slid her attention across the collage of looking glasses. Her eyes fell upon a small, triangular shard with pearlescent sheen. She tossed her head in an imperceptible motion towards the incriminating fragment.

***

When the party departed for the hotel, the alleged doctor took Pasha graciously by the hand. They stood on the front porch in the setting twilight.

"You mentioned you had a penchant for horseracing, Mr. Lapochkov."

"I did indeed."

Cottonmouth took a section of the newspaper from his suit jacket and unfolded it for Pasha to see.

"There's a particularly interesting race being held this Saturday at Churchill Downs. I've been getting up a party with Mr. Letcher and Mr. Clay. Would you and your lovely lady friends be interested in joining us this weekend?"

"Absolutely, we would love to."

Cottonmouth pulled him aside more closely. "Now, I feel compelled to make you aware, Mr. Lapochkov, there are some expectations should you join us this Saturday. Your participation in the revelry would be most welcome."

"I thought my intentions were obvious." Pasha stroked his chin with a furtive smile.

Cottonmouth pointed a finger and broke into laughter.

"I knew I could count on you, Mr. Lapochkov. Now you mentioned you like to gamble with valuables other than money? What would you say to staking a little …" he held up Pasha's wrist and indicated to the seam of blue vein running beneath his skin, "vitality, for a good cause?"

Pasha leaned against the railing and sucked his teeth. "It would have to be worth my while."

"You mentioned you had an interest in artwork."

Pasha tapped at his chin. "If I win, you let my wife pick out any piece she wants from your collection."

"A fine wager." He leaned closer so only Pasha could hear. Cottonmouth nodded towards Cicada and Faina. They pretended to admire the crepe myrtle hanging from the eaves.

"You don't suppose you could persuade your wife and Miss Butler to make a contribution as well, do you?"

Pasha folded his hands behind his back and paced across the top stair. "I might be able to, if …"

"If what, Mr. Lapochkov?"

"If you threw in the 1908 and 1915 bottles of Chevalsky."

Cottonmouth sank his teeth into his bottom lip. "You drive a hard bargain."

"Do I? Two bottles of sparkling for two pints of sweet? I thought I was being fairly reasonable."

Cottonmouth's shoulders shook as he repressed a chuckle.

"I like the way you talk, 'two pints of sweet,' they are sweet indeed, aren't they?" His vision narrowed hawk-like on the blush of sun which weather had kissed upon Faina and Cicada's cheeks. He held out his hand to Pasha.

"We have a deal."

They shook hands, a challenge sewn into their gaze.

***

"You bet what?" Cicada roared as they pulled up to the Seelbach.

"Shhh, not so loud." Pasha held open the door and tipped the valet. "What's the matter, Cicada? I thought you were always up for anything dangerous."

"It's only 'dangerous' when a given amount of uncertainty is present. In this case, what you agreed to is 'very dangerous.'"

Faina chewed on her lip. "I have to agree with Cicada." They made their way towards the lift. "Staking the shard over a horse race wasn't the best move."

Pasha rolled his eyes. "I see, and what was I supposed to bet on?"

"Cards!" Cicada threw out her hands. "You were supposed to bet on cards!"

"And how is that any more certain than a horse race?"

"I can control the outcome of a card game, I know how to cheat. You can't expect me to rig a horse race!"

"My point exactly, *you* know how to cheat at cards. *I* don't! Cottonmouth is expecting me to participate, not you two!"

Faina stamped her foot. "In that case, you should've just made the bet on Cicada's or my ability to win! That would've been a lot safer!"

"Are you kidding? He'd have known we were cheating! Look, if there's one thing I do know, I know horses! My family was breeding race-horses before I was born. I grew up in the saddle. Trust me, I know how to pick a horse."

The group remained silent for some time. It wasn't until they had made it back to their rooms that Pasha finally spoke.

"Well, at least we don't have to worry about him growing suspicious." He fiddled with the keys. "Did you see the size of that shard? He'll think we want one of those stained glass windowpanes."

Faina flexed her eyebrows. "Personally, I wouldn't mind having that horse head."

"Or one of those suncatchers," added Cicada.

Chapter 25:

Glassblowing

"Honestly, Evangeline, of all days to be hauled up in your studio!" Theo leaned against the window and fanned himself with his hand.

It was the peak of July and the summer heat had reached its pinnacle in Karkinos.

"Why not put it off until nightfall? You'll give yourself heatstroke." Evangeline hauled the tip of a long pipe from the furnace.

"You are always babying me."

Sweat poured down from the soft part of her neck and trickled between her shoulder blades. Blots of moisture formed on the cotton of the men's shirt she was wearing. Her arms were sheathed to the elbow in tough hide gloves that, to Staccato, appeared most uncomfortable in such an atmosphere. And yet, her face never displayed anything but perfect contentment.

Theo snickered. "You're the youngest. Consider it your birthright."

"Pardon me, Staccato," Evangeline murmured, turning around. "I don't want to burn you."

Staccato struck his head. "Right, my apologies."

It was a wonder Staccato's distraction hadn't led him to stumble right into the furnace. He was certain that being inside Evangeline's studio was the closest thing on earth to being inside her colorful, inventive mind. Things he didn't think were possible to form from glass filled in the space with bright, dizzying shapes. There were trees, *entire trees*, with twinkling crystal leaves, and rippling bark.

Animals appeared to be a favorite subject of the artist and littered the corners and ceiling with hardened feathers and fur. There were birds, deer, and an elephant head that, as far as Staccato could tell, was true to size. But the most impressive spectacle by far was the blue whale, less true to size, suspended from the ceiling. How it was possible to craft such a large piece from blown glass, Staccato did not know.

"She's a great lover of fauna," remarked Theo with a snicker, "as you can probably tell. She's made each and every one of us a personal statue of our favorite animal."

"A lion for Theo," Evangeline recited, "an owl for Javaid, and a rabbit for Estella. You'll have to let me know what your favorite animal is, Staccato, so I can get one started for you."

"I'm afraid that's rather a hard choice for me. ..." he trailed off, too amazed to finish his sentence as he watched her blow into her pipe, and the molten bubble crowning the pinnacle swell. She twirled the rod like a baton in her hands, then, seating herself at a special bench, laid the glass end of the pipe on a metal table and began rolling it back and forth. She pointed to an object on the table.

"Pass me that jack, would you, Staccato dear?"

Staccato beamed at the idea of Evangeline calling him "dear," even if she referred to everybody as such. He looked back at the assortment of tools, intimidated.

"Which one is that?"

"The one that looks like a pair of scissors."

Staccato held up an instrument that was something akin to tongs. Evangeline smiled and nodded.

"That's the one, thank you."

Staccato willed it to float towards her. Using the contraption, she pinched the end of the bubble until it achieved an hourglass silhouette. She worked the jack back and forth, twisting and prodding. At last, she pinched her lips with her teeth as she examined the effect.

Staccato was transfixed with curiosity. "What is it?"

"I shall require some assistance." She sat up. "Staccato, would you care to blow into the pipe for me?"

Staccato dropped his shoulders, dumbfounded.

"Me? Oh, I don't know if that's a good idea. I know very little of artistic process. I wouldn't want to upset anything. What about Theo? He's watched you do it so many times, surely he'd be more useful."

Evangeline cocked an eyebrow and pointed her gaze at her brother.

"Last time I asked for Theo's help, the glass exploded." She giggled. "Too full of hot air, I suppose."

Theo shook his head. "Very clever."

Staccato managed a smile. "Somehow that does little to ease my apprehension."

Evangeline reached for his hand and pulled him towards the bench. "Nonsense, you'll be fine. Now hurry before it cools."

He knelt down at the head of the pipe. "Anything special I need to know?"

"It just needs to be short."

Staccato nodded his head and blew into the rod. He winced and peered over the other side of the bench.

"Did I break it?"

Evangeline tittered. "No, silly. You've done well. That was perfect.

Now don't run off just yet, I may need you to do it again." She twisted the bubble with the jack.

Staccato craned his head over the steel marver. "What is it going to be?"

Evangeline shrugged as a damp curl fell out of her bun and brushed across her forehead.

"I'm not quite certain yet, something pretty." She crossed her eyes and blew at the hair. Theo reached behind her and tucked it behind her ear.

"Is this your gift to Queen Ursula?"

"That was my original intention. The poor dear. Can you imagine having nearly your entire family taken from you in one single moment? Her husband and seven sons. Everyone but Bruin." Her nose stiffened. She blinked the moisture from her eyes.

No one would have blamed Evangeline if she had burst into sobs. Only weeks ago, eight members of the Northstar family were assassinated during Mathgemain's coronation. As was tradition, the Soters had been part of the ceremony. Estella herself was to christen the new king, her fiancé, with honey and salt water: the two foods that never spoil. Unfortunately, the ceremony never came that far.

Like the Ursine kings of generations past, each member of the Northstar family was asked to place a silver ring on their finger during the commencement. Eight Northstars fell dead on the spot, including the King-to-be. The memory was forever seared into the shadows of Staccato's mind. They had looked like marionettes whose strings had been suddenly cut. One moment they were standing, the next they were on the ground.

When authorities removed the rings, they found marks burnt into the victims' flesh. The image of a serpent wound round their fingers and sank its teeth into its own tail. It was the C.O.N.'s ensign, the ouroboros. At the time, Staccato had been standing near enough to detect the smell of charred human skin, faint though it was. Whenever the incident was brought up, the aroma always seemed to resurface, a dirty trick of his mind.

The King and seven heirs had been the victims of an assassination. Only two family members survived: Queen Ursula, whose ring had been too small, and Bruin. How Bruin survived remained a mystery. In the end, he had walked away with nothing more than a snake-shaped scar.

"And poor Estella." Evangeline sniffed. "Mathgemain was to be her husband, his brothers our brothers."

Theo reached for her arm. "Don't think about it, Evangeline, you'll get yourself worked up again. Some time has passed now, and we must carry on."

"You're right." She took up the jack once more. "Everyone needs cheering up. Queen Ursula especially." She glanced hopelessly at the bubble crowning her pipe. "Though I doubt a silly old vase will make much difference."

Theo patted her shoulder. "The vase may not, but your kindness will." He kissed the top of her head.

A silence followed. Staccato could tell Evangeline was struggling to repress a question.

"Looks like a storm cloud has rolled in."

Evangeline whirled round to gaze at the cloudless sky out the window. She threw Staccato a questioning look. He laughed into the back of his sleeve.

"That's not what I meant." He tapped his forehead. "Penny for your thoughts?"

Evangeline's cheeks dimpled in amusement. "I love the way you speak."

Staccato ducked his head to conceal his oncoming blush.

"Do share with us what's on your mind."

She knit her brows together. "It's just … I'm a little worried about Bruin."

Staccato fell back on his haunches. Meanwhile, Theo pretended to observe a suncatcher.

"Why is that, Evangeline?" Staccato finally asked, forcing himself to engage.

"Ever since the death of his father and brothers, Bruin's been struggling to make sense of it all. He says Cobra Samael has been calling on them. You see, because the attack was carried out in the name of Primal Instinct, Samael feels he should come to Bruin and Ursula as an ambassador for his people. He doesn't want the Northstars to get the wrong impression of Draconians, I suppose."

"And this worries you because …?"

"Because I'm concerned Samael will take advantage of Bruin during his grief. Ursula refuses to see the Cobra, but Bruin wishes to hear what he has to say."

Theo could help himself no longer as he turned and rolled his eyes.

"Bruin would feel that way!"

"He's just trying to be open-minded." Evangeline lowered her head.

Staccato leaned forward with a sigh. "No, he wants to be *perceived* as open-minded."

Theo nodded his head in agreement.

"Precisely. Honestly, Bruin and Samael would get along quite nicely. They both have a penchant for keeping up deceitful appearances."

Evangeline held up her hand, determined they should hear her out.

"But Theo, stop and think for a minute. Bruin is now set to inherit the throne. His mother is too old to have any more children, and when she passes, Bruin will be crowned king of the most powerful nation in Voiler. He has seen seven brothers and his own father perish before his very eyes. He's afraid. He's depressed. He needs counsel! I'm sure I needn't remind you of the danger Bruin will face if a sorrow this severe goes untreated."

Theo leaned back against the wall with his arms crossed. "Ever the weeping mermaid, aren't we, sister? You're really afraid Bruin will become a fury?"

Staccato watched with intrigue as Evangeline lifted her chin and struggled to hold Theo's gaze.

"That is how one becomes a fury, is it not? Through some deep-seeded depression or other. I've been reading about the epidemic that's broken out over Therion, and talking to Empress Tsu. She says because of our empathetic talents, mermaids are one of the few beings powerful enough to tranquilize furies. We can heal them."

Theo scoffed. "That's impressive coming from Empress Tsu, since Scorpius has spent the last two years warring against the furies of Therion. They may need medical attention, it's true, but they certainly aren't getting any from Scorpius."

Staccato cleared his throat. "You forget, Theo, the Scorpions have set up several military clinics in Therion, completely free to those who desire it. Trouble is, they all want to run off into the wilderness and live out their passions, thanks to the rubbish Samael is pandering about giving into one's basest desires. Many of the furies in Therion don't want help."

Theo fought against the smile creeping in at the corners of his mouth.

"Regardless, I doubt Bruin is in danger of becoming a fury! There are other risk factors involved, you know."

"Unless that's part of Samael's plan." Evangeline's eyes burned with conviction. "We know Samael puppeteers the C.O.N. We know he ordered those attacks on the Northstars. And yet, Bruin survived. What if he was left alive on purpose? It wouldn't have behooved Samael to kill off the entire line of Northstars, because Ursa would have fallen under our stewardship, and he's less likely to infiltrate a kingdom ruled by Fay. Bruin was the least prepared to assume the throne. He is also the most willing to negotiate with ophidians and Primals. He is ripe for temptation! Staccato said it himself, many of the furies in Therion are resisting treatment because Primal Instinct has encouraged them to embrace a violent nature. Perhaps Samael wants to exploit Bruin in his weakness."

Theo cocked an imperious eyebrow, but it was clear he was giving some thought to what Evangeline had said.

"What would you have me do?"

"Counsel him!" She squeezed her apron between her fingers. "Take him under your wing before Samael has a chance to ensnare him."

Theo stared at her for a moment, then released a long exhale. "I will try."

Evangeline rose and clapped her hands together. "Really, Theo? You will?"

Theo tried to remain stern. "But don't get your hopes up. It's no secret that Bruin isn't fond of me, nor I of him. It's doubtful I'll get very far."

Evangeline nodded. "That's very true. I've always had far better luck with Bruin than you have, perhaps I could—"

"No, no!" Theo drew himself up to his full height. "If what you say is true, I don't want you getting involved."

Staccato sat up and smirked. "I suppose Bruin has something real to sulk about now."

Theo snickered, but Evangeline turned to him in shock.

"You shouldn't say such things, Staccato. They make you sound cruel."

Staccato's smile retracted. "Forgive me, Evangeline. You're right. I do not wish to be cruel."

Evangeline managed a weak smile. "No." She rose from her bench and returned to the furnace. "We wouldn't want that. You're far too handsome to behave ugly."

Staccato blushed and fumbled for an answer. "On the contrary, I've met several highly attractive people with rather wanton personalities."

Theo nudged his shoulder and whispered, "I believe you took that far too literally."

But Evangeline seemed to find the remark intriguing.

"As have I, unfortunately. Which makes you all the more a rarity." She looked into his eyes with precious sincerity.

As Staccato and Theo left Evangeline's studio, Theo halted in front of him with a mischievous grin.

"So, when are you going to ask me?"

Staccato assumed a comical expression. "Ask you what?"

"If you may court my sister!"

Staccato shrank away with a blush and tried to meander around his friend. "Very funny, Theo."

Theo reached up and hung from a tree branch, blocking his path. "You like her, don't you?"

Staccato opened his mouth, then snapped it shut. Theo threw back his head and jerked a thumb at his chest.

"Empath, remember?"

"Yes, as you remind me on a regular basis." Staccato threw up his hands. "I suppose there's no point in hiding it. Yes, I like her."

Theo let go of the tree branch and grinned. "I know."

"I suppose she knows as well?"

Theo shook his head. "Remember how I said her compassion can cloud her judgement?"

Staccato raised an eyebrow. "It's that bad?"

"I know, I mean, it has to be pretty impaired for her not to notice your interest."

Staccato eye's rolled skywards. "You're quite amusing. Is that normal for mermaids?"

"It occurs more frequently than one might imagine. Grief, trauma, pride, there are many things that can upset a mermaid's empathy and cause their powers to go haywire. Anyway, you better get a jump on it before rumors form, and you know how they like to form in the mermaid kingdoms."

Staccato knit his brows together. "What rumors? What are you talking about?"

Theo sank his teeth into a smile and dusted his hands. "Well, the pair of you have spent a lot of time together this summer, laughing, talking, wandering off. …"

It was true, Staccato and Evangeline had spent a considerable amount of time together. Only three days ago, the five of them had swum to a nearby island for a picnic. Evangeline had favored Staccato with bold attention. She'd grabbed his hand and dragged him down hidden paths. In the water, she'd teased him and tried to get him to chase her. And while everyone was nodding off after their meal, she'd laid her head in his lap and sunned herself.

"Not to mention you certainly seem to argue a lot when you think no one is looking. One might think you were having a little lover's spat."

"Well, she's an intellectual. It's only natural we debate from time to time … and she is rather enchanting when she's in a passion."

"Enchanting, you say?"

Staccato shrugged and tried to remain impassive.

"I don't even know if she thinks of me that way. …"

The truth was, Staccato was only half certain Evangeline might have feelings for him. It would be easy to mistake her bubbly personality for flirtatious advances. Furthermore, mermaids were notorious for being physically affectionate, it was a cultural trademark. As a result, he was compelled to analyze every touchy-feely gesture she extended to him.

A rascally glint fell into Theo's eye. "But I know."

Staccato froze. He stared at Theo for a long time. "Isn't that considered bad form to employ your powers in such a manner?"

"Terrible form. Appalling, really, but I'm willing to make an exception for you."

Staccato took a step forward. "I see … and?"

Theo ushered Staccato farther down the path and made a show of looking over his shoulder.

"She's absolutely infatuated with you."

Chapter 26:
A Visit From Mother

Pyro spun his wheels down the long chamber leading from the public archives. "Honestly, Melodious, I don't see why you had to come with me. It's not like you can help read the records."

"Sonata wanted me to accompany you to help you get around."

Pyro scoffed. "Well, now, what a capital idea! The blind leading the lame!"

Before Pyro could stop himself, his wheels tipped over the edge of a long, winding staircase. Pyro let out a squeak. Melodious seized the handles.

"The ramp is that way." Melodious pointed to the right. Grumbling, Pyro allowed him to steer him down the incline.

"You think I am not capable of pushing a wheelchair?"

Pyro waved his hand. "You know that's not what I meant. It's that *I'm* perfectly capable. It can't be any fun for you to drive me around. Why is it you always get stuck with the boring jobs?"

"Because I am the only person who doesn't complain about it."

"Doesn't that bother you?"

Melodious shook his head. "You should know by now, Pyro, I am easily contented."

"Alright, preacher man. As long as you don't mind shuffling through file cabinets with me for a few days." Pyro sighed. "I knew we weren't going to find anything in those bloody archives. You'd think being a former government official, Staccato would've had a better idea of how many Voilerian migrants go undocumented."

Melodious shrugged. "The search isn't over yet. There are still the records in Hexmark Folkman's office."

Pyro threw back his head and snorted. "Hexmark Folkman! He's lucky Thayer hasn't given him the death penalty for high treason, voting in Samael's favor, and all."

"That is a little extreme. The man was elected to do what he thought was best for his country, was he not? Besides, didn't he lose his job?"

"You bet he did! He was in such a hurry to disappear, he didn't even bother to clean out his office or hand in the key. Oh well, the lady at the desk said they're in the process of making a new one. Should be ready by Monday. Seems like a long time to make a new key if you ask me."

"Libra is famous for their excellent security, being a place of such international importance. It won't take just any key."

"You're right." Pyro scratched his chin as they cut to the ground floor. "Well, I wonder how the trial went. I had been looking forward to seeing Ol' Furny, but thanks to Cici—"

"Pyro, there you are!" Sonata raced towards them, Lydia in tow. "I'll take it from here, Melodious. See if you can get Lydia back to the hotel without any interference from the press. I'm afraid there will be plenty."

"Is Staccato present?"

Lydia looped her arm through his elbow and led him away. "I'll explain everything on the way there."

Pyro tilted his head back to look at Sonata. "I take it the trial didn't go well, then?"

Sonata put a hand to her forehead. "It was a disaster. Any luck in the archives?"

"None whatsoever, but I told you it was a useless idea, didn't I?"

"Does that mean you didn't try?" She pushed him towards the entrance of Aries's box.

"Where are we going?"

"Someone wants to see you."

Pyro sat up tall. "Is it Furny?"

As Sonata was about to open the door, a towering woman spotted with freckles appeared before them. Pyro's face fell.

"Ma! What are you doing here?"

Her rosy lips stretched into a grin, calling out the fine wrinkles around her eyes which somehow made her appear younger.

"Good to see you, too! Honestly, is that any way to greet your mother?"

In a display of affection which bordered on violent, she pinned him to her chest and kissed his head and cheeks over and over.

"Ma! Ma! My hair!"

The Queen sighed and sucked her teeth. "Yes, alright. You'll have to excuse my eagerness. But I haven't seen you in eight months!"

Pyro craned his head back towards Sonata. "I demand a new driver!"

"Poor Sonata! He must be running you ragged."

Sonata beamed. "Really, Bravery, I don't mind."

Pyro was still reeling from shock. "But what happened to Furny?"

Bravery placed her hands on her hips. "When I heard you'd be here, my son, my only surviving son," she added with bitter emphasis, "whom I never seem to have the privilege of seeing—honestly, not coming home for Christmas, and then to find out you were just over the bay—"

Pyro waved his arms. "Get to the point, Ma."

Bravery pressed her lips together and drew a long inhale through her thin, delicate nose. "When I heard you'd be here, I decided to represent Aries myself."

"So you're not here to support Pasha, you're just here to see me?"

"Well, of course I'll support Pasha! As though Aries would ever endorse Samael."

With his blood rising to a nice low boil, Pyro reached for his cigarette case in his pocket. Finding it wasn't there, he leaned back to look pleadingly at Sonata. Sonata shook her head. At last, he sighed.

"But it's not why you're here?"

"No, I mainly came to see how you were doing. Since you never come home anymore, it seems I must pursue you." She glanced around him as though looking for someone. "Well?"

Pyro eyed her as though she had lost her mind. "What? Well what?"

"Where is she?"

"Who, Ma?"

"The girl."

"What girl?"

"The girl, the igneous, the little freckled thing you've taken a shine to! I've read all about her in the papers."

Pyro groaned and rubbed his mouth in an exasperated fashion. "I'm sure you have."

"Well, where is she?"

"She's not here right now. She's off taking care of official company business. What's your interest anyway?"

The Queen observed her fingernails. Pyro grew suspicious.

"Ma, why are you so interested?"

"Well, it seems … I mean, I wondered, with you taking her under your wing and all … I thought perhaps she might be … my granddaughter?"

Pyro choked. "What? You think Faina is my daughter?"

Bravery assumed a withdrawn air. "I'm certain I don't know. I don't know anything about you, really!"

"Is that why you're here? Because you wanted to meet your alleged granddaughter?"

Bravery threw her hands on her hips. "Is that so wrong? Is it so wrong that an old woman might travel all the way to Libra to see her one and only son and granddaughter?"

Pyro stared at her with burning eyes. "Let's get one thing straight: Faina is not my daughter. I have no children to speak of."

"You say that, but do you know it?"

Pyro gaped at her in disbelief. "Seriously, Ma?"

Bravery drew a long breath. "Well, I don't know what skirt you're sniffing up these days, but I do know you've had your nose up several!"

"She's from Russia, Ma!"

"Well, you do get around, after all."

"What is it you think I've been doing all these years? Where do you think I've been?"

"I don't know!" Her nostrils flared. "You don't call, you don't write. For all I know you could be selling pickled spooglies on some street corner in Procyon!"

Pyro threw up his hands and pulled his hair. "She's not mine, okay? Trust me on that. Her parents are dead. They were killed in some war, or something."

"So you're considering adopting?"

Pyro's eyes glowed like molten coals. Sonata put a soothing hand on his shoulder, pacifying him into a somewhat compliant mood.

"No," he finally sighed.

"Well," Bravery smoothed her skirt, "I should like to meet her all the same. If anything, I can determine for myself." She patted Pyro's head and kissed his cheek. "By the way, we're meeting for lunch this Saturday."

"Says who?"

Bravery started towards the exit and waved an airy hand.

"Sonata arranged everything."

Once his mother was out of earshot, Pyro tugged on a lock of Sonata's hair.

"Who do you think you are, my nanny?"

But Sonata did not indulge his attitude. "You need to spend more time with your mother."

"That's for me to decide, isn't it? I'm beginning to think this wheelchair is just a way for you to control me."

Sonata kept her voice even and tranquil. "Now, don't get yourself worked up. It's almost time for your medicine."

Pyro crossed his arms and hunched his shoulders, but Sonata smiled in his ear.

"If you're good, I'll get you ice cream from that place around the corner you like."

Pyro glanced at her hopefully from the corner of his eye. "The kind with the cinnamon candies?"

"Yes, I'll get you the kind with the cinnamon candies."

Pyro tilted back with a saccharine grin. "Did I ever tell you you're my favorite nurse?"

Chapter 27:
Sins of the Father

The blue twilight pressed against the fevered brow of the red horizon. Evening subdued the rabid heat that had plagued the afternoon. Staccato was winding about on his penny-farthing through the olive grove that ran along the peppered beach. His thoughts lingered on Evangeline and how best to win her affections, when a broken sob ebbed over the roar of the waves. He looked around and, seeing no one, continued on his way. Farther down the path, he heard it again, this time clearer and closer.

Bending his head around the dappled blue shadows, he caught sight of Evangeline. She was curled between the roots of a large tree, as if seated in an armchair. Her head was buried in her hands. He would have to approach with caution, which was no easy feat when dismounting a penny-farthing, but Staccato had become a master.

Coasting, he waited until the right moment, then stepped back on the mount and lowered his foot to the ground as a break. Unfortunately, he did not consider the embankment and was immediately thrown off balance. Staccato grapevined for some ways until he at last tripped over his own legs and somersaulted backwards, coming to a stop at Evangeline's side.

Evangeline jumped, forgetting her own troubles and hurrying to inspect him for injuries.

"Staccato! Oh, dear! Are you alright?"

When he saw her face, his mouth fell open in shock. An enormous bruise was welling across her cheek.

"Am I alright? I believe I should be asking you that question!"

Evangeline gasped and immediately tried to hide the injury.

"What happened?" He tried to peel her hands away from her face, but she resisted. He sighed. "It's no use, I already saw it."

She brought her head up to look at him. He was no stranger to these sorts of injuries.

"Your mother struck you."

"Please, I don't want Theo to find out. I've been trying to heal the bruises but," her voice broke into an impassioned sob, "it just won't work!"

Staccato pressed his lips in a grim line and, taking her arm, examined the purple spots pressed into her skin.

"My mother couldn't heal properly either once she'd worked herself into a panic."

Evangeline looked up at him and sniffed. "That's right, your mother was a mermaid, wasn't she?"

Staccato mustered a weak smile and nodded. Evangeline smudged her tears with the back of her hand.

"Please don't tell Theo, please! Nor Estella or Javaid. It would—"

"It would just make things worse."

Evangeline looked him over with her glittering eyes. "You seem to understand perfectly."

Staccato ran his fingers up and down her arm. "Well, I know from experience."

When he didn't elaborate further, she continued to stare after him. Staccato drew a deep breath. Looking away, he pushed his fingers through his hair.

"My father beat me whenever he was drunk, which was often. When he finished I would hide, because I knew if my mother saw she would try to heal me, even though my father had forbidden it. If he found out, he would beat her. So, my brother and I knew it was always better to lay low and keep quiet rather than risk making things worse. Not that I'm encouraging you to do the same."

"How old were you when he started beating you?"

Staccato shrugged. "Don't remember."

"Did no one help you?"

Staccato snickered and laid his head against the trunk of the tree.

"Someone did. Two friends of mine. They happened to be visiting relatives after I'd endured a particularly nasty beating. They told their aunt of the suffering I had been made to endure, and, well, she being Queen of Pisces at the time, my father was finally sent to jail."

Evangeline's lips spread into a knowing smile. "Theo and Javaid?"

"Theo and Javaid."

Evangeline edged closer and took his hand in hers. "I won't tell anyone."

"You needn't worry about that. My skeletons are no secret. That's what happens when you come from one of the most prolific Fay families in Voiler, or at least what was once one of the most prolific." He scoffed. "Dysfunction runs in the family. If the Nimbuses aren't beating their children, or drinking themselves into oblivion, they're squandering money, philandering, or heaven knows what. Well, I shouldn't say all the Nimbuses. My favorite aunt, Aunt Poppy, her family ended up migrating to the Other to study endangered unicorns. That, and to distance themselves from the toxic family name."

Evangeline's eyes beheld him with an innocence. "And you. You're not like that."

Staccato paused for a moment and considered.

"No. I'll never be like that. What I'd like more than anything is for my children to be the first Nimbuses not to come from a broken home plagued by scandal and vice."

Evangeline squeezed his hand. She had not let go of it since promising not to tell anyone about his family.

"That's why you've worked so hard to make something of yourself, isn't it?"

Staccato dared to meet her gaze. Evangeline saw so much of him through her strange eyes.

"Yes. That's why."

Summoning his courage, he gave her a squeeze back and felt her warmth spreading up his arm. Evangeline rested her head against his shoulder and closed her eyes.

"Most young men are too wild to think about things that matter." She smirked. "I don't know any boy my age who thinks about his future family, or who strives to be the first at anything outside a sporting event. I wish there were more young men like you, Staccato Nimbus. You're rather special."

Staccato ducked his chin to his chest. Inwardly he was beaming. He wanted nothing more than to lay at her feet with his heart open. He wanted her to excavate treasures within him he never knew existed, beauty only she could unearth. He wanted to be molded and transformed like her glassworks.

Staccato closed his eyes and drew a heavy breath through his nose.

"You know I can't promise not to tell Theo."

Evangeline's lower lip trembled as she looked away. "I know. I realize that's a lot to ask."

"I could never turn a blind eye when someone I care about has been hurt."

"No, I don't believe you could."

Staccato looked down at the bruises dotting her arm.

"Look, they're starting to heal." He put a hand up to the bruise scaring her cheek. The swelling had gone down tremendously. "See? All you had to do was calm down."

Evangeline lowered her eyes as she grinned, looking very bashful.

"Oh no, I think it was you. I think you must've inherited a healing presence from your mother."

Staccato felt his cheeks grow red as he helped her to her feet. "Come, let's take you to Theo."

Chapter 28:
Reunion

In the empty hallway of the hotel, Lydia knocked on Staccato's door with a soft fist.

"Mr. Nimbus?"

For the second time there was no answer. He was determined to hide. She inched closer to the door, pressing her cheek against the wood and dropping her voice.

"Please?"

There was a stirring from within. Lydia drew back. The door opened and Staccato gestured for her to enter. Lydia stepped across the threshold, and he latched the entry behind her.

Staccato turned and faced her, his only discernible expression one of fatigue. She searched his eyes in desperation for the thing which had stirred the memory within her. She wasn't finding it. Her eyes dropped to the charm laying against his chest.

"Mrs. Chevalsky, I apologize for toda—"

Lydia reached forward and ripped the necklace from around his collar. Staccato did not resist. He made no attempt to hide, no attempt to retreat. He remained open before her, allowing her to study his face for the first time.

She took in the clever, mellow eyes, the long eyelashes. She traced the sharp angles of his face hiding beneath the scruffy iron beard. She couldn't believe she had missed it. After a long moment of silence, Staccato knit his brows together. He looked like he was expecting some sort of reprimand.

Lydia's voice was soft. "It is you, isn't it?"

Their eyes met. She could see him breaking, feel his desire to reach out and touch her face.

"Papa?"

The muscles at the corners of his mouth twitched as he fought for composure. His voice cracked.

"Yes, Lydie, it's me."

Everything happened at once. Lydia ran to him. Staccato caught her in his arms. They sank to the carpet in a mangle of overwhelmed tears. Lydia sobbed into his neck, clenching the material of his shirt between her fingers.

"You are alive!"

Staccato clutched the back of her head against his chest and buried his nose in her hair.

"I am."

"You hid from me! You lied to me!" She held up the filigree charm. "You used this—this—thing, didn't you? Were you wearing this in Pisces? Were you wearing this when I first saw you in Voiler?"

Staccato dragged his head up and down. "Yes, I'm afraid I was."

"It does something! It makes me not recognize you!"

She threw it across the room. When she looked back at Staccato his eyes seemed to sink open in the weight of their sorrow. Tears dragged in the creases of his face. Staccato, her father, had always been an impenetrable fortress of secrets. Never had she seen him so vulnerable, so desperately open.

"I'm sorry, darling, I'm so sorry! I didn't mean to hurt you! I was trying to protect you!"

Lydia continued gaping at him through bleary, tear-stained eyes. She was so caught up in her own shock she couldn't think of how to react, or even remember she was capable of responding. Her silence must've stung him for Staccato's face grew more and more pained.

"You have every right to hate me, and I understand if you never want to see me again."

Lydia's hair whipped around her face as she shook her head.

"No, Papa! Please don't go away! I don't hate you! I still love you!"

Staccato's tears thickened and drenched her hair as he wrapped his arms around her.

"Oh, Lydia!" He kissed her forehead. "I love you so much. You have no idea how badly I've missed you. I feel like I haven't breathed in seventeen years."

As her body absorbed his emotions, she knew at once he meant what he said. She could feel the years of ache, of self-loathing brought on by their separation. She became aware of the tears he'd shed for her, of the countless dreams he'd built around her, of the love that cut inside him until it hurt. Her voice came out in a strained whisper.

"Why did you leave? It was that awful job, wasn't it?" She pulled away, trying to make sense of it all. "The one you would never tell me about!"

"I had enemies, Lydie!" He reached out for her chin and turned her head towards him. "My presence was putting you in danger. Even after I retired from spying on the C.O.N. they were hunting me! I knew it was only a matter of time before they traced me to Siberia where I was taking care of you."

She stared at him, allowing the reality of the moment to sink in. Staccato must have taken her silence for anger, for his voice rose with a sense of urgency.

"Lydia, they would've hurt you to get to me! You, the person I loved more than anything in the world! I could never let that happen!"

Lydia sniffed. "But I don't understand. After quitting your job you stayed home for three years. Everything was fine. What changed that made you feel you had to leave?"

"Lydia, I left because they *did* come!" His voice was grave.

Lydia's eyes widened with astonishment. "They came for you in Siberia?"

Staccato's mouth formed a thin line. "It only had to happen once." He softened. "I wasn't going to let it happen a second time."

Lydia's breathing grew regular again. She wiped away a tear with her sleeve.

"I got married, Papa."

Staccato's eyebrows lowered a bit. His voice was gentle but sour. "I know … At sixteen."

"Seventeen," she quickly corrected him.

Their eyes locked briefly, drawn by a tension neither wished to acknowledge. Lydia cleared her throat and looked away.

"We were married in 1907. I was seventeen."

Staccato swallowed and put on an expression of mild disinterest that was clearly forced.

"Are you certain? Because I distinctly remember receiving a letter from *Tetya* informing me of your elopement shortly before my thirty-sixth birthday."

"It was your thirty-seventh," she snapped. Lydia immediately lowered her head, blushing. She hadn't meant to sound so forceful.

Staccato chewed on the inside of his bottom lip and sat up a little straighter.

"Well, I must say I'm surprised. Discovering your child is going to be a wife and a mother before she's finished growing herself isn't exactly forgettable."

Lydia felt a surge of adrenaline burst forth from her chest and pop like hot grease down her veins.

"Do you really want to discuss this now?"

Staccato took a deep breath and covered his eyes. "You're right. I apologize, it's just … I know this isn't the right time, but I just want to understand why. I want to know why you did it."

Lydia set her shoulders, and pushed her hair away from her forehead.

"I suppose that is fair."

Staccato shook his head in confusion. "Running away with your employer's son at seventeen? Surely, you knew what was going to happen."

Lydia scowled at the floor. "I didn't think Ruslan's parents would allow him to retain his title. I thought they would disown him. They certainly wanted to."

"Well, they weren't going to welcome you with open arms, that was for sure, especially not after Ruslan converted for you!" He shook his head. "Different stations, different upbringings, different religions, for heaven's sake! They don't take such matters lightly in the Other, you know."

Lydia crossed her arms. "First of all, Israelites of the New Covenant do not consider themselves converts. *Maaminim*, believers, are what they are called. Second, it had nothing to do with me! Ruslan had been following the teachings of Rabbi Joseph Rabbinowitz long before I met him."

Staccato sniffed. "It's my own fault. I didn't expose you enough to the real world. How were you to know life outside the hedge was different than the ones in your storybooks?"

"Then why didn't you stop me?"

The glower in Staccato's eyes eroded into one of shock as he turned and gawked at his daughter.

"What?"

Lydia tried to appear distant. She threw up her shoulders, glancing off to the side.

"If you were so greatly opposed, why didn't you show up and do something about it?"

"Lydia, you aren't suggesting … Y—you mean you ran off with Ruslan hoping I would reappear and stop you?"

Lydia struggled to keep her mouth pursed, but her lower lip trembled. She nodded. "I never really believed you were dead." She took a deep breathe then split open like a dam. "It was a terrible, wicked, false thing to do! I'm ashamed of it every day!"

"You mean you didn't love him?"

Lydia tucked her chin against her chest, unable to face her remorse.

"Maybe not as much as I should have at first, but oh, Papa! I truly was fortunate things turned out the way they did because I grew to love him more and more every day! I fell in love with him in a way I didn't even know was possible!"

Staccato's brows knit together. "Oh, Lydia." He scooted towards her on his knees and gathered her into his arms, letting her cry on his shoulder. "I'm sorry I wasn't there."

"I was a fool to behave in such a way! I was so selfish! And then after everything happened Pasha came early, and we almost lost him, and everyone thought I … everyone thought …"

He stroked the back of her head. "I know, Lydia. You don't have to tell me, sweetheart. I know."

"We almost lost Katya! I lost three altogether!"

Staccato's voice was strained with agony, as he again said, "I know." She didn't have to explain what the "three" were. He cupped her face with both hands and pressed his forehead against hers. "Every day without you has been like walking on knives."

Lydia swallowed and tried to catch her breath.

"I still don't understand. You came back for us. You came to New York to restore Pasha to the throne. Why didn't you just come to me? Why didn't you tell me who you were? Surely, you weren't still worried about your enemies."

Staccato bowed his head. "There were other things I was trying to protect you from." He drew his hand across his eyes. "All this, for example, the trial, the scandal … my association has completely compromised Pasha's position."

Ignoring this remark, Lydia shifted in his arms so she could get a better look at him.

"Papa, did you shave your head and grow out your beard so I wouldn't recognize you?"

Staccato's eyes widened. She had caught him off guard. His lips flexed into a guilty expression.

"Maybe. …"

She ran her hand along his clean-shaven scalp, and burst into laughter. Staccato pinched his eyes closed and smirked.

"I look like a pharaoh, don't I?"

Lydia unsuccessfully stifled a giggle. "Oh, no!" She kissed the top of his head. "I think you look very handsome this way. Very rugged."

Staccato laughed out loud and pulled her close once more. "You have always been kinder to me than I deserved." He pressed his cheek against her head and breathed her in. "My Lydie."

With her tears finally dried, she laid her head against his shoulder and smiled.

"Is Staccato your Fay name, then?"

"It is. How does it feel to be Lydia Nimbus?"

"I think I would have liked that name growing up. Not that Kingsley isn't nice too." Her eyes fell upon the staff propped against the wall. "Your staff has changed."

He wound a curl around his finger. "I had to take a lot of precautions. You're very perceptive, you know."

"If only *Tetya* had known you were alive before she died. It would have been such a comfort to her. She was planning on moving to America, you know."

Staccato pressed his lips in an awkward line.

"Papa," Lydia drew back, her hands on her hips, "what are you hiding now?"

Stalling, Staccato summoned the necklace Lydia had tossed across the room back into his hand.

"An ambiguous—as this is known—can be quite powerful when made properly. Unfortunately, I was never really any good at it, and they're quite expensive. ..."

She snatched the necklace out of his hand and pitched it into the waste basket.

"Papa!"

"Alright, alright. *Tetya* didn't die, she moved to New York, and her name isn't Baba Yaga, it's Poppy. Aunt Poppy."

Lydia stared at him with her mouth agape. "Miss Pumpkin Potemkin? Aunt Poppy Potemkin? You mean, for the past ten years, *Tetya* was living just down the hall? And I didn't know because," she pointed an irate finger at the trashcan, "because one of those stupid ambigu—things? When the war broke out I wrote to her, and her neighbors told me she had died at the hands of the Red Army!"

Staccato cracked his knuckles. "She faked her death to avoid capture, but she escaped to America. Funny coincidence, really, that you ended up in the same tenement building. I couldn't have planned it better myself. Made it a lot easier for me to keep an eye on you." He wrapped his arm around her and kissed her cheek. "Why are we still sitting on the floor?" He helped Lydia up by the elbow. "Come, let's sit on the sofa."

Together they sat down on the cushions in peaceful silence. Staccato glanced around, bewildered.

"Well, what would you like to do? I can order a cup of tea if you like, or if you're hungry we can get something to eat. If you'd like to get out of the hotel, I do have a few tricks for avoiding the press. …"

But Lydia simply beamed and, lowering her head into her father's lap, closed her eyes. She could hear the grin in Staccato's voice.

"Or we can just stay like this. It's up to you."

Lydia was silent. At length, he took her left hand and kissed the inside of her wrist.

Chapter 29:
Love and War

The only reason Pasha even condescended to tolerate Roman's presence was because he wanted to find out more about Anastas. As the four breakfasted in the Oakroom Friday morning, Pasha could not quell his questions.

"So, any recent sightings of Anastas?"

Roman swallowed his coffee, then leaned over the table. "He's been hanging down by the riverfront the last couple of days. Supervising shipments."

Faina made a dramatic attempt to clear her throat. "Pasha, could you pass the butter, please?"

Pasha turned to her with an apologetic smile and handed her the butter. He waited until Faina's mouth was full before he started again in a low voice.

"What about Vadim?"

Faina slammed her coffee mug onto the coaster, nearly splashing Pasha. Roman pretended not to notice.

"We think Vadim's been in New Albany working inventory."

Pasha cupped his hand over his mouth. "But Anastas is definitely here, right?"

Faina threw down her napkin in obvious vexation.

"I'm gonna excuse myself to the ladies room. Hopefully, when I come back, you boys will have finished discussing that unspeakable person."

She rose and stared at Cicada who glanced around, dumbfounded. Faina placed her hands on her hips.

"You coming, Cici?"

Cicada managed an awkward smile. "Excuse us, fellas."

As Faina led her away, Pasha heard Faina whisper.

"We're women, we're supposed to go to the bathroom together."

"Why?"

Faina nudged her. "Because … I don't know, that's just what we do!"

Cicada sighed, exasperated. "Nothing you people do makes sense. …"

Pasha turned his attention back to Roman. "Faina is still … sensitive about all that."

Roman shrugged. "Naturally. Anastas intimidated her, killed her family, kidnapped her, then left her for dead."

As Roman rattled off the list, Pasha felt his chest flush with rage-fueled adrenaline. He looked up at Roman, determination glaring in his eyes. Before he could open his mouth, Roman had read his mind.

"You wanna take him out yourself, don't you?"

"Nothing would make me happier."

Roman leaned back and lit a cigar. "Can't say I blame you." He whipped out a pen from the inside of his jacket and scribbled a time and location onto a napkin. When he finished, he slid the napkin across the table towards Pasha.

"You'll find him there. Pretty secluded that time of day, so you shouldn't have any trouble. Just make sure you show up before the shipment. Don't want any Butcher interference."

"Certainly not." Pasha tucked the napkin into his pocket while Roman cleared his throat.

"So, uh, I been meaning to ask … is there anything going on between you and Faina?"

Pasha bit the inside of his lip. He'd been dreading this question for some time. He decided to remain vague.

"Why do you say that?"

"Well, there's that whole pretending to be a married couple thing."

"That was Cici's idea, we didn't know she was gonna introduce us that way."

"And I noticed you two have adjoining suites."

Pasha threw up his shoulders. "So?"

Roman stared at Pasha, then waggled his eyebrows. Pasha glanced to the right, then to the left. Roman pinched his forehead and sniggered as though addressing a twelve-year-old.

"Pasha, there's only one reason anyone ever gets adjoining suites."

Pasha's eyes bulged as it dawned on him. "Oh." He felt like an idiot.

Roman smirked as he threw up his hands in a nonchalant manner. "It's okay, I get it. You're casual."

Pasha stared at him in confusion again. Casual? What was casual? Should he just pretend like he knew? There was no mistaking Roman's exasperation this time.

"Casual! As in barney-mugging with no strings attached!"

Pasha's cheeks turned red. "No! No, we're not like that. That's … that's not why we have adjoining suites."

"You and the blonde then?"

Pasha rolled his eyes. "No! Nobody is having the … nobody is … no." He pursed his lips, trying not to scowl. Roman leaned back in his chair and chuckled.

"You sure you're up to taking down Anastas?"

Pasha's face grew hot. "Why wouldn't I be?"

A fly buzzed between them. Roman smacked his hands together but missed. It lighted on the table. Before Roman could raise his hand again, Pasha snared it in an empty cup. Their eyes met.

Before they could continue, Faina and Cicada returned.

Pasha rubbed his hands together. "Look who's back!"

Roman's eyes trained on Faina as she returned to her seat.

"Have you moved on to a more stimulating subject now?"

As Pasha was about to answer, Roman interrupted.

"Hey, Faina, how's about you and me go for dinner at the Brown this evening? Just the two of us!"

Faina's eyes grew wide with surprise. She glanced back at Pasha, who turned to glare out the window.

"C'mon," Roman urged. "You wouldn't wanna miss out on a Kentucky Hot Brown while you're down here, would you?"

"No, I suppose not." She turned to Cicada. "Didn't we have something planned this evening?"

Cicada fumbled for an answer. "Uh, um, the park maybe? Wasn't that it?"

"Aw, you can go to the park any old time," Roman insisted. "Have dinner with me tonight. I won't take no for an answer!"

Pasha felt Faina's knees touch his as she turned towards him in her seat. "Pasha? Wasn't there something you wanted to do this evening?"

Pasha flicked a crumb with his finger towards the window in a bitter manner. "Nope! Can't think of a thing!"

As soon as he said it he regretted it. Eyes wide, Pasha twisted around in his seat to change his answer, but Roman cut him off.

"It's settled then! We'll meet down in the lobby at five!"

For a moment, Pasha's eyes locked with Faina's. Something had cooled in the burning autumn-brown color, and the unmistakable disappointment in her expression caused him physical pain.

She turned to Roman, but her eyes were trained on her plate. "A— alright then."

Roman leaned back in his seat with an overly-large, arrogant smile.

"Swell!"

***

When the time came for Faina to meet Roman down in the lobby, Pasha lay on his bed and stared at the ceiling. He could hear the heels of Faina's shoes on the other side of the wall.

"Well, I guess I better get going. I'll try to be back in an hour."

"You aren't staying longer?" he heard Cicada remark.

Faina dropped her voice so Pasha couldn't quite make out what she was saying. Her heels clicked towards the adjoining door.

"I'm gonna tell Pasha I'm leaving."

"I think he's asleep."

She stopped short. "Oh." There was a long pause. Her voice faded away as she moved towards the hall. "I won't wake him. I'll be back, Cici."

Pasha listened to the front door close behind her. When he was certain she had gone, Pasha rolled off the bed and crawled to his suitcase in the corner. From the bottom compartment he unearthed a pistol. He deposited the ammunition into the chamber, savoring each metallic clink. Once he had locked the compartment he enclosed his fingers around the handle.

He stared down at his hands. It seemed as though they belonged to someone else. He craned his neck back and covered his eyes. What was wrong with him? Any other man wouldn't hesitate. He summoned the memory of Faina tied to the chair. Her face caked with blood. Her body slumped over. Her lips tinged blue.

He imagined his mother screaming as they careened down the Bowery. He thought of his nine-year-old sister dodging bullets and flying glass. He pictured the body of Faina's uncle lain out on the pavement. He envisioned Anya's lonely burial. He thought of Leo and the dynamite-filled cart, and of the two lives dependent on him.

Pasha saw himself lifting the barrel of his gun against Anastas's temple. He thought about how satisfying it would be to pull the trigger. He opened his eyes and stared down at the firearm. The satisfaction disappeared.

Pasha shook his head. He'd force himself if he had to. He tucked the revolver into the waist of his pants and covered it with his shirttail. Throwing on his coat and hat, he rapped on the door of the adjoining suite.

"I'm going to the drugstore, Cici, I'll be back."

She mumbled a response, but Pasha didn't wait around to hear. He hastened out the door.

***

It was a twenty-minute walk to the riverfront. The air had grown chillier in the twilight. It was cooler still near the shores of the Ohio. Anastas would be waiting at some old warehouse, probably flicking cigarette butts onto the gravel. Pasha followed Roman's directions down to the steamboat docks. The crowds and street lamps thinned to a sparse string until there were no people at all. Only the distant ebb of a single light remained.

Crickets chirped across the seam of bluegrass. Water soughed at the coarse banks of sediment. Pasha crept forward beneath the frigid shade of a loading ramp. As the river heaved a thoughtful sigh, the stench of loamy tobacco drifted his way. Someone was standing at the water's edge.

Pasha peered around the wall. Anastas had one hand shoved in his coat pocket, and the other holding a cigarette. As he turned to look down the river, Pasha could see the burn scars coming down from Anastas's hairline. His curls had been cut short. No doubt he'd had to shave it after Faina used her powers to light him on fire. At length, Anastas checked his watch and, putting out his cigarette, strode towards the front of the building.

Pasha backed out from beneath the ramp and made his way up the platform. Keeping himself close against the outer wall, he tailed Anastas to the loading bay lift. Pasha stood at the opening. Anastas was a few feet below him. Pasha reached under his shirttail and enclosed his fingers around the handle of the gun. With both hands, he raised the revolver and crept forward.

He was about to order Anastas to turn around, when a man walking his dog came wandering up the waterfront. Pasha edged back into the shadows, pinning himself to the inside of the doorway. He trained his eyes on the broken window, and waited for them to pass. When the figures had shrunk to an appropriate distance, he pivoted onto the loading bay, revolver raised.

"Turn around, you—"

But Anastas was gone. Pasha kept his hand steady and looked around. Anastas was about a hundred yards away, headed back towards the downtown area. Pasha vaulted off the side of the lift. He was not about to miss his chance! He'd corner him in an alleyway if he had to!

With long, hurried strides, Pasha managed to come close enough to Anastas without him noticing. The flow of pedestrians picked up, the volume of noise rising to a roar just loud enough to cover Pasha's footsteps. He dared closer.

At Fourth Street, Anastas slipped between two buildings. Pulling the brim of his fedora down over his eyes, Pasha darted in zigzags from dumpster to fire escape. His heart was eagerly nursing adrenaline into his veins now. His face flushed. Anastas turned into a dead alley with a single locked door. He hesitated, fishing for the keys in his pocket. The windows sat in vacant rows of darkness. There was no better time. No witnesses. Nowhere for Anastas to run.

Anastas inserted the key into the slot. There was a metallic, rubbing commotion as the key jammed in the lock. Pasha unsheathed the revolver from his waist and stretched it over his head. Anastas grunted. Pasha smiled. Anastas cursed. Pasha stepped towards the passage. Anastas swore again. Pasha opened his mouth. A hand slammed down over his lips.

Someone grabbed him from behind and wrenched him back into the adjacent alleyway. Pasha was thrown up against the wall. Faina stared down at him from under the rim of her cloche. With one hand pasted across his face, she put a finger to her lips. They listened as a door swung open in the alleyway, followed by the chime of keys being shoved into a pocket. A limn of yellow light pooled across the bricks on the opposite wall. It vanished as Anastas shut the door behind him and bolted the lock. Faina ripped the gun from Pasha's hands and knocked her sleeve across the top of his head.

"What is wrong with you?" Without waiting for an answer she wrapped her hands around his wrist and towed him back to the sidewalk. "You could've gotten yourself killed!"

"That wasn't gonna happen!"

They stopped in front of a boarded-up shop.

"We didn't come here to kill Anastas!" she hissed.

"Why waste an opportunity?"

Faina grabbed his coat collar and shoved him back in frustration.

"You've spent the past four months trying to distance yourself from your criminal record, and right before your hearing comes up you decide it's a good idea to pop a slug in someone's head?"

The adrenaline was still rich in his veins, and he couldn't help but shout.

"Think of it as doing my civic duty!"

Faina pulled at her hair from beneath her hat and growled. "You sound so stupid right now! This isn't what we came here for!"

Pasha's jaw dropped. "Stupid?"

Faina smacked his shoulder with her hat. "What if he fired at you?"

"I had him cornered! He was three feet away! There's no way I could've missed!"

"Pasha, let's be honest, you couldn't hit Anastas if he were standing three inches away!" She was practically spitting. "And even if you did, how were you gonna evade the police?" She threw her hands up over her eyes. "My gosh, you didn't even have a silencer!"

Pasha fumed. He didn't want Faina to make sense. He clung to his anger.

"He's dangerous, Faina! He murdered your family! He hurt you! I can't just turn a blind eye when someone I care about has been hurt!"

"You're not a thug! Quit trying to be one! You weren't a thug when you joined the Breadwinners and you aren't one now! You're Pasha! And that's all you need to be! It's not your job to kill Anastas—"

"You're right, it's my pleasure!"

"Stop it!" she screamed, attracting the attention of several passersby. Her hands crumpled around her forehead, and her voice broke with desperation. "Stop talking like that!" Tears squeezed from her eyes as she staggered forward and wrapped her arms around his waist. "Please, please, Pasha, I don't wanna talk about it anymore! Let's just go back to the hotel, please!"

Pasha's mouth fell open in shock. He held her close, her tears soaking his shirtfront.

"It scares me! I know what he's capable of, Pasha! Please, I don't wanna talk about it! I don't wanna think about it! I just wanna forget it ever happened!"

Pasha was awestruck. This was Faina, the same girl who jumped trains, who bargained with mobsters, who fearlessly faced a bunch of well-known gangsters just to save his mother. This was Faina, who had only ever been afraid of fire, and who could now control it like some volcanic goddess. She'd even shot and killed the Siberian, one of the most wanted criminals in all of Manhattan! Never in his life had he seen her have such a reaction, never had he known her to be this terrified of anything. He stroked the back of her head.

"Alright, calm down. We'll go back to the hotel, okay? Just try to calm down."

Before he had left, Faina would've gladly spit in Anastas's eye if given the opportunity. Now, the mere mention of him sent her spiraling into a panic attack.

She lifted her head up and looked him in the eye. "Promise me you won't do this again."

Pasha stiffened. He looked off to the side, fumbling for an answer. Faina squeezed him authoritatively.

"I don't need you to avenge me! I need you to be you. Promise me!"

She held his gaze, coaxing a softness into his eyes, his shoulders. He couldn't stand to see her hurt like this. Pasha held her against his heartbeat as he struggled to surrender.

"I promise."

"Thieves' Honor?"

Pasha drew his lips tight and managed to force out the words.

"May I, Pasha Chevalsky, be betrayed into the hands of my enemies if I ever forsake Faina Spichkin."

"And may I, Faina Spichkin, burn in my own fire if I ever forsake Pasha Chevalsky."

Pasha cupped her face in his hand and wiped away her tears with his thumb.

"Let's get you back to the hotel. You look like you need a coke."

"With peanuts?"

Pasha chuckled. "The only way to drink it."

Faina giggled as he replaced her cloche on top of her head, and looped his arm through hers.

"Where's Roman?" he asked, remembering she was supposed to be having dinner with him at the Brown.

Faina frowned and kicked a can with the toe of her shoe. "We ate, and he went back to the hotel. I told him I wanted some time to myself."

Pasha lowered his head to get a better look at her. "Did everything go alright?"

She shrugged casually. "He got a little pushy. I didn't wanna go in the first place. I'm not into Roman. I only flirted with him back in New York because—"

"Because you wanted some fun." Pasha's eyes grew bitter. "I get it."

Faina ground to a halt. "No!" She threw up her hands and glared at him. "Geez, Chevalsky! Don't you know me?"

Pasha lowered his head. "I know you like to flirt."

"Pasha!" She drew her fingers through her hair, clearly upset now. "You sound like the girls who used to bully me at school!"

Pasha closed his eyes and unwound his shoulders. "You're right. I'm sorry."

"I only flirted with Roman because we needed the car. I was desperate, I didn't know what else to do. And I only accepted his invitation tonight to avoid any tension. That, and I couldn't come up with a convincing excuse."

Suddenly, Pasha understood. He recalled the way Faina had pretended to flirt with Solokov at the Thanksgiving Parade to steal his gun, and how his mother had described her charming a roomful of gangsters to poison and disarm them when they escaped the Butchers.

"Faina, if he's bothering you I can tell him to back off."

She sighed. "No, don't do that. Look, after we leave we're probably never gonna see him again, right? So what's the harm in being friendly?"

Pasha cocked an eyebrow. "How friendly we talking?"

"You don't have to kiss him if that's what you're worried about."

Pasha laughed and stretched an arm around her shoulder. "Well, that's a relief."

Chapter 30:
The Poison Garden

Staccato shielded his face with his elbow and laughed as Theo's golden tail kicked up a shower of salt water.

"Sure you don't want to get in, Staccato?"

The family was taking their customary post-dinner coffee in the wet parlor, a semi-open-air conservatory where water from the bay was ushered into a large pool that took up more than half the room. Several bowl-shaped islands connected by teakwood platforms were sunken in the water for anyone wishing to stay dry. Each had their own fire pit surrounded by piles of luxurious cushions and silk floor pillows.

Staccato was sitting on the edge of one of these islands with his legs dangling in the water. He looked out at the fiery late November foliage between two columns.

"I'm quite comfortable where I am, thank you." He leaned back towards the heat of the fire.

Evangeline swam up and grabbed his ankles. "The water is heated, you know."

Her light and airy laughter seemed to reverberate through his sternum and turn his ears pink.

"But it will be freezing when I get out."

With a coquettish smile she lifted herself halfway out of the water and leaned forward.

"I could always warm you back up."

She was so close, the water droplets from her hair soaked through his shirtsleeves.

"Evangeline!"

Staccato jumped so high he almost kicked Evangeline in the face. Atergatis's petite shadow appeared leaning over the gallery railing. Evangeline threw herself back into the water and bowed her head.

"Yes, Mother?"

"Enough fooling around!" She made her way down the staircase. "Your sister has finally cried herself to sleep, bless her, and you'll wake her."

Evangeline's eyes didn't dare flick up from the water. "She's still upset over Queen Ursula's death?"

Atergatis stopped at the edge of the pool and took off her wrap. As the fabric was removed from her skin, Staccato could detect a subtly acidic fragrance. He had yet to know a day when Atergatis did not smell like poison, and with good reason.

There are many who would assume cosmetic achievement would involve very little brain power, and still more would be surprised by the considerable amount of science that goes into the field. Thus, Atergatis was not the air-headed simpleton one might suppose her to be. She was a prodigious chemist and an accomplished businesswoman, but her true calling lay in toxicology.

It was that very passion that made her cosmetics such a success: her beauty products were laced with a variety of poisons. Her wrinkle cream was riddled with nightshade, her rouge was seasoned with sea snapper venom. Never enough to kill, mind you, but just enough to tighten the skin, or deepen a blush. Atergatis was truly a poisonous woman.

"It appears so." She scoffed as she slid into the water, white scales forming on her pale legs. "I told her she's the only woman I know to grieve so piteously over a potential mother-in-law." She brushed her abundance of hair over one shoulder. It seemed fitting that with one blonde daughter, and the other red-headed, Atergatis's hair color should rest somewhere in-between. It was a perfect shade of strawberry blonde, with a single platinum highlight growing near the front of her head.

The differences in appearance between Atergatis and her husband's late wife, Timpani, were jarring. In fact, many were nothing short of surprised when King Nereus had announced his engagement to the Cassiopeian merchant.

Like most Pisceans, Timpani had the dark, even complexion of a beautiful volcanic rock, rich and black. Atergatis was as fair as a white pearl. Timpani had been built like a warrior goddess, tall and solid. Atergatis was almost fairylike in her delicacy, and was hardly above five feet tall. Timpani had favored styles and fashions of a more natural and earthy flavor; Atergatis preferred glamor, and her taste was exquisite. Even now at forty-four years old, she still managed to stun strangers with her elegance and beauty.

Had the differences been only skin deep, it is possible no one would have batted an eye; a person may have many tastes, after all. But shortly after the engagement was announced, it became overwhelmingly evident that two more opposite women could not have existed. Timpani was kind. You could never trust Atergatis's kindness, for it was only ever a means to an end. Timpani had a sense of humor. Any sense of humor Atergatis possessed often came at the expense of others. Above all things Timpani loved her family. Though Atergatis might have gone through many pains to control her family, one could not really say that she loved them.

For weeks King Nereus and his new bride circulated with alacrity through every gossip column of every newspaper from Sheritan to Sham. And it only grew worse when, in the wake of their marriage, Nereus managed to make a series of bad financial decisions costing Karkinos thousands of taxpayer dollars.

Could it be that the death of his first wife Timpani had driven him mad? Staccato never entertained such rumors until he had the opportunity of meeting Atergatis himself, but he wouldn't dare admit it for fear of hurting any of the Soters.

Sneering, Theo propped himself against a rock and faced his stepmother.

"Glad to know someone in this household is still in touch with their compassionate nature."

Atergatis lifted herself onto one of the islands and lounged against the pillows.

"Do stop your moralizing, Theo. What's the use of having a heart if you haven't got a brain to control it? Your poor father knew that."

Evangeline inched forward ever so slightly. "But Mother, the Northstars were to be Estella's family. You can't expect her to get over it that easily."

Atergatis's nose pleated with disdain. "Ugh, child, quit hunching your shoulders; it makes your stomach stick out even more."

Keeping in mind Atergatis was an empath, Staccato fixed his eyes on the back of her head and stoked up as many hateful feelings as he could muster.

Atergatis regarded eating—or not eating—as a competitive sport, in which everyone was a player, and she the champion. Had it not been for this quirk, she likely would have been shaped more like her youngest. Instead, her daughters' bodies served as favored targets for Atergatis, for neither were as thin as she would've liked them to be.

Embarrassed, Evangeline folded her hands in front of her stomach and straightened her shoulders.

"Honestly, your waist and Estella's thighs! I should've put you in a corset when you were younger. At least yours could've been helped!" Atergatis reached forward and caressed her daughter's chin. "You can't expect to cheer Bruin up with that posture." Atergatis painted her mouth with a caring grin. "You'll want to look pretty to please His Majesty."

"W—what?" Evangeline stared back at her with unfocused eyes.

Javaid, who had been floating on his back with Ulysses sitting on his chest, lifted his head.

"The man just lost his entire family. I doubt she can expect to cheer him up at all."

"Nonsense." Atergatis slid back into the water and took Evangeline's hands. "Men are not like women." She tucked a hair behind Evangeline's ear. "When a woman's heart breaks it remains that way forever, but a man will forget his grief in the presence of a Venus."

Staccato could not help but think of how Nereus had married so soon after Timpani's passing. Theo towered out of the water. He was never good at holding his temper.

"What are you suggesting, Atergatis?"

At the sound of Theo's voice she pursed her lips and paused, as though thinking of a way to persuade an unruly toddler into an act of obedience.

"Now that Bruin is to be King of Ursa, the alliance between our two kingdoms sits on thin ice. Unfortunately, Ursula and Uther neglected their duties when it came to preparing their youngest to deal with matters of state. And there's no use pretending the boy wasn't unstable to begin with. We can only imagine what the death of his family has done to his mind. Karkinos needs insurance; we need to make sure the bond between Ursa and our kingdom is secure. What better way to do that than a marriage?"

Theo smacked the water. "You're suggesting we use Evangeline as a pawn?"

"Don't be so dramatic, Theo. Monarchies in the Other have been doing it for ages."

"But not Voilerians, and especially not mermaids! It's a breach of our virtues—we marry for love, not advantage."

"You don't think Bruin could learn to love our Evangeline?" She held Evangeline close and patted her cheek.

Theo forced a softness into his manners. "Evangeline, could you give us a moment, please?"

She turned back towards the stairs, but Atergatis wrenched her back by her wrist.

"I'm the girl's mother; I can decide whether or not she stays or goes."

"Well, I am King!" Theo's voice echoed off the high ceiling.

Frowning, Atergatis released her daughter, who floundered out of the water and raced down the hall. Staccato resisted the urge to get up and run after her.

Theo faced Atergatis, Javaid standing boldly behind him.

"Have you considered her feelings at all?"

At this remark, Atergatis tossed back her head and laughed.

"Please, Evangeline is a Titania, she'd fall in love with an ass if it gave her its life story!" She stabbed a glance at Staccato with her stinging, metallic silver eyes, which, rather than lend itself to her beauty, made her appear cold and distant.

Javaid clenched his fists. "You said it yourself! Bruin is unstable! You'd really sell your daughter to an unpredictable brute just for security?"

"You all make me out to be rather callous, don't you? It may surprise you boys, but I've given the matter much consideration. If I'm as careless with my children as you suggest, why am I not throwing Estella at Bruin? Evangeline will be happy no matter what happens. She is gifted with an unconditional love for all people, an advantage in this case."

Theo ground his teeth together. "Bruin is a scoundrel! I tried reasoning with him all summer, offered him advice on taking his father's place. He told me I had no business telling him how to run his kingdom. He spends all his time in the company of the Cobra, taking his cues from the very man who ordered his family's execution! He wears that scar like it's a tattoo! Do you know Samael sends Bruin women from the brothels in Draco?"

Javaid lowered his chin. "I've even heard he's taken to dining on *saignants* with the Draconian nobility. They say he's become a blood drinker, that he's dabbling in Primal Instinct."

Atergatis shrugged her shoulders and swam back towards the island.

"The child is as gullible as a puppy. As long as he keeps it quiet she'll have nothing to cry over, and even if she does find out, you know Evangeline, she's as forgiving as a spring morning."

Theo threw back his shoulders. "I will not allow you to throw Evangeline to the lions!"

Atergatis smiled. "That's not really up to you, is it?"

Javaid narrowed his eyes. "Nor you!"

"You're right, Javaid. It's up to Evangeline."

***

The moment the family adjourned from the parlor, Staccato ran off towards Evangeline's quarters. If given the chance, Atergatis would convince Evangeline she would be saving the kingdom if she married Bruin,—

even if she didn't want to.

Perhaps if Evangeline knew about Staccato's love for her, she would be less inclined to listen to her mother. Was it possible Evangeline loved him as well? If she did, surely she wouldn't throw away such happiness to please her abusive mother.

Just as he was rounding the corner to Evangeline's bedroom, he stopped. He looked around the hallway as though he'd walked there in his sleep. It occurred to him for the first time exactly what he was doing. He was acting on impulse. He was defying the Queen Mother. He was breaking the rules.

He stared at the double doors of Evangeline's bedroom, frozen with fear. Steeling himself, he strode forward to knock.

A rippling sound drew his attention over his shoulder. Atergatis's sycophant maid, Ms. Conch, appeared. The penetrating glare of her thin violet eyes aroused such a feeling of exposure in Staccato, he was tempted to shield himself. Ms. Conch tossed her voluminous braid over her shoulder, looking like a painting. Atergatis had a rule that all her personal servants must meet her exacting standards of beauty, and Ms. Conch was no exception.

"Her highness, Queen Atergatis, wishes to see you in her greenhouse."

Staccato's shoulders bowed forward as he coughed into the back of his hand.

"Oh, um, yes. Thank you, Ms. Conch. You may inform Her Highness that I'll come at once."

He had expected her to leave, giving him an opportunity to speak to Evangeline first, but Ms. Conch was a shrewd woman. They remained staring at each other in awkward silence. At last her gaze rinsed him over with a disapproving sneer.

"I thought you said you were coming at once."

"Right," he turned the other way, "let me just get my bicy—"

"Her Highness requests that you leave the contraption behind."

There was nothing else to do. Defeated, Staccato released an irritable sigh and headed down the corridor, Ms. Conch swimming alongside him.

Atergatis's private greenhouse was easy enough to spot in the darkening twilight. It lit up the garden like a bioluminescent sea urchin, and was shaped like one, too, complete with spikes. Theo and Javaid appropriately referred to it as the Poison Garden, for it was just that, the place where

Atergatis housed the deadly ingredients for her homemade beauty products.

Spiny plants of all varieties cast lithe, twisting shadows in the frosted, violet glass. The noise of crickets and starlings thinned to an overpowering silence as Staccato neared. Nature itself wanted nothing to do with the place.

Staccato stopped abruptly at the footbridge. His hand clenched the railing. Thousands upon thousands of poisonous jellyfish lit the moat surrounding the greenhouse like a galaxy of pale moons. Time and again, Theo had ordered Atergatis to have a protective barrier built over the enclosure as a safety precaution. When she did not comply, Theo had one built for her. Atergatis then proceeded to tear it down in a fit of rage. After that, Theo let it go. She was the mother of his sisters, and for their sake he tried to keep the peace as best he could.

Holding his breath, Staccato put one foot on the platform. The stream of hollow, ballooning figures glided inauspiciously beneath his feet like the river Styx, separating the land of the living from the realm of Hades.

Staccato forced himself to look away, and, recovering his nerve, plowed across the bridge. Sweet fragrances of citrus bled seductively into his sinuses from the trees flanking the entrance. To the casual garden-party observer they were simply olive trees, the national tree of Karkinos, two of thousands growing on the estate. But Staccato's Aquarian upbringing had given him an eye for this particular variety of tree. He recognized them at once as oleander, a tree which, like everything else in Atergatis's garden, was incredibly poisonous.

Staccato raised his fist to knock.

"You may enter, Mr. Nimbus."

Staccato staggered back slightly. Atergatis must have seen his shadow through the glass doorway. Sighing, he reached for the golden latch, trying desperately to avoid the overabundance of unidentified ivy curling around the handle.

A million saccharine odors hit him at once as he stepped across the threshold. It was like being in an oversized perfume bottle. Atergatis was just paddling up from the depths of a pool in the floor, a pair of shears in hand.

"I was just trimming up my reef garden." Her glittering white fins trailed behind her like a cathedral train on a wedding dress. As she drifted towards the stairs, trading her tail for legs, her top lengthened magically to form a sheer white robe. Staccato cleared his throat.

"Ms. Conch said you wished to speak with me."

"Yes." Atergatis smoothed her long hair over her chest and opened a cabinet filled with phials of liquid. "Tell me, Staccato, when Theo comes to you for advice, how do you go about divining the right path for him to follow?"

Staccato rubbed the back of his neck. "W—well, I help him to weigh the options and choose what's best for the most people."

"I see." She uncorked a container of vivid periwinkle fluid and extracted a drop or two with a pipette. "And when you were sworn in as my stepson's advisor, what was it you promised to do?"

"To put the country's needs ahead of my own."

A solicitous smile unraveled across her delicate features like a snake sliding along the sand.

"I need you to advise me, Staccato."

"Your Highness?"

She lifted a clear jar of silken cream to the light. Staccato couldn't help but notice how red the nostrils of her upturned nose were against her snowy skin. He thought it made her look like a rabbit.

"How would Karkinos benefit from Bruin and Evangeline's marriage?"

Staccato released a heavy exhale. "As long as Bruin were married to Evangeline, he'd be unlikely to ever break the alliance. Karkinos and Ursa would continue to share resources and would never have to fear war."

Feeling she'd made her point, she nodded. "Precisely." Two drops of the periwinkle substance went into the cream.

"But does Karkinos really need Ursa?"

Atergatis set aside the pipette and raised an eyebrow. "They're the wealthiest and most powerful nation in Voiler." She plucked a glass stirrer from her workstation and set about folding the elixir into the jelly.

"Exceeding Karkinos only marginally," Staccato went on. "Ursa is every bit as dependent on Karkinos as Karkinos is on Ursa, if not more so. We control the waterways; do you realize how vital that is to a country?" He hesitated momentarily as Atergatis dipped her hands into the ointment and began rubbing it into her skin. "A land kingdom without water will not survive, but a mermaid kingdom without land? It's a minor inconvenience. There'd be some drawbacks, but overall Karkinos would be fine. Your Highness, I understand your trepidations concerning Karkinos's future with Ursa, but it's hardly worth throwing away your daughter."

Atergatis turned upon him with a malignant glower.

"You think I don't love my daughter? You think I don't care about her happiness? Really, Staccato, as a law student I had expected better of you. As Queen, I too am expected to make sacrifices for the good of the kingdom."

Inwardly, Staccato was rolling his eyes. The sheer vanity of this woman! She must have sensed his cynicism, for her eyes softened with feigned understanding.

"You and I have more in common than you would think, Staccato." She fingered the leaves of a potted hemlock. "I too was born into less-than-ideal circumstances. Mummy dug for clams while Daddy drifted from one odd job to the next, and despite their struggling bank account, the pair bred like rabbits. When I was ten years old, my Auntie Emerald died and left my family her vast fortune. I thought all our troubles were over. We could once and for all stop scrounging for mudbugs and live like a real family.

"But my parents squandered every last penny on a string of ridiculous investments and temporary luxuries until everything was right back to the way it was, only worse. I tried to advise them. I tried to point them in the right direction, but as usual no one would listen to me. In the end I was forced to watch my favorite brother succumb to starvation. He was only six years old. I had no control. The only thing I could do was try to comfort him in his final moments, all because my parents refused to put their children first."

Before he could stop her she had grabbed him by the chin and was turning his head down towards her.

"You swore to put the country's needs ahead of your own." The smell of toxins lingered faintly beneath the smothering of perfume. "Just remember that. You swore. Stay away from my Evangeline!"

She let go, and Staccato nearly tripped backwards into the reef garden. A knock at the door drew Atergatis's attention away from him.

"Your Highness?" Staccato could see Phrygia's outline at the door. "You sent for me?"

Atergatis put on her false smile once more. "Yes, Phrygia darling, come in!"

With her head ducked shyly towards the ground, Phrygia entered the garden. Atergatis floated towards her with her arms outstretched.

"There you are, my dear!" She glanced at Staccato over her shoulder. "You're dismissed, Mr. Nimbus."

Staccato hastily nodded and headed towards the door. Atergatis continued on as though he weren't even in the room.

"I would be delighted if you would test this new lip rouge I've just formulated. I believe the color would be absolutely ravishing with your lovely skin. …"

Chapter 31:
Sadie Salome

When Pasha exited the lift Saturday morning with Cicada and Faina, Roman received him with an unmistakable look of surprise.

"Pasha!"

Pasha glanced between his two female companions. Roman shook his head as though to throw off the morning's leftover fatigue.

"And Cici, and Faina! Don't you three look swell!"

They had each dressed for the occasion. Pasha was in a white suit and panama, and the girls matched in cream-colored chiffon.

"Let me guess, you must be on your way to Churchill Downs?"

Pasha was impatient to get out the door. "You guessed correctly."

"Picked you out a horse yet?"

"Don the Man," Cicada answered for him, forgoing her accent in a moment of panic. She'd been running through the numbers all morning and had stuffed her head with every piece of available information she could find on horseracing.

Roman bounced his chin. "Ah, the favorite. Playing it safe, huh, Chevalsky?"

Pasha glared at Cicada from the corner of his eye. "I haven't decided for sure."

Cicada smacked him with her palmetto fan. "Trust me, Pasha, honey, Don the Man is the way to go. You forget my family bred racehorses."

"So did mine." Only Pasha was telling the truth.

Roman coughed into his elbow. "Uh, before you go, Pasha, I have something that might interest you."

He stared at Cicada and Faina. Faina rolled her eyes.

"Come on, Cici. We'll have them bring the car around." And grabbing her arm, Faina dragged her out the door, leaving Pasha and Roman alone.

Roman dropped his voice. "How'd it go last night?"

Pasha rocked back on his heels. "I, uh, lost him." He coughed into his sleeve. "It's alright though. I mean, maybe I should just leave it to Mr. Barinsky. I'm done with the Breadwinners anyway."

Roman raised his eyebrows. "Pasha, how many chances you gonna get like this? What are the odds the two of you would happen to show up in the same place?"

Pasha sighed and shoved his hands into his pockets. "I made a promise to someone, alright?"

Roman gave a condescending snigger. "Let me guess? Faina shed a few tears and you went soft? C'mon Pasha, you're tougher than that! Besides, she doesn't have to know."

Pasha straightened his tie and glanced restlessly towards the door. "That's our car. See you around, Roman."

***

On the way to Churchill Downs, Cicada was relentless.

"Pasha, I've calculated the odds a hundred times! Don the Man has everything in his favor! He's the fastest! He has the best position, an immaculate bloodline! Not to mention he was the most expensive contestant purchased!"

"I heard you the first fifty times, Cicada."

She threw down her newspaper in a fit of exasperation. "Then why won't you say you're betting on Don the Man?"

"I'll make my decision after I've seen my options."

Faina pulled up in front of the track. "Alright, Cicada, even you have to admit that's reasonable."

Cicada tangled her arms across her chest and hunched down in the seat.

"Fine."

"Cottonmouth said to meet him down in the paddock, so we can check out the horses first thing." Faina held open the door, and Cicada slunk out.

Cottonmouth was easy to spot in a yellow seersucker and straw boater.

"Well, good afternoon, friends! So nice to see you on this fine spring day!"

They exchanged greetings, and together the party made their way to the pen. As they brushed towards the stall of Don the Man, Cottonmouth shook hands with a well-dressed fellow in a pink tie.

"Mr. and Mrs. Lapochkov, Miss Butler, I'd like to introduce you to Mr. Edmund Decker, the owner of Don the Man."

The horse owner tipped his hat. "Pleased to meet ya'll."

"The pleasure is ours." Pasha stretched out his hand with his most confident manners. "How long have you been sponsoring racehorses, Mr. Decker?"

"Oh, I'm fairly new to the racing game. Don here is only the second racehorse I've backed."

"I see, well, you must have an eye for breeding, in that case. Making the favorite is no small achievement."

"Well, as they say, quality never does come cheap. Once I saw the price tag, I knew I had me a winner."

Cicada's eyes pinned on Pasha, completely unable to settle her nerves.

"You hear that, Paul? Mr. Decker shelled out a lot of money for Don the Man."

"Yes, I heard." Pasha drifted towards the stall to observe the horse up close.

Cicada turned back to Mr. Decker. "I heard you laid down a fortune just to bring him down from New York."

"Yes siree, best accommodations money can buy. I tell you, that horse lives like a king."

Pasha looked over his shoulder. "When did you arrive?"

"Late yesterday afternoon. There was a small delay on the train coming down. Hasn't seemed to bother him one bit, just look at him!"

Don the Man was tossing his head and pawing at the straw on the ground. Sweat had gathered on his hindquarters.

"He's champin' at the bit!"

Pasha resisted the urge to roll his eyes. As the others conversed, Pasha wandered across the paddock towards the stall of a dappled gray just like Harpagos. There wasn't anything particularly special about her. She was of no great size or unique strength. Her behavior wasn't erratic, nor was it especially subdued. But confidence was carried like a torch in her eyes.

Faina joined him in front of the stall. Pasha stroked his chin. "That one. She's got it."

Faina leaned over his shoulder and squinted at the nameplate.

"Her name is Sadie Salome! Just like the Irving Berlin song!" She bounced on her heels. "Pasha, it's a sign!"

He put his arm around her. "You bet it is."

Cottonmouth and Cicada approached from behind. "Found yourself a horse, Mr. Lapochkov?"

Pasha smiled and reached forward to stroke Sadie's nose. "I believe I have, Dr. Cottonmouth."

Sadie nickered and pressed her nose affectionately against Pasha's palm.

***

Cicada pinched her temples as they made their way towards the box.

"Let me get this straight. You're staking the shard on a long shot just because she's named after some Irving Berlin song?"

Faina dropped her chin. "That's not the only reason."

"Oh, I'm sorry, and she's got 'the look,' unlike Don the Man, who's got the odds!"

Pasha gritted his teeth. "Cicada, Decker doesn't know the first thing about horses. I've seen these types before. These moneyed snobs think they can buy their way into horseracing by purchasing the most expensive animal, paying for the most expensive trainer, and shelling out the most expensive equipment. They base everything on price tag alone, paying no attention to the horse itself."

"Okay, but did *you* actually pay any attention to the horse itself? You heard Decker, he was 'champin' at the bit.'"

"Decker doesn't know what he's talking about, I've seen dope fiends less anxious than that horse. Mr. Decker mentioned the train arrived late yesterday. Don the Man has had absolutely no time to settle in to his surroundings."

"You do realize Sadie is a filly, right? Statistically speaking, fillies rarely win."

"That doesn't matter."

"Have you looked at her odds? She's in the bottom!"

"Cicada, I know what I'm doing, trust me."

She threw the paper over her shoulder. "Alright, look. Your horse doesn't even have to win, right? As long as it beats Cottonmouth's choice, which is Don the Man. I'm begging you, choose a horse with better odds! How about Make Mine a Double? Bat in The Belfry? Quotin' Moses? Take your pick!"

Pasha stopped just short of their box and turned to look at her.

"Cici, I've made up my mind. I'm betting on Sadie Salome."

When the time finally rolled around for Don and Sadie to race, Pasha was feeling confident. By the looks of it, so was Sadie Salome. She was positively prancing as she was escorted to the gate. Cottonmouth didn't seem to notice. He leaned in his chair and folded his large hands in his lap.

"Just so you're aware, it's best to consume a large breakfast on the morning of your appointment to give blood. Helps prevent fainting."

Pasha put down the binoculars, and together he and Cottonmouth laughed. He would let Cottonmouth think what he wanted. He would allow him this brief moment of security. Cottonmouth didn't stand a chance. With a crooked smile, Pasha turned and offered the binoculars to Cicada.

"Don't you wanna take a look, Cici?"

Cicada wrinkled her nose and downed another shot of illegal whiskey. Pasha threw back his head and chuckled. The horses lined up in their gates.

Cottonmouth crossed one leg over the other. "So you and Mrs. Lapochkov are fans of Irving Berlin?"

"Oh, yes!" Faina gazed into her so-called husband's eyes dreamily. "We danced to *A Pretty Girl is Like a Melody* at our wedding."

Pasha drew his arm around her. "Ol' Izzy is sort of our good luck charm."

Cottonmouth snickered into his shirt collar.

"In that case, I'd say you've made a wise decision, because luck is something you're gonna need."

Overhead, the announcer barked into the loudspeaker. "Lining up now. Clash of Arms a little slow to the gate. There goes Mooney on Make Mine a Double. …"

Faina squeezed his arm, but Pasha was as cool as sweet iced tea.

"And they're off! Make Mine a Double quickly takes the lead, Don the Man close to follow. Magic Carpet off to a good start. Pass the Salt coming up on the inside. Making House Calls on the far outside. Don the Man takes the lead while Sadie Salome kicks up the rear with California Cotton."

Clay scoffed. "Sounds like Sadie Salome should go home!"

Cicada held her head in her hands. Pasha didn't bother to turn around.

"Just you wait. Best to let the horse pace itself."

"Leapin' Locust is riding the rail while Make Mine a Double and Don the Man duke it out for the lead. California Cotton coming up fast. They're rounding the first turn and here comes Of Great Worth, taking the place right between Make Mine a Double and Don the Man. Sadie Salome still behind."

Meanwhile, Letcher and Clay chanted the refrain to *Sadie Salome*.
"Oy! Such a sad disgrace
No one looks in your face
Sadie Salome, go home!"

Cottonmouth guffawed along. Still, Pasha remained collected with a sly smirk at the corner of his lips.

"Starting on the second lap now. Pass the Salt falling back along with Of Great Worth. Don the Man looks as though he's beginning to wan, and here comes Sadie up on the outside!"

The mobsters ceased their laughter. Cicada peeked open an eye.

"She's passing Leapin' Locust, Bat in the Belfry, Pass the Salt. Sadie Salome neck and neck with Of Great Worth. Don the Man retreats to seventh place. They're going round the bend. Sadie Salome moves to second place. Spick-and-Span now ahead of Don the Man, followed by Quotin' Moses. Sadie Salome moves to first! Oh boy, folks, look at her go! 'The only real Salome—y, baby!'"

Faina was on her feet. "Go, Sadie, go!"

Cottonmouth dropped his iced tea. Glass shattered beneath the seats while Sadie Salome moved one, six, eight, ten lengths ahead of the other horses!

"*And Sadie Salome wins by twelve lengths!*"

Faina and Cicada erupted into squeals of rapture. Forgetting her accent, Cicada tossed her cloche in the air.

"God bless Irving Berlin!"

Letcher slapped Pasha on the back. "Well, what do you know! Paulie here knows what he's doing after all!"

"You saw it here, folks: Sadie Salome, the long-shot filly brought up right here in the 'Old Kentucky Home,' wins the race!"

While Pasha lifted a triumphant glass to Cottonmouth, Faina threw her arms around him and kissed his cheek. Pasha's eyes bulged. He could feel his face turning as pink as the flowers pinned to Faina's dress.

"You did it, darling!"

He wound one of her curls around his finger.

"All for you, my *kolibrishka*." My little hummingbird.

He turned back to Cottonmouth. "No hard feelings, Doctor, but I am afraid we will not be making a donation to your blood bank after all."

Cottonmouth smiled placidly. "You're a clever man, Mr. Lapochkov. I applaud you. If you'll drop by my house, let's say, tomorrow evening? You and your wife may claim your prize."

Chapter 32:
Mistletoe

In the mermaid kingdoms one is never far from a body of water in one form or another. The library at Alveare was no exception. The room itself was a series of book-filled islands. Channels ran between the bookshelves like roads in an ancient floating city. Water sluiced down the walls in a soothing rhythm. Even the galleries had fountains running down the bottom of the railing.

Like the wet parlor, the library boasted a series of islets, only considerably larger and more accommodating. And rather than being fully open and littered with floor cushions, they were built like pavilions, with thick columns and draped canopies. Traditional furnishings filled in the space with their cozy, overstuffed shadows and gold embroidery thread. Fires roared in brass bowl fire pits, cooking the fragrances of the early winter air until they blended together in a comforting bath.

Reclining on one of the plush, velvet chaises, Staccato held a newspaper over his head and tried to read the headline for the third time.

"*Wode's Virus Casualties Increase as Epidemic Ravages Karkinos*." A photograph of an overfilled sick ward accompanied the title. "*First appearing in Acubens back in September, Wode's Virus has been making its way across Karkinos as a sort of Angel of Death. The disease has claimed roughly 32,000 victims so far. Symptoms often mimic kidney failure, and can include severe muscle cramps in the lower back and extremities, lethargy, high fever, shortness of breath, and loss of consciousness.*"

Staccato sighed and folded the paper in his lap. It wasn't exactly new information. He and Theo had been monitoring the epidemic for weeks. He could hardly expect to distract himself with old news, but what was left? Atergatis's warning had been plaguing his attention for a week and nothing seemed to divert it.

That isn't to say he was afraid of Atergatis. If anything, she was a woman desperate for control, but she had none, not as long as she lived under Theo's rule. Still, he could not help but dwell on the truth of her reminder. Staccato had sworn to put the country's needs ahead of his own. He did not agree that Karkinos needed Evangeline to marry Bruin, not in the least. But was it appropriate for Staccato to pursue a relationship with a woman who was also his sovereign ruler?

A bit of movement drew his eyes towards the entrance of the library. Atergatis sauntered down the middle aisle, her head swiveling between the bookshelves. In her right hand she carried a jeweled hair comb.

Staccato sank farther behind his newspaper. By the looks of it she was searching for Evangeline, who had no doubt run off to avoid some pretentious outing.

"Ah, Staccato!"

Staccato cringed as he slowly brought his eyes up over the edge of his newspaper.

"May I help you, Your Highness?"

Atergatis swung round the column with one hand, an oddly energetic gesture for her, and bent low over the chaise, leaving no place for Staccato to hide.

"You wouldn't happen to have seen my Evangeline, would you?"

Staccato stared dully back at her. "Can't say that I have."

Atergatis's lips curled with a boastful smile. "She's supposed to be attending a Christmas luncheon this afternoon at Alfbern Hall. King Bruin was adamant she attend."

Staccato couldn't help but notice that she now referred to Bruin exclusively as King Bruin, especially when Staccato was within hearing range. She turned the comb over in her hands.

"I thought it would be nice if she wore this lovely comb I got her for her birthday last week. It suits her far better than that Aquarian peasant garb, don't you think?"

She was referring, of course, to the gift he'd given to Evangeline for her birthday: a headband made with Aquarian indigo dye. She'd worn it nearly every day since.

"I quite disagree," he replied in a bored manner. "I think the violet color complements the gold of her hair superbly. Furthermore, it would be a shame to overwhelm her natural beauty with such ostentatious ornaments."

Atergatis looked him over with a mocking simper.

"Well, I suppose your tastes are a bit more rustic, what with your upbringing. It's all very well for a penniless missionary in Sadalmelik who has her elbows plunged in a dye pit every day, but a princess of Karkinos needs something a little more refined."

Staccato pretended to be reading his newspaper, but inside he was seething. It was one thing to insult his upbringing, but it was very much another to insult his mother. Never mind that Aquarian indigo silk was a highly sought after, and expensive commodity.

"Well," she sighed, turning back towards the opposite exit, "if you should run into her, do send her my way. We wouldn't want her to be late for the party."

Staccato said nothing, hoping she would leave it at that, but she stood there staring at him.

"Staccato, did you hear me?"

Staccato bit the inside of his lip. "Yes, Your Highness, I will do that."

"See that you do." She turned and left the room.

The moment she was gone, Staccato let out a long growl and got to his feet. The nerve of that woman! He could hardly bear it! He was just about to start pacing when a bit of movement beneath the platform caught his eye.

Something long and wavy was undulating in the surf. He leaned over the edge and smirked. It was a lock of golden blonde hair. Staccato dropped on all fours and crept a measured total of five feet and five inches from the tendril. Steadying himself, he plunged his hand under the surface and tugged Evangeline out by her fins.

Evangeline's face appeared under a mask of popping round bubbles as she let out a startled squeal.

"Well, well," Staccato chuckled, "if it isn't our lost princess!"

Evangeline rose up out of the water, giggling, and planted her elbows on the surface.

"I am not going to that Christmas party!"

Staccato snickered and sat back on his haunches.

"Really, well that's quite a costume for a quiet afternoon at home."

Evidence of her mother's aesthetic touch were everywhere. Above her seashells, a thick white cravat was tied about her throat and pinned with a sand dollar brooch. A bustle cage without the bustle was fastened around her waist and bounced on her backside. To top it all off, there was a faint whiff of poison about her cheeks and mouth that no doubt had something to do with the dabs of rouge that had been put there. Staccato eyed her with a teasing smile.

"Is that oleander I smell?"

Evangeline groaned and, snatching the cravat from her throat, began rubbing violently at her cheeks.

"Mother insisted I wear it! It itches dreadfully!" She drew the neckerchief away and looked down at the clean material. "Ugh! It's waterproof!" She smoothed her tresses over her shoulder with a flushed smile. "You won't tell mother I'm hiding, will you?"

"Of course not!" He leaned forward and folded his hands together. "Tell me, if you aren't going to spend the day merrymaking at Alfbern Hall, just what is it you're planning on doing?"

Evangeline's finger flew to her mouth as she bounced onto the island with uncontainable joy.

"It's a secret! You have to promise not to tell anyone!"

Staccato held up his right hand. "Not a soul."

Evangeline flattened a hand over her heart and drew in a deep breath. "Alright then."

She crooked her finger at Staccato, beckoning him to come closer. Staccato could feel the hair raising up on the back of his neck. Trying to keep his smile within the limits of an appropriate size, he leaned towards her. The scent of wildflowers and salt water hung heavy in her hair. She put her lips beside his ear.

"I'm going to see Cavatina D'Sirena live at the Softshell Brewing Company in Black Beach!" she squealed.

Staccato jumped back in alarm, nearly falling into the water. Evangeline's hands flew up over her mouth.

"Oh, I'm sorry, did I scare you?"

Staccato rubbed his ringing ear. "I thought you were going to whisper it."

Water droplets ran down the incline of her nose as she pushed back her hair and smiled apologetically.

"Sorry! Everyone tells me I have a tendency to get a little overexcited!"

Staccato chuckled and scooted closer to her. "A little?"

Evangeline bit her lip and fooled with a lock of her hair so as to hide behind it. Staccato batted her hand back down. He'd grown bolder as of late.

"I'm sorry, dear, I didn't mean to embarrass you." Staccato drew her hair away from her face and tucked it behind her ear. "There's no need to cover up that pretty smile of yours."

She abated, letting her hands fall into her lap and leaning closer to him.

"Let me see if I understand," he began again. "You're going to attend a musical performance on the other side of town?"

Evangeline stuck out her chin with an overly confident smile. "Mhm!"

"In an old brewery warehouse—"

"It's been renovated—"

"—Into a pub."

Evangeline sucked her teeth with an air of impatience. "Not a pub, a coffeehouse!"

Staccato couldn't help but smirk a little. "Evangeline, they serve alcohol."

Evangeline widened her eyes as though doing so would drive home her point. "And coffee!"

"With whiskey in it."

"And where does it say a coffeehouse can't also serve alcohol? Does it really matter?"

Truth be told, he was really more concerned about keeping her out of trouble with her mother, but he wasn't sure how well Evangeline would respond to that.

"I would say it matters a great deal where you're concerned. One might argue that a renovated brewing company is no place for a princess on her own."

At this point it was useless for him to try and hide his oversized grin. To Staccato, pushing Evangeline's buttons was as delightful as cake. That little nose of hers would wrinkle up with the wrath of a vengeful goddess, and next thing he knew the mouth with the sweet smile would be cutting him up with an intellect so sharp it could scratch steel. Her shoulders were drawing up to her ears now.

"Might I point out that I have spent the past four years away at boarding school quite on my own, thank you very much! And if the idea of my frequenting such an establishment is so offensive to you, then I daresay you'd find my time away in Cassiopeia quite shocking! I may be a princess, but I am also an artist, and the Softshell Brewing Company happens to be a place of culture and—"

"Alright, alright!" He grabbed both her hands, laughing. "I didn't mean to insult your bohemian existence! I perfectly understand why you want to attend the performance."

Evangeline's cheeks colored as she drew a breath. "Mother can't know! It's to be an absolute secret from her!"

"Yes, but is your brother aware of this little outing?"

Evangeline bit her lip. "Which one?"

"You know which one."

Evangeline's shoulders rolled forward slightly. "Well, no, Theo doesn't know … But I wasn't planning on going alone!"

Staccato snickered and crossed his arms. "Weren't you?"

"No …" Hooking a stray hair behind her ear, she sidled closer to him. "I was hoping you would come with me. ..."

"You want me to chaperone you?"

"Well, not chaperone exactly. ..." She looked up at him from beneath her eyelashes.

Staccato froze. He could feel his heart racing. He and Evangeline may have strayed off the path during outings with her brothers and sister, but they never ventured far enough to raise any sort of alarm. Evangeline curled a hair around her finger and drew her shoulders together.

"You know Theo wouldn't mind!" She blushed even deeper. "After all, you're like our brother. ..."

Staccato's heart gave a disappointed throb. Like her brother? Had her feelings changed towards him?

"Oh," was all he could manage for the time being. Evangeline looked down at her lap and wrung her hands.

"Well, perhaps not like a brother, not a brother to me, a brother to my siblings, what I mean is ... B—but we ... we don't even have to go to the Softshell Brewing Company! We could do something else instead!"

Staccato piqued his head, his thoughts flying in several different directions.

"I thought the whole point of skipping the Christmas Luncheon was to see Cavatina D'Sirena."

"Well, no, the point was ... the real point was just to be with ... ." Her eyes seemed to be searching for a placc to land; finally, she looked up. Evangeline's whole body froze. Her face appeared to brighten.

"Perfect. ..." Her voice was just a whisper.

Staccato raised an eyebrow.

"What? What is it?"

His gaze followed hers. There, dangling from the molding on the column, was a sprig of mistletoe. Staccato furrowed his eyebrows in astonishment. Where had it come from? Surely, he would've seen it before while he was lying on the lounge; indeed, he'd stopped to stare at the ceiling several times during his musings, and yet he hadn't noticed it before.

As he continued to gape stupidly at the branch, Evangeline sprang forward, and the next thing he knew her lips were cupping his. Staccato was so stunned he could hardly move. All he could do was shut his eyes and allow the thrill to flow through his veins. At last she released him, sliding her fingers down his arms, then clasping both his hands.

"Evangeline, I ..." he opened his eyes. There, behind Evangeline, was a pale figure glaring at him from the doorway.

Staccato staggered back from Evangeline so quickly he almost fell into the water. It was Ms. Conch, and by the looks of it, she had been watching the two for some time. Her head was leaned forward as if to catch every detail of the exchange. There was no question she had seen the kiss.

"Ah," Staccato exclaimed loudly for Ms. Conch's benefit, "I, uh, I did not realize there was mistletoe there. Well, it would be a shame to break with tradition, wouldn't it? We must do as the rules say regardless of who's standing under it!"

Evangeline stared at him with uncomprehending eyes. Staccato made a discreet gesture for her to look over her shoulder but she didn't seem to catch it. Before he could make her understand, Theo was calling for him from the opposite doorway. Staccato quailed inwardly. He couldn't bear the look of injury staining Evangeline's countenance, but he would have to explain it all later. He hastily made his excuses and dashed out the door, leaving Evangeline alone.

As he skidded into the hallway, he nearly ran straight into Theo's trident.

"Ah, Staccato! There you are!" He looked Staccato over from head to toe, then frowned. "What's the matter with you? You're upset about something. …" He tilted his head to one side, examining him. " …Yet also excited."

Staccato quickly turned him round and marched him in the opposite direction.

"I'll tell you every detail as soon as we get to the absolute most opposite part of the castle as possible."

Theo dug his heels into the ground, and tossed Staccato a wry grin over his shoulder.

"This has something to do with Evangeline, doesn't it?"

"Will you just move?" He scratched at his mouth. "Please! It's not funny!"

"Oh, but I beg to differ!"

Staccato opened his mouth for a retort and found that his lips felt slightly sore. He was sure they had become chapped in the frigid weather. His eyes bulged. What if Evangeline noticed? Giving up, Staccato veered around Theo and took off at a brisk pace down the passage. He rubbed at the space between his eyebrows. The whole ordeal was making his head pound.

"Staccato, slow down!" He could hear Theo's feet slapping the floor as he ran after him. "I was only joking!"

"Yes, well, let me tell you it was no laughing matter!" The pain in his head hammered harder and Staccato was forced to stop and steady himself against a pillar. Theo grabbed hold of his elbow.

"Staccato, are you feeling alright?"

Staccato let out an involuntary gasp as the muscles in his arms and shoulders cramped with unbearable tension. He slumped forward on his knees, still bracing himself against the column. The last thing he could remember before blacking out was Theo kneeling beside him and calling for help.

***

The weeks followed in a feverish blur. Staccato was not kept in the Advisory Quarters, but was placed in a bedroom nearer the family. The way the bed sank into the watery floor was almost boat-like. Breezy curtains of white chiffon surrounded him on all sides like the veils of ghosts, and he sometimes thought, in his delirium, that he was out to sea.

In the beginning, caims were constantly about him, placing their hands on his head and chanting. Always the air was smoky and spiced with incense and healing oils. Oftentimes Staccato could hear his own cries of agony erupting through choruses of mermaid singing. It felt as though someone were pulling all the ligaments in his arms, legs, and back until he thought every muscle in his body would tear.

A terrible sense of dread plagued him, and he was certain of his own death. The sensation could only be described as laying beneath a guillotine for hours at a time, never knowing when the deadly blade was going to drop. The anticipation nearly drove him mad, until he pleaded with the doctors to kill him, unable to endure the terror of waiting.

The voices of the Soters were always floating nearby with soothing words and loving gestures. When the pain was most excruciating, they were his greatest comfort.

"Now hold still, Staccato," Estella would say. "Hold still while I put this cloth on your head."

"Everything will be fine," Theo reassured him as Staccato drifted in and out of consciousness. "The pain will pass, I'll call upon every doctor in the kingdom if I have to!"

Javaid, who was a skilled healer, often woke him when he braced his hands on Staccato's shoulders and spoke in the strange language known as Healer's Tongue.

Evangeline was present most of all, even sneaking in during the night. She would turn over his arms and massage the muscles near the crook of his elbow with some sort of invigorating oil. He could remember her whispering things to him but could never actually remember anything she said.

When the first few days had passed, the worst of the illness ebbed away. The cramps and the dread were erased, but Staccato remained feverish and continued to drift in and out of consciousness. As a result, he was often confused in his waking moments. Gradually, he became aware that Theo had not visited him for some time. When he at last managed to grab a moment of fleeting alertness, he was able to ask where the eldest Soter had disappeared to.

"He's … fallen ill," Evangeline hastily explained with her eyes cast downwards.

As Evangeline spoke, Staccato noticed Javaid watching her with an acute intensity.

"Evangeline, why don't you go check on Theo?" Estella suggested authoritatively.

Staccato hadn't been aware of Evangeline holding his hand until it slipped away. Waves sloshed around the bed as she lowered herself into the water and swam out into the corridor.

"Are Theo and I both ill?" Staccato managed to get out, his mouth feeling dry.

Estella reached over and wiped his forehead with a damp handkerchief.

"I'm afraid so, pet."

"With what?"

"You caught Wode's Virus."

Panic struck hard in his chest. He struggled to sit up. "If that's true, then you shouldn't be near—"

"It's alright," she assured him, gently pushing him back against the pillows. "The three of us have an immunity."

"An immunity?" Staccato raised his eyebrows. "Really?"

Estella managed a weak smile and nodded. Javaid did nothing.

Evangeline visited him again later that evening around the time when everyone else was preparing for bed. Light had slid from the lamp when she turned the dial, and Staccato's eyes fluttered open. He hadn't been far from sleep, but when he saw Evangeline poised on the edge of the bed he didn't mind the disturbance.

Staccato was too foggy to think of anything to say just then, and Evangeline did not break the silence. She went straight into her routine, turning up his left palm as she often did before massaging the muscle, only this time she took his wrist and lifted it to her lips.

"Did your mother ever give you mermaid kisses as a child, Staccato?"

"She did," he answered in a vague, distant voice. "I could feel all her love spread over me in this sense of uncontainable joy." He paused for a moment, feeling noticeably more open than usual. "It must be nice to be able to do that. If ever someone doubted your affections you could always reassure them simply by kissing the underside of their wrist."

Evangeline stared at him for a long while before smiling suddenly.

"I suppose you're right."

Without another word she bent down and pressed her lips to the tender flesh beneath his palm. For a moment, Staccato's spirit seemed to lift out of his body entirely. A lightness reached every corner of his soul, filling even the emptiest of places. It was somehow different from the mermaid kisses his mother had given him, in that it was a different kind of love.

When she drew away, Staccato was speechless. She placed her fingers on the side of his neck and began tranquilizing him into sleep.

"Now you'll never have to doubt my affection for you."

Staccato was never able to make a reply, he had fallen asleep too quickly.

***

When the second week finally dawned, Staccato awoke tired but pain-free. A cold sweat clung to his body. The fever had broken. His eyes travelled to the windowpanes overhead. Snowy crystals were knitting themselves in chains across the glass. He pulled the bedclothes closer around his shoulders and shivered.

Ripples formed in the doorway, and he could just make out Estella's lavender tail as she swam under the walkway and up to his bedside. Slowly, her eyes appeared over the edge of the bedframe.

"It's alright, Estella," he laughed. "I'm awake, and I believe my fever has broken."

A smile pinched the corners of her eyes as she rose up.

"Truly?" She hoisted herself onto the edge of the platform, reached out, and placed her hand on his forehead. "So it has!" She grabbed both his hands, yanked him forward, and threw her arms around his neck. "Oh, dearest Staccato, you have no idea how glad I am!"

Tears fell like hot raindrops onto his shoulder, and her last words came out in loud sobs. Though Estella was known for her excellent ability to keep her head in a crisis, the moment everything was safe she fell into absolute histrionics.

"To think you could have almost died! Oh, I can hardly bear it!"

Staccato's head throbbed; his fever may have broken, but he was still weak. As she squeezed him tighter he gave an involuntary grunt.

"Oh, pet, I'm sorry!" She dropped him at once, letting his head flop back on the pillows. "I shouldn't have had you sit up yet."

Staccato held up his hand to steady her as well as to ward her off. "It's fine, really. Still a bit weak, is all." He glanced up at the sprig of bushy red Sylose pinned to the bedpost. "I take it you're responsible for this?"

Estella smiled bashfully and cast her eyes down. "It's supposed to help with inflammation."

"And what indigenous tribe invented that remedy?" He smirked knowingly at her. "The Zakis-Aja of the Wakenoro?"

"The Abojo, actually, of the Smoke Plains." Her eyes beamed with pride.

"Ah, I see. I shall have to make a pilgrimage one day to thank them. Or perhaps you can do it for me when you visit someday. They can make you their patron saint."

"Don't tell mother!" she quickly warned him.

"Why not? She does have a penchant for applying botany to pharmaceuticals, does she not?"

Estella glanced off to the side. "She would say it was superstition, and you know how she feels about my interest in travel … or what she calls, 'travel to uncivilized places.'"

Staccato let out a fatigued sigh. "Well, then, you know me. I won't say a word." He offered her a weak smile. "How is Theo?"

"His fever broke yesterday. He didn't seem to have had the virus as badly as you. That isn't to say we weren't afraid for his life at times, as well."

She smoothed his covers in her neat manner and checked the coals in one of the fire pits hanging near the bed. With Staccato's newfound awareness, the gravity of his situation sank in for the first time. He had contracted the Wode's Virus, a disease that claimed the lives of 32,000 people, and he had almost died. He was hardly an adult, and he had faced mortality.

His thoughts drifted to Evangeline. The memory of the mermaid kiss rose to the front of his mind. It was as though she had kissed him all over again. Joy flooded his veins as he was struck with an overpowering

urge to see her. As he turned his head to ask Estella where the youngest Soter had gone off to, a small glass ornament resting on the windowsill caught
his eye. It was the figure of a breathtaking white bird with gorgeous quills
spilling from the crown of its head, almost like an ornate headdress. It must
have been some sort of waterfowl, for the legs were rather long.

"Evangeline made that for you while you were ill," explained Estella, placing it in his hand.

Staccato held the figure to the light, turning it this way and that, and
smiling in admiration.

"It's beautiful."

"It's a secretary bird."

Staccato smirked. "It resembles her in a way, don't you think?"

Estella turned to give him a one-armed hug and laughed. "How silly
you are! What makes you say such a thing, pet?"

Staccato blushed slightly, too shy to offer an explanation. "Where is
Evangeline?"

Estella was just lighting a stick of incense when the mention of her
sister nearly caused her to drop the rod.

"Evangeline? You want to know where Evangeline is?"

"Yes, I would very much like to see her."

Estella held the stalk of incense over the smoking bowl until a little
yellow flame appeared at the end.

"I'm afraid she's rather busy this morning." She waved the fire out
until it was a mere glow, then placed the incense in its holder. "But never
you fret, I'll tell her you sent for her, and I'm sure she will come as soon as
she gets a chance."

But Evangeline did not come. She did not come for three days. Everyone made her excuses as often as they could. She was at a party, she had
an exhibition, she was invited to a concert.

Soon Staccato was well enough to get back on his feet and join the
family at the breakfast table. He had been waiting for this moment for some
time, faithfully doing as the caim said, religiously taking his medicine, all
so he could see Evangeline and confess his feelings for her.

His near-death experience had been like a sieve, straining all his pri-
orities until only the most valuable things remained. The largest of those
treasures was Evangeline. If it was truly wrong for the advisor to love the
princess then so be it; he would resign. But he was now convinced that a
life with Evangeline was far more precious than the prestige of his job.
When he finished washing and dressing, Staccato raced down to breakfast.

The dining room was a wide vaulted space like most rooms in the palace. The table itself was a fountain, with trays of food floating atop a shallow pool while water gushed down the front in a continuous waterfall. Surrounding the table on three sides was a series of cushioned lounges called triclinium. Mermaids always dined on triclinium, laying out on their stomachs so their tails could dangle into the water.

Atergatis was already reclining at the head of the table, her dainty fingers picking at a plate of orange slices. Estella and Javaid were on her left side. Theo was just laying down. He had a silken robe thrown over his bare chest and was rubbing his hands up and down his arms. In truth, he did not look as recovered as Staccato. His skin had paled into a sallow greenish color and there were dark circles under his eyes. At the sight of Staccato, his lips parted in a feeble smile.

"Ah, look who it is!"

Staccato chuckled and took the chaise beside him. "Are you sure you feel well enough to be up and about, Theo?"

"Me?" Theo patted his shoulder and laughed. "From what I hear, you were far worse off than I was."

Estella held out a bowl of eggs and immediately began spooning them onto Theo and Staccato's plates.

"Here, you boys eat up, you need your strength."

Javaid put his hand on Estella's shoulder and tried to pull her back.

"Yes, alright, Mother Hen, they're grown men, they can feed themselves."

But Estella shook him off. "Even grown men need a little extra care from time to time."

Staccato glanced at the remaining empty seat. "Shouldn't we wait for Evangeline?"

A noticeable silence fell over the table. Estella seemed to scrape the eggs out quicker, Javaid hid his mouth in his coffee, and Theo's face grew dark. Only Atergatis maintained her high spirits.

"Oh, she'll be along shortly—Estella, must you scrape that bowl so loudly?—She stays busy at her vanity these days."

She examined the slice of orange at the end of her fork like a cat admiring a particularly large mouse she'd just caught.

"Oh?" Staccato had a feeling she was baiting him, but he was delighted by the idea that Evangeline might be primping for him, and decided to ignore his suspicions. "Why is that?"

Atergatis opened her mouth to answer, but Theo slammed down his fork.

"No reason. There is no reason why Evangeline would be spending more time at her vanity than usual. It wouldn't surprise me if she overslept, what with all her worrying lately." He nodded to Staccato. "She hardly left your side, you know."

Staccato scanned the collage of faces circling the table. It was clear something had happened that nobody wished to talk about, nobody except Atergatis. Could it have been that Evangeline had fallen ill? No, there would be no reason to keep that a secret.

Soft footsteps echoed in the doorway. Staccato turned and looked over his shoulder. Evangeline was making her way down the stairs in a rose-colored dressing gown. Staccato instinctively stood, though no one else at the table did.

"Ah, there she is, dear girl!"

At the sight of him, Evangeline took a step back, but Staccato didn't think much of it. He took her hand and pressed his lips against the soft skin.

"Theo tells me you were quite the little nurse during my illness. And here I was thinking the lovely angel at my bedside was just a dre—"

"Evangeline, come and sit down at once!" Atergatis threw down her fork. "You've kept everyone waiting long enough with your dawdling!"

Staccato was tempted to point out that Atergatis had indeed not waited for her daughter and was already halfway through her plate, but it wasn't worth the strife. Evangeline slipped out of Staccato's grasp without even looking at him and hurried to the table. When everyone was settled, Staccato immediately resumed his charm.

"I see it snowed quite a bit while I was sick." He smirked. "It's perfect weather for reading. Evangeline, perhaps you could help me find something in the library later."

Turning his head, he threw her a discreet wink. When he faced the table again, Javaid was staring at him with a raised eyebrow. Staccato blushed. His flirting skills really were not what they should have been. Atergatis pushed back her plate.

"Evangeline, where's your ring?"

Evangeline's shoulders tensed. She stared at her mother with wide eyes.

"M—my—"

"Where is your ring? Why aren't you wearing your engagement ring?"

And there it was, the secret. Theo drew a deep inhale through his nostrils and threw his napkin down.

"I—I needed to—that is, it needs cleaning," she managed to get out.

Staccato felt as though his spirit were leaking through a hole in his chest.

"Cleaning?" Atergatis tossed her head back and laughed. "Well, that is like you. In the future, you must strive to take better care of it. I'm sure Mr. Nimbus would have loved to have seen it this morning, seeing as this is the first he's hearing of the engagement." She reached across the table for Staccato's hand, as though he were suddenly an old friend. "It happened just a few days ago."

"I wouldn't lament, Staccato," Theo hissed, pouring himself more coffee. "I too knew nothing about the engagement until recently. You see, I was unable to involve myself in the marriage negotiations due to my indisposition. Otherwise I can assure you things would've turned out quite differently. That being said, I did have Javaid and Estella to serve in my place. …"

Atergatis sucked her teeth. "Hardly a necessary procedure, I must say, given that I am Queen."

"Queen Mother," Theo corrected her, "Queen Stepmother, actually."

"Well, I'm not Evangeline's stepmother, am I? The rest of you needn't concern yourselves with the affair. Evangeline is my daughter, and from here on out I will oversee the wedding plans."

"You most certainly will not," Theo snarled. "You tried your best, Atergatis. You took advantage of my absence, and you forced Evangeline to accept Bruin's proposal. I do not doubt you were counting on my demise, but unfortunately for you I did not perish. Javaid and Estella may not be willing to stand up to you—"

"Theo," Javaid began with a groan, but Theo did not stop.

"But I am! Evangeline will not be marrying Bruin against her will."

Staccato could not help but notice the look of shame infecting Estella's eyes.

Javaid lowered his eyebrows and hissed in a quiet voice. "Theo, this is hardly the time or place!"

"Nonsense, seeing as you failed to deal with this issue in my absence, I must set the matter right at once!"

"Careful, brother, you don't know everything yet. …"

Atergatis sat up, appalled. "Evangeline isn't marrying anyone against her will! The child wants to marry Bruin, don't you, dearest?"

Evangeline bent her head to her chest. Before she could answer, Theo turned on her like a vengeful lion.

"You don't have to lie for her, Evangeline!"

Evangeline's chest was heaving now; she fingered the ribbon on her collar and finally managed to meet Theo's gaze.

"Sh—she's not lying. I want to marry Bruin. I do!"

Javaid looked at Theo and threw up his shoulders as though to say, "What am I supposed to do about that?"

Theo narrowed his eyes suspiciously. "You want to marry Bruin? Why?"

Staccato could hardly bear to remain at the table, and yet he wanted so badly for Theo to be right. Surely, Evangeline had not willingly consented to this marriage.

"Because … Because I love Bruin!" Evangeline shook her head back and forth. "That's all there is to it."

But Theo still wasn't buying it. "What could you possibly love about that overly dramatic scoundrel?"

"He's poetic," she scratched the space behind her ear. "He's artistic, deep, thoughtful. Why wouldn't I want to marry him? We're so alike, he and I. It will be a perfect match, don't you agree?"

"Evangeline, if Atergatis has threatened you in any way, if she has forced you through violence or threat of violence, you can tell me. I swear by my trident I will not let her hurt you. And you needn't feel that you have to protect her. I have not forgotten that she is your mother, and you can rest assured I will deal with her mercifully."

Atergatis's red, fleshy nostrils flared as she rose up and pointed an incensed finger in Theo's face.

"How dare you!"

But Evangeline was on her feet in an instant.

"Stop this, Theo! That's enough! I know my heart, and can't bear to have you questioning my feelings any longer! I realize as King you are accustomed to getting your own way, but the fact remains that I am in love with this man you call a scoundrel, and I'm afraid you'll have to accept that."

And with that, she fled the dining room in tears. Staccato pushed his plate back. He could not eat. In fact, if he didn't know any better, he would've said his illness had rebounded. Evangeline did not love him, she loved Bruin. The incident with the mistletoe meant nothing. It was not out of her character, after all, to flirt and play, to kiss the person standing under the mistletoe regardless of who it was. He wondered too if she hadn't been using him as a way to sneak off to a concert she was forbidden from seeing. And as for the mermaid kiss? Well, it must have been a dream.

Chapter 33:
Tea with Mother

On the sidewalk outside the hotel, Sonata leaned over the back of Pyro's wheelchair and fussed with his tie.

"Ow! Sonata, cut it out!"

"Don't you want to look nice for lunch?"

Pyro fiddled with the knot. "It's just Ma, it's not like we're meeting with the judicial secretary of Betelgeuse or something."

Sonata balked at him. "She's the Queen of Aries, and you should want to look nice for her regardless."

Pyro shrugged. "She don't care."

"And can you please try to talk with a little more refinement? You know how she hates that."

"If she wanted me to sound posh like her, she shouldn't have sent me away to that boarding school in the Pan."

Sonata pinched the space between her eyebrows. "I know you resent her for that, but she didn't know what else to do. You were out of control."

"Look, Sonata, I know you care and all that, but it's not your job to patch things up between me and my family."

The moment it became safe to cross the street, Pyro sat up and glued his hands to the wheels.

"And for goodness' sake, I can drive myself!"

Sonata seized the handles, preventing Pyro from going anywhere.

"Need I remind you how you busted your head yesterday? You were doing wheelies in the lobby."

Pyro threw up his hands and sputtered. "You fixed me up fine!"

"Lucky for me, you have a thick skull. That was a nasty fall, and Staccato gave me strict orders not to let it happen again."

"*Oi*, my parents pay Staccato, he can't tell me what to do."

"In that case, why don't you try changing your bandages tonight and see how that goes?" She let go of the chair and allowed him to propel himself to the other sidewalk.

"Maybe I will!"

"And you can lay out your clothes for tomorrow."

Pyro waved his hand. "That's easy."

"I put your suitcase on the top shelf of the closet."

He nodded his head. "Fine, fine."

"You're about to hit a pothole."

Pyro whipped around. "What'd you say?"

Pyro's left wheel dipped into a large hole. He soared onto the sidewalk where he collided with a trashcan full of cinderblocks. The trashcan swayed, then tumbled over onto his injured foot. A string of curses sprang from Pyro's mouth as he sat on the pavement clutching his foot. Sonata stood at his side and waited for him to finish.

"Would you like me to make it better?"

Pyro thrust out his lower lip. "Yes!"

Sonata unstuck the chair from the hole, helped him back into the seat, and set about dulling the pain.

***

Moments later they sat across from Pyro's merry-faced mother in the Archimedes. She had taken the liberty of ordering Pyro's tea. It arrived shortly after they sat.

Pyro took a moody sip. He paused. He looked down at his cup with pleasant surprise. Bravery reached across the table and patted his cheek.

"Cinnamon chai with a drop of whiskey. You didn't think I had forgotten, did you?"

Pyro coughed into his elbow and set the cup aside.

"Well, no wonder you're always complaining about forgetting things, Ma. You're too busy remembering silly things that don't matter."

Bravery appeared unperturbed by her son's brash behavior as she unfolded her napkin and laid it in her lap.

"So, when are you coming down to see the baby?"

Pyro glanced dully over the top of his menu. "What baby?"

"Candescence had her third last month."

Pyro nearly fell out of his wheelchair. "Dessa had another baby?"

Sonata laid her hand on Pyro's elbow. "Don't you remember, Pyro? Your mother wrote last month with the news. I laid it on your dresser."

Pyro cocked an eyebrow. "No. ..."

Sonata tightened her jaw and leaned forward with emphasis.

"Yes, remember how excited you were for your sister?"

But the damage had already been done. Bravery's spritely eyes were crestfallen.

"It's alright, Sonata. You don't have to cover for him. He never read the letter."

Her lower lip trembled. Pyro surged across the table for her hand.

"Ma! Come on, Ma, don't start that!"

Before he could say any more, a shrill bird-like whimper escaped Bravery's throat. All at once she erupted in a shower of loud, sopping sobs.

People at the bar turned to stare. Waiters' eyes slid furtively to their little table in the corner.

"Ma," Pyro pleaded, "you're making a scene!"

Bravery choked through her tears. "How is it that when Arson died I lost two sons?"

Confusing the table cloth with the napkin in her lap, she dabbed violently at her eyes. Pyro winced.

"Ma, don't talk about it!"

Her mood took a hairpin turn and she slammed her fist on the table. "We need to talk about it! You think I don't know the real reason why you won't come home?"

Pyro kept his head low between his shoulders. His eyebrows knitted together with pain. He was determined not to move an inch.

"Well, I didn't think you wanted me around much, since you decided I'd be better off overseas at that stupid academy!"

"Your father and I agreed you needed structure."

"How about a family structure?"

"Pyro, you know we did everything we could to provide you with stability. But you were bent on destroying yourself!"

"Then you should have let me finish!"

Sonata and Bravery both froze, but Bravery stared back at him, nonplused by his declaration.

"What happened to Arson wasn't your fault."

"It was completely my fault." His voice was strident and dark. "I'm the one who got Dessa and me caught, and Arson died to get us out. It was a prisoner exchange!"

Bravery matched him with equal fervor. "Well, the fact of the matter is you're here now. Your brother didn't give his life so you could waste yours apart from your family. We love you, Pyro, and we miss you."

Pyro sat with his head bowed low over the table. Half a minute passed before he moved, and when he did he wheeled himself away from the table and out the door.

Chapter 34:
Breaking the Rules

The sound of pages of notes turning in the Judge's hands fluttered into the microphone as Staccato awaited the next question.

"So, you never at any point before Evangeline's marriage to Bruin made your affections known to the girl?"

Staccato gave a testy shrug. "No."

The Judge stared at him in genuine astonishment.

"Never?" The appalled manner in which she gaped at him made Staccato uncomfortable.

"As I said, no. Is this question really necessary?"

Samael scrambled for his microphone, sending a whirlwind of papers across the box. Feedback pierced the court's ears.

"It's absolutely necessary! It's vital that the Council understands the nature of your relationship with this woman so we can determine whether or not your …" his eyes narrowed on Lydia, "'adopted daughter' isn't really your lovechild with the Queen, Mr. David Kingsley."

He drew out his words, emphasizing Staccato's birth name. Several of the Fay covered their mouths, appalled. Judge Alba pounded on her gavel.

"Cobra Samael, I ask that you please refrain from using Mr. Nimbus's birth name in the courtroom. Most Fay take offense to that."

Samael held up a hand. "My apologies, Your Honor. I was merely trying to emphasize the deceit employed to construct Mr. Nimbus's double life."

Staccato slammed his fist down on the desk. "Can you even prove I had relations with Her Highness?"

Samael smiled and gleefully opened to another entry in the diary. "*March twenty-first, 1889. …*"

***

Staccato watched as Evangeline propped her elbows against the side of the boat. She stared forlornly at the trail of moonlight falling across the water. Behind him, Javaid and Theo popped champagne bottles and laughed.

All around them the mermaids luxuriated in the plush excess of their canopied keels. The bay encompassed them in a wreath of festive music as all Karkinos swam to the surface to lend their hand in the merrymaking.

Javaid nudged his sister's shoulder and offered her a glass of champagne. She mumbled a decline. Theo uncorked a bottle with a little more force than was necessary.

"Nice for Bruin to finally let you come out and see your family, Evangeline." When she made no reply, he went on. "And don't try to give me any of that 'he misses me while I'm away' rubbish."

"No, he's with his whore, as usual." Her words were slow and measured, portioned out like spoonfuls of medicine. "But I shouldn't call her that. The poor girl probably doesn't know any better. I doubt she knows his real identity, or that he's married."

Theo placed a hand on her shoulder and tilted her chin up to look him in the eye.

"Don't go back."

Evangeline rolled her eyes and turned away.

"That's stupid, Theo. The Senate isn't going to approve your proposal to terminate the treaty to preserve something as trivial as domestic bliss."

Theo rubbed the side of his face. "At this point, even if you weren't married to Bruin, he's caused enough trouble to justify the destruction of the alliance. 'No disciple of Primal Instinct shall be held responsible for breaking the common law in accordance with their beliefs'? He's given the Primals license to do whatever they please!"

Evangeline shrugged. "It's all that awful Samael. He has Bruin convinced the attack on his family would never have happened if Ursine law allowed more freedom for Primals to practice their rituals. He said the oppressive nature of the legal system is responsible for creating a generation of zealots."

As usual, Javaid's voice was softer than Theo's. "I hear he's removing all Fay representation from chancery."

Evangeline didn't even try to argue, nor could she hide the contempt in her voice.

"Yes, he's considered that."

Theo held up a warning finger. "You realize he's one bad move away from me shredding our treaty, don't you?"

Out in the water, Constanza called flirtatiously to the two brothers.

"Javaid! Theo! We're getting up a game of Treasure Hunt! Come play with us!" She winked. "Javaid, you can be my captain!"

Theo and Javaid exchanged coltish glances. Without another word they dove into the water. As the couples' laughter died away, Staccato took a seat next to Evangeline amongst the overstuffed floor cushions.

"Didn't you want to play?"

"Treasure Hunt?" She scoffed. "Not interested."

Staccato frowned. "You missed one."

She looked at him over her shoulder. With a gentle hand he brushed away her long cascade of hair to point to a bruise on her lower back. Sighing, she reached around and pressed a finger against the injury. When the golden light failed to evaporate the blue shadow, she turned around in defeat. Staccato laid a blanket over her shoulders.

"You look lovely."

Evangeline winced as though the sentiment caused her physical pain. "Don't talk like that."

Staccato edged away shyly. "I didn't mean anything by it."

She twisted around, the bridge of her nose drawn tight with exasperation.

"That's the part which frustrates me. You shouldn't say things you don't mean. It confuses people."

"Perhaps that wasn't the best choice of words. When I said I didn't mean anything by it, I meant my intention was not to upset you. When I said you looked lovely, I meant just that."

She blinked her long lashes. "Lovely?"

Staccato nodded his head with impatience. "Yes! I may not be the most articulate person in the world, but I thought that was pretty straightforward."

Crossing his arms, he watched as she opened her mouth to correct him, then stopped and smiled instead. It was a broken smile, but a smile nonetheless. Staccato sipped his champagne and looked back at the stars through the thin, gauzy drapery.

"Don't go back," he discovered himself saying. He didn't recall giving this thought permission to leave his brain. But there it was, hanging suspended in the air. "Your brother's just waiting for an excuse to break the alliance anyway. Your marriage will be annulled. Don't go back."

"All of you say that as though it's so simple."

He shrugged. "Seems pretty simple to me."

"Of course it does, when you're only saying the words." She turned back around. There was a dare glimmering in her eyes that Staccato found irresistible. He examined the champagne in his glass in a bored manner.

"Does it? You wouldn't even have to say anything. Let Theo do all the talking for you while you stay here." He glanced back at her and was pleased to discover a scintillating spark of delicious anger.

"How is my marriage any of your business?"

By now Staccato's appetite for an argument had flowered to maturity, and he craved a reaction.

"I'm the King's counselor. Political analyzing is a part of my job, and considering your marriage to Bruin was motivated by little more than a sense of bureaucratic responsibility, I take an enthusiastic interest."

Evangeline glowered at him. "How dare you presume to know my reason for marrying anybody!"

"Forgive me, I'm afraid I'm being much too closed-minded. If it wasn't for political gain, tell me, why would you pledge yourself to an unfaithful brute? Why did you do it, Evangeline? Because I refuse to believe you ever loved that cad! Why did you let your mother talk you into something so detestable? Didn't you want to be happy?"

He massaged his forehead, unable to keep his words from flying out into the night. What was he doing? Evangeline was married, and yet here he was provoking her for no other reason than the thrill of her temper.

Her nostrils flared. A forced coolness washed over her. She smoothed her hair over her bare shoulders, refusing to make eye contact with him.

"I had my reasons, and that's all you need to know. Besides, it wasn't as though I had any better options waiting for me."

Staccato slunk down over his glass. "You had plenty of options."

Evangeline snatched the champagne glass out of his hands and splashed it in his face. Staccato stared at her dumbfounded as well as charmed. Evangeline sizzled.

"I think you've had enough."

Staccato blinked slowly and pretended not to have noticed what just happened.

"Do you have some sort of response?"

She chucked the wineglass over her shoulder in exasperation. "Alright, I'll bite. What options?"

"Me."

Evangeline sneered and turned away from him. "You're drunk."

"Actually that was my first glass of the evening. I had hoped to finish it, but you dumped it over my head."

Evangeline whipped round to glare at him.

"I'm quite sober." He sat up straighter. "You can test me if you like. I'll walk a straight line and everything. I'll do whatever you ask."

She faced him, a hint of suspicion in her expression. "Funny, I seem to recall you running away in horror after I kissed you in the library."

"That was because your mother's little henchman was standing in the doorway and had seen everything. I was planning on explaining later but I never got the chance."

"Never got the chance? You could have come and talked to me at any time!"

"I was on my deathbed!"

"After that, then!"

"You were engaged after that!"

"So? If I mattered so much to you, then why didn't you fight for me? Why didn't you make your feelings known? Or did you mean to say you were just offering yourself as a political alternative? Sounds like something you'd do."

Staccato sighed and pushed back his hair. His voice grew quieter. "If you haven't figured it out by now, feelings aren't exactly my forte."

"That's not true."

"Expressing them, then." He pressed his lips together and stared down at his feet. Evangeline edged closer.

"Why don't you give it a try now?"

Staccato felt something inside his chest pulling him towards her.

"I love you." He bowed his head, afraid to look in her eyes.

"You love me?" Her voice was almost hollow sounding, as though the meaning of the words had yet to reach her.

He nodded his head.

"And when did you discover this?"

Staccato closed his eyes and struggled to wind back his memory to the precise moment when he'd fallen in love with Evangeline.

"It's hard to pinpoint, really. I think perhaps it was when you said you wished there were more people like me. Or maybe it was when you told me to stop sounding so cruel. It could've been earlier, I suppose. Perhaps when you corrected me about the Empress of Scorpius, but then I didn't really know you yet. I'm not the best at recognizing these sorts of things. But I do know by the time your mother took it upon herself to throw you at Bruin, I loved you with an exhausting, relentless frustration."

He chanced a glimpse at her and was surprised to find her scowling. Her gilded eyes seemed to radiate a molten heat like the glass she heated inside her furnace. Tears burned wet trails down her cheeks.

"You loved me then?"

"I did."

"Why didn't you say something?"

"Because by the time I had decided to speak up you had already pledged yourself to Bruin." Staccato summoned his cup back to his hand and poured himself another glass of champagne. He hunched down with his arms crossed. "Anyway, it was selfish to pursue you."

"It's never selfish to love somebody."

Staccato gave a sharp scoff. "I don't know about that. I studied law; there's very little I do that doesn't revolve around a sense of self-importance." He was expecting her to laugh. "That was a joke."

She stared at him in a concerned manner. He looked down at his glass. Maybe he *was* drunk. He thought of his father. His shoulders bowed.

"I suppose it was all for the best. I did swear to put the country's needs ahead of my own, after all. Involving myself with you would have been wrong."

"Why do you keep saying that? That's ridiculous and you know it is!"

Staccato rubbed his temples and ground his jaw together. "Yes, but it's easier than facing the truth."

"What truth?"

He stared ahead of him. "If I had told you that I loved you then, what would you have done?"

"I would have told you I loved you too."

Staccato's nose wrinkled with a bitter, cynical laugh as he took another swig from his glass.

"Why on earth are you laughing?"

"Because you never loved me. If you did, you wouldn't have married Bruin."

Evangeline's mouth fell open in surprise. "How can you say such a thing after what happened between us?"

Staccato stared at her uncomprehendingly. "What? What happened?"

Slowly, she shut her eyes and nodded. "Of course, you don't remember. You were too sick."

His mind drifted back to the kiss Evangeline had planted on his wrist. He fingered his collar.

"I didn't leave you without letting you know how I felt. …"

"No," he whispered, half to himself. "You gave me a mermaid kiss." He stared down at the floor, embarrassed. "I thought it was a dream."

Staccato felt a warm, revitalizing flush over his shoulders that had nothing to do with the champagne. Not wanting to look like a fool, he forced his face to remain hard.

"But I still don't understand. If that's how you felt, then why did you decide to marry Bruin practically the next day?"

"Because if I didn't Mother would have killed you!"

Staccato's eyebrows rose. "Kill me?" In spite of himself he actually laughed. "Evangeline, I know your mother is a conniving harpy, but do you honestly think she could get away with murder? Murder right under the King's nose?"

There was true terror in her face now. "You have no idea what she's capable of!" Her tears thickened and she wiped at her eyes with the corner of her skirt.

Staccato offered her his handkerchief. "Dear girl, you let her get into your head! Atergatis could never actually kill me!"

Evangeline pushed the handkerchief away and threw up her hands.

"For the love of stars, Staccato, she already tried!"

Staccato blinked at her in amazement. "What?"

"Don't you understand? You never had Wode's Virus! She poisoned you, and in the cruelest way!"

Staccato leaned against the side of the boat, thinking. Had she poisoned his food? No, that would've been too obvious. His coffee? With as much as he drank she would have had several opportunities.

"The day you fell ill was the Christmas Luncheon," she explained. "I was hiding because I knew Bruin was going to propose to me. I had planned to confess my feelings to you that very morning. Well, I can't say my behavior wasn't predictable. Mother foresaw everything. She planted the mistletoe in the library when she went looking for me. She knew I would be hiding wherever you were."

Staccato held up his hand in confusion. "Wait, what has mistletoe got to do with anything?"

"The poison was in the lip rouge! Somehow she concocted the formula so that the poison could only be activated through the touch of another's lips."

"But it didn't poison you?"

Evangeline pinched the space between her eyes and waved her hand.

"Something to do with pheromones, and the jellyfish's immunity to poison oneself, I don't know, she explained it all to me but I didn't understand a word of it!"

"You mean she confessed? Why didn't you tell Theo?"

"She got to him before I ever had a chance!"

Staccato recoiled in disgust. "Your mother kissed Theo?"

"No! Theo kissed Phrygia!"

Staccato was completely blindsided. "Phrygia? The maid?"

Evangeline covered her eyes and groaned. "They've been seeing each other in secret for quite some time, as a matter of fact. Nothing unsavory, mind you. Theo is nothing if not a gentleman."

Staccato recalled how he'd seen Phrygia in the Poison Garden, how Atergatis had said she'd concocted a lip rouge that she thought would complement her skin. Staccato shuddered. He never would have suspected it. Evangeline went on.

"The Wode's epidemic gave her the perfect opportunity. All she had to do was find a poison that mimicked the disease."

"What did she use?"

Evangeline bit her lip. "Her jellyfish."

All Staccato could do was sit back, stunned. "I imagine even after Theo pulled through, you were too frightened to take action."

Evangeline's voice broke. "Exactly. Could anyone have figured out such a scheme? If I had refused to marry Bruin then surely she would have found a way to finish you off. She won't hurt you now, or Theo. She only poisoned Theo to frighten me into silence."

"Did Estella know?"

Evangeline nodded. "Oh, yes. Estella suspected Mother from the very beginning. Javaid sensed it but he could never prove anything." She reached forward and placed her hand on his knee. "That is the only reason I married Bruin, I promise. It was you I wanted to be with."

Staccato didn't know what to say. His eyes fixed on the floor.

"Don't you find me overly ambitious?"

"I find you careful and responsible."

"What about awkward?"

She giggled. "Your brain moves faster than your mouth, is all. I'm afraid for most people it's the other way around."

As Staccato turned to look at her, his eyes swelled. She gave him a desire to be known through and through. To his surprise, he found himself reaching for her hand. She laid her head on his shoulder.

"Do you think I'm a coward for not telling anyone about my mother?"

Staccato couldn't stop himself from wrapping his arms around her, from burying his nose in her hair.

"You married a monster to save my life, how could that be cowardly? I'm the coward. I couldn't even summon the courage to confess my love for you."

"But you did today. Now I'll always know that you loved me."

"Love," he corrected her. "I still … well, here."

He turned over her left arm and caressed the inside of her wrist with his lips. Evangeline closed her eyes and inhaled, overcome with emotion. Her cheeks lifted with a smile. Staccato wiped a tear from her face.

"I still love you."

They looked into each other's eyes, then everything combusted. Staccato wasn't sure which of them had moved first. He now found her lips were on his. His fingers tangled in her hair. Her arms encircled his waist.

"I love you, Staccato!"

"I love you," he murmured between kisses. "I love you, Evangeline." He repeated it over and over as she pulled him towards the floor of the boat.

Chapter 35:
Caught

Staccato was red-faced. He closed his eyes and pinched his temples, waiting for it all to be over. He couldn't bear to look Lydia in the eye and wished there was a way to have her excused from the court, but that was a hopeless endeavor. Sonata smacked him on the shoulder.

"'Can you prove it?' Do you even remember what you wrote in that stupid diary?" Her voice was barely above a whisper.

Staccato threw up his shoulders. "It was over thirty years ago!" He pinched the place between his eyebrows. "Sonata, I believe it's time you excused yourself for the remainder of the hearing. You've heard enough."

"Codfish!" she scoffed. "I'll do no such thing! I'm made of sterner stuff than that."

Samael closed the diary and sniggered. Before Staccato could respond, Sonata leaned across him and seized the microphone.

"That letter was written in March of 1889, a full year before Mrs. Chevalsky was born. It proves nothing. Mathematically speaking, Staccato and Evangeline would have to have been …" she fumbled for the word, "intimate … in June of 1889 for there even to be a chance Staccato fathered Lydia."

Samael opened the diary again. "*June seventeenth, 1889. …*"

Staccato flashed Sonata a look, who shriveled into her seat.

***

Staccato pinned his chin on Evangeline's shoulder and wrapped his arms around her from behind. Sighing, she sank her head back and lightly kissed his jaw. Salt water sloshed beneath the windows as wave after wave was ushered into Evangeline's bedroom at Alveare. The moon was plowing for a June tempest. Evangeline spent weeks at a time back home now. Bruin hardly noticed her absence.

She turned so they faced each other. The strap of her cotton night-gown had slid off one shoulder. She traced a finger lovingly over Staccato's lips.

"I'll tell Bruin I'm leaving while you're visiting your mother in Aquarius."

Staccato frowned. "Darling, Theo said as soon as Bruin makes another slip-up he's using it as justification to end the alliance. You know he can hardly go a week without causing trouble. Just wait."

"It's been three months and so far he's done nothing worth breaking a treaty."

"But you know he will. You don't want to go making unnecessary difficulties."

She combed back his bangs and sighed. "I want to get it over with."

"I know, but it's dangerous. Not only because of Bruin, but because of your mother."

Evangeline didn't seem to be paying attention. She was concentrating on outlining a patch of freckles with her finger just below his collarbone. He clasped her hands and willed her to look at him.

"Eve, listen! Wait until I get back from Aquarius."

She turned away from him and yanked the covers up over her shoulders. "I'm tired of waiting!"

Staccato couldn't help but smile. He laid his cheek against hers and stroked a finger down her spine as thunder rattled the windowpanes.

"You're rather impatient, did you know that?"

"Am I?" She tilted her head back and tossed him a teasing glance.

"You can't bear delayed gratification."

She sat up and stretched her arms over her head. "Example?"

"How about right now? If we get caught, there could be serious consequences."

Evangeline yawned in a careless manner. "Darling, if they haven't discovered us by now they're not going to."

Staccato propped himself up on his elbows and sighed.

"That's not a guarantee." A feeling of uneasiness twisted inside his chest. "Stars, we're in a house full of empaths!"

"And yet no one suspects a thing. Theo attributes your happiness to the prospect of my marriage being annulled. And as for me …" her eyes fell to the floor, and the smug little smirk vanished from the corners of her lips. "Well, I don't suppose anything is all that out of the ordinary." She fingered the collar of her nightgown and swallowed. "Not yet anyway."

Staccato shook his head. "If Bruin has any suspicions that you've been unfaithful it will look as though you were solely responsible for the alliance breaking."

Evangeline snorted. "You think just because I had an affair all Bruin's transgressions will be forgotten?"

"Unfortunately that's the reality of a scandal. Once it happens it's the only thing that matters. It's the only thing people remember."

Evangeline crossed her arms. "I don't care what people think of me."

Staccato rolled his eyes. For all her intelligence, she could be exhaustingly childish at times. He leaned over her, bracketing her with his arms.

"That's easy to say when you've never been at the center of one. Besides, if word got out, you're not the only one who would be affected. There's your brother to think about."

"How is my behavior Theo's fault?"

"It doesn't have to be his fault for people to blame him. Evangeline, the public as a whole isn't reasonable and forgiving. You're being naive. It won't be much longer now until the alliance breaks. You'll be released from any obligation to Bruin, and you and I can get married. Don't go rushing to tell Bruin you're leaving him. Stay at Alveare."

Thinking about the consequences burnt a hole of guilt within him. They were behaving irresponsibly, but something about Evangeline compelled him to defy his own nature.

Evangeline's shoulders stiffened. There was something fearful in the way she bit at her nails.

"Staccato, I want to get it over with now! He frightens me! I just want it to be over so I don't ever have to think of Bruin again!"

Staccato winced as a pang of remorse struck him from within.

"I know." He cradled his head in his hands and sighed. Evangeline reached out and pulled him into her arms.

"I'm sorry. I don't wish to frighten you. If it means that much I won't say anything yet." She reached across the bed and opened a drawer in her nightstand. "As for Mother, I know exactly how to deal with her." She rummaged around until she came across a pot of rouge. She held it up for Staccato to see. "I stole the rouge my mother gave to Phrygia, not only for everyone's safety but for evidence. When the time comes for my marriage to be annulled I'll show this to Theo and explain everything."

Staccato instinctively edged away from the container. "Are you sure you shouldn't be handling it with gloves or something?"

Evangeline giggled and, taking her handkerchief from the tabletop, wrapped it around the jar.

"If it makes you feel better." Carefully and quietly she returned the rouge to the drawer and sat back on the bed. "Do I really have a problem with delayed gratification?"

He chuckled. "You're a spoiled little princess." He began kissing his way up her arm. "An unbearable tease …" He reached her shoulder. "And I just can't help overindulging you!" He buried his face in her neck and squeezed her shoulders. Evangeline squealed and batted him away.

"Your hands are freezing! Let me get you another blanket."

She crossed to the dresser and flipped her hair haughtily over her shoulder.

"Now if I remember correctly, it was you who came into my room."

"You invited me."

She cocked her hand on her hip. "Perhaps you should learn to tell me no." She took a clean sheet from the drawer and draped it around her shoulders. Scoffing, Staccato slid off the bed.

"Have you met you?"

He staggered towards her. She pulled him into the sheet and rubbed her nose against his.

"You're not exactly easy to say no to, Eve."

"Alright, well, let's practice, shall we? I'll ask you to kiss me, and you tell me no."

He ran a finger beneath her chin. "That's impossible."

She threw back her head and puckered her lips. "Go on, kiss me."

Without even trying, Staccato dipped down to kiss her, but she pulled away. Evangeline stuck a finger in his face, trying not to smile.

"No."

Staccato grinned mischievously and pulled her in closer. Giggling, Evangeline covered her mouth and shook her head. Staccato wrenched her arms back and scooped her up. Evangeline laughed and kicked as he kissed her lips. The door swung open. Ms. Conch stood with a satisfied smile on the threshold.

"I knew it!"

Staccato nearly dropped Evangeline on the floor. Evangeline's mouth fell open in horror as the maid turned and dashed up the corridor.

"No!" She shook her head back and forth. "No, no!"

She hustled to shut the door and swiveled around, running her hands through her hair. Staccato threw on his shirt and scrambled to her side.

"What should I do? Where should I go?"

Evangeline looked more stork-like than ever, standing there frozen with her skinny shoulders hunched, her belly pushed forward, and her long legs locked. Her brows ran together as she took shallow breaths through her open mouth.

"Evangeline, darling!"

When she didn't answer, he turned to the churning pool beneath the window. Perhaps he could swim out beneath the wall and into the open water. Just as he was about to dive forward, Evangeline wrenched him back.

"No! There's lightning! You'll get electrocuted!"

The door burst open. Atergatis was pale with rage. She seized Evangeline by the wrist and wrested her around to face her.

"You little slut!"

Atergatis slapped her daughter so hard she stumbled back into the dresser. Bawling, Evangeline curled into herself on the floor. Atergatis grabbed her by the back of her hair and dragged her to her knees, forcing the girl to cry out.

Staccato slammed down his foot. "Stop it!"

The shelves shook in their brackets. Several of Evangeline's vases popped one by one into a shower of splinters. Atergatis paid Staccato no attention.

"I'm sorry, Mother," Evangeline pleaded, "I'm sorr—"

Atergatis backhanded her across the cheek. Evangeline flew backwards into the cheval mirror, and slipped onto the floor. The mirror rocked forwards and shattered over her head. Cuts materialized all over her body. Staccato threw himself in front of her.

"Stop it! You'll kill her!"

Outside, the waves roiled with a clap of thunder. Atergatis's fleshy pink nostrils flared.

"Get away from my daughter! Get out!"

Evangeline pinched Staccato's hand in desperation. "No! Don't go!"

"Evangeline, you will leave this house immediately!" Atergatis's hands shook. "You will go back to Polaris, and you will stay with your husband!"

"No! I'm never going back!"

"You insolent little snake! Do you realize what you're doing? Do you realize how this could impact our kingdom?"

"I deserve to be loved! Staccato loves me, and I love him!"

Footsteps echoed down the hall as Estella, Javaid, and Theo all came running towards the source of the noise, followed by four guards.

Theo ground to a halt at the threshold. He took in the scene with his commanding, authoritative gaze. He glanced from Atergatis frothing with rage, to the bedsheet on the floor. Fistfuls of Evangeline's hair were strewn amongst the mirror shards. He took in the image of Evangeline cowering in her nightgown, to Staccato in his unbuttoned shirt. Theo's eyes widened. He had grasped everything. Staccato couldn't bear to look him in the eye.

Theo's lips curled back as he turned to Atergatis. "You dare raise a hand to my sister?"

Atergatis pointed to Staccato. "Didn't I tell you to get rid of him?" Lightning fissured outside the window. "Now look what's happened! Your sister has become an adulterous little tart!"

Javaid and Estella crouched down beside Evangeline and set about healing the wounds her mother had inflicted.

"None of this would have happened if you hadn't practically forced her down the aisle in the first place!"

Atergatis pushed Staccato and reached for the back of Evangeline's neck.

"Get up!"

Staccato flew in front of Atergatis. Thunder crashed through the floors. Atergatis soared back against the wall. Staccato's mouth dropped. He hadn't meant to do it. He hadn't even lifted his hands, but his powers were out of control. Atergatis rose to her feet. Her eyes sizzled in their sockets.

"You dare attack your queen?"

Staccato shook his head, edging away from her. Theo stepped between them and leaned into Atergatis's face.

"You are not the authority here!"

"So what if he did attack you?" Estella challenged, stepping forward. "It would've been self-defense!"

Atergatis turned and sneered at her eldest daughter. "What are you insinuating?"

Estella held her head high. "I know what you did, Mother. Evangeline told me everything."

Theo looked from Estella to Evangeline. "Told you what?"

"You and Staccato never had Wode's virus," Estella explained. "When Mother saw Evangeline was in love with Staccato and not Bruin, she decided to poison him."

"I knew it!" exclaimed Javaid.

"And just to make sure Evangeline didn't go running off to tell you, she poisoned you as well. We were afraid to say anything! Afraid of what she might do if she could poison the both of you so easily!"

Atergatis tossed her head back and laughed. "What a ridiculous story!"

Theo held up his hand to silence her. "I wouldn't say that. After all,

I've never known either of my sisters to lie." He turned and pointed his trident at Atergatis's throat. "You on the other hand. ..."

Atergatis threw up her hands in submission. "You don't have any proof."

Evangeline nearly yanked the drawer from the nightstand. "Yes, I do!" She plunged her hand into the clutter and produced the jar of rouge. "This is the pot of lip rouge she gave to Phrygia. The poison is transferred to the victim through a kiss."

Theo's eyes ran off to the side. "Ph—Phrygia?"

Atergatis rolled her eyes. "Don't act like such a fool, Theo. Everyone knows about your little infatuation with the maid."

"The very same I was wearing when I kissed Staccato, minutes before he fell ill," continued Evangeline. "You can test it if you like, it's filled with toxins."

Atergatis rolled her eyes. "All my cosmetics are filled with toxins! It's perfectly safe!"

"Not in heavy doses. I'm certain you'll find the poison in this jar far exceeds the regular amount."

"Please," Atergatis scoffed. "All she's trying to do is cover her own guilt, the ungrateful little tramp! Do you realize what will happen if word gets out that she's been unfaithful? It will destroy the alliance!"

"The alliance is already destroyed, Atergatis," roared Theo, "and there was nothing Evangeline could have done to save it. I shall accept no more insults from Bruin, and his next offense will be justification for the Senate to approve my annulment of this treaty." Theo turned and pointed his trident at Atergatis. "And as for you, I've tolerated your abuse of my family enough over the years, and now that I am King I shall allow it no longer."

"You needn't worry about special treatment, Theo." Estella looked down at her mother in disgust. "You deal with her the same way you would any other criminal. Isn't that right, Evangeline?"

Evangeline nodded her head. "She can rot in prison for all I care!"

Theo nodded to the guards standing by the door. "Arrest this woman!"

Before Atergatis could move she was taken up by two sentries and bound in handcuffs. She looked around, speechless. Theo continued to point his trident at her.

"Atergatis, you are hereby charged with attempted murder and assassination of the King. May the courts deal with you justly!"

"Fine, fine!" She shouted as they tried to restrain her. "The kingdom will never last under your leadership, Theo! And do you know why? Because you're not willing to sacrifice, not like me! I laid my husband on the altar for this country!"

"What are you saying?" Theo managed to get out, his voice shaking.

"I would rather have seen your father dead than let him make one more harmful decision against the kingdom's welfare! And so I poisoned him, for the good of the family name, for the good of my daughters, and the good of the people! I killed your father!"

Staccato let out a gasp. Estella's knees went weak. Javaid braced himself against the wall, and Evangeline sobbed. For a moment, Theo's face was pale, then he pulled back his trident and charged forward with an angry cry. Javaid held him back.

"Take her away! Quickly! And send Ms. Conch with her!"

The guards shut the door behind them, leaving them all to wonder in silence. Evangeline continued to weep quietly in the corner. After a while, Estella got to her feet and helped her into her bed. Theo kept his face covered for some time. Staccato was sure at any moment he would burst into tears, but he did not. At length, he set his shoulders and turned to stare at Staccato.

Staccato struggled to gather the appropriate words. "Theo, I …"

Theo held up his hand and shook his head. He helped Staccato to his feet, and motioned for Javaid.

"See to the girls. We'll return in a moment."

Staccato followed Theo outside to the garden in the storm, weaving beneath the covered walkway. They stopped near a rose hedge. The Poison Garden sat mere feet away. With the breeze stirring the trees, Staccato could smell the oleander stronger than ever.

Rain pattered off the roof and sluiced down the columns on either side of them.

"You have endangered my sister." Lightning flickered, casting shadows across Theo's grave expression.

Staccato burned with shame. "I know, I should never have—"

"You have compromised her virtue! You have risked her reputation! How long has this been going on?"

Staccato looked down at the ground, his voice barely audible. "Three months."

Theo's eyes bulged. "Three months? Staccato, you could have—she could be—"

Theo pressed a hand over his mouth and released a heavy exhale. Staccato knelt before his king with heavy remorse.

"I'm so very sorry. I betrayed your trust. I have scandalized your family. I exposed your sister to adultery, and by doing so I did not treat her with the love and respect she deserves. And I certainly knew better. I have been very selfish, and I hope you will come to forgive me. I know I deserve banishment. I'm willing to accept whatever punishment you feel appropriate."

Theo stared at him in hard, unrelenting silence. When at last he spoke there was a subtle gentleness running beneath the supremacy in his voice.

"Until the alliance is shattered you are not to enter my sister's company unchaperoned. I've spoken with the Senate, our contract with Ursa shall terminate upon the next offense, at which time the two of you are free to marry if you so desire. But until you wed, you shall not lie with her. You shall not touch her in any manner less than befitting that of a gentleman, nor may you look at her without the purest of intentions." He was stern but merciful. "There shall be no punishment beyond this. You are lucky I am a mermaid and thus have the power to know you love her most sincerely. If this were not so, you would have great reason to fear my retribution. As it is, I forgive you. You will remain in this house, remain in my service, and remain my brother whom I love."

Staccato's mouth fell open. He couldn't believe what he was hearing. With his head still bowed, he nodded.

"Yes, Your Majesty, thank you."

Theo's voice remained steady as he corrected him.

"If you call me 'Your Majesty' one more time, I may be forced to change my mind." He yanked Staccato to his feet. "Prepare yourself, for there will always be natural consequences to our bad choices. But you will not face them alone. It is all behind us, Staccato. You are forgiven."

They stood in silence for some time before Staccato cleared his throat in an attempt to lighten the mood.

"So, you and Phrygia. …"

Theo raised an eyebrow but smiled at the same time. "You really want to bring that up now?"

Watery footsteps splashed towards them as Estella made her way across the garden.

"Estella," Theo scolded, "you shouldn't be out—"

Ignoring him, Estella reared her hand back and slapped Staccato in the face.

"What were you thinking?" At once her face softened and she pulled him into a hug. "Oh, come here you dear, stupid thing!" She kissed the stinging place where she had slapped him and squeezed his hands. "At least I know you love her, and I know you'll do right by her."

Staccato's voice was deep and sincere. "I promise I will!"

The three of them jumped as a bash of thunder echoed across the sky. Out of the dark a figure flew at them. It was Atergatis, her mouth open in rage, her wet hair falling in stringy clumps around her shoulders. With a wild cry she hooked her tethered hands around Staccato's neck and began choking him.

Staccato clutched at his throat, gagging and gasping. He threw himself forward. Atergatis soared over his shoulders, somersaulted across the flagstones, and fell straight into the moat of jellyfish surrounding the Poison Garden.

A white cloud formed as the ghostly figures swarmed about her, attaching themselves to her body and pumping their toxins into her blood. For a split-second a convulsing Atergatis breeched the surface, screaming and clawing at her skin. Theo threw his arm around Estella and hid her face against his shoulder.

It was over in seconds. There was nothing they could have done. The adrenaline was more than her heart could take.

Atergatis was dead.

Chapter 36:
Triumph

Back at the hotel, Pasha, Cicada, and Faina crowded into Pasha's sitting room and giggled over cokes with peanuts. Faina hung upside down from the couch with her stocking feet propped against the wall. Her hair brushed the rug. Pasha lay on his back beneath her. Above them, Cicada floated in her glittery cloud.

Faina pointed her toes. "How do you think the hearing is going?"

Pasha shrugged and rubbed the back of his head. "Gee, we've been so busy with the shard I completely forgot about the hearing."

Faina gestured to the mirror lying on the counter. "We could always check in. To be honest, I'm surprised no one's called us."

Cicada swooped towards the kitchen and retrieved the calling glass. "Shall I ring for Staccato?"

Pasha threw her a thumbs up. Cicada held the mirror at arm's length and turned around.

"Staccato … Staccato … Staccato …"

"What time is it in Voiler right now?" asked Faina, looking back at Pasha over her shoulder.

"About nine o'clock. Everyone should be settled for the night."

Meanwhile, Cicada was growing more and more frustrated with every turn. "Staccato! Staccato! Staccato!"

Pasha threw up his hand. "Cici, calm down before you make yourself dizzy. Try Sonata."

Groaning, Cicada gave it another go. After six turns there was a fumbling noise. Cicada's reflection disappeared, and a voice reverberated into the glass.

"Shhh," hissed Sonata, "it's Pasha!"

Pasha climbed onto the sofa as Cicada settled between them. "Hello?"

Cicada lit up. "Good evening, Sonata!"

Pasha and Faina leaned over her shoulders and waved. There was a strange clamor from Sonata's end, as though someone were struggling with a door. Sonata glanced off to the side, and turned the mirror towards the ceiling.

"Pull, not push!"

She directed the mirror towards her face again and smiled.

"Just wondering how the hearing is going," said Pasha, clearing his throat.

Sonata's eyebrows rose. "The hearing? You want to know about the hearing?"

Pasha eyed her. "Yeah, that's what I said. …"

"Have you gotten the shard yet?"

"We won the bet against Cottonmouth, and we're picking it up tomorrow evening."

"Splendid! I knew you could do it!"

Pasha leaned closer to the mirror. "And the hearing?"

Sonata blinked as though she hadn't understood him. "Hmm?"

Pasha threw up his hands in aggravation. "Alright, Sonata, what is it you're not telling us?"

There was another commotion as the door opened and shut. Sonata rolled her eyes.

"Honestly, Pasha, you get worked up so easily! Everything is fi—" Before she could finish her sentence someone was taking the mirror out of her hands.

"Is that my darlings I hear?" came the panicked voice of Pasha's mother. Lydia's face appeared in the glass, looking pale and frantic. She laid a hand over her heart.

"Oh, my babies!"

"Hey, Ma!" Pasha huffed with impatience. Faina shouldered Cicada out of the way to blow Lydia a kiss.

"Hello, Mama Lydia! We miss you!"

"I miss you too, my sweethearts!" Her eyes darted from one face to the next. "Are you alright? You aren't hurt, are you?"

Pasha shook his head. "Of course not! In fact we just picked up the shard this afternoon. But we probably won't leave until tomorrow evening. There's still a lot that we haven't gotten to see yet, after all."

Cicada threw him a questioning glance. Before she could open her mouth, Pasha stamped on her foot. Lydia raised her eyebrows in surprise.

"You did? Already?"

Pasha stuck out his chin with a false but cheerful grin. "Yep! We won it fair and square betting on a horserace. Didn't have any trouble at all."

He wasn't at all confident that his mother would fall for the ruse, but either she was too desperate to believe him, or their physical distance had dulled her intuitive perception. Her shoulders immediately relaxed as she threw her head back and heaved a sigh of relief.

"Thank goodness! Really, I wouldn't mind if you never went back to the Other ever again!”

"How's the trial going?" Pasha was eager to move on to a new subject.

He watched his mother carefully as she shrugged and glanced disinterestedly off to the side.

"The hearing is taking a little longer than we planned, but hopefully it will all be over by the time you get back."

Pasha narrowed his eyes slightly. He was having difficulty reading her. On the surface everything seemed fine. But Pasha couldn't help but wonder if her calm demeanor was merely an attempt to put him at ease. Lydia leaned forward into the mirror and puckered her lips.

"Now let me kiss you both."

Faina flew forward, nearly elbowing Cicada in the face, and threw Lydia another kiss.

"That's my *Fayishka*." Lydia turned to her son. "*Patulya*?"

Pasha's cheeks colored. He uncrossed his arms and made a kissing noise into the mirror. "Love you, Ma."

"Love you too, my babies! Bye-bye now, my darlings."

When Lydia's reflection disappeared, Pasha snorted and laid his head against the sofa.

"Well, that was a wealth of information!"

"Why did you lie and say we already had the shard?" asked Cicada, completely dumbfounded.

"I don't see any use in worrying her unnecessarily," Pasha explained. "Especially with the hearing going on."

Faina popped another peanut into her mouth and shrugged. "Well, according to her it sounds like it's all going well."

"But she did say it was taking longer than they expected."

"You know what I don't understand?" Faina laid her head in Cicada's lap. They'd grown rather chummy the past couple of days. "Why don't they just ask Mother Genesis if you have a bona fide right to the throne? I mean, since she's supposed to know everything it seems like a given."

Cicada played with the bottle cap from her soda. "Oh, Mother rarely gets involved in legal trials. Too messy."

"But she does do it?"

"Now and then. But she hasn't testified in a courtroom for a hundred years. It has to be super important for her to get involved."

Faina sprang forward with a look of gossip glimmering in her eyes.

"Hey, do you think that was Pyro sneaking out of Sonata's room when she picked up?"

Cicada shuddered and made a gagging sound. "What? Ew! No way!"

Pasha leaned back and took another swig from his coke. "That wasn't Pyro, that was just Ma. Face it, Faina. You're alone on this one. They're too different."

The truth was, he was half lying. At this point, not even he could deny there seemed to be something between the pair, but just this once he would've loved to prove Faina wrong.

"Wanna bet?" Faina challenged him.

"You're on! If you prove Pyro and Sonata are a couple, I'll buy you coke for an entire year!" His hand instinctively flinched towards his wallet in his back pocket, as though this would somehow protect it.

Cicada jiggled her hands as though the very idea were contaminated. "What would Sonata even see in Pyro?"

"Lots of things," Faina insisted. "He's funny, isn't he? And brave. He's passionate, has a strong sense of right and wrong. I know he may act kind of goofy, but he's actually pretty smart. And don't you think it's a little suspicious that everyone on the team is single?"

Pasha shrugged. "Not especially. Melodious is a widower. I'm pretty sure Pyro gets around. Sonata is too focused on rebel work. As for Skelter, well, it's a little hard to get to know a girl if you can't talk to her, isn't it?"

"And Staccato?"

Pasha threw back his head and laughed. "You think Staccato has a girlfriend?"

"Well, Queen Calliope sure was hitting on him hard the other day. Do you think they have a history?"

Pasha couldn't keep a straight face. "Staccato and Calliope? No way." He threw the pillow back at her.

"Well, he must have had someone at some point. Don't you think?"

"I don't know. Staccato strikes me as the married-to-his-job type. You know, the kind that always says they'll settle down. Then one day they realize they're old, and it's too late."

"So, you think Staccato never had a wife or children?"

"He said he's never had any children of his own. Even if he did, why would he keep it a secret?"

Faina flashed him a mischievous smile. He shook his head.

"Alright, so Staccato keeps everything a secret. But what kind of woman would be interested in Staccato? Other than Calliope, that is. He's a little odd. I mean, have you noticed that weird humming thing he does?"

"What humming thing?"

"Whenever Staccato hums, he only hums one particular set of notes. Sometimes he arranges them in a different order, but they're always the same twelve notes."

Cicada glanced up. "Oh, you mean the Lydian Mode?"

Pasha stopped and stared at her. Sensing his miscomprehension, she sat up straight and leaned forward.

"A mode is a set of musical notes that create a scale. Wasn't that what your mother was named after?"

Pasha furrowed his brow. "I don't know, was she?"

Cicada's eyes glazed over. "Mermaids love to name their children something musical. The modes are always a popular choice: Phrygia, Dorian, Ione, Locria, and most popular of all: Lydia."

Pasha sat back, dumbfounded. "Gosh, I never really thought about it before. That makes a lot of sense. But … why would Staccato be humming the Lydian Mode?"

Chapter 37:
Theo Writes

June 30th, 1889

Dear Staccato,

Something monstrous has happened, and we need you to return at once. A week ago our beloved Evangeline went missing, only to return the next morning severely brutalized and barely conscious. She had gone to confront Bruin at Alfbern Hall, who was entertaining guests from Draco at the time, the Cobra among them. In their inebriated state they forced her into submission for their own amusement. Amongst the atrocities imposed upon her, they cut open her veins and drank her blood. The wound is so deep it is beyond the caim's natural ability to heal, and Evangeline has had to receive stitches.

My dear Staccato, my brother, I must advise you to steel yourself, for this is unfortunately not the worst of the brutalities visited upon our Evangeline. With the Cobra's encouragement, I'm afraid Bruin—it's hard to find the appropriate words—Bruin took advantage of Evangeline. She escaped by jumping from the north tower into the sea, and swam back to Alveare.

Thankfully, she will sustain no permanent damage and in time will recover. Much blood was lost, but by the grace of God she has survived. Do not be upset with us for choosing not to inform you immediately. Once it was confirmed Evangeline was going to recuperate, we thought it best to wait until your return. We didn't want to worry you unnecessarily and spoil your visit. However, during her follow-up examination this morning, the caim made a discovery we feel should be brought to your attention. There's no need to worry for her safety, Evangeline is quite alright. Please come home soon, we all miss you very much.

Your faithful friend,

Theo

P.S. Shortly after Evangeline returned, it was discovered Bruin had stolen the sword Sarmentum from the Library of Kings, the sword given to Karkinos by the first King of Ursa when our kingdoms were joined centuries ago. As a consequence, the alliance has officially been severed. Karkinos shall no longer serve Ursa, and Evangeline's marriage to Bruin has been annulled. I have demanded as payment for the theft that Sea-Splitter, the trident my forefathers bequeathed to Ursa, be returned as well, but as you can imagine I have yet to see that demand fulfilled.

Chapter 38:
Collecting the Shard

Pasha, Cicada, and Faina remained unusually still during their drive to Edom Cottonmouth's manor. They had each armed themselves before departing from the hotel. Faina had her lighter, Pasha had his revolver, and Cicada was ready to glow.

The drapery of bougainvillea, which had once seemed so bucolic in the light, became limp, haggard bushels of shadow once the sun had gone down. They pulled up the gravel drive and found Cottonmouth awaiting them on the front porch.

The moment Faina shut off the engine, the ophidian came to help the ladies from their automobile. The obligatory greetings were made, and at last Cottonmouth turned to Faina.

"Well, have you given a thought as to what piece you'll be taking home?"

Faina managed a cool smile. "I have indeed, Doctor. It was a hard choice but I believe I've made my decision."

"Who knows," started Pasha in an attempt to throw him off, "she may change her mind once she gets down there."

As they made their way into the foyer, Pasha could not help but feel an even greater sense of unease. A lithe, slithery woman was watching them from the stairwell. A black silk kimono was draped over her pale, languid arms. A matching turban capped off her lacquered, brunette, curls which had been rolled at the nape of her neck. When she caught Pasha staring, she slunk farther down the steps, her perfumed hands trailing the polished bannister.

Cottonmouth cleared his throat. "I don't believe I've had the pleasure of introducing my wife, Mrs. Laudine Cottonmouth."

Cicada threw her hands on her hips and laughed. "Why, Doctor! I didn't know you were a married man!"

Cottonmouth smiled and reached out a hand to help his wife down the bottom stair.

"Oh now, Miss Butler, don't you go getting me into trouble."

"A pleasure, truly." Laudine took her time unfolding her words as though she were laying them down in a coffin. "The Doctor has told me all about ya'll." Bit by bit she turned her head towards Cicada. "I hear your Granddaddy was a Breckinridge."

"That's right." Cicada forced a lighthearted giggle.

Laudine did not laugh nor did she smile, but kept her large, doll-like eyes trained on Cicada.

"My mother was Alvinia Talmidge, the painter from Bowling Green. She was friends with Eulalie Breckinridge as a girl. She captured your family's property beautifully in a watercolor I keep upstairs. Why don't you let me show it to you while Edom here takes Mr. and Mrs. Lapochkov to the gallery."

The three exchanged unsettled glances. Cottonmouth wouldn't go down without a fight. Before Cicada could open her mouth, Laudine spoke again.

"I insist." It was practically a command.

Cicada shuffled in her T-strap heels, and allowed Laudine to lead her up the winding staircase. Cicada took one last look over her shoulder and disappeared down the hall.

Pasha and Faina laced their hands. They followed Cottonmouth to the cellar door. He retrieved his cane, lit a torch, and together they descended into the basement.

"The snakes shouldn't be too much of a problem this evening." The stairs creaked beneath Cottonmouth's enormous frame. "They recently supped, and they typically take their repose about an hour after dinnertime."

Pasha glanced at Faina. She had lost her appetite for conversation. He cleared his throat.

"I see." They flowed towards the catacomb-like hallway. "And where is Henri this evening?"

"Oh, I'm quite certain he's about. Probably nestled somewhere in the rafters where he can digest his meal peacefully."

As they passed the laboratory, Pasha forced himself to look away. Faina did the same. The farther they travelled, the colder the air seem to wane. An unnatural chill pierced their blood and bones. Cottonmouth paused outside the gallery to set the torch in its holster. He unlocked the door, switched on the lights, and ushered them over the threshold.

"Well, Mrs. Lapochkov, what'll it be?" Cottonmouth indicated to the glass horse head. "I noticed you were admiring my stallion upon your previous visit."

Pasha forced a smile. "Because we have something quite similar back home. Isn't that right, darling?"

Faina nodded her head. "Uh, yes. Very similar, in fact."

Cottonmouth rubbed his chin and gestured towards a stained glass window with a scene from Genesis when Adam and Eve were in the garden. The Serpent loomed overhead.

"Perhaps one of the stained glass windowpanes?"

Faina shook her head. Trying to appear confident, she brushed a curl away from her face and pointed to the shard on the ceiling.

"I do not know why exactly, but something about that piece seems to speak to me."

Cottonmouth dropped his smile. His eyes followed to the spot where Faina was pointing.

"Is it an artifact of some type? I thought perhaps because it was merely a fragment. …"

She trailed off. There was a long pause in which Pasha felt it necessary to tighten his grip around Faina's arm. All at once Cottonmouth broke into amused laughter.

"You mean that little shard right up there? Oh, that's nothing. Just some broken glass I happened upon while strolling across Myrtle Beach last summer." He shrugged. "Nothing special."

Pasha rubbed his hand up and down Faina's arm. "Is that really what you want, darling?" He hoped this made it sound more convincing.

Faina set her jaw and nodded. "That is the one."

Pasha pasted on a grin. "Well, I suppose that's a relief for you, Dr. Cottonmouth. I'm afraid we won't be walking away with anything you'll miss."

He made eye contact with their adversary. A moment passed between the two. Cottonmouth had figured them out. The doctor's mouth stretched into a grin. Without moving forward he extended his hand towards Pasha.

"It's a deal."

As Cottonmouth's enormous fingers enclosed around Pasha's hand, something slithered over the ceiling. Pasha looked up. It was Henri the rattlesnake. Henri wedged himself under a mirror and, with a twist, pushed the glass out of its bracket. With his hand still grasping Pasha's, Cottonmouth yanked him forward. The mirror came smashing down over Pasha's head, encasing him in a stinging shower of silvery shards. Faina let out a scream.

The moment the twinkling chimes of broken glass had ceased, Pasha peeked open an eye. Faina was hunched over him, horrified. He became aware of faint stings all over his body. Something warm trickled down his forehead, and in the space in front of his ear, and the inside of his elbow. He lifted his head. A sprinkle of crystal dust fell from his hair. The room was spinning.

"Don't rush to get up now," Cottonmouth warned with feigned concern. "You're losing blood quick."

Faina knelt down behind Pasha and wrapped her arms protectively around his neck. He couldn't help but worry over the motes of glass that were surely being embedded into her knees. She whimpered. Tears fell onto his shoulder.

"Don't cry now, honey. I'm a doctor, remember? I tell you what, it's a good thing this happened here and not somewhere else. By the looks of it he's gonna need a transfusion."

Pasha felt the lighter go off in Faina's hand. A wall of fire sprang up around them in a protective barrier. Faina lowered her head.

"Stay back! Or I'll melt right through that Sunday suit of yours!"

The heat from the flames distorted Cottonmouth's grin.

"Voilerian spies. I figured as much."

Pasha's head lolled back in Faina's lap as the warmth of her fire made him sleepy. She shot her hand towards Cottonmouth. Cottonmouth's pupils shrank as the flames charged at him like obedient hounds. With nowhere else to go, he raced out of the gallery and slammed the door. Faina's blaze chewed away at the wood.

The inferno made its way across the room, cooking the vases into combustible ballistics. Flecks of pulsing embers spat at Pasha's cheeks and burned. He coughed on the thick clouds of smoke.

"Faina!" He reached for her hand. "The smoke—I can't breathe!"

Faina's eyes widened. She put out the blazes in her palm, but the wildfire remained. She stretched out her fingers.

"Oh, no!" She whipped her head around. "No, I—I can fix it. …" Desperate, she dug her hands through the fire, but the blazes might as well have been smoke. She could not contain them.

Pasha's eyes watered. His muscles trembled as he succumbed to horrible fits of coughing. Faina grabbed fistfuls of her hair. Pasha could feel her pulse quickening. She bent over him, chest heaving, scared breathless. At last she resorted to screaming at it.

"Stop! Back!" With every word she sobbed harder, and with every sob the flames grew higher.

"Faina, don't—" Pasha gagged on his own words. He could hardly speak. "You're making it worse!"

His body shuddered. He was losing strength. Desperate to escape the smoke, he buried his face in Faina's lap. It was closing in on them now. The heat drew sweat from his pores and scorched his skin. Faina got to her feet. Looping her hands under his arms, she dragged him out of the pile of glass and lay over him as a fireproof shield. Just as Pasha was about to close his eyes, a lissome figure appeared in the doorway. A flood of water flushed over them as Pasha blacked out.

Chapter 39:

The Rooster

Pyro hobbled on his crutches towards the locked door of Hexmark Folkman's former office. Melodious took the key from Pyro and jammed it into the lock.

"I'll get that."

Pyro hunched his shoulders. "When is everyone going to stop coddling me? Sonata finally let me graduate out of that torchin' chair, and I'm still not allowed to do anything."

"I think perhaps you are seeing the situation the wrong way." Melodious opened the door. "No one is trying to baby you, we're taking care of you, just like you would take care of us."

He groped for the light switch. Bulbs flickered on the ceiling. Pyro raised an eyebrow.

"Did I hear you right, Melodious?"

"Did you hear me say that you are a caring person?"

"Uh-huh."

"Then you heard me correctly."

Pyro tossed his head. "Mel, I believe you have me confused with Sonata, or Skelter, or Pasha even. I'm not exactly the mother hen type."

Melodious threw back his head and let out a genuine, jovial laugh. Pyro bristled.

"What exactly are you trying to say, Reverend?"

"Forgive me, my friend, but you are not … how should I say it? You are not very self-aware. You are Father Hen."

Pyro dusted his hands and leaned against the wall.

"That's not a saying, Melodious. There is no 'Father Hen,' there's just a rooster, and all he does is strut around and show off."

"You do that too." Melodious chuckled to himself. "I have known you a long time now, Pyro. Over the years it has come to my attention that you are quite a warmhearted person. You're always worrying that Staccato gives Sonata more than she can handle."

"Can't say she appreciates me for that."

"And fussing over her when you think she's in danger."

"Again, not real appreciative of that."

"You have spent a considerable amount of time the past few months training Pasha and Faina. You make them laugh. You boost their confidence." He pulled at his mustache. "I have to say, I had never pictured you as the paternal type. Now I believe I am correct in saying you would make an excellent father."

In a moment of passion, Pyro almost threw down his crutches. "Torch it all, Melodious, you've been talking to my mother, haven't you?"

Melodious waved a hand and lowered himself into a plush armchair. "Forgive me, I did not mean anything by it."

Pyro rummaged through a file cabinet. "But you did hear about all that?"

Melodious sighed and folded his hands into his lap. "I did."

Pyro frowned and shook his head. "She has some pretty wild ideas about me."

"She does not know you. What can her opinions of you be but ideas when you do not allow her into your life?"

Pyro stabbed a crutch in Melodious's direction.

"Let's get something straight, here." He staggered forward. "Before you go all preacher man on me, you should know I love my family. I do. Despite what anyone says, I love my parents. I love my sister. I love my grandfather. And I love my nephews."

Melodious crossed his legs and leaned one elbow on the chair.

"I know you love your family. You love them a great deal. How else could you justify distancing yourself from them?"

Without being aware of it, Pyro fell back into the chair at the desk, dumbfounded. Melodious leaned forward with his hands folded.

"I will tell you a secret, my friend. If you wish to hide something, don't build a giant wall around it for everyone to see. People guard what is vulnerable."

Pyro reached into his pocket for a cigarette, and, sighing, remembered he was trying to cut back. Melodious continued.

"The problem isn't that you don't love your family. You hate yourself. You do not think you are worthy of love. This is true, *ja*?"

Pyro stared at Melodious for several drawn-out seconds. At last he gave a solid blink.

"Yeah."

"Then I'm afraid I must correct you, my friend. You are worthy."

They sat there in silence, unflinching for a full minute. Pyro got up from his chair, limped to the set of drawers next to Melodious, and patted him on the shoulder. He paged through several old documents. After thumbing through the first stack, Pyro huffed, somewhat annoyed.

"He wasn't exactly organized, was he? Hexmark, that is."

Melodious gestured to the cluttered space around him. "I could sense the room was somewhat unbalanced."

"It's a right mare's nest. You know it has to be, if I think it is."

"You did say he left in a hurry."

Pyro shook his head and poked at an overturned trashcan with his crutch.

"Must have. Boxes overturned, papers strewn across the floor …" The flowery script of a crumpled letter caught his eye. He tapped the floor next to it. "Melodious, hand me that balled up piece of paper, will you?"

Melodious fumbled forward, grabbed the paper, and handed it to Pyro. Pyro unraveled the epistle and read it silently to himself.

"You're aware of my connections, Mr. Folkman. Assuming you received the message I left in your kitchen sink, you now have no reason to doubt I will employ the advantages of that relationship, should you choose to vote in favor of guilty this coming Thursday. Choose your actions wisely."

He may not have signed his name, but it was undeniably Samael's hand. Furthermore, it was dated just before the conclusion of the trial concerning the Firebird.

"Melodious, look!"

Melodious lowered his eyebrows. "I can't, remember?"

Ignoring him, Pyro clutched the letter to his chest. "This changes everything!"

"What does?"

If it weren't for his foot he would've hopped up and down.

"Melodious, do you realize what this means?"

"No, because you have yet to tell me what you have found!"

Pyro cocked his head. "Huh? Oh yeah, right, sorry."

He read the letter to Melodious, who seized a hand to his heart.

"We must tell Sonata at once! Whatever you do, do not lose that letter!"

Chapter 40:
The Blood Bank

Pasha's arms prickled with cold. He tried to wiggle his fingers, but they were stiff with chill. The sterile odor of alcohol filled his senses. It was underlined with rust and damp. Even more overpowering was the intimate aroma of blood. Behind him, something like an aquarium or tank was beating out a bubbled chug.

Pasha opened his eyes. His gaze met with the high-ceilinged shadows of Cottonmouth's laboratory. He tried to sit up but something was restraining him. A chill ran down his spine. He was strapped to the hospital bed. He arched his head back and found himself staring at Faina. She was fully submerged inside an enormous, wheeled water tank. Her wrists and ankles were bound, and an oxygen mask had been fitted over her nose and mouth.

A hazy yellow glare struck in the corner of his eye. He craned his head as much as the restraints would allow and spied a glass lantern on the edge of Cottonmouth's desk. A blanket was thrown over the top to dim the light. It darted in angry zigzag patterns. So they'd trapped Cicada! Pasha wasn't surprised.

Something long and cusped traced over his ankle. Pasha started with a jolt. He looked down towards his feet expecting to see a snake caressing his leg with its fangs. Instead it was Laudine running her nails over his flesh.

"You awake yet, handsome?"

Pasha forced himself to take a long, deep inhale. She circled around to his head and massaged her fingers through his hair.

"The Doctor's stitched you up real good."

Pasha blinked his eyes, confused. They'd given him stitches? He tried to glance down at his arms. Was the charade still going on?

"You didn't take my blood?"

Cottonmouth cleared his throat from somewhere on the opposite side of the room.

"I'm afraid, Mr. Lapochkov, if that's even your real name, as much as we'd like to go ahead and harvest your blood, there are a few questions we need to ask you before you proceed to the pearly gates." His face appeared at Pasha's side. He had lost the pince-nez, and his hair had come untied, falling loose about his shoulders. "Unfortunately, my wife's methods of interrogation had no effect on your friends. We're hoping your resistance will be a little more negotiable."

He felt Laudine's fingertips drop to his neck. "Brace yourself, darling. I can make a hornet's sting feel like a kiss." She was noticeably more animated now that jig was up, flirtatious even.

Pasha's body was seized with a sensation of hellish terror. The branch of veins throughout his body burned as though his blood had turned into magma. His body wrenched and contorted itself. He cried out in anguish.

Once he had suffered enough, Laudine stepped away. The pain ceased. Sweat trickled down Pasha's temple as he gasped for breath. Laudine's eyes swelled with recognition.

"Well, what do you know? We're in the presence of royalty!" She tapped a finger on the end of Pasha's nose. "I knew I'd seen you somewhere."

Cottonmouth raised an eyebrow. "You've met before?"

Laudine rubbed Pasha's shoulders. "Oh, no, we've never been introduced. But I've seen you in the papers. You're the boy who's gonna take back the throne of Ursa. Pasha Chevalsky."

Her fingertips grew hot on his skin once more. Pasha groaned with pain. A sprinkle of water rained down on his nose. Behind him, Faina was thrashing in protest. Laudine knocked on the tank.

"Hush now, baby doll, or you'll be swimming with the water mocs."

Faina settled down. Pasha watched the dim light of the pendant lamp shimmer across the black silk of Laudine's robe.

"What are you? You're not an ophidian."

"I'm a lilith, honey. A wife of the devil. All the powers of a miraculous except deadlier, darker, and of course, I didn't come by my abilities naturally. I had to work for my talent. Bargain, if you will. You know, the old 'sell your soul' bit. But enough about little old Laudine."

She set her hands on Pasha's chest. Her voice became alive with a chorus of howls.

"How did you find out about the shard?"

Pasha fused his jaw together, refusing to speak. He clenched his fists. His hands shook. He withstood until he could feel himself drifting out of consciousness. Cottonmouth pulled his wife away.

"Don't overdo it, honey, or else we'll have to wait for him to come to again."

The darkness sucked away at the single pendant light, dimming it so it was just a glow. Laudine groaned and snapped a finger towards the desk.

"Edom, darling, go light a candle. My other senses are not as keen as yours. I have got to have my sight."

"What about the igneous?"

Laudine waved her hand. "She's waterlogged, there's nothing she can do to hurt us."

A bead of hope blossomed inside Pasha's chest. Pyro's palm lighter had worked! They thought Faina was a full-blooded igneous and couldn't control fire when wet! And the light? Cicada must have sapped the power!

Pasha listened to the scratch of a matchstick against sandpaper. Faint cylinders of light feebly lit the space around them. Pasha chanced a glance at Faina. Her eyes fixed on the candles. Cottonmouth jammed his hand around Pasha's throat and bent low over his head.

"Now I believe we can conclude Staccato Nimbus sent you, but how did he find out about the shard? Answer me, boy!"

With no way to fight back, Pasha's lungs felt suffocated. He wrinkled his nose in defiance as he tried to breathe. A pale ray of firelight rippled around the blanket covering Cicada's jar. It set to work eating away at the fabric. Cottonmouth released Pasha and jerked around to Laudine.

"Put it out!"

Laudine ripped the burning material from Cicada's lantern and made to stomp it out on the floor. Cottonmouth threw a hand over his face.

"The water, you crazy woman!"

"What? And release the igneous?"

Cicada's covering was gone. She was free to charge up her light. Pasha squeezed his eyes shut and smiled as he waited for Cicada's blinding glare. Through the shadows of his eyelids he could feel a faint sting of white hot brightness. Laudine shrieked.

"My eyes! She's blinded me!"

"Relax, sugar," hissed Cottonmouth, "I have my other perceptions."

Pasha watched as Cicada whipped a trail of light about the room in several directions. Blinded, Cottonmouth followed the trail of heat. His head darted back and forth like a cat with a flashlight. Lifting her hands, Cicada yanked the stream of light towards her like a yoyo. Cottonmouth pounced at the desk, knocking over her prison and breaking it into a million pieces. Cicada blossomed to her full size. She snatched a jar of blood from the shelf and hurled it at Cottonmouth and Laudine. Laudine shielded her face from the breaking glass. Cottonmouth sniffed at the air, his senses clouded by the flickering light and smells. He reached for the end of the bed. Before he could grab Pasha, Faina ripped a wall of flame between them. The fire singed Cottonmouth's hand. He flew back, writhing in pain.

With Cottonmouth and Laudine blocked off, Cicada unbuckled Pasha's restraints. He sat up, still a little faint, but anxious to escape. Laudine stretched out a hand and the hum of Faina's oxygen tank went silent. Pasha whipped round in panic. Faina clutched her throat. She banged on the glass. Pasha hurried to finish unlacing himself. His eyes flicked over the room, looking for something to break the walls of the tank. His gaze fell upon an old IV stand. He held out a hand to Cicada.

"Stay back!"

He picked up the stand and swung it like a baseball bat into the tank. The glass fissured and leaked. He gave it another strike. Faina's prison shattered. A flood of water pooled across the laboratory, sloughing off the protective barrier of fire. Pasha removed Faina's mask. She stood trembling, her ankles still tied to the metal ring of the tank floor.

Cottonmouth rose to his feet. Laudine's hands surged with power. The hospital bed flew into the air of its own accord. Laudine gave a flourish of her hands, and the floating bed careened towards them.

Cicada took up the IV stand and blocked the furniture as though engaged in a sword fight. Pasha fished in his pockets for his knife, but all his weapons had been removed. Desperate, he picked up a shard of glass and sawed away at Faina's bonds. Faina shook her head.

"Pasha, you'll cut yourself more!"

"Got any better ideas?"

Cicada tossed a suture from the rolling cart his way. It landed at Pasha's feet.

"That'll work!"

There was no more fire to manipulate, and Faina's lighter was soaked. The pair was defenseless as Cottonmouth barreled towards them on all fours. Cicada swung at his head. Cottonmouth ducked beneath her, his jaws unhinging as he reached for Pasha's pant leg. Faina's bonds broke. Pasha leapt onto the wheeled platform. Cottonmouth collided with the base, pushing it backwards. Pasha and Faina sped across the laboratory, struggling to keep their balance.

Cottonmouth slipped through the broken shards of the tank to his feet, desperate to go after his prey. Abandoning her fight with Laudine, Cicada resumed pitching jars at Cottonmouth in an attempt to draw him away.

Laudine groped her way forward. Her neck strained as though doing so would enable her to hear better. With a wicked grin, she faced Pasha and Faina shivering on the remnants of the tank. Laudine crooked her finger. The wheeled platform raced forward. Pasha and Faina screamed as they zoomed towards Cottonmouth's venomous canines.

Mustering up his strength, Pasha hoisted Faina onto his back. At the last second, he leapt over Cottonmouth's head, and sprang across his broad back as if it were a bridge.

Pasha ground to a halt as Laudine blocked their path. Faina pulled back on Pasha's shoulders and thrust her leg into the air. The lilith flew backwards over the desk as Faina kicked her upside the head.

"Take that, you nasty old witch!"

Cicada grabbed the box of matches and set to work lighting them and tossing them about the room. With her wrists stuck together, Faina butterflied her hands, nursing the flames until they climbed up Cottonmouth's shoulders and caught in his long hair. A scream scraped out of his lungs. Cicada threw open the door, and the three scattered into the passage. Laudine raced to her husband's aid.

"Edom! Edom, no!"

They slammed the door shut and headed off to the gallery.

Pasha's back strained under Faina's weight. "Is the shard still there?"

Cicada was panting. "It should be. The mirror isn't susceptible to fire, so no matter how damaged the room may be it should still survive."

The door was barely in existence, having been burnt down to the hinges. Cicada floated over the smoking wreckage and flew up to the ceiling.

"It's still here!" With some effort she managed to dislodge it from its hanging. Down the hall, Laudine's screams grew louder and louder. Pasha bit his lip.

"Hurry!"

Together they dashed up the corridor and into the main room of the basement. At the exit they ground to a halt. All the commotion had upset the snakes. They now covered the floor in a knotted frenzy. Faina threw back her head.

"You have got to be kidding me!"

Pasha's eyes wound round the room. "What about your fire?"

"You saw what happened in the gallery, what if I lose control?"

"Just stay calm, you make it worse by getting upset!"

"How can I stay calm when we're all about to get eaten alive? Look, it's like Cottonmouth said, they're more afraid of us than we are of them."

Pasha's eyes flew skywards. "Somehow I doubt that."

He tiptoed around the writhing adders. They danced away from him.

Pasha let out an involuntary whimper. A large rattlesnake reared up and hissed at them, causing Pasha to jump and fumble backwards between the aisles of bloody wine.

Down the hall, someone threw themselves against the laboratory door. A handle clicked. Faina jiggled her hands.

"Pasha, you have to run!"

Cicada waved her arms. "You can do it, Pasha!"

"Easy for you to say, you're floating!"

"Oh, for goodness' sake!" Faina wriggled her shoeless feet to the ground and unhooked herself from around Pasha's neck.

"What are you doing?"

Faina pulled back her fist and punched Pasha in the lower abdomen. Pasha gave a cry and bowed forward. The moment he lowered himself, she hooked him sideways over her back, bowing so low under his weight her hair brushed the ground. It was taking every ounce of muscle she had to hold him up, but what she lacked in strength she made up for in sheer force of will.

She took off at an awkward gait down the aisle. The snakes fled in countless directions. The moment they reached the steps, Pasha scrambled back onto his feet. In seconds they had made it to the top of the stairs. They burst out the door, tripping over each other and slipping on the polished wood floors. They skidded into the foyer. Faina's eyes widened.

"Where are the keys?"

Cicada bustled around the hooks on the wall and tossed Pasha the key ring. They staggered onto the front porch, leapt down the stairs, and flew towards their parked car. Pasha fiddled with the keys on the driver's side. Faina gritted her teeth.

"Hurry!"

With shaking hands, Pasha thrust the key into the lock and swung open the door. He shoved Cicada towards the backseat.

"No time to unlock the other doors, just go!"

He tossed Faina like a duffel bag into the passenger seat, and climbed in after her. Her feet hung over the console. Pasha jammed the key into the ignition. The headlights flickered. The engine stalled.

"*Chort!* It's not starting!"

Light rippled across the glass of the front door as Laudine groped her way onto the porch. Her robe hung in scorched tatters. Soot and blood were ground into a muddy paste across her cheeks. Her long, dark hair tumbled out from her turban. Cicada rang with an ear-piercing scream.

"We're gonna die! We're gonna die!"

Pasha wrested the key back and forth until at last the car came alive. He hurled the gear into reverse, pounding on the gas and nearly hitting the edge of the fountain. Laudine swayed down the drive.

Faina kicked her legs. "Pasha! Drive!"

Pasha tossed the gear forward and, flooring the car, sped away from the manor. His body seized with unbearable pain as Laudine's sorcery filled his veins. His head pinned against the seat. His fingers curled in on themselves. He couldn't move.

Grabbing him by the back of the collar, Cicada pitched him into the passenger seat with Faina, and took the wheel. Making a U-turn at the fountain, she drove the car straight at blinded Laudine. Laudine was thrown up into the air, landing on the hood of the car. Pasha's pain ceased. Eyes narrowed, Cicada stepped on the gas. Laudine, injured, but still alive, rolled off the front of the vehicle. Cicada raced them out of the neighborhood towards the Seelbach.

Once they were far from Cottonmouth's manor, Pasha finally allowed himself to breathe. His back was shoved up against the passenger door, with one foot on the dash and the other on Cicada's headrest. He sat directly on top of Faina, who squirmed.

"You're crushing me!"

Pasha rolled over as Faina wriggled into an upright position, and propped her feet on the console. Pasha grabbed the receptacle of the cigarette lighter and burned through the ties around her wrists. Closing his eyes, he laid his head against the seat. Faina put a hand on his arm.

"How are you feeling?"

"Like I wanna go home and hug my mother."

"Sounds like you could use a drink."

Something cold and heavy plopped in his lap. Pasha opened his eyes. His jaw dropped. It was the two bottles of Chevalsky vintage, the 1908 and the 1915.

"Faina, I can't believe it! When did you—"

Faina waved her hand. "Oh, I grabbed them on the way out."

He looked over her tattered dress and torn stockings with a cocked eyebrow.

"But where did you …? Aw, it doesn't matter! You're an angel, Faina!"

"Ain't I, though?"

He snatched her around the waist and hugged her tight, causing

Faina to accidentally kick Cicada. The car swerved.

"Hey! Watch it, you two!"

Pasha smiled sheepishly. "Sorry, Cici. You're doing a great job, by the way."

"I told you all you should've let me drive."

Chapter 41:
Consequences

"A baby? Really? Oh, Evangeline, darling, that's wonderful!"

Staccato knelt at Evangeline's feet and pressed her hands to his lips. He beamed with joy, but Evangeline remained emotionless.

"Evangeline?" Staccato clasped her shoulders and tilted her chin. "Darling, what's wrong?"

Her eyes were in a daze as she sank farther back into the armchair she was sitting in. "What do I do now?"

"What do you do?" Staccato laughed. "Do what you love! Go sit in the sunshine, go create in your studio! We'll make plans for the wedding, and then we'll start planning for our baby."

"Our?" Her voice was hollow. "How do we know it's ours?"

Staccato drew his eyebrows together and scoffed.

"Don't be silly, of course it's ours! I know what happened with Bruin was—but, I mean, that was only one time!" He lowered his voice. "And we, well, we spent a lot of time loving each other, didn't we?"

She nodded, her eyes distant. Panic dammed in Staccato's chest.

"Evangeline, I'm the baby's father. Even …" he drew a long breath. "Even if I wasn't the one who—even if it is Bruin's, I will be the father! I will! I promise! A—a—and we'll get married, and we'll care for the baby, and we—we'll have more children, and we'll be so happy!"

Evangeline looked at him for the first time. Tears spun down her cheeks.

"Really? You mean it?"

He cupped her face in his hands. "Of course I do! It doesn't matter to me how this baby came into our lives. I'm just happy it came to us. And you know there is no earthly power that could stop me from loving anything that carried a piece of you! Is that all you're worried about?"

Her eyes dropped to the floor. She fiddled with the bandages on her arm.

"No. Not exactly. It's just … What are we going to do about Bruin?"

Theo stepped in, his face clouded with suspicion. "What do you mean?"

Evangeline's head sank further between her shoulders. Theo pressed on.

"Eve, what about Bruin?"

"I wrote to him and told him I was expecting."

Theo's face contorted with rage. "You told him you were expecting?"

Estella stared at Theo, a warning in her silvery eyes. As Evangeline opened her mouth to explain, she was gagged into silence by a stream of sobs. Staccato rushed forward and gathered her up in his arms. Estella put a hand on the side of her sister's neck to subdue her into coherency.

"I wanted to … I wanted …"

"Well?" Theo's voice was like far-off thunder.

"I wanted to make him sorry for what he did!"

Staccato fell back. Estella steeled a hand over her heart. Javaid's eyes widened. Theo was practically frothing at the mouth.

"What ungodly power would possess you to do such a stupid thing?"

Evangeline's hands flew to her forehead and bunched in her hair as she sobbed.

"I was angry …"

"You always let your emotions get in the way of your better judgement! Do you realize what's going to happen now? If you had stayed silent, you could've married Staccato quickly and quietly. You would've announced your family situation, and no one would've questioned it! I doubt even Bruin would have questioned it! Now we have a paternity case on our hands!"

Evangeline wrung her hands. "I know, I know! I didn't think until after the damage had been done!"

"That's what's wrong with you, Evangeline! You never think until after the damage is done!"

Estella huddled protectively around Evangeline. "Theo, calm down."

"No! Evangeline is always making foolish decisions that we have to fish her out of later, whether it's entering into a marriage that was doomed from the start, or carrying on with an affair, or sneaking off without telling anyone to try and negotiate with a dangerous lunatic! She needs to be made aware of what she has done! This cycle has to end!"

"She is aware, Theo! What good will it do to berate her like this?"

"It will get her attention, that's what it will do!"

"For goodness' sake, show some mercy!"

Theo wrenched towards his youngest sister, who had been reduced to a pitiful crumple of bitter weeping.

"I told you to stay at Alveare! I told you not to return to Alfbern!

Did I not promise I would deal with Bruin myself? And yet you were so impatient, so willful, so determined to have your way that you disregarded everything I said and walked headlong into danger! And now out of sheer spite you have created an entirely new dilemma!"

From his place in the corner where he had been sitting silently, Javaid spoke up.

"Theo, it's true what Evangeline did was thoughtless, and yes, it is a problem, but can we at least postpone this discussion until the more recent trauma has subsided?"

Theo let out a groan and walked away from them with his hands thrown upwards.

"Do what you want! I don't know how one can carry on a discussion with someone who lacks basic reasoning, but you may certainly try."

Javaid stared back at Theo, unimpressed. "The bravado is hardly necessary, Theo."

"You think you're so dignified, don't you, Javaid?"

Estella beat her hand on the side table. "Theo, stop it!"

Evangeline squinted through her tears. "All of you are being too hard on Theo!"

Javaid clutched at the arms of his chair. "This is the thanks I get for coming to your defense?"

Theo threw himself upon the couch and scoffed. "What did I tell you? It's no use when she's made up her mind to play the child."

Staccato edged back as he watched the loving family he'd revered crumble like monuments of clay. What had he done? He clutched at his heart, feeling as though poison were running through his veins. The gravity of everything that had passed settled on his chest. Because of their rash behavior, he and Evangeline's child would be made to suffer the scorn of scandal. They would have ugly names thrown at them from the mouths of people they did not know. It would be recorded in history books. Centuries from now it would be taught in classrooms: Staccato Nimbus had an affair with Queen Evangeline Soter.

He had vowed his children would never know a broken home, and yet his actions had secured their inheritance of undeserved shame. They would suffer for his sins. He got up and fled the room.

***

The Judge's spectacles slid down the bridge of her nose as she scanned the old letter Javaid had presented her.

"So, according to the letter presented by King Javaid, written by former King Thessalos to Staccato Nimbus in June of 1889, Evangeline was taken advantage of by her then-husband King Bruin?"

Javaid nodded his head. "That is correct, Your Honor."

Her eyes fell upon Samael. "And Cobra Samael, were you present when this happened?"

Samael remained cool. "No, Your Honor."

The muscles in Javaid's shoulders swelled with rage. "That is a lie!"

Samael leaned forward and propped his chin upon his wrists. "Is it now?"

Javaid was on his feet, roaring into the microphone. "Admit it! It was you who instigated the whole affair!"

Before the Judge could intercede, Samael answered him.

"I see. Well, perhaps if you hadn't been so concerned with covering up the lurid details of your sister's affair you might have managed to scrape up some proof of that assertion. As it is, I take it you have no more to offer than this correspondence between Staccato and your brother?"

Javaid's head sank between his shoulders as Constanza pulled him back towards his chair.

"No, I do not."

"Then it is your word against mine." Samael's sleeve swept the top of the desk as he pointed a finger at Staccato across the way. "Your Honor, by presenting his daughter to the Council and trying to pass her off as the heir to the throne of Ursa, this man has committed perjury in front of an international court!"

Staccato almost yanked the microphone from its wire.

"Your Honor, I have not committed perjury. I have lied about nothing. I never denied having an affair with Evangeline, I only asked if there was proof." He gestured to the stenographer. "Check the transcripts if you don't believe me. Furthermore, despite the circumstances I have full reason to believe Lydia's son has biological claim to the throne."

The Judge rubbed her temples as though disappointed. "You mean to say you do not believe Mrs. Chevasky is your blood daughter?"

"As much as I would love for that to be true, I know it isn't. What I am about to share with the court, I never shared with my wife. You won't find it in the diary either. After Evangeline made the mistake of informing Bruin she was pregnant, we were faced with two choices. We could either come clean about the affair, exposing the family and the child to scandal, or we could say the child was Bruin's and attempt to secure full custody. Unsure of what to do, I went back to Aquarius to ask Mother Genesis who had fathered Lydia. Before I go any further, I must inform the Council that I did not ask her directly. As you can imagine, I was a little apprehensive about finding out the truth. But the answer given led me to believe Lydia was not my blood offspring."

"What did you ask Mother Genesis?"

Staccato paused as though trying to numb himself from his own words.

"I asked her, 'Should I have married Evangeline when Atergatis decided to fling her at Bruin?'"

"And what did she say?"

"She said, 'No. Ursa needed an heir, and therefore you should not have married Evangeline at that time. But do marry her now.'"

The council members all turned to whisper to each other as the Judge pounded the gavel.

"Did she say anything else?"

Staccato bit the inside of his lip and shifted in his seat.

"When I became upset, I took it out on her. I asked her what was the point in answering me if it was only to make me miserable. She said, 'My ways are not your ways. The finite cannot hope to understand the infinite.' She told me not to be afraid because I would love the child, that it wouldn't matter to me who fathered the baby because in my heart she would be my own."

As his eyes scanned the crowd of officials, he could see he had made his perspective understood. Samael flew to the microphone.

"Your Honor, we aren't really going to take an old tree's testament seriously, are we? I mean, I understand that, to many Fay demographics throughout Voiler, Mother Genesis is perceived as some sort of divine prophet, but … well, we aren't all Fay, need I remind you?"

The Judge slipped Samael an obligatory smile.

"I completely understand your concerns for equality, Cobra. However, I'm afraid I'm going to have to overrule you. The fact of the matter is, Mother Genesis holds a long-standing record for accurately predicting several historical events, even ones which predate the Ecliptic Council. I think in order to bring this hearing to a close, Mother Genesis needs to be called in to testify."

She punctuated the order with a pound of her gavel.

"B—b—but Your Honor, Mother Genesis is not likely to attend.

Rarely does she ever involve herself in legal matters. It's been a century since she last conceded to show up in court."

The Judge shrugged. "Well, there's no harm in asking, now is there? Court is adjourned."

Chapter 42:
Double-Crossed

Pasha, Cicada, and Faina made an unusual party sneaking through the lobby of the Seelbach. Not only were their clothes scorched, but they were covered in blood. They wasted no time in rushing upstairs, showering, and packing up. As they descended down the lift, all three armed should they run in to anymore unsavory characters, Cicada and Faina refused to let Pasha carry the luggage. He had lost a lot of blood, after all.

Pasha didn't like this one bit. "I'm gonna look like a jerk if I just stand here doing nothing!"

The caged doors of the elevator parted. To their surprise, Roman, Clay, and Letcher sat in the lobby. Roman snuffed his cigarette in the ashtray and rose to his feet.

"Don't tell me you three were gonna leave without saying good-bye?"

They instinctively took a step back.

"What if Cottonmouth rang him a warning?" Pasha heard Cicada whisper to Faina.

"Nonsense, Roman doesn't work for Cottonmouth. He's an associate of an associate for the Breadwinners. Klokov may be a violent madman, but he's still a man of his word. He'd have a kitten if Roman tried to hurt us."

Cicada nearly crossed her eyes. "He can do that?"

"No! I'll explain later."

Pasha shrugged, trying to remain casual. "We have done what we came to do, and now it is time to head home." With Clay and Letcher present, he thought it best to maintain his Russian accent.

Roman tipped back his fedora. "In that case, allow us to help you with your luggage."

Pasha shook his head. "Thank you, but I believe we have a handle on it."

Roman waved Letcher forward. "I insist."

It was odd to see these seasoned gangsters taking orders from someone as young as Roman. Something had to be up. Roman snapped at the doorman.

"Hey, my buddy needs his car brought around."

Pasha coughed into the back of his hand. "Black Rolls Royce, Pav …" He stopped. The car was under his real name. The doorman smiled and nodded.

"I remember, sir."

Pasha drew a sigh of relief. Roman reached around Faina's shoulder to get her attention.

"I just remembered. I have a gift for you. Come back inside. I'd like to give it to you personally."

Pasha whipped his head around. "What gift?"

"Just a little something for the lady to remember me by. Nothing to get excited about. I'll have her back in a jiff."

The Rolls Royce pulled round to the front. Faina glanced at Pasha and shrugged.

"We'll be quick." She allowed Roman to lead her back inside.

Cicada looked warily at Pasha as Letcher and Clay loaded their luggage into the backseat. At length, Letcher held out the driver's side door for Pasha to get in.

"Well, it's been a pleasure, Paulie."

"Same to you, Mr. Letcher. Mr. Clay."

He thanked them and climbed into the driver's seat. He wondered why they hadn't opened the passenger side for Cicada. The door slammed shut. The barrel of a gun was pressed to the side of Pasha's head.

"Drive," ordered a familiar voice.

Pasha glanced into the rearview mirror, and found himself staring into the cold, scarred face of Anastas. Outside, Letcher and Clay grabbed Cicada's wrists.

So they'd been set up. Everyone had their prize. Anastas had Pasha. Letcher and Clay had their card shark. Roman had Faina. Anastas pressed the gun harder against his skull.

"I said drive!"

Pasha stuck the key into the ignition as calmly as he could, trying to think of a way out of his situation. He kept his voice dull.

"Where do you want me to go?"

"The warehouse on the riverfront. You should remember."

Pasha put his foot on the gas and took off down the road.

"I take it you saw me that day, then?"

"I was waiting for you."

"So, Roman tipped you off."

"After you arrived we both realized we could be of some benefit to the other. By delivering you into my hands, Roman would receive substantial payment from the Butchers, with interest. He'd also be eliminating the competition."

"Competition for what?"

"For Spichkin, you idiot!"

Pasha couldn't help but snort. "Well, I'm proud of you, Anastas. Realizing you didn't have a chance with Faina is the first step towards accepting you're an unhealthy maniac."

Anastas lashed the gun against the side of Pasha's head.

"Don't get smart with me, Chevalsky."

Pasha tapped his forehead. "That's right, I forgot, you can't understand intelligent conversation."

Anastas cocked the gun. "I don't think you're in a position to make personal remarks right now."

From that moment on, Pasha resolved to be silent.

Suddenly, shots rang out in front of the Seelbach, followed by cries of "She's a ghost!"

Anastas jumped, accidentally throwing his pistol. Pasha caught it, swerved behind a building, and threw the car into park. With both hands he pointed the gun at Anastas, ignoring the commotion from up the road.

Anastas didn't even flinch. "Go ahead. You don't have it in you."

Pasha fired into Anastas's right shoulder. Anastas yelped. He shriveled back, clutching his arm, and cursing. Pasha narrowed his eyes.

"It's true, I don't like violence. I may not be as bloodthirsty as you. I may not even be as tough as you. But I know what you're capable of. You murdered my good friends. You endangered my mother and sister. Don't think for one second I would hesitate to shoot you in order to defend the people I love. Oh, and one more thing. You made my girl cry." Pasha whipped the handle across Anastas's skull. "What's Roman done with her?"

At that moment, he looked up to see Cicada sprinting down the sidewalk. Bullet holes had torn straight through her blue dress and coat. As she came closer, Pasha could see her figure had become transparent.

Before Pasha could stop her, she swung open the back door of the car. Anastas reared up and kicked her in the side of the face, causing Cicada to fall over on the pavement. Pasha shot at Anastas's back but Anastas ducked out of the way. The passenger window shattered, and Anastas took off down the alley in a sprint. Pasha scrambled out of the driver's side, firing in his wake, but missing every time.

Cicada wrenched the pistol from his grasp.

"Give me that!" She took aim and fired the gun. Nothing happened. She opened the barrel. "Out of ammo." She tossed it aside. "You really are a terrible shot, aren't you?"

"Hey, I shot him in the shoulder, didn't I? Are you okay?"

Cicada shrugged and tossed her hair over her shoulder. "I'm fine. What do we do about Faina?"

"Roman handed me over to Anastas because he thinks I'm Faina's beau."

"If that's true we can safely assume he won't hurt her. If he really wants Faina he wouldn't want her to know he ordered your execution."

At that moment, Faina's voice rang up the street as shrill as a firework.

"Get lost, Roman!" She had just come out of the Seelbach and was twisting her arm out of his grip.

"But Faina, baby, I did it for us!"

"Us? I hardly know you! You tried to have Pasha and Cici killed!"

"What can I say? I'm the jealous type."

"More like the crazy type!"

"Hey, a real man is territorial."

Faina pivoted on her heel with such fury Pasha thought she might spit fire in his face, which was totally within the realm of possibility.

"Territory? Is that what you think I am? Your property?"

Before Cicada could stop him, Pasha hustled up the street to Faina's aid. He grabbed her by the shoulders and pulled her back.

"Faina! I'm right here."

Faina whipped round in relief. "Pasha!" She threw her arms around his neck. Behind her, Roman shrugged as though he had planned the whole thing.

"See? Everything's fine. He's right here."

Faina drew her own gun from her coat and pointed it at Roman, who threw up his hands. Pasha pushed her arm back down.

"Woah, woah! Alright, Faina. Put the gun away, he's not worth it." He put a comforting arm around her shoulder and turned her towards the direction of the car. "I survived, and Roman is just a worthless simp." Pasha slipped him a smug smile as Roman watched them depart with his arms tangled across his chest.

The moment they turned their backs, a gun fired. They jumped. Pasha's hat fell to the sidewalk and settled at his feet. A bullet hole was burnt through the brim. Roman grinned as he pointed his gun. Pasha seized Faina's hand.

"Run!"

Roman chased them down the street. Faina reached back over her shoulder and shot, narrowly missing the toe of his boot while Cicada came speeding up the road in the Rolls Royce. Pasha and Faina dashed out of the way as she drove onto the sidewalk. Roman scuttled against the wall. Cicada stopped just short of crushing him, and laid on the horn. Roman covered his ears and writhed. He dropped the gun as Pasha and Faina threw open the door and climbed into the backseat.

"Enough of this craziness!" Pasha slammed the door behind them. "Cici, take us home!"

"You got it, Your Majesty!"

And throwing the car into reverse, they took off towards the outskirts of Louisville, headed for the Pope Lick Trestle.

Chapter 43:
Conspiracy Theories

After Staccato and Evangeline were married, Evangeline spent an unprecedented amount of time in her studio. At first, everyone delighted to see her engaging in her passions. But it wasn't long before worry replaced rejoicing. Evangeline did not sleep. She did not eat. What's more, strange packages arrived at Alveare with peculiar messages attached to them.

Dear E.,

Here are the two gallons of Ichor harvested from Fornax like you requested. The Vine Dresser is working on your hurranical petrichor as we speak. Our hopes rest in you.

-The Acolyte.

When Staccato inquired about the letters, Evangeline claimed they were old schoolmates, advising her on her latest project, a mirror. When he asked what kind of mirror she simply replied, "A round one."

But it was an old book she'd stashed away that prompted Staccato to worry. Once, he awoke in the middle of the night to find Evangeline's nose buried in what he considered quite a ridiculous reading choice.

"Evangeline, what on earth are you reading?" He peered over her shoulder and snorted.

Evangeline jumped, dropping the book. Staccato picked it up with two fingers and turned it over in his hands.

"*The Search for Caiman Asterias's Lost Diary?*" He threw back his head and laughed. "Evangeline, you can't be serious!"

Evangeline lowered her head. "What? What's so funny?"

Staccato scanned through the pages. "Eve, this is nothing but conspiracy theories! You don't really believe ophidians are demons sent to destroy all magic, do you?"

Evangeline folded her hands in her lap. "Is that so hard to believe when they're actively promoting Fay genocide?"

Staccato balked at her for a moment, then scoffed, as though he couldn't believe what she was saying.

"Well, yes, as a matter of fact, it is. I can accept that they're tyrants, but actual demons? Come now, darling!"

Evangeline crossed her arms over her chest and hunched down in her pillows.

"Caiman Asterias saw it for himself while he was held captive during the Liberty Wars. He wrote everything down in his diary, which was discovered centuries later by the famous archaeologist Koto Yosai."

"Which mysteriously disappeared before anyone could legitimize its authenticity."

Evangeline sat bolt upright. "Because it was stolen by the C.O.N.!"

Staccato set the book aside and pulled her into his arms so her head was in his lap. "Evangeline!" He snickered. "Everyone knows the diary of Caiman Asterias is a silly old legend."

Evangeline held very still for a moment. Sighing, she shut her eyes. Her arms curled beneath her chin as though protecting a fragile pearl.

Staccato brushed her hair back. "You need your rest after such a long day in the studio. Why are you working so hard, anyway?"

There was something forced and almost disappointed about the weak smile she gave him.

"Just being silly, I guess."

He laid his palm against the gentle slope of her belly. She had only recently begun to show.

"Between carrying the baby and spending all your time in the studio, you should be worn out."

"I should be, but I'm not."

Staccato ran a finger down her side. "Then allow me to offer my assistance. ..." He gave her a squeeze.

"Staccato!" She giggled and swatted at his arm. Rolling over, she stamped his chin with a kiss.

***

The following morning she was back in her studio before Staccato was even awake. The mirror was becoming a point of obsession for Evangeline. No one knew why. She worked herself to exhaustion. Several times Staccato and the family had to beg her to leave her workplace. It was suspected that once the baby grew heavy enough, Evangeline would slow down. But even when she could hardly walk, Evangeline was caught trying to hobble her way to her art. When at twenty-eight weeks she was discovered unconscious, having fainted on the floor of her studio, it was locked up. A close eye was kept on Evangeline from then on.

Chapter 44:

The Goat Man

Most of the drive was peaceful. Pasha and Faina even had time to fret over how they were going to jump off a ninety-foot bridge.

Faina bit her nails. "Maybe we should call Staccato and make sure that's what we're supposed to do."

Cicada tossed her hand. "What are you all making such a fuss about? You're jumping off a bridge. Nothing to it!"

Pasha leaned against the seat and scoffed. "There's a sentence you don't hear every day."

"That's easy for you to say," interjected Faina. "Cicada, you can basically fly!"

When they made it back to Fisherville, the traffic thinned. One car remained on the road, an old Model T that had been tailing them for twelve miles. Pasha cracked his knuckles.

"Hey, you don't think that car is following us, do you?"

Faina glanced through the back windshield. "That old Ford? Surely not."

A bang tore through the air. Pasha pinned Faina to the floor of the car as the windshield shattered. Cicada pounded her foot against the gas. It was difficult to tell who was inside the car. It was too plain for Letcher and Clay, and Cicada had scared them off anyway. Roman would have had a fancy car from the dealership, which left one person: Anastas. Faina trembled.

"I thought you shot him!"

"I did, he must have Vadim with him!"

The farther they drove into the country, the fewer streetlights appeared. They could only see as far as their headlights would allow. The gun pounded a second time. Cicada swerved out of the way.

"Cici, the trestle," Faina shouted. "We have to stop!"

"Stop? Are you nuts? I've got a better idea!"

She jerked the car off the side of the road and into the trees. Pasha and Faina tossed around the backseat, screaming. Branches smacked the windshield until at last the car took a nosedive into an unseen ditch. Cicada turned off the car and threw open the door.

"Get out! Quick! It's only a matter of time before they catch up!"

They scrambled into the bushes amongst the crickets and frogs. Somewhere in the distance a train horn blared. Headlights skimmed across the road. They could hear the Model T being parked. Two doors slammed.

"They couldn't have made it very far," Vadim was saying.

Cicada pushed them forward. "Just keep running!"

At last they stood below the trestle. Breathless, Cicada grabbed their luggage. Keeping her light off, she hovered into the air.

"Well, what are you waiting for? Climb!"

Pasha and Faina braced themselves against the stinging chill of the rusted iron. The trestle quaked. Cicada waved her arms.

"Come on, we have to beat the train!"

Soon Pasha and Faina stood at the top of the tracks. They hunched down against the overwhelming strength of the breeze, fearing they might blow away.

Faina pulled her jacket closer around her shoulders and shivered. "Do you think they're gone?"

A force knocked Pasha forward across the tracks, his head banging against the rail. It was Anastas. He couldn't have climbed with his shoulder injured; he had to have run up the tracks. Vadim held Faina and Cicada at gunpoint.

"Don't move!"

Anastas was pinching Pasha's throat when all of a sudden a shadow rose up before them. The train's headlights pooled around an enormous horned figure seven feet away. It seemed to keep growing.

Anastas went limp. Sweat dripped down his forehead. The creature stepped forward and the trestle strained. Anastas released Pasha. Vadim gaped at him, his back turned to the monster.

"What are you doing?" Anastas fired at the figure but it hardly flinched. He flew to his feet and tugged Vadim in the opposite direction.

"Let's go!"

Vadim resisted. "Have you lost your mind?" He ran towards them, gun drawn. He was so focused on his target that he never even saw the horned shadow.

Faina pulled Pasha to his feet and dragged him to the edge of the track.

"*Raz ... dva ... tri!*"

The three grabbed hold of each other and leapt off the bridge as the figure vanished and the train struck Vadim head-on.

***

Pasha and Faina were still screaming and clutching each other as they lay prostrate on the marble floor of the Citescape. They were too terrified to open their eyes.

Cicada slammed a hand over their mouths.

"Will you two pipe down already? We made it!"

She stretched her arms over her head in jubilation. Pasha and Faina blinked their eyes open. They were back in Alrisha, surrounded by magnificent depictions of the world's most amazing places. Overhead, the moon was shining bright over Louisville in its frame. It was as though they had fallen asleep there beneath the painting, and everything had been a dream. They were back home at last.

Chapter 45:
Mirror Mania

The unfortunate truth about appeasing radicals is one can never be radical enough. Such was the case when the C.O.N. docked their boats on Polaris's shores, salivating for blood. Embracing Primal Instinct hadn't been enough to keep Bruin safe; they had come for him all the same.

At Theo's instruction, Karkinos did not lift a finger. As far as he was concerned, Bruin had brought this upon himself. Stella Real was evacuated, the mermaids driven beneath the surface, and non-mermaid citizens into the vivariums. Crowds gathered in the underwater streets to watch the enormous ships drift past like storm clouds.

Staccato and Evangeline stayed in a suite at the State Manor inside the vivarium. Even amongst the uncertainty of their circumstances it was easy to feel at home. There was an excellent view of the reef from their quarters, and the floors housed spacious saltwater pools to accommodate Evangeline. It was in one of these pools at the turn of the season that she gave birth to Lydia.

Mother Genesis's words had proved true; the moment Staccato heard Lydia cry for the first time, he was moved to tears. He was completely captivated by his little girl, savoring each little breath, celebrating every smile. He forgot about Bruin. He forgot about the evacuation. He even forgot about the mirror.

When Lydia was a week old, Staccato awoke one night to the baby's hungry cries. He yawned and stretched his arms. To his surprise, the other side of the bed was empty. He assumed Evangeline had risen to tend to Lydia. But when the crying continued without the soft hushing of his wife, Staccato summoned the lamp on. He sneezed from the sudden brightness. When his eyes adjusted he looked about the dimness of the room. Evangeline was absent. Perhaps she'd gone down the hall for a drink of water.

Rubbing his eyes, Staccato rolled out of bed and made his way towards the crib. He grabbed a towel from the dresser and lifted Lydia from the shallow pool of her seashell cradle. Her pink tail shrank away to two kicking legs.

"Hello, darling." He folded the towel around her. "Are you hungry?" He sat with her at the edge of the pool. "Mama will be right back. Why don't we wait for her together?"

Lydia stared up at him with penetrating eyes. He took her little hand and kissed the inside of her left wrist. Lydia stretched her toes with a happy hum, and cuddled her head against his chest. Staccato gave a soft laugh, utterly delighted. He counted himself lucky to have a mermaid for a daughter, for he could always share this special gesture of affection with her, and watch her face light up as she felt his love for her.

"That's my Lydie."

Five minutes passed, and Lydia became fussy again. With the baby still in his arms, Staccato got up and looked for Evangeline. He poked his head into the hallway and called her name. Everything was quiet. As he passed the open door of the bathroom, a bit of movement drew his eye. Spinning round, he found himself face to face with his own reflection. His chest sank. The mirror.

Staccato left Lydia with the maid, and ran up to Alveare in search of Evangeline. From a distance he could see the light of her furnace illuminating the midnight air. Rolling his eyes, he made a dash for the studio. Sure enough, there was Evangeline like a feminine Hephaestus. Heavy apron thrown over her nightgown, hands thrust into her large leather gloves, and a glassblowing pipe javelined into the hearth as though she had just slain a dragon. Staccato was outraged.

"Evangeline! What are you doing?"

Evangeline gave a start. "Staccato?"

"You're not supposed to be on the surface, it could be dangerous! It's your brother's orders!"

She pulled the pipe out of the fireplace and drizzled molten hot liquid over the looking glass.

"The C.O.N. aren't going to come anywhere near Alveare. Their war is with Bruin. I have to finish the mirror!"

"Will you forget about this blasted mirror!" He would've taken the pipe out of her hands if he had any idea how to handle it. "You're obsessed, Eve! This isn't art anymore, it's mania!"

Evangeline set the pipe aside and turned to face Staccato, fumbling for an explanation.

"I know this seems a bit mad, but Staccato, you have to trust me! This project is very important."

"Yes, I know! It's so important that you're willing to risk your safety to finish it! By the way, Lydia is beneath the surface crying because it's time for her to feed!"

Evangeline furrowed her brow and covered her face. "I lost track of time, I could hardly bring her up here with me."

"That's right, you couldn't because it's technically a war zone! Not to mention you just had a baby! You hardly get enough sleep as it is, what with Lydia only a week old. You'll make yourself sick this way."

"But, Staccato, I have to finish this while the C.O.N. remains in Ursa."

Staccato threw up his hands in exasperation.

"Why?" His voice echoed throughout the studio. "What is all this about, Evangeline? Do you hear yourself when you're talking? You are risking your life over a mirror! Do you not see how that's a problem?"

"If it's a problem, it's my problem and not yours!"

Staccato could feel the back of his neck turning red with anger.

"Why are you always so immature? Everything always has to be your way no matter how ridiculous it is! No matter how dangerous it is!"

Evangeline's nostrils flared. "Why are you always so controlling?"

"I wouldn't be so controlling if you weren't so careless and stubborn! It's just like Theo says, you're always making foolish decisions that people have to come drag you out of! Coming up here was dangerous! You could've been hurt! You could've been killed! But you did it anyway! And since you are so childish it may be above your maturity level to understand, but your safety does affect other people, Evangeline, especially those you love!"

The tables shook. Evangeline's eyes widened in panic as she looked back at the mirror trembling on the marver. The movement stopped. Evangeline grabbed Staccato by the shoulders and began pushing him out of the studio.

"Oh, no! Until you get a hold of yourself you'll have to leave, I don't want you breaking my mirror!"

Staccato dug his heels into the ground. "Are you kidding? I have half a mind to shatter that blasted thing just to free you from this insanity!"

Evangeline thrust a threatening finger in his face. "Staccato Nimbus, if you dare break that mirror—"

Staccato reached out his hand. The mirror zipped into his grasp. Horrified, Evangeline flew to Staccato's side.

"Staccato, no!" She tugged at his elbow.

He lifted the mirror high over his head. Evangeline threw her arms around his waist and begged him.

"Please, Staccato! Please don't break it! I've worked so hard!"

He told himself not to look down, but he couldn't help it. Tears ran down her face.

"Please!"

Staccato's shoulders fell. He couldn't do it. It would be wrong. It was her art, after all; she'd labored over it for months. Perhaps it was all the stress from having the baby. He'd heard of such things happening before. Sighing, he released the mirror and let it float back to the marver.

"As much as I'd love to, I'm not going to break the mirror." His voice was cold. "But I'm not leaving this studio without you!"

Evangeline stared back at him with conflicted eyes. Staccato rubbed a hand over his face.

"Evangeline, our daughter needs you. I need you. You can't be so reckless."

Her lower lip trembled. "I know. I'm sorry. It was selfish to come here. I'll try to do better. I made a mistake."

He gathered her into his arms and stroked her hair.

"You're exhausted, that's all this is. Carrying Lydia put a lot of stress on you." With an outstretched hand he snuffed the furnace. "Come, show me what needs to be put away, it'll go faster if I do it."

The next day a caim was called upon to examine Evangeline. She was diagnosed with puerperal mania, psychosis brought on from the trauma of birth. The doctor thought it best to make accommodations for Evangeline to finish her mirror, so a makeshift studio was set up in the vivarium.

***

By late May it seemed as though the C.O.N.'s ships had become permanent fixtures in the landscape. Ursa was doing far better than any of the mermaids had expected. Everyone longed for a victory, eager to see the light of day again. The Soters even discussed the possibility of sending the new family to stay in Aquarius with Staccato's mother.

When Theo showed up unexpectedly at Staccato and Evangeline's door, they thought he had come for this very reason. Unfortunately, it was much more urgent.

"Make no mistake," Theo stared gravely at the two, "the C.O.N. has made several attempts to target Bruin exclusively. They will not rest until they've killed off the King. In order for Samael to gain a chance at winning Ursa, he needs to ensure the line of Northstars is finished." A light of horror came into Staccato's eyes.

"Oh, no …"

Evangeline glanced between the two. "What? What has that got to do with us?"

Staccato reached for Evangeline's hand. "Everyone believes Lydia is Bruin's daughter; in other words, she is the heir to the throne of Ursa."

A darkness gathered in Theo's eyes. "Whether or not Ursa emerges from this war victorious, Lydia is in great danger."

Evangeline shrugged. "Then we'll tell everyone about the affair, convince them she's Staccato's. She is anyways, I know she is!" She reached across Theo's lap and brushed a brunette curl from Lydia's forehead with a loving smile. "Look at those eyes! She doesn't even look like me. She's entirely her father."

Staccato stared down at his knees, wishing it were true, trying to forget Bruin's dark hair.

Evangeline straightened herself with dignity.

"I don't care what people say about me. Let them call me a harlot, a tart, whatever name they want, as long as Lydia is safe. I'll make a public announcement. I'll admit to everything."

Theo shook his head. "I'm afraid that's not enough. The fact of the matter is, we still don't know for sure who Lydia's biological father is. There's no definitive way to completely rule out one over the other, not one that would satisfy the C.O.N. anyway. As long as the *possibility* remains, there will be a price on her head."

He stroked his niece's cheek. Lydia wrapped her hand around his finger.

Evangeline was breathless. "What should we do?"

"Until things improve, I think it would be best if you relocated to the Other, somewhere remote where you're less likely to be hunted down."

"Leave Voiler?"

Evangeline stared at him, mouth agape. She looked as though she half expected Theo to burst into laughter and tell them it was all a joke. But Theo was far from joking.

"It's your best option right now."

"And live in a world without magic? Amongst those cruel people with all their savage ideas? I mean, have you seen the women? They're not even allowed to show their legs! How am I supposed to get out of the ocean without showing my legs?"

"You'll have to do your swimming in strict secrecy."

Staccato patted Evangeline's shoulder. "It's alright, Eve. We wouldn't be the only Voilerians living out there in the Other. Why, I hear in New York there are whole secret societies for Fay and Voilerians. And there is an abundance of mermaids living in the Other. As a matter of fact, many of them have gone on to have successful singing careers. Some even have indoor saltwater pools so they can stretch their fins in privacy."

"In other words, an aquarium! A pool isn't the ocean!"

Staccato snapped his fingers. "My Aunt Poppy! She lives in Siberia!"

Evangeline edged away. "Siberia?"

"Yes, yes. She grew up there, remember? She's with the naturalists, the ones who went to study the unicorns in Lake Baikal! There are all kinds of creatures hiding in Russia! It will be just like home! And Siberia is hardly touched by human hands, hiding would hardly be an issue!"

Theo bobbed his head in approval. "Not to mention it receives very few Voilerian migrants despite being one of the few magical touchstones."

Staccato gripped Evangeline's hands tighter. "I know it's frightening, darling, but think of the baby. We need to do what's best for Lydia. It's dangerous here."

Evangeline looked back at her brother with frightened, pleading eyes.

"Would we ever come back?"

Theo steeled his jaw and shut his eyes. "Ideally, the C.O.N.'s power will have to diminish considerably before I would deem it safe for you to return."

Evangeline bit her lip and looked around as though she wanted to strike something.

"This is all that horrible Samael's doing! He has driven us from our home! How can Bruin be so blind? He's let this monster infect his mind, infect his kingdom, our kingdom, and now our lives. He has to be stopped!"

Staccato put his hands on her shoulders and lowered her back into the chair. Theo rubbed at his forehead.

"We're doing everything in our power, Evangeline."

"Really? Why aren't we driving back the C.O.N.?"

"Because we no longer have an alliance with Ursa. To be honest, we're practically enemies."

"But who is the bigger enemy? We know the C.O.N. is secretly acting on Samael's command. Shouldn't we be stopping them?"

"I have tried to reason with Bruin. I told him the C.O.N. has been taking orders from the Cobra, but he wouldn't listen."

"Then we have to do something! We have to fight for our own country's sake! For our way of life! Regardless of your feelings towards Bruin, Polaris is the brightest star in the sky! Its light shines upon all of us. We can't allow it to grow dim."

She looked to Staccato, her eyes rallying for his support. But he cast his attention to the floor and rubbed the back of his neck. Theo stared at her. At last Lydia broke the dead of silence with her cooing. Theo cleared his throat and nodded towards Staccato.

"Talk to your aunt. Let me know when you've made arrangements."

And with his last command, he departed. The moment the door shut, Evangeline turned on Staccato with wounded outrage.

"Thank you for the support!"

Staccato gaped back at her in alarm. "What are you angry at me for? You want Karkinos to send out an army to defend a kingdom that's showed them no respect? You ask too much of your own people, Evangeline."

"It's not about defending Ursa, it's about defending Karkinos! Our alliance is broken. If Bruin dies, the kingdom won't fall under our steward-ship, it will fall under Draco's! It's already been written in Bruin's will! Sa-mael can't have that kind of power! He would use it to oppress as many Fay as possible!"

Staccato sucked his teeth. "You're overthinking things."

"You and Theo obviously aren't thinking enough!" She collapsed to the sofa in a fit of exasperation.

Staccato straightened himself and smiled down at her with amuse-ment.

"Evangeline, darling, your mind is all over the place these days. You just worry about our baby and leave the politics to your brother and me."

He deposited Lydia in her arms. Pain reflected in Evangeline's eyes. The statement echoed back to him. He saw the stabbing arrogance with which he had punctuated his words. His mouth fell open.

"Dear, I'm terribly sorry!"

He reached out for her, but Evangeline wrenched back with Lydia in her arms.

"I *am* worrying about our baby! That's what makes this so frustrat-ing! But I'm forgetting I've been pinned as a mad woman!"

Staccato rubbed his hand over his face and sank to his knees beside her.

"Darling, you know I say a lot of stupid things, and that was one of them. Don't pay any attention to it, please, I beg you, forgive me."

Evangeline relented somewhat. Her lips sagged. She was tired, too tired to fight.

"You used to love it when I shared my opinion. You used to ask me what I thought about things. Now you never ask. If I give my opinion you tell me I shouldn't worry myself with such things."

Staccato furrowed his brow. His posture dissolved. "I'm so sorry." Sighing, he wilted into her lap. "I didn't know it bothered you, my love, I'm so sorry."

"It makes me feel like you think I'm stupid."

"Oh, no! Darling, I don't think that at all! You're wonderfully intelligent. I've been afraid of overwhelming you is all, what with the stress carrying Lydia put on your body—"

Evangeline grit her teeth together. "I wish you'd quit saying that! It's been nearly two months! My body is fine!" She clicked her tongue. "It wouldn't surprise me one bit if one of these days I woke up to find you and Theo had me committed!"

Staccato clutched her hands. "I'm sorry! I'll try to do better! I didn't mean to belittle you."

A moment passed. He felt her fingers running through his hair.

"I forgive you."

He rolled to his side to look up at her. She was soft once more, forgiving. Yet something remained broken in her eyes, and its fragments were being cauterized with a spiritual fire.

Chapter 46:

Breaking News

Though they had escaped Louisville late at night, it was only mid-afternoon when Pasha, Faina, and Cicada returned to Pisces. They were given plenty of time to recover. Pasha's wounds were nursed out of existence, and Cicada and Faina changed clothes and relaxed.

They spent the night at the embassy in Alrisha as Queen Calliope's personal guests. Once they made it to their rooms, they fell asleep before dinner, and didn't have a chance to catch up on the latest news.

Monday morning, Pasha was jolted from his dreams as Faina galloped into his bedroom and shook his shoulders.

"Pasha! Wake up! You have to hear this!"

Pasha pulled his covers over his head and rubbed his eyes.

"Ugh, Faina, can't you let me sleep an hour longer?"

She wrenched back the blankets. "This is serious!"

Cicada flowed into the room, throbbing with a fresh glow. Pasha had to shield his eyes. She handed him a cup of coffee.

"Take this, you're going to need it."

She crossed to the radio and flipped on the dial. The static sewed itself together until the voice of the news anchor at *The Morning Star* was discernible.

"For those of you just tuning in this morning, we're here at the Ecliptic Court in Zubenschamli where the case to determine Lydia Chevalsky's royal blood status will continue Tuesday morning. When we last left off, Cobra Samael presented evidence that Lydia Chevalsky is not the offspring of former King Bruin, but the illegitimate child of Queen Evangeline and Sir Staccato Nimbus."

Coffee fountained out of Pasha's mouth. "What?"

"An old diary belonging to the miraculous reveals Evangeline carried out an affair with her brother's former advisor. The tryst lasted from March 1889 to June of that same year, when Evangeline's marriage to Bruin was annulled and she and Staccato Nimbus were secretly married."

Pasha was clutching his chest in horror. "They had an affair? Are you serious?" He buried his face in his hands.

"The entries read before the court detail the passionate nature of the couple's affections ..."

Pasha cringed. "Ugh! Turn it off!"

But Faina and Cicada were too engrossed.

"... but despite the Queen's liaisons with Staccato Nimbus, it should be noted the Queen was forcibly violated by King Bruin that same month. Thus, the paternity of Mrs. Chevalsky is somewhat difficult to determine. That being said, given the sheer frequency of Mr. Nimbus and Queen Evangeline's dalliances, the odds rest with the miraculous at an estimated twenty-seven to one."

Pasha crammed his pillow over his ears. "Turn it off now!"

Faina flipped the switch. She took a seat at the end of Pasha's bed and squeezed the lump where his foot was.

"Well, look on the bright side, at least you know what the big secret is now."

Cicada plopped down beside her. "Yep! Looks like Staccato Nimbus knocked up your grandma!"

Pasha shook his head and made a disgusted face. "Cici, do me a favor and never ever use those words in a sentence ever again."

Chapter 47:
The Mirror Goes Missing

When Evangeline presented the finished mirror to Staccato, he had just returned home after an exhausting day with Theo. Lydia had awoken from her nap when he walked in the door, delighted to see her father. As usual, one of the first things he did when he greeted her was give her a mermaid kiss. Almost four months old now, Lydia giggled and squealed, and held her arm out for more.

Staccato laughed right along with her, and happily obliged. When at last she had settled down once more, he sat with her on the sofa, cradling her in his arms. Lydia stared up at him, humming contentedly and gnawing on a seashell rattle. Softly, he began to sing her the lullaby which his mother had sung to him.

"Lucifer of the fiery coals
had a handsome face and an ugly soul
he charmed two-thirds of the angel host
and the stars came tumbling down. ..."

Evangeline stood in the doorway holding the mirror with a timid smile. "It's finished."

Staccato turned around. "What is, darling?"

She inched forward. "The mirror."

Staccato's face fell. "Oh." He returned his attention to Lydia. "Well, thank goodness."

Evangeline remained rooted to the spot, staring after him. "Staccato, I want us to talk about it."

"What for? What's there to talk about?"

She edged closer. "Don't you want to know what it's for?"

"No, I don't. It's done. I don't care what you do with it, so long as I never have to look at it."

"But Staccato—"

"I said no, Evangeline! Never mention it again!"

It had sat on the vanity ever since, safely tucked away in its padded box. Despite his declaration, he did look at it once. Even he had to admit it was remarkable. The frame was frosted glass, almost soft to the touch. Light softened as it shone through the edges like sunshine refracted through ice. The frame was formed like the outstretched wings of a bird with its handle shaped like the body.

Even the reflection seemed crafted, if such a thing were possible, perfecting the symmetry of the subject's features, brightening their complexions. Staccato could've sworn it had diminished a blemish on his forehead, irritating him to no end. It was a ruddy masterpiece and he hated it all the more for that very reason. Every time Staccato passed it he caught himself glaring at it, as though it were a living thing and could discern how he loathed it.

Much to everyone's disappointment, the completion of the looking glass had not eradicated Evangeline's unstable behavior. She was distracted, pensive. Some days she stared out at the reef for hours, twisting her hair as though wringing out water. Her hands shook. She burst into sobs at random. The queerest part of all was how she tried to pretend everything was normal. Theo concluded it was leaving Voiler that caused her such pain. This seemed reasonable, and so Staccato tried not to worry.

The most uncomfortable aspect in preparing for their departure was having to fake Lydia's death. Days before, they took one last stroll around the reef together. Staccato followed along the glass walls of the vivarium as his wife and daughter swam outside. They'd enjoyed many walks like this before. But it was clear Evangeline received no consolation from this final outing.

Theo made up a false announcement and released it to *The Daily Compass*. Staccato and Evangeline couldn't bear to play along. They spent their last week in Voiler, hidden in their suite.

Most everything had been loaded into boxes or trunks. Evangeline's art supplies had been the first thing to get packed, but she kept a few materials to amuse herself. It was a relief to see her covered in charcoal for once, instead of sheathed in her hot leather apron and gloves.

One afternoon, Staccato lay on the bed while Evangeline nursed Lydia in the rocking chair. Out of nowhere they both burst into laughter. Staccato sat up in alarm. It'd been so long since he'd heard his wife laugh that the sound startled him. He stared at the two. Evangeline's waves of hair fell over her chest and wrapped Lydia in a golden halo. There was paint under her fingernails. They hadn't seen the surface in months and yet Staccato could make out the faint remnants of a tan line stenciled into her shoulder. The colors of the reef outside the window framed them in a prism of magnificent light and splendor. He couldn't look away.

When Evangeline caught him staring, she smiled and carried Lydia over to the bed. She placed Lydia on Staccato's chest. The baby settled her ear over his heart as though it were the perfect place for an after-lunch nap. Staccato chuckled.

"Well, she looks like she knows what she's doing."

Evangeline stroked her fingers through his hair and kissed his cheek. "I hope you don't mind staying put for a while."

Staccato laid his head on the pillows and yawned. "Of course not. I was just thinking our little girl has the right idea." He laid a hand on the small of her back, and the infant began drifting off. "What do you say, Lydie? Shall we give your Mama a well-deserved break?"

Evangeline's hair canopied around them as she pressed her lips to Staccato's.

"I was thinking I might go for one last swim."

He reached up to caress her cheek. "You don't want to stay and join us?"

Evangeline smirked and ran a finger beneath his chin. "Maybe when I get back."

"Be careful, dearest."

"I will." She lingered, tracing a nail down the side of his face and looking into his eyes with a new depth. Staccato lifted an eyebrow.

"Are you alright?"

A soft but unconvincing laugh escaped her lips. "I love you."

He could feel the warmth of her breath beneath his nose as their lips touched again. They carried on for several moments, then a faint light fell on his shoulder. It was coming from Evangeline's hand. His head fell back.

"What are you doing?" He practically laughed, feeling sleepy and giddy all at once.

She bit her lip as she giggled. "I'm helping you fall asleep, silly."

Staccato's eyes grew heavy. He put his arm around her waist.

"Don't go." His vision was blurry.

"Staccato, I love you so much." The golden light bathed her silhouette. She lifted his left hand and kissed the inside of his wrist. Staccato's breath swelled in a euphoric wave.

"I love you, Evangeline." He descended into sleep.

***

Staccato awoke an hour and a half later with Lydia asleep on his chest. The light had grown dim outside the window. Perhaps a storm had settled over the surface. He glanced back at the clock and wondered if Evangeline had been back long. He arched his neck in a sleepy stretch, trying not to disturb Lydia. Maybe Evangeline had gone off to visit with Javaid, Estella, or even Theo if he wasn't busy.

Staccato was about to close his eyes once more when he noticed the mirror was no longer on the vanity. He stared at the empty space for a moment, letting the dark fog of apprehension settle over his brain. Something was wrong, and Evangeline was where she wasn't supposed to be.

Staccato hastened to get up, stirring Lydia from her sleep. As he headed out the door with the baby in his arms, he noticed a folded letter lying in place of the box. Staccato's hands trembled. Fearing he might drop Lydia, he set her back on the bed, and picked up the paper.

My Love,

I realize what I am endeavoring to do will likely be the subject of a considerable and quite appropriate quarrel when I return, but I cannot sit idly by and watch as our home is taken from us. As you know, I've spent a lot of time reading up on Caiman Asterias's diary. I know the diary disappeared before anyone could legitimize its authenticity, and I know it's widely believed to be little more than a silly legend. But I have reason to believe the diary existed, and its records are true.

Asterias claimed the only way to cast the ophidians back into the abyss was through the use of a magic mirror called Amnos. Desperate to do something, I dug up the instructions from antiquity and began crafting the mirror. If I finished, I could stop Samael from corrupting Bruin any more than he had already, drive back the C.O.N., and save Voiler. I believe I've managed to successfully recreate the looking glass spoken of in legend. Its capabilities are far beyond what I had planned. I'm still discovering all of its powers for myself. I've wanted to discuss this with you, but I understand why you would prefer to avoid the subject.

Anyway, I've gone to see Bruin. If I can get him to look into the mirror everything will be made right again, and we won't have to leave our home. Please do not mistake this as an attempt to rescue a man whose only achievement in life was to abuse and cut down everyone in his path. Whether we like Bruin or not, the preservation of his life is in the kingdom's best interest. If Bruin perishes, Samael will inherit the kingdom. We will have granted the very man who craves our child's death power above all nations. Can you imagine anything worse than the leader of the C.O.N. sitting at our doorstep poised to devour our child the moment she surfaced from the sea?

Though Bruin is a terrible despot, I desperately hope to avoid replacing him with the Cobra. If all goes well, I should be back in time to feed Lydia. But if not, know that I love you and Lydia more than anything.

-Evangeline

Staccato put a hand out to steady himself. His chest felt like the epicenter of an enormous strain that pulled everything inward on a tight, unyielding cable. Evangeline thought she could reason with Bruin. She had completely lost touch with reality, and now she was putting herself in danger.

Struggling to catch his breath, Staccato stuffed the letter into his pocket. He summoned the maid to watch Lydia, and sent word to Javaid and Theo. Without waiting, he headed to the surface in search of Evangeline, hoping to find her alive.

Chapter 48:
The Forgery

Pasha, Faina, and Cicada power-walked down the pier towards Ti-aki. Bodyguards flanked them on all sides. The shard remained safely hidden with Cicada, while Faina couldn't stop ranting about the latest details of the hearing.

"To think all these years he kept his love for Evangeline a secret, just like in *The Great Gatsby*! And then a secret wedding! It's so romantic! Do you think Staccato has pictures?"

Pasha rolled his eyes. "Give it a rest, Faina! This isn't one of your novels! This is serious! You're forgetting what's at stake here! We want Bruin to have been Ma's father, otherwise I can't take back the throne!"

Cicada shrugged. "Gotta say, Pasha, the numbers are against you."

Pasha moaned. "Don't say that!"

"What about the resemblance?" Faina suggested. "Have you ever noticed any similarities between Staccato and your mother?"

Pasha rubbed the back of his neck. "Now that you mention it, they both have those deep-set eyes with the heavy lids."

"Strong cheekbones, strong jawline."

"They take their tea the same," observed Cicada. "And what about the similarities between Pasha and Staccato?"

Pasha whipped around in a fury. "What similarities?"

"You're kidding, right? You two are so alike! You both get that snooty, condescending look on your face whenever you're mad, for instance."

Cicada doubled over in laughter. Pasha hunched his shoulders. "What condescending look?"

Faina couldn't contain her giggles. "You're doing it now!"

Pasha's eyes crossed as Cicada poked a finger in his face. "And your nose!"

Pasha waved her away. "I do not have Staccato's nose! His is all pointy and long!"

"That's just because he's old. Yours will be that way too by the time you're his age."

"Just because—"

"Don't forget the jaw!" Faina pinched his chin.

"Plus, they're both tall."

"Will you two stop with the poking, and the pinching, and the grabbing?" Pasha roared. "I am not like Staccato! I'm nothing like Staccato!

We're not related! Staccato is a liar, and a status seeker, and apparently a philanderer! I'm nothing like him!"

Cicada leaned towards Faina and cupped a hand over her mouth. "They're both touchy."

"Enough!" Pasha was shouting now. "Do either of you realize how big of a problem this is? Everything I've worked for is about to be for nothing, thanks to Staccato and his wild youth! And all you two can do is sit here and make jokes! It's not funny!"

Suddenly, Faina let out a gasp. "Now I know why those old pictures of Staccato looked so familiar! They look just like you!"

Pasha froze, recalling how Faina had referred to Staccato as a sheik. "Well, maybe we do look a little alike…"

Unfortunately, their conversation was cut short as Katya raced out the front door.

"You're back!"

Skelter followed behind her trying to keep ahold of Mammoth on his leash. Pasha turned and, masking his worry behind a smile, held out his arms for his little sister. She lowered her mouth to his ear.

"Did you get the you-know-what?"

Pasha scooped her into his arms and laughed. "You bet I did."

Katya pulled back to take a thorough look at him. She frowned.

"Why are you so upset, Pasha? Aren't you glad to be home?"

Pasha sighed. He threw Skelter a look as though inquiring, "How much does she know?"

Skelter made a cutting motion across his neck and shook his head. So she knew nothing. Pasha scuffled her hair.

"Of course I'm glad to be home, silly!"

"Then what's wrong?"

Pasha craned his head and groaned. "This is gonna be fun to explain …" He set Katya down. "It's nothing for you to worry about. Now let's go find King Lahar so he can take a look at this shard. Once that's done we'll all go to Libra and see Mama."

They followed their escorts through the grand foyer to the wide windowed room that was the King's study. Lahar was seated at his large koa wood desk, thumbing through an enormous ancient volume. He glanced up and erupted into a broad smile.

"Ah, my friends! You're back!"

Lahar patted Mammoth's head as he galumphed to his side. Pasha couldn't help but notice that, next to Melodious, King Lahar was the only person large enough to make Mammoth seem like a conventionally sized dog. Lahar pulled out a chair for each of them.

"I am so sorry you could not have returned to better news."

Pasha cleared his throat and tossed his head towards Katya. Skelter patted Katya on the shoulder and gestured for her to go play in the hall. Katya did as instructed.

"Forgive me," sighed Lahar, pinching his temples. "I did not consider the girl."

"It's fine." Pasha reassured him. "We'll have to figure out some way to explain things to her by the time we get to Libra."

"Which reminds me, I've made arrangements for you and your friends to travel in my own personal coach so you won't have to bother with the press. Armed escorts will accompany you to and from the terminal. The horses and caravan are being transported to Karkinos."

"We appreciate that, Your Majesty. Security from the press is quite a relief, as you know, under the circumstances."

He gestured to Cicada, who took out a small protective case from her purse. She unhinged the clasp and revealed the shard.

Lahar dropped his jaw and leaned in closer, studying the fragment with squinted eyes. He took it between his massive fingers and laid it atop a clean fold of linen on the desk. He picked up the magnifying glass, shielding it between his face and the chip, then turned to his impressive anthology and stumbled through the pages. Reaching into a desk drawer, he removed a loupe and held it to his eye.

"Genuine Cassiopeian gold, a good sign … the ash used in the glaze, however, is from Horned Heights, a pair of volcanoes in Mesarthim."

Cicada and Skelter nodded their heads while Pasha and Faina exchanged confused glances.

"Uh, what exactly does that mean?" Pasha scratched the back of his neck.

"Evangeline's mirror contained ash from nine different volcanoes; unfortunately, none of them were Horned Heights."

Cicada hung her head and groaned. Faina had to anchor herself to her chair.

"You mean we took the wrong shard?"

"No, not exactly." He gave the loupe another twist and pointed his finger to an almost imperceptible anomaly. "You won't find many imperfections in Princess Evangeline's glassworks, but the few that do make their way into the pieces are rather unique. Some may even consider it her trade-mark. Whoever crafted this specimen was making a deliberate attempt to imitate those distinctive blemishes."

Skelter's hands passed over his face like a mask. Lahar bobbed his head.

"Exactly, Skelter. In all likelihood this is a decoy meant to deceive the C.O.N."

Pasha bowed his head, trying to gage exactly what Lahar was attempting to say.

"You mean someone else stole the shard and replaced it with a fake?"

"I believe that is what happened."

"But how do you know it wasn't a decoy made by the C.O.N. to deceive thieves?" interposed Faina.

"Because this was made by an igneous. Not only is glassblowing a craft popular amongst mermaids, but it enjoys special attention from igneous who heat the works with their own bodily fire. It gives a whole new meaning to the term 'glassblowing.'"

Cicada rubbed her chin. "And no doubt interacts with the chemical properties of the materials."

Lahar nodded. "… Often lending the art its own unique attributes. Some differences are more understated than others. This artisan was particularly careful not to give himself away, another reason to believe this is a decoy."

Pasha shook his head in disbelief. "But who was it that stole the original? Where do you think it could be?"

Lahar removed the loupe and shook his head. "Unfortunately, I'm not the person to ask. Staccato, however, should be greatly intrigued."

Chapter 49:

Pasha Faces Staccato

Pasha and the others arrived in Chamali close to dinner time. They were told they'd find the rest of the company awaiting them in the private sitting room on the second floor. Pasha was so eager to go after Staccato, he ran ahead of his own security as soon as they exited the lift.

"Pasha, don't," Faina pleaded after him.

But Pasha refused to listen. He wrenched open the heavy oak door and fled into the warmth of a wide, posh room. Sonata, Melodious, Lydia, and Pyro conversed quietly amongst themselves. Staccato was nowhere to be found. Pasha didn't even bother to greet anyone.

"Where is he?"

Everyone jumped and turned. Pyro slapped his knee and groped for his crutches.

"Well, look who finally made it back!"

Lydia's face lit up. "Pasha, my love!"

But Pasha had already entered battle mode. "Where's Staccato?"

Lydia dropped her smile and scurried to her son, embarrassed. She took his hands and whispered to him in Russian.

"Don't do this."

"I wanna know where he is."

Lydia squeezed his hands tighter. "Pasha, not now!"

"Does he realize how difficult it was trying to get Katya on the train? People pointing at us, whispering … we're lucky she isn't traumatized!"

"Shhh! I will deal with Katya, and you and I will talk about this later. But right now you need to calm down and say hello to everybody."

"Not until I find Staccato."

Lydia gritted her teeth. "Will you keep your voice down?"

"Relax, they can't understand us!"

"I did not raise you to behave this way!"

But Pasha was adamant. "He's humiliated our family, Ma!"

"Right now you are humiliating our family by acting like a crazy person! Besides, just what do you think you're going to do when you see him?"

Without thinking, Pasha relapsed into English. "I'll knock him into next Thursday, is what I'll do!"

An elegant voice redolent with sarcasm leaked around the corner. "Could you make it Wednesday? Business to attend to, and all. I'd hate to miss an entire week."

Staccato appeared from behind the kitchen door, stirring his coffee in a dignified manner. He stared Pasha down with an unimpressed sense of authority. For a moment Pasha blanched. Regaining his strength, he drew his eyebrows together and turned to his mother.

"*Spasibo, Ma! Ty mog by skazat' mne, chto on stoyal tam!*" Thanks, Ma! You could have told me he was standing there!

Staccato plowed forward, and addressed Pasha in Russian. "Don't speak to your mother like that!"

Pasha threw up his hands, and continued in his own language.

"Oh no, you are not my grandfather! Don't think you can start using that to try and control me! I refuse to accept you as part of our family!"

Lydia gasped, shocked. But Staccato only narrowed his eyes further.

"Whether you accept it or not, your mother is my daughter, and I will not allow her to be disrespected by a skinny little brat with an overactive temper!"

"If you wanted to be a part of our lives you shouldn't have abandoned her!"

The others' eyes traveled between the pair, completely oblivious as to what they were saying.

The door flew open. Skelter, Faina, Mammoth, and Cicada collapsed one after another over the threshold. Katya sauntered past them and made a beeline for her mother.

"Mama!" She threw herself around Lydia's waist and buried her face in the folds of her skirt.

Staccato glared at Pasha. "Well, are you going to make a scene in front of your little sister?"

Pasha scowled back at him. Staccato rolled his eyes, and set aside his coffee. He grabbed his staff, and, taking Pasha roughly by the arm, led him towards the door.

"In that case, I suggest we adjourn to a more private setting, and we'll see if your arm has the power to break the space-time continuum."

Pasha followed Staccato back to his room and waited until they were inside. Staccato closed the door.

"Now what is it you would like to say?"

"How could you lie to me about something like this? Do you realize how embarrassing this is?"

Staccato leaned his head back with a bitter laugh. "Believe me, Pasha, however embarrassing it is for you, it is a thousand times more embarrassing for me. Take comfort in that."

"You had an affair with my grandmother!"

Staccato lowered himself into a chair. "Yes, we had an affair!" He gestured for Pasha to sit, but he was too irate.

"And you documented it for anyone to find!"

"Yes, I did."

Pasha paused and looked up at Staccato in confusion. Why wasn't he putting up more of a fight?

"Is this some kind of trick?"

Staccato shrugged and shook his head. "No. I am merely confirming the truth of your statements."

"Don't you have something to say for all this?"

"For the time being I'd rather keep quiet and let you get it all out. I realize there's a therapeutic quality to shouting the sins of my youth back at me."

"Don't be such a martyr!" Pasha's nostrils flared. "You show up out of nowhere and tell me I'm heir to some powerful kingdom in a magical world! You spend months preparing me to take the throne, teaching me about my country. Then it turns out none of it's true! It's not my country, is it, Staccato? Your country is my country, because apparently you're my …" He didn't want to say the word "grandfather," no, he wanted something colder, stiffer. "You're my mother's biological father!"

Pasha was panting. Staccato merely stared at him, vexing him further.

"Do you realize how big of a lie that is? I mean, why? Why would you try to pass me off as something I'm not?"

Staccato sighed and closed his eyes. "I did not try to pass you off as something I believe you are not."

Pasha forced a sarcastic laugh. "Oh, you mean because of that one time with Bruin?" He covered his face. "Are you serious? Even if I did end up being Bruin's heir, do you think anyone's going to pay attention? No! All they're gonna care about is the scandal! This isn't even a hearing about my mother anymore, it's a hearing about Staccato Nimbus!" At last he collapsed to a seat and buried his head in his hands.

At length Staccato spoke, his voice somewhat softened. "I never meant for that to happen."

Pasha peered through his fingers. "You really believe Bruin is my mother's real father, don't you?"

"Did you hear about Mother Genesis?"

Pasha nodded and rubbed his eyes with the heels of his hands. "That doesn't mean anything. Mother Genesis never makes any sense."

"You and I made the mistake of not listening to Mother Genesis last December. Remember that? We relied too much on our own understanding."

"But Mother Genesis has a convoluted way of speaking. She never says exactly what she means." He trailed off and looked up at Staccato. "Your eyes are shaped like my mother's."

Staccato shrugged. "Lots of people have deep-set eyes."

"You and Katya leave your spoons in your teacup."

Staccato raised his eyebrows in mild surprise. "Does she do that? I never noticed."

"Faina and Cicada think we have the same nose."

Staccato tossed his head with a weak scoff. "I don't know about that. Mine is much too long. If anything you have Evangeline's nose."

But Staccato's rebuttals weren't enough for Pasha. "We both have a talent for learning foreign languages. We're both allergic to damp. You're the only other person I know who sneezes when a bright light is shined in their face."

They remained silent for a moment. When Pasha finally did speak again, he had regained some of his old fuel.

"Why did you abandon my mother?"

Staccato's face dropped; the words smarted in his eyes. A grave shadow came over his features.

"Pasha, I have always loved your mother. From the moment I laid eyes on her I knew she would have my heart for eternity. I never intended for us to part, but circumstance drove me to it."

Eager for real answers, Pasha leaned forward. "What do you mean?"

"Pasha, do you think I could relinquish my own daughter so easily?" He sighed and turned his attention to the floor. "When your mother was about four years old, I began my first job with the resistance. I worked for King Thayer as a spy. As someone who worked in politics, it was easy for me to gain access into private circles and collect information. They needed someone like me. Theo was the one who recommended it. Javaid wasn't so keen on the idea. He would've much rather me stayed in Siberia and devoted all my time to your mother. He was more than willing to provide us with whatever we needed, and naturally it was an enticing offer.

The problem was, I felt I had an obligation to fulfill. Theo thought so too.

"You see, it broke Evangeline's heart to leave Voiler. In the end, she gave her life thinking she could stop the C.O.N. and save everyone. She had Samael's plan figured out from the beginning. She knew he had left Bruin alive so he could manipulate him. Theo and I didn't listen to her. And when she pleaded with us to drive back the C.O.N., we dismissed her." His face assumed a bitter air.

"As you know, your grandmother was … not well. In fact, I'm not convinced it was puerperal mania only she suffered from. She was struggling before that. She'd have bouts of melancholy followed by manic episodes that could last for days. After the baby was born she only grew worse. I began treating Evangeline's opinions as though they were quaint, little fancies, something to be humored. I thought I was protecting her. But at the same time I believe Evangeline's frailty inflated my sense of self-worth. I took pride in her dependence on me, so much so I diminished her role into that of some naive, helpless invalid.

"It is a husband's job to love his wife and to make her feel loved. I belittled Evangeline. I put myself first. Because of me, Evangeline became desperate to the point of delusion. Because of me, she took that blasted mirror to Bruin, thinking she could singlehandedly save the world. Because of me, Evangeline is dead."

Staccato regarded his own hands with such a narrowed, scathing eye, Pasha felt he wanted nothing more than to cut them off. The memory of Staccato yelling at his bloodied hands drifted to the forefront of his mind. "What have I done?" he had repeated over and over. Staccato had not murdered Evangeline, but he still felt responsible for her death. Yet something didn't sit right with the way Staccato had described Theo's attitude towards his espionage.

"Is that how Theo felt?"

Staccato's shoulders stiffened. For a brief moment his eyes widened. He made a deliberate attempt to look settled, moving with such purpose it was clearly unnatural.

"Theo brought some things to my attention which I had failed to address during my marriage…"

Pasha looked Staccato directly in the eye. "Was this before or after Theo abdicated?"

Staccato hesitated for a moment. He released a heavy sigh. "After."

Pasha's mouth turned sour. "Theo guilted you into working as a mercenary, didn't he?"

Staccato pursed his lips. It was some time before he answered.

"Even if he did, that still doesn't absolve me of the hand I played in Evangeline's death." He rubbed at the corners of his eyes. "As much as I would have loved to devote my time exclusively to your mother, I owed something to Evangeline. In addition to being an Ecliptic Council member, I became a spy, and a rather good one. Good enough to make enemies. Good enough to earn a price on my head."

Chapter 50:

The Madness of King Theo

Staccato sat in the parlor at Alveare with his broken leg propped on an ottoman. His crutches were leaned neatly against the arm of the chair. Two days had passed since he'd been rescued from the C.O.N., injured and half-starved.

Javaid had charged three-year-old Sonata with tending to her uncle through the use of her healing presence, for young mermaids often have a potent therapeutic power. Sonata was overjoyed to oblige him. She curled comfortably in Staccato's lap. Her eyes closed and her head draped across his shoulder. Any minute she would fall asleep. But any chance of such a pleasure was dashed at the sound of Theo's harsh, grating voice. Sonata jumped and rubbed her eyes as her uncle started another rant.

"Have you heard the latest?"

It seemed that whenever Staccato saw Theo he was more and more tense. Even his shoulders seemed to roll progressively forward as though huddling around a seed of bitterness.

"Members of the C.O.N. have been rooting out migrant Fay in the Other and killing them like vermin." He brandished a newspaper. "Did you hear about this poor chap Melodious Krüner? Son of a well-known Fay family? Apparently, he'd been living peacefully in Bavaria for the past twenty-some-odd years as a reverend. Hadn't seen Voiler since he was an infant. One night, the C.O.N. shows up out of nowhere accusing him of withholding some sort of artifact they needed. Naturally, the man had no idea what they were talking about. When he denied it, the C.O.N. set fire to his church and attacked his congregation. Killed everyone, even his wife and children."

Sonata looked back at her father with frightful eyes. Javaid, impatient with Theo's attitude, massaged his forehead. With his free hand he signaled for Sonata to go out and play on the lanai. She complied and left them.

Javaid had always been a soft-spoken, gentle merman, with none of his brother's commanding presence or Estella's queenly dignity. Nor had he Evangeline's inclinations for flying off into passionate tangents. Instead, Javaid was introspective and almost withdrawn. When Theo made the decision to abdicate, many had feared Karkinos might fall as easily as Ursa. But Javaid had surprised them all.

Theo and Javaid argued endlessly these days. They'd crossed horns several times over what was to be done with Lydia, rendering Staccato uncomfortable whenever the two were together in a room. And Estella spent so much of her time traveling these days she was never there to straighten them out. It only seemed to worsen as time went on.

Staccato coughed into his sleeve. "Yes, I did read about that. Terrible shame. I can't imagine what that poor man must be going through right now."

Theo's eyes remained scathing. "This is exactly why it would've been better if you'd put Lydia in an orphanage."

Staccato could see the muscles in Javaid's shoulders tightening.

"If it makes such little difference whether or not she's here or in the Other, we might as well bring her back home."

Before Staccato could answer, Theo had cut in for him. "No, we will not bring Lydia back yet. Not as long as the C.O.N. remains as strong as it is. Besides, how would it look? Staccato raising our niece? People will figure it out in seconds!"

Staccato had already had enough of Theo referring to him as though he weren't in the room.

"No one knows about the affair." Staccato tried to keep his voice steady. "And why is it so ridiculous that I would be Lydia's guardian when I've served this family faithfully over the years? It isn't as though you or Javaid or Estella could have gone away to raise her."

Theo narrowed his eyes. "Don't you realize that if a male heir is born within Lydia's lifetime, you will have to escort her back to Voiler for a legitimacy hearing at the Ecliptic Courts? They won't just set her descendant back on the throne without checking to see if she has any real claim. And when they ask who raised her she'll point to you and say, that man right there! Staccato Nimbus, looking after Evangeline Soter's child! How do you think the court will react to that?"

Staccato was just about to correct Theo for not saying Evangeline *Nimbus*, when Javaid threw himself up in a passion.

"As though it even matters! Ursa is thriving under our stewardship, they do not need an heir to restore them. Bring the child back, let her live a normal life; why lay the burden of producing an heir on one so young when it is needless?"

Theo drew his ringed fingers into a fist. "We can't bring her back! Whether or not Ursa needs an heir, the fact remains that as long as the C.O.N. survives, Lydia is in danger."

Staccato pinched the space between his eyebrows and closed his eyes. "Well, she's hidden away in Siberia. You have your way, so there's nothing to fear."

Theo whipped round to glare at Staccato. "If I had my way, Lydia would have actually been up for adoption, not living out some convoluted fantasy with her real father pretending to be her adopted parent!"

"Need I remind you that telling Lydia she was adopted, and that I had no relationship with her mother, was *your* idea!" His nose wrinkled. "You've forgotten what Mother Genesis said, I presume."

Theo waved his hand with a sneer. "I thought you didn't believe what Mother Genesis said."

"I …" Staccato's voice faded. He sank his head into his hands. "I don't know anymore."

"I would think if you did believe her it would've been easy to give her up, if you really believed she was that monstrous Bruin's child."

Staccato winced. Theo was so cold now, there was none of his old compassion left in him.

"What happened isn't Lydia's fault. She didn't decide how she came into this world. Either way, I love her, and I couldn't bear being separated from her. I can hardly stand it as it is."

Javaid nodded understandingly. "I can only imagine. It would break my heart if I couldn't see Sonata every day."

"Do either of you ever think clearly?" snipped Theo. "The C.O.N. has been hunting down Fay migrants in the Other. Staccato endangers Lydia by association! He has enemies now!"

Javaid turned, almost knocking over a vase. "And whose fault is that, Theo? It was you who bullied him into giving service to your rebel groups!"

"I bullied no one! Staccato is honored to serve in Evangeline's memory! Don't you see? The C.O.N. is already keeping tabs on Staccato. If he continues to see Lydia on a regular basis they will trace him back to her, and use her as a means to weaken him."

Staccato tightened his jaw as he tried to ignore the infectious anxiety in Theo's statement. Javaid stepped in front of him like a barrier.

"How can you ask him to leave his daughter, Theo? Has your grief rendered you so heartless you would abandon all sense of empathy and compassion?"

"Would you have her die, brother? Die like Evangeline just for the sake of a little sentimentality?"

"You have no children, you don't understand! You can't!"

Theo's chest swelled as he rose from his chair and descended upon Javaid.

"How dare you address your king in such a way!"

Staccato knit his brows together, as though he hadn't heard Theo correctly. But when he looked up at his old friend, there was a misguided conviction in his eyes.

"You are not the King here!" thundered Javaid.

And despite himself, Theo stumbled back. Though he tried to hide it, there was fear in his eyes. Javaid pressed on in a more controlled tone.

"You forsook that title years ago. In your grief, you cast it aside, and it is I who sit in your place now. It is I who make the decisions for this country. And you are a sad, lonely, shell of a man! You have let your grief and your guilt poison you with fear, such fear that you would banish your niece to a foreign land and call it protection! You would have her orphaned and alone and call it security! You have manipulated the man you once called your brother into spying on the C.O.N. when he could be at home with his daughter! You do these things because you do not want the responsibility of failure! You cannot forgive yourself for what happened to Evangeline, and so you use others to absolve you of your own sense of guilt!"

Theo's nostrils flared as he looked past Javaid's shoulder to stare expectantly at Staccato. Staccato could not help but pity him.

"I know you mean well, Theo. But I will not be parted from my daughter. Ever."

Theo's brows lowered over his eyes as he threw back his head with haughty pride and drew away from them.

"Fine! Have it your way! I withhold my counsel from this day forth."

And, turning, he swept out of the parlor, strode down the stairs, and disappeared into the water. Staccato steadied his hand over his chest. Javaid surveyed him with a penetrating sense of apprehension.

"You say you will not be separated from Lydia, and yet you let him frighten you all the same. I can feel it."

Staccato cradled his head in his hands. "Theo may be ill, but his fears are not unfounded. This Krüner fellow is not the first of his kind. There have been many such stories like his in *The Daily Compass* as of late, and I am well known to the C.O.N. I hear they've put a price on my head."

Javaid sat beside him and laid a comforting hand on his shoulder.

"Then put aside this rebel business. Resign from your position on the Council. Go back to Siberia and devote your time to Lydia."

Staccato shut his eyes, letting the thought sink into his skin. He smiled.

"Yes. I think you're right, Javaid. That is what I will do."

Chapter 51:

The Pieces Fall Together

Pasha leaned forward with his folded hands resting in front of his mouth. He was staring sober-eyed at the tips of his shoes. He recalled how Sonata had said if Pasha knew the details of Staccato's story he wouldn't resent him so. His insults stained a bitter taste on his tongue. He wished he'd never doubted Staccato.

"Someone found you in Siberia, didn't they?"

"One night, when your mother was sixteen, a bounty hunter sent by the C.O.N. came looking for me. Aunt Poppy and I fought her off. Your mother never knew about it. She was safe in the hedge, asleep. After interrogating the assassin, Poppy and I concluded she didn't know about Lydia. She had only come looking for me. She hadn't even made it into the hedge. I knew I couldn't stay with your mother. I would be endangering her life if I remained. If the C.O.N. found out about her existence, they would've used her to get to me. And if they found out she had any claim on Ursa's throne, they certainly would've killed her.

"So, I left," the word seemed to throb through him, "and I didn't come back. I was told it tore her apart. After a month had passed she went down to the lake and cried out for me until her voice was hoarse. I told Poppy to let her think I was dead. But Lydia didn't seem to believe it. I'm sure it was her intuition which told her I was alive. She thought I had abandoned her."

He stopped to catch his breath. The story was taking a physical toll on him.

"After that I didn't want to live anymore." He bore his eyes into a blank space on the wall. "Your mother made losing Evangeline bearable. And without her I couldn't go on."

"What stopped you?"

The question flew out of Pasha's mouth before he could think. But it was too late, the words were already out there, floating in the space between them.

Staccato looked him over, flummoxed. "Stopped me from what?"

Pasha held his breath for a moment. Biting his lip, he answered. "I mean, what made you change your mind?"

Staccato gawked at Pasha for a moment or two. His eyes glazed over with a knowing suspicion.

"Pasha, what do you know that you're not supposed to?"

Out of excuses, Pasha explained how Faina had been struck with a memory of Staccato trying to take his own life after Pasha had broken his staff. Staccato blinked once or twice, as though he couldn't quite decide how to react. Finally, he folded his hands in his lap, and looked Pasha in the eye.

"Javaid found me before any permanent damage could be done." He smoothed the material of his trousers with his hands. "Javaid and Constanza went out of their way to heal me. They looked after me. Sonata too, little as she was. I learned to look outside myself for hope, for wisdom, for direction. That's when things became a little easier.

"I went out of my way to make as many public appearances in Voiler as I could, so the C.O.N. wouldn't go looking for me in the Other. After a year had passed, I began checking up on your mother in secret. I'd watch her from a distance, remain hidden."

"She never saw you? Never recognized you?"

Staccato smirked. "I was very careful to stay out of sight. As you know, I do have the advantage of being a miraculous, so there are ways to ensure concealment. The necklace, for example. You obviously had that one figured out. Plus, I haven't always had this beard …" His eyes rolled towards his scalp. "And I used to have hair."

Pasha gaped at him in shock. "You shaved your head and grew a beard just to make sure Mama couldn't identify you?"

He nodded. "I was still fairly young, too. About thirty-eight. I'll never forget everyone's reactions. Sonata told me I looked like a pirate."

Pasha found his lips curling into an amused smile. Staccato snickered.

"She was just a baby then." He busied himself with a loose string on the upholstery. "But I kept an eye on your mother. I was there when she married your father, or at least when they had their public ceremony. I wasn't happy about it, mind you, under the circumstances, but I was there. I was a little late checking in after you were born, but you were a little early."

Everything came together in Pasha's head. A new light dawned in his eyes as he gazed at Staccato.

"You were there when the Reds came for us! It wasn't Evangeline, it was you! You made the soldiers hallucinate, didn't you?"

Staccato bowed his head in a grim manner. "Had I known, I would have come sooner. Yes, I made the soldiers hallucinate. Fortunately, the Other is more susceptible to Fay powers, having been less exposed to magic. I was able to start picking soldiers off at random, and I held the illusion long enough for you to make your getaway. I could never do that with

Voilerians. Once they were in a sufficient uproar, I loosened your mother's bonds. I planted the revolver where your mother was sitting. She shot the soldier who was tying the noose, and I shot the one who retaliated. Pyro pulled Katya out of the fire—"

Pasha had to stop him there. "Woah, wait, you had Pyro with you? He's known about all of this? *Pyro*?"

Staccato chuckled. "You'd be surprised at the secrets Pyro can keep. He did used to work for the Saighdeoir, remember. And being fireproof of course, Pyro was able to run into the house and gather what you needed."

A thought occurred to Pasha. "You bought Harpagos from the gypsies, didn't you?"

"I did. I saw how it tore you apart to lose your pet, and I couldn't bear it. I brought him to Voiler so someday I could return him to you."

At this stage, Pasha could hardly contain himself. He scooted his chair closer to Staccato as he continued on.

"As for the Breadwinners, well, I was very busy in 1920. When your mother started working at the speakeasy I was being held prisoner in Crux. I wasn't released until after the first stage of your initiation had already taken place, otherwise I would have stopped you, and I would've taken care of Piyakov myself. If it hadn't been for the Land Lock I would have brought you all home after Katya was born. I tried several times before but your mother was always expecting, and given her tendency to miscarry I was afraid such a shock might cause her to lose the baby. I had been planning on returning when you were still a small child. I never dreamed I would have to wait until you were sixteen!"

Pasha stared at him, dumbfounded. Staccato didn't seem to notice.

"I am sorry I lied to you, Pasha. You're right, that was a considerably large detail to keep secret. I'm sorry for the damage I've done to your reputation. I'm sorry I scandalized you and your sister. I'm sorry I wasn't there for your mother enough."

"I forgive you."

Staccato did a double take. "What?"

"I forgive you. I understand why you did what you did. I'm sorry for judging you when I knew nothing about you."

Staccato pressed his lips together and gave a half-hearted smile. "It's alright. Had I been in your position, I know I would have reacted the same way."

"But there's still something I don't understand," Pasha leaned back in his chair and folded his arms across his chest. "After you brought us to

Voiler, why didn't you just tell us who you were? Why did you try to keep it a secret? Instead of coming to me, you should've just gone to Ma and told her you'd come back for her. You were willing to face the Ecliptic Council when Ma was a child, why did you change your mind?"

Staccato dragged his fingers through his beard. "There are many reasons why I hid the truth from you, Pasha. The most important being that by keeping my identity a secret, I could keep the affair a secret … or so I thought anyway. No one would know I raised your mother, and no one would question why."

Pasha studied Staccato with unblinking eyes. "But you never planned to tell us who you were. I heard you say so to Sonata."

It was clear as Staccato bent forward with his head bowed that Pasha had cornered him. He let his hands fall open in his lap.

"I didn't want to hurt you with the truth." The wrinkles around his eyes strained like the drawstrings of a heavy purse that might spill at any moment. "Pasha, I've made many mistakes in my life." The corner of his mouth twitched with an acidic smirk. "All this business with the Ecliptic Council, the hearing, it just goes to show I have nothing to offer your family but shame. You don't need me tarnishing your future."

Pasha instinctively drew towards him. He flowed like water until he found he was kneeling at the side of Staccato's chair.

"That's not true." Pasha reached out and placed his hand on Staccato's arm. "I have only myself to be ashamed of. I refused to trust you. I mocked you. I disrespected you, when my whole life you've been fighting for my good. I'm sorry for everything, Staccato. Please don't go away from us because of the things I said."

As Staccato sat up to look at Pasha, he moved as a man freed. Pasha glanced up at Staccato with a cheeky smile.

"You know, Katya is gonna be really excited."

Staccato fingered his collar. "She will be?"

Pasha chuckled and smacked the arm of the chair. "Are you kidding? I guarantee you it'll be all she talks about for weeks. So, what do you say? Will you stick around? For her sake at least, and Mama's?"

Bit by bit, Staccato smiled, and the more he smiled the more he lowered his head to hide it. "If you insist."

Pasha beamed at Staccato as he fell back into a sitting position at the foot of the chair.

"You loved Evangeline."

Staccato bobbed his head in agreement, but remained silent.

"Last Christmas, when I told you a mermaid named Eve, who said she knew you, showed me how to break the Land Lock, you knew it was Evangeline, didn't you?"

"Yes." His voice was strained.

"You thought she might somehow be alive."

"I did."

"But you were afraid to believe me, just like I was afraid to believe in the Firebird. Neither of us wanted to be disappointed."

Staccato bent forward to stare at Pasha questioningly with his elbows on his knees.

"Faina is right," Pasha admitted. "We really are just alike." He paused and bit his lip. "Sorry I threatened to knock you into next week, by the way."

Staccato's eyes met Pasha's. He began to laugh. "It's quite alright. I daresay I made many a similar threat when I was your age."

Pasha snorted. "Did you ever manage to punch anyone through time?"

"No, but I did manage to make a boy croak like a frog for a week once after hitting him." He flexed his fingers. "Miraculous problems."

Chapter 52:
A Bigger Mystery

"Well, Pasha, did you knock him into next week?" scoffed Pyro as Staccato and Pasha reemerged, both looking quite at peace.

Sonata smacked his shoulder. "Don't tease him about such things!"

Lydia had disappeared to help Katya settle in, and Faina had gone off to change into comfortable clothing. Everyone seemed to be in a relaxed mood despite everything they'd gone through.

"Ah, lighten up, Sonny," Pyro groaned. "I for one am glad it's all out in the open, and I don't have to keep a secret anymore."

Pasha tapped the back of his chair. "Thanks for helping save our lives, by the way."

"Don't sweat it, kid!" He hooked his arm around Pasha's neck and scuffled his hair. "I couldn't let you die without growing out of those chubby cheeks first."

Pasha laughed and squirmed away. "I can't believe you of all people managed to keep a secret that long!"

"Why is everyone so surprised by that? I used to be a government-hired hit man! There was once a time when I could name every skeleton in every closet of every senator, alderman, and council member ever to hold office! And just so you know, I did know that alcohol was banned in the United States!"

"I knew it!"

Staccato rolled his eyes. "Yes, it looks like I won't have to fire you after all."

"You wouldn't fire me," scoffed Pyro. "I know too much!"

"I suppose you're right." Staccato stroked his beard. "Besides, I wouldn't want to put a family man like you out of a job."

Pyro narrowed his eyes. "What are you getting at, Staccato?"

Staccato lowered himself into an armchair. "I hear your mother is interested in meeting her granddaughter."

"What's this now?" buzzed Pasha curiously.

Pyro held up a warning finger. "Don't you dare …"

But Staccato could hardly contain his laughter. "His mother thinks Faina is secretly Pyro's daughter."

Pasha made an absurd sputtering noise, then burst into laughter.

"It's not funny!" Pyro tangled his arms across his chest, but Pasha and Staccato couldn't help themselves. Just then, the door opened and Faina emerged in a comfortable pair of slacks. Pyro turned to Pasha.

"If you mention any of this to Faina, I swear—"

"Hey, Pops!" Faina chortled, hugging Pyro's neck. Pyro turned red.

"I didn't say anything!" Pasha assured him.

"Mama Lydia told me." Faina gave Pyro's head a conciliatory pat as he scoffed.

"As if I could ever spawn such a nuisance."

"Aw, now, is that any way to speak to your little girl?"

Pyro shooed her away with a good-natured laugh. "You're not a little girl, you're a hairy little beast! For all I know, you hatched out of an egg!"

"An egg you laid!"

Unable to hold it in any longer, Skelter stood up and began gesticulating in a most bitter attitude.

"Aw, don't feel bad, Skelly!" Pyro clicked his tongue. "Melodious didn't know about Staccato's secret either."

Melodious cleared his throat. "Actually, I have known for quite some time."

Staccato did a double take. "What? What do you mean?" He flashed Pyro a look.

"Why do you always suspect me? It could have been Sonata!"

"Please, no one had to tell me." Melodious tapped at his ears. "One thing you should always remember: a blind man hears everything. I do not wish to embarrass you, but there is hardly a whisper I cannot perceive."

Everyone shrank back in horror, trying not to think of all the private comments and secrets they'd muttered in a false sense of privacy. Pyro was the first to speak.

"Does that mean there's no such thing as 'silent but deadly'?"

Sonata was ready to rip out her hair. "Pyro!"

Everyone fell into a fit of hysterics, everyone except Staccato and Sonata, that is. In order to call the rowdy party back into compliance, Staccato had to change the subject.

"Did you get the shard?"

Pasha bit his lip and glanced at Cicada, who removed the case from her purse and laid it in his hands.

"Kinda."

Pyro cocked an eyebrow. "What do you mean, 'kinda'?"

Pasha opened the latch and held up the fragment for all to see.

"Lahar says it isn't genuine. He thinks the real shard was stolen by an igneous who made this decoy."

Staccato whipped out a pocket handkerchief and took the shard between his thumb and index finger. He squinted close. With a bilious sigh he unsheathed his spectacles from his pocket and slid them over the long bridge of his nose.

"I'm afraid he's right. This is not a piece of Evangeline's work, however it's quite a deliberate forgery. It's clear someone was making an attempt to imitate her." Removing his glasses, Staccato held out the shard to Pyro. "What do you think?"

Pyro held it up to the light and furrowed his brow. Hardly a second passed before he made his conclusion.

"Oh, yeah. That's igneous-made alright."

Pasha was taken aback. "I get you're an igneous and all, but do you actually know anything about glassblowing?"

"My brother dabbled in it. Ma wanted each of us to excel at some igneous art form, and Arson got saddled with glassblowing. He was good enough to get by, I suppose, but his real passion was geology. He had a penchant for volcanic minerals, the formation of gems and all that. So yeah, you could say I know a thing or two."

Staccato leaned forward with his elbows on his knees and pressed his fingertips together.

"I must say I'm surprised you came back with anything at all. However did you manage it?"

Pasha looked surprised. "Didn't Sonata tell you?"

Staccato frowned slightly and leaned away. "I'm afraid I've been so caught up in your mother's hearing, I haven't given her the chance."

Pasha went on to recount the story from start to finish. There was no mistaking the expression of horror on Staccato's face as he sat back in his chair, clenching his staff, and staring blankly at the wall.

"What's the matter?" inquired Pasha, tilting his head to one side. "You seem upset."

Staccato passed a hand over his face and took a deep breath.

"You could've died …" his voice was hardly above a whisper. He seemed to be saying it more to himself than anyone else.

At length, he managed to look Pasha in the eye.

"I'm afraid I have another confession to make. Pasha, the real reason I didn't want you to go to Louisville alone was because I didn't believe it was safe. Even if the incident with the gun hadn't happened, I couldn't justify putting you in harm's way, especially not for something as silly as one of those shards." He rolled his eyes. "You see, when Theo admitted his suspicions that Evangeline's mirror might be Amnos, I thought the idea perfectly ridiculous. I still do, to tell you the truth. Evangeline's mirror may have been a feat of enchantment, but Amnos is only a legend." He shook his head several times, still trying to throw off the shock. "Rest assured I won't be sending you off on any more missions alone, not until you've had more training at least."

Again, Pasha was struck with a pang of guilt. Staccato had cancelled Pasha and Faina's trip to protect them, not because he thought they were incompetent. And yet Pasha had gotten angry with him.

"I'd like to discuss what happened between Pasha and this Laudine person," declared Staccato, changing the subject. "You said Laudine was able to read your thoughts?"

"Something like that; at any rate, she was able to find out who I was just by causing me pain. Cicada and Faina didn't tell her anything."

"How do you know they didn't find out from the newspapers or a tip-off?" posed Melodious. "I mean, I understand they're living in the Other, but surely they aren't that isolated from everything happening in Voiler."

Faina threw up her shoulders. "After she tortured Pasha, she did say she recognized him from the papers. But before that they had no idea. While Pasha was out, she kept trying to interrogate Cicada and me about who sent us."

Everyone exchanged fearful glances while Pasha wrung his hands.

"That's never happened to anyone else?"

Staccato bit his lip. "I've been tortured by the C.O.N. twice and never have I been exposed to the power you're describing."

Pyro shrugged. "Me neither." His eyes settled on Skelter, who shook his head. Sonata looked down at her hands.

"I've never even heard of anything like that happening before. It has to be something new."

"That's the problem with liliths," observed Staccato. "Their powers come from forces of darkness, making their range of abilities nearly impossible to predict. It could be such capabilities have existed for some time, and they're just rare."

"Or perhaps it's difficult to find someone susceptible. After all, Laudine was able to use her sorcery on Pasha, but was unsuccessful with Cicada and Faina. Could it be that it only affects men?"

"No," Staccato shut his eyes and stroked the end of his beard. "Whatever it is, it has to be more specific, otherwise we'd have heard about it before."

"But what?" Melodious wondered aloud. "What could it be that makes Pasha vulnerable when Cicada and Faina are immune?"

Staccato let out a frustrated sigh. "I just don't know. I suppose for the time being we'll just have to keep wondering and searching for an answer."

"Well, that's just great!" Pyro blustered. "We don't know who stole the shard, we don't know who made the decoy, and we don't know how the lilith read Pasha's mind! Not only that, but we still don't know how Evangeline appeared to Pasha in the grotto as herself and not as the Firebird!"

Staccato pressed his fingertips together.

"Yes, about that … now that everything is out in the open I may have something to add to that. After the Land Lock was placed, I used to have dreams of Evangeline telling me to go to the hidden library of St. Jorah, or the library in the grotto. She never said why, but she kept pleading with me to go there."

Pyro blinked slowly. "Are you saying for ten years you've known where to find the instructions for breaking the Land Lock, and you didn't say anything?"

"Well, I didn't know that's why she was telling me to go there."

"But you're a miraculous! Isn't that how your encounters with the dead work? They show up in your dreams and tell you to do something, and then you go do it?"

Pasha held up his hand. "Hang on, how does that have anything to do with the Land Lock? That just sounds like a weird dream to me. If she was actually trying to tell you how to break the curse, why didn't she just tell you?"

"Don't you remember the last thing Evangeline told you, Pasha? The dead tell no tales. That's why Evangeline had to show you where to find the instructions for breaking the curse. She couldn't tell you."

"Not even to miraculous?"

"Not even to miraculous."

Staccato had barely finished his sentence when Faina threw out her hands and blurted, "Who cares about all that! We still haven't talked about the Goat Man!"

Pyro drew back his head. "The Goat Man?"

"Yes! We didn't get to tell you what happened when we went back to the trestle!"

With trembling hands she retold their mysterious encounter with the horned figure on the bridge. When she ended the story, Sonata stared down at her lap, trying not to laugh. Staccato hid behind his hand with a snort.

"And just what is so funny about all that?" Faina placed her hands on her hips. "We're probably gonna have nightmares for the rest of our lives!"

Staccato smoothed his waistcoat. "His name is Aruncus Dioicus."

Pasha turned round so quickly he almost gave himself whiplash. "You know him?"

Recognition fell into Pyro's eyes as he smiled. "Oh, you ran into ol' Arny!"

"Is this another one of your weird family friends?"

Giggling, Sonata shook her head. "I don't believe we ever explained it to you. Every gateway has a guard, you see, just like Angelo in New York. Aruncus and his family have guarded the trestle for generations."

"And he's a goat man?"

"Of course not, he's a sylph! The horns on his head are just branches. He's the one who arranged for your car. When he isn't guarding the trestle he walks about like an ordinary citizen."

Faina was irate. "You two knew this the whole time, and you didn't stop to tell us?"

Sonata and Staccato glanced at one another and dissolved into laughter.

"Say, wait a minute!" Pasha narrowed his eyes. "You two did this on purpose, didn't you? You thought it would be funny!"

Sonata finally managed to catch her breath long enough to explain. "He's the man you talked with after you arrived. Staccato and I thought it would be funny if he gave you a good scare."

Faina shook her head. "Who would've thought the pair of prudes could pull off such a prank!"

Staccato leaned back in his chair. "Well, we can't let you and Pasha have all the fun."

Chapter 53:
Mother Genesis Testifies

Everyone was tense when they shuffled through the gargantuan doors of the courthouse Monday morning. The overwhelming onslaught of press did little to comfort them. Everywhere reporters spat back the juicy details of Staccato and Evangeline's affair. It seemed impossible to ignore them.

As they passed through the lobby, Pyro extracted an extraordinarily tall woman from the nearby crowd. She was showered in merry freckles and looked somewhat surprised to see him. Pyro smiled.

"You know, you never did say if Dessa had a boy or a girl."

Pasha knew at once this had to be Pyro's mother. The woman's face lit up. She wrapped an arm around her son's shoulders.

"It's another boy."

Pyro pumped his fist into the air. "Ha! I knew it!"

Scarcely had the words left Pyro's lips when his mother let out a shrill gasp. She was covering her mouth with both hands, and staring at Faina, who had gone to get a drink from the water fountain.

"Oh my! Oh my!"

Pyro was in a panic. "Ma! Ma! Calm down!"

The Queen of Aries pressed a handkerchief to her mouth.

"What on earth are you crying for, woman?" Pyro's face was bright red.

"She has the freckles!"

"So what? They're freckles! There are millions of people with freckles!"

Pasha stared at them dumbfounded. Staccato hadn't been exaggerating. The Queen was wholeheartedly convinced Faina was her granddaughter.

"Those aren't just any freckles, Pyro! Those are Anomaly freckles, and you know it! I knew you were keeping something from me!"

Pasha glanced back at Staccato, who was finding it difficult to keep a straight face.

"Should I help him?"

Skelter placed a hand over Pasha's mouth and shook his head, while Staccato held up a hand. "No, no, I want to see what happens."

Pyro moaned and covered his face in abject exasperation. "Oh, for the love of shrapnel! She is not mine! Do you hear me? Not mine!"

Melodious sucked his teeth, but was trying not to laugh. "Poor

Pyro."

Pasha glanced back at Faina to see if she had noticed anything. Her attention was absorbed in a painting on the wall.

"She even has your eyes!"

"I think you're seeing what you want to see," Pyro insisted.

"Nonsense, I have a sixth sense about these things. It's in my blood. My great-grandmother was a mermaid, you know."

"This is Voiler, everyone's got a little mermaid in them somewhere."

But the Queen wasn't listening. "My mother always used to say to me, she'd say, 'Bravery, you got your Nan's mermaid intuition.' And I have enough fish sense about me to know that that girl right there is my granddaughter!"

She elbowed her way through the crowd. Pyro was aghast. He limped after her in a horrified hurry.

"What do you think you're doing? Get back here!"

But Bravery would not listen; she headed straight for Faina. As she was turning around, the giant willowy lady stretched out a hand for her.

"Why, hello! You must be Faina! How lovely it is to meet you, dearie."

Faina looked delighted as she bent into a curtsy. "Hello, Your Majesty. It's wonderful to finally meet Pyro's mother."

Bravery shook her head and, chucking her under the chin, raised her to an upright position.

"You needn't bow, nor call me by my title. You can call me—"

"Ma!" Pyro sprang forward. "I swear, if you say—"

"Bravery."

Pyro sucked his lips over his teeth. Faina beamed.

"Bravery. How lovely."

Bravery took Faina's arm and led her towards the large bay windows overlooking the National Garden.

"Tell me, sweetheart, what is that you're reading there? I'm a bit of a bookworm myself, you know…"

Sonata hooked her arm through Pyro's and shepherded him back to the group.

"Relax," Pasha could hear her whispering. "Your mother may be a bit emotional, but she isn't crazy."

Pyro ducked his chin against his chest. "That's what you think."

Pasha shoved his hands into his pockets, pretending not to hear them as they made their way to the box.

"Pyro," said Sonata, dropping her voice lower still, "I was just wondering … *ahem*, there isn't any chance you could be Faina's father, right?"

Pasha had to beat his chest to keep from choking. Pyro nearly dropped his crutch.

"Oh no! Not you too! What is this?"

"Well, it's not as though it's completely out of the question."

Pasha wanted to turn around and assure them it was, but it felt awkward to interrupt.

"You were rather a wild card in your day."

"This is ludicrous! Sonata, don't you think if I had a daughter I would know about it?"

She answered him with a lengthy stare of silence. Pyro huffed.

"Fine, you aren't convinced? Let's do the math. Faina is seventeen years old, meaning—"

"She was born in 1908. Which would've made you …"

Pyro counted back on his fingers. "Sixteen! Ha! See? Too young!"

Sonata looked him over skeptically until at last Pyro threw up his hands. "Look, she's not my kid, okay?"

Soon, Faina rejoined them, and they took their seat inside the courtroom. The Judge soared silently through the oak doors. As Pasha stood, his knees shook beneath him. Behind him, Cicada munched noisily on a bag of peanuts, the papery peels crackling between her fingers. The subtle scent of salt seemed out of place in the courtroom, and Pasha couldn't help but feel it was all just some big circus they were looking down on. It did nothing for his nerves.

The Judge cleared her throat and began reviewing everything that had happened so far. When she was through, she turned to Staccato.

"Mr. Nimbus, would you like to make a final statement?"

Staccato rubbed his hands together and looked down at the microphone.

"I've made many confessions in the past week: that I had an affair with the former Queen of Ursa, that we were secretly married after the alliance broke, that I was an accomplice in faking Mrs. Chevalsky's death, and that I raised her as my own child in Siberia to the age of sixteen. However, based on my conversation with Mother Genesis in June of 1889, I do not believe I am Mrs. Chevalsky's biological father. Everything I have done, the measures I have taken to ensure her son could claim the throne, were all because I truly believed he had every right to do so by international law."

The Judge addressed the council members. "Would anyone else like to make a statement before we begin?"

Samael seized his microphone. Feedback squealed through the speakers.

"I would like to make a statement, Your Honor!"

"Surprise, surprise," grumbled Pyro.

"As lovely as Staccato's little story of the self-sacrificing father figure is, I feel the need to remind the court of the much more likely reality. Staccato Nimbus is a power-hungry social climber. He was born into a family that once boasted one of the most prestigious names in Voiler, but with alcohol, addiction, and scandal, the Nimbuses have long since been a disgrace.

"Staccato Nimbus is a man of ambition as well as skill. I believe we can all agree to that. He is one of only three miraculous in all of history to wield his powers to their full extent without a staff. He was first knighted at the age of ten. He received a full ride to Sadatoni Charter at the age of eleven, where he finished early. He was immediately accepted into Mankib Fay University, became a member of Kappa Aurigae, and graduated top of his class at seventeen. Curious he did not pursue a profession where he could better employ his exceptional talent as a miraculous. But then, perhaps it's not so curious.

"When Staccato was commissioned as King Thessalos's federal advisor he became the first non-mermaid counselor to serve a mermaid king. To this day he holds the record for youngest appointed government official. All this he had accomplished by the age of eighteen. That isn't to say his methods of securing such a position were entirely honorable. His classmates described him as competitive, cunning, and decidedly opportunistic. And let's not forget, he was King Thessalos's correspondent and childhood playmate before he was ever his employee. A little favoritism can go a long way.

"Ladies and gentleman of the Ecliptic Council, it is my belief that Staccato Nimbus sought a position in government for the sole purpose of seducing a monarch and producing an heir with a claim to the throne, thus restoring his family name to its former glory! He wanted nothing more than to establish a legacy by beguiling Princess Evangeline, and this woman," he pointed to Lydia, "is the product of that affair."

To Pasha's horror, many council members nodded their heads in sound agreement. Some sort of wrapping crinkled behind him. Cicada threw her bag of peanuts into the air, dousing Pasha in a deluge of crushed nuts.

"That's ludicrous!"

Everyone in the courtroom turned, their eyes wide with shock. The Judge hammered her gavel.

"Staccato Nimbus, may I remind you that a council member is speaking. Please get a hold of your party before I hold them in contempt of court."

Staccato's face was bright red. "Yes, of course, forgive me, Your Honor." He turned to hiss at Cicada. "Will you please control yourself?"

Samael seemed to find it all quite droll. Flipping his silky hair over his shoulder, he laughed into the microphone.

"No, no, it's quite all right, Your Honor. By all means, let the esperite speak. I'd love to hear what she has to say."

Cicada floated over Pasha's head and grabbed the microphone.

"Thank you. Samael says Staccato Nimbus set out to seduce Evangeline so he could establish a legacy, and you all actually believe him? I mean, what is wrong with you people?"

"Cicada …" growled Staccato under his breath. Cicada drifted down towards the center of the room, straining the microphone as she went.

"I mean, you actually listen to him? Has no one stopped to consider the appalling sense of logic to that story? No one? No one?" She poked her head questioningly at several council members.

The Judge cocked an incredulous eyebrow. "I'm sorry, but who exactly are you?"

Cicada waved a hand. "Oh, I'm Cicada Sycamore, daughter of Mother Genesis and all that."

Samael scoffed. "Of course you are! And what gives you the authority to speak of such matters? Is it because your mother is supposedly the tree of all knowledge?"

Cicada shoved a finger in his face. "For starters, I seem to be the only person here with a brain. I'd say that makes me more qualified than half the court! I mean, looking around, it obviously doesn't take much to secure a seat on the Ecliptic Council. That being said, it took your country centuries to gain representation! What does that say about you?"

Many of the council members snickered. Samael turned to the Judge with a sneer and pointed an accusatory finger at Cicada.

"Your Honor, I demand this nuisance be removed from the court at once!"

The Judge pounded her gavel. "Overruled. I want to hear what she has to say." She cleared her throat and motioned to the esperite. "Go ahead, Miss Sycamore. You were saying?"

"Well, if Staccato was planning to seduce the Queen so he could produce an heir with a claim to the throne, why on earth would he work for a male ruler? It wasn't as if the opportunities to work for a female weren't on the table. What about Queen Calliope, for example? Or Empress Tsunami? Those were all real options for Staccato, and yet he chose to work for King Thessalos."

Samael bent low over the podium. "Who's to say he wasn't simply playing Claudius to Theo's Hamlet the First? How do you know he didn't seduce Evangeline the way Claudius seduced Queen Gertrude?"

Cicada winced as though his lapse of reason had caused her physical pain.

"Really? That's your argument? If you're going to draw comparisons between Staccato's situation and *Hamlet,* I suggest you familiarize yourself with the play. Claudius killed his brother and married his sister-in-law to become king. Staccato married the youngest princess of four, there were three people ahead of her for the throne. To say Staccato seduced Evangeline to gain a position is grasping."

"Evangeline married Bruin, didn't she? Ruler of the most powerful kingdom in Voiler? Though Staccato claims to have been in love with Evangeline he made no effort to stop her from marrying someone else. Obviously, he was waiting for her to secure a better position before he made his move."

"That's ridiculous! If Staccato's plan was to establish a legacy, he'd have to be a complete idiot to conceive a child with a married woman whose only legal claim to any kingdom was through marriage to her husband! Furthermore, how could Staccato make a name for himself by trying to pass his daughter off as someone else's child? If Lydia is Staccato's daughter, Pasha Chevalsky cannot inherit the throne. But if she *is* Bruin's daughter, Pasha has every right to rule, biologically and legally, and Staccato has nothing to do with it. He's effectively nobody! Just some bum who knocked up the Queen."

Several of the council members gasped and covered their mouths with handkerchiefs. Staccato glared at Cicada from the box.

"Er … maybe just nobody." Cicada popped a peanut between her teeth. "So, I uh, rest my case. I guess."

She flew back to her seat as the Judge was clearing her throat.

"Anything else you'd like to add, Cobra Samael?"

Samael crossed his arms and gestured to the door. "Just bring in the tree already."

The heavy oak doors peeled back. A seraph dressed in trailing robes carried a potted bonsai to the center of the court. He laid it on the podium and stepped back. Everyone fell silent, their attention trained on the shrubbery. The Judge leaned forward as though she were almost afraid.

"Mother Genesis? Are you there?"

A breeze spiraled round the perimeter of the court. The branches gave a twinge, then a twist. The trunk stretched to life.

"Greetings, Council Members! I've come at la—" Mother Genesis stopped and looked down at her torso. Exasperated, she turned to the seraph and crooked a twig his way. The Seraph looked over his shoulder. Realizing she was beckoning to him, he inched forward. Mother Genesis shoved her hands high on her wooden hips.

"A bonsai? Really?"

The seraph shrugged apologetically. "It was the most convenient thing on hand, Madame."

"Last time I was here they wheeled out an entire boxelder to accommodate me!" She heaved a heavy sigh and brushed the moss from her shoulders. "Times certainly have changed." She flashed Samael a nasty look. "Along with standards."

The Judge folded her hands. "Mother Genesis, do you know why we've asked you here today?"

"Well, of course I do, dear! I wouldn't have agreed to uproot myself without knowing the cause! I understand there's been a bit of a hold-up where reinstating the heir of Ursa is concerned."

The Judge nodded. "We'd like to know who fathered Mrs. Chevalsky."

"I see. Well, no matter. I'll settle this nonsense. The rightful and legal heir to the throne of Ursa is Pavlo Ruslanovitch Chevalsky of Balalchik, son of Princess Lydia Sylvia Chevalsky and Baron Ruslan Dareko Chevalsky. That darling boy sitting right there."

She pointed a branch at Pasha. Sonata covered her mouth to keep from giggling with glee. Faina hugged Pasha's shoulders and beamed. Melodious gave a prayer of thanks under his breath.

"Take that, you bloody serpent," Pyro guffawed, and Skelter stuck out his tongue while Cicada stuck her fingers in her mouth and made a face.

Staccato remained impassive. Pasha watched his mother reach for Staccato's hand and give his fingers a squeeze. The Judge pounded her gavel.

"Quiet! Everyone settle down. Now that Mother Genesis has spoken, the court will decide whether or not they should recognize Mrs. Chevalsky as the daughter of King Bruin. Those who wish to acknowledge Mrs. Chevalsky as Princess of Ursa, raise your right hand."

To Pasha's astonishment over half the Council raised their hand in approval. His chest swelled as Judge Tyto Alba slipped him a smile and lifted her own hand into the air. Samael was seething but silent.

"Let it be known then," thundered Judge Alba, rising to her feet, "that the Ecliptic Council hereby recognizes Princess Lydia Sylvia Chevalsky as the daughter of King Bruin Halborn Northstar and Princess Evangeline Ophelia Nimbus. Case closed."

The moment her gavel struck the podium, the court leapt into the air with shouts of excitement. Everyone reached over to hug Pasha and pat him on the shoulder, while Cicada descended to the floor to retrieve her mother and sat her next to the microphone in their own box.

"Well, crown me with blossoms and call me a dogwood!" Mother Genesis fanned herself with her fronds. "That was rather exhausting! Cicada, darling, might I have a sip of water, please?"

"Yes, Mother." Cicada reached for the water pitcher and poured it over her roots. Mother Genesis sighed with relief.

"Thank you, dear, that's much better!"

Before the court could get up to leave, the Judge tapped her gavel once more.

"Now, with that settled, I suggest we move on to Mr. Chevalsky. Beginning now, the court will decide whether or not Mr. Chevalsky possesses the aptitude to ascend the throne. Mr. Chevalsky, would you please take the stand?"

Pasha's eyes wove through his friends. Sonata patted him forward.

"You can do it, Pasha."

Pasha swallowed hard. Running his fingers over his bangs, he made his way down the steps and up to the podium. The Judge smiled down at him.

"Well, Pasha, congratulations, you are the rightful heir to the throne of Ursa."

Pasha bobbed his head and grasped for something to say. "Thank you, Your Honor," was all he could get out.

"Council, the floor is now open for questions. You know the rules."

A mermaid from Scorpius with an elaborately braided hairdo

pounded her gavel.

"Ondine Oracle," the Judge acknowledged, "you have the floor."

"As King, do you plan to reinstate joint rule with Karkinos?"

Pasha grinned as though this were a silly question. "Of course I do! Ursa needs Karkinos, our kingdom can't survive without the mermaids."

A stiff-looking sylph craned his head over the podium, snapping his joints as he did, and struck his gavel.

"Deciduous Larch, go on."

"What about the Senate? Your grandfather obliterated Ursa's constitution in 1889 and turned the kingdom into an absolute monarchy. Do you plan to carry on this way?"

"No, sir. I plan to reinstate Ursa as a constitutional monarchy the moment it is within my power." He tossed his head with a cheeky smile. "I am an American, after all."

A thread of laughter hummed through the court. They all seemed quite taken with him, and to his own surprise, Pasha felt quite at ease. Perhaps he could do this.

Samael beat his gavel so hard a fissure formed in the stem. Pasha turned with surprise. Samael's bright blue eyes clouded with wrath.

"Cobra Samael, you may speak." There was a hint of reluctance in the Judge's voice. Samael swiveled to his feet, looking very much like a snake lifting its head to strike.

"And what do you plan to do with the Draconians who have settled in Ursa? And the Primals?"

Pasha tried not to narrow his eyes. "They're welcome to stay so long as they abide by the laws like everyone else."

"Laws which will prevent them from practicing their beliefs, no doubt."

Pasha folded his hands behind his back and lifted his chin. "I'm sorry, you'll have to be more specific, which laws are you referring to?"

"You know precisely what I am referring to. My people have long been blood drinkers and devoted disciples of Primal Instinct. King Bruin made it so no Primal could be condemned in a court of law for taking part in their own practices. If you were King, would you not put up laws that prevent them from acting on their beliefs?"

"Make no mistake, Cobra Samael, I will not permit murder and bloodshed in my kingdom. I will hold all people equally responsible for upholding the laws of the land regardless of their personal practice. Anyone who can't abide by those laws may leave. After all, Draco doesn't seem to have a problem tolerating savagery."

Samael's fangs glistened in a sickening grin. "Forgive me, I didn't realize you were so averse to violence, being a former gang member and all. Didn't you used to street fight for money?"

Pasha nodded his head. "I did. I've never lied to the public about my history, about what I had to do to keep my family alive. Because of my past I'm determined to bring my people opportunity. Doors will be open to them no matter where they were born, what their first language is, or what kind of accent they have. They won't have to subject themselves to danger and humiliation just to put bread on the table."

"You play the progressive, and yet you would rob my people of the freedom to exercise their customs!"

"I would when your customs rob the innocent of the freedom to live without fear!"

"What you are suggesting is the abolishment of their rights!"

"And what rights would those be? The right to homicide? The right to steal? The right to murder children and drink their blood? A right that interferes with the human rights of others isn't a right, it's an abomination! I can assure you that when I ascend the throne, your doctrine will not be upheld in my courts!"

Samael clicked his tongue piteously. "I wouldn't expect you to understand our ways, Master Pavlo, therefore I cannot expect you to understand our laws."

"Laws? What laws?"

"The law of the heart's desire."

Pasha could have thrown up for the ridiculous, soppy expression Samael dressed himself with.

"There is nothing more pure than the ancient Draconian belief of fulfilling the soul."

"Is there now? Please, Cobra Samael, enlighten me. Let's say I have a case brought before me in which a young girl was murdered by her neighbor. What would you have me do as King?"

"What was the motivation?"

Pasha shrugged. "To steal money."

"Then the girl's family would be expected to exact revenge. That's not even a federal case."

"That's how you would justify the matter? Revenge? What about taking steps to prevent the murder from happening in the first place?"

"It wouldn't be necessary if everyone simply lived in accordance with the ideology."

"You think you'd have less cases like this if everyone just did as they pleased? The court may not be aware of this, but Draco has the highest murder rate of any other country in Voiler."

Here Samael snorted. "Oh, yes, I'm sure you hear about it in the news all the time."

A few of the council members snickered. Mega Cabral, Capricorn's representative, rolled her eyes. "Probably read it in *The Daily Compass*."

Those who had laughed at Samael's remark found this even funnier. Pasha ignored them.

"You don't hear about it in the news because they go unreported. Murder is legal in Draco. You won't find the number under criminal statistics, because it isn't a crime. Instead, it's listed under 'Casualties of Passion.' That's the Draconian term for murder victim, 'Casualty of Passion.'" He smirked. "To be honest, I'm surprised Samael even has a people to rule over! I don't know how they haven't all killed each other!"

The courtroom roared with laughter; a few even clapped. Samael waited for their clamor to subside. He aimed a murderous glare at Pasha.

"Is a lion to be held responsible when it slays the cubs of the fallen alpha to make room for his own progenies? Is the fox to be imprisoned for murdering the hen to feed its pups? Primal Instinct is the way of nature!"

"The way of nature?" Pasha paused and chuckled sarcastically. "That's the stupidest thing I've ever heard!"

A collective gasp rang through the audience. Staccato's eyes nearly left his skull as he stared at Pasha, mouth agape. Amongst the murmurs, the words "insult," "disrespect," and "bigot" could be discerned.

"Survival of the fittest," Pasha went on, "the basic building block of Samael's beliefs. What are we trying to survive? We're not cavemen! We don't have to resort to such atrocities to live. The human race is past that, or at least it should be, especially in Voiler. Voiler has thrived because of its respect for the sanctity of life in all creatures. There are currently over two thousand species of animals in Voiler that no longer exist in the Other because they've been hunted to extinction. Over two thousand! This may sound funny to most of you, but I've never seen a wooly mammoth in my lifetime. Ever."

There was enough giggling in the room that one might have thought Pasha had said he'd never seen a squirrel.

"When my friend and I, who's also from the Other, discovered that wooly mammoths are not only alive in Voiler but plentiful, we could hardly contain ourselves!"

The giggling grew to laughter, and Pasha too had to laugh a little, for the whole conversation felt peculiar.

"The animals that have survived in Voiler but not in the Other survived because they were protected by the laws of the people. And I believe human life too should be protected by the law, because life deserves respect. Primal Instinct has no respect for life, and so it has no place in a court of law, or amongst intelligent, civilized beings. You don't get a free pass to murder, steal, and violate just because that's what's done where you come from! So to answer your question, Cobra Samael, no, I will not uphold your doctrine in my kingdom."

Pasha permitted his eyes to scan across the surrounding crowd. The shock had been erased from the council members' faces and replaced with mild expressions of respect.

"Is this who you all think should be King?" Samael threw out his hands towards Pasha. "This narrow-minded boy, hardly old enough to shave? This intolerant bigot who would censor those who don't conform to his conventional definition of moral goodness? You're an insult to progress, standing there with your moral superiority, composing righteous speeches about a place you only learned existed a couple of months ago! Why, you're nothing but an uneducated immigrant!"

Queen Bravery pounded her gavel. "Uneducated is not the same as unintelligent, Cobra Samael."

From the upper tier a seraph struck in. "Well, he certainly doesn't seem uneducated to me! As far as I can see the boy is well-read, eloquent, and incredibly intelligent for someone of his age and background."

"Indeed," agreed an esperite. "And what could be more impressive than being *self*-educated? The boy is perfectly admirable!"

Deciduous Larch cleared his gravelly throat.

"'True intelligence is not something that can be measured by a piece of paper in a frame upon the wall, nor can it be determined by tests of academia and scholastic principle, only by the suffering and trials of life.' Boxwood Pottinghouse said that, 1895, while giving his address to the United Arboreal Timbers of the Southern Copse."

"And what does it matter if he's an immigrant?" thundered Javaid. "Where is the shame in that? If anything it gives him an appreciation for our world that no others have! When was the last time any of us spotted a wooly mammoth, or a dragon, and stopped to appreciate its wonder? Or walked into the Subaquatic Rail with a sense of awe? I think we can all agree Pasha possesses a unique sense of respect for Voiler, one that would set him apart from other rulers. I believe I'm correct in saying Pasha would work hard to preserve what's good about our world."

The Judge looked from one side of the court to the other.

"I take it the Council is ready to make a decision. Those who wish to acknowledge Pasha Chevalsky as the Sovereign King of Ursa, raise your right hand."

Pasha held his breath. He sank his teeth into his lower lip. Nearly every representative from every country and every district raised their right hand. Pasha was powerless against the grin that spread across his face. The Judge smiled at him.

"Then let it be known throughout history that on this day the international authority of the Ecliptic Council recognizes Pavlo Ruslanovitch Chevalsky as the true King of Ursa and all its districts." The gavel resounded with triumph.

Chapter 54:
A Celebration

As the company gathered into the sitting room that evening, Pasha felt as though it were the first time he had breathed in months. Everyone was chattering away and pouring champagne. Pyro and his mother sat in the corner laughing at *The Morning Star*'s broadcast as the anchors cried over the fact that Ursa would now be taken from Draco's administration.

Cicada, Faina, and Katya amused themselves with making up songs about Pasha's triumph over Samael, while Melodious and Skelter accompanied them on the accordion and violin. Glasses clinked as Lydia and Constanza giggled over glasses of champagne, Staccato and Javaid sat conversing in the corner, and Sonata quickly chopped up a tray of celebratory strawberries at the bar.

Notes sagged as Melodious and Skelter's merry tarantella reached an end, and Cicada raise a glass.

"May we never forget this day when justice was served! The day when Ursa was freed, and Pasha's inheritance was restored! By blood and by law, the throne belongs to Pasha Chevalsky!"

"By blood?" echoed Pyro. "Don't you mean by law? Mother Genesis said Pasha is the true and legal heir of Ursa. So Lydia had to be Bruin's daughter."

"No," insisted Cicada. "By law and by blood. He has both."

Staccato stared at Cicada incredulously. "What do you mean? Lydia may be my daughter, I'm the one who raised her. But I did not father her. That was Bruin."

"Staccato, no wonder you drive Mother crazy!" Cicada exclaimed. "Look, it's simple: whose name is on Lydia's birth certificate? Staccato's or Bruin's?"

When no one answered, Staccato glanced around embarrassed. "Bruin's."

"Thus, Bruin is Lydia's legal father which makes Pasha the legal heir. It has nothing to do with blood."

Pasha held out his hand. "But wait, that still doesn't prove Staccato is Ma's real father."

"Staccato, when you went to see Mother before Lydia was born, what did you ask her?"

Staccato closed his eyes, trying to shut out the present situation. "I asked her if I should have married Evangeline when Atergatis was plotting to have her marry Bruin."

"And she said no, because Ursa needed an heir. If you had married Evangeline you would've had Lydia regardless, and she would've been born without any claim on Ursa at all. But because she married Bruin, and you and Evangeline had a secret affair, everyone believed she was Bruin's daughter. If Lydia hadn't have been conceived out of wedlock, no one would ever have had any reason to try and cover it up, and Evangeline would never have written Bruin's name on Lydia's birth certificate."

Pasha's jaw fell open. The room was dead silent. Staccato sat up in his seat.

"So, Lydia is my biological daughter?"

"Well, of course she's your biological daughter! Bruin was impotent!"

Pyro leapt up from his seat by the radio. "How on earth did you come to that conclusion?"

"Why do you think no one else has challenged Pasha for the throne? Bruin was a serial adulterer! You'd think after all the affairs he had with other women he would've at least impregnated one of them! And if he had, Samael would've known about it! If you don't believe me, I asked Mother, and she said it was true. Bruin couldn't have children."

"Well, congratulations, Staccato," announced Pyro, "it's a girl!"

"And no one can take her away from you," added Javaid.

Staccato blushed and looked down at his shoes as a smile slipped in at the corners of his mouth.

"Mama," Katya piped up with wide, innocent eyes, "what does 'impotent' mean?"

Pasha's eyebrows rose to his hairline. Eager for a distraction, he hastened to the bar where he had hidden the two bottles of Chevalsky. When he presented the vintages to his mother, Lydia was so overjoyed tears spilled from her eyes.

"*Oi,*" Pyro smacked him jokingly on the arm, "you mean you didn't bring anything back for your old pal Pyro who you shot in the foot?"

Faina smiled mischievously. "Actually, we did." She ran around to the kitchen and laid a box of bourbon balls in his lap.

"I was only joking, you know," he said with a smile. "You didn't really have to get me anything."

"I know, but since you were supposed to go with us in the first place it only seemed fair."

Pasha glanced at Faina over his shoulder. She met his eye with a rascally wink.

"I still don't understand how Sonata managed to get locked in the kitchen closet of all places!" Staccato approached the door of the private sitting room with harried strides. "I didn't even know that closet had a lock."

Pasha nodded his head in agreement. "Yeah, why would it even need one?"

Faina shrugged. "I don't know. Maybe the hotel's got a problem with people stealing cutlery."

Pasha watched as Faina crossed her fingers behind her back. He raised an eyebrow. What was she up to now? Pasha held open the door. As Faina passed, he threw her a questioning look. Faina's lips slipped into a sideways smile. She threw him a wink.

Together they rounded the corner into the kitchen. Pasha was just about to suggest they look for a key in the drawer, when his ears faintly detected Sonata's voice from behind the closet door.

"This is all your fault," hissed Sonata, "downing those bourbon balls one after the other!"

Staccato cocked an eyebrow, and knocked on the door with the tip of his staff. "Sonata? Who are you talking to in there? Faina said you were stuck in the closet."

No answer. He and Pasha exchanged worried glances but Faina didn't appear at all concerned.

"Sonata?" Staccato knocked on the door a second time.

When no one answered, he turned the knob. Just as the door was opening, someone from the other side forced it shut. Staccato jumped back in alarm.

"I'm fine," Sonata finally called back. It sounded as though she were covering her mouth with her hand. "I'll be with you in a moment!"

Pyro's voice leaked through the door, somewhat stifled. "What do you mean you'll be with them in a moment? What are we going to do?"

"Shut up!"

Pasha's mouth fell open. He swiveled around to look at Faina. She stared up at the ceiling with an innocent simper. Staccato's face grew pale with indignation. His shoulders swelled like a tidal wave as he drew himself up to his full height.

"Sonata Undine Soter," there was a slight tremor in his voice that reminded Pasha of distant thunder, "open this door right now, young lady, and bring that red-headed ingrate with you!"

"What redheaded ingrate?"

Staccato's hand shot towards the handle a second time, desperately trying to pry it open.

"Don't play games with me! Open this door now!"

"No one is in here, really, Staccato!"

Staccato took a step back, his nostrils flared. "Is that so?"

"It is indeed!"

Staccato placed his hands on his hips. "Pyro, is anyone in there?"

"No," was Pyro's dull reply. "Wait, I mean—oh, torch it all!"

Staccato motioned for Pasha and Faina to step back as he raised his staff and pointed it at the door handle like a firearm. The lock made a popping noise, and the door swung open with such force one might have thought Staccato had kicked it. There sat Sonata and Pyro, perched on top of a crate with Pyro's injured leg on a bucket, their lips glued together in a permanent kiss.

Faina fell to the floor in a fit of laughter. Pasha flashed her a look.

"You laced those bourbon balls with burning bush, didn't you?"

Pyro pointed a threatening finger in her face. "You just wait until I get ahold of you, beastie!"

But Staccato would hear none of it. "Oh, no, Mr. Anomaly. You just wait until I get ahold of the both of you!"

Faina jumped to her feet and looped her arm through Pasha's. "Sorry, folks! Gotta run! Pasha here owes me a coke!"

And together, Pasha and Faina ran out of the sitting room, leaving Pyro and Sonata at the mercy of Staccato.

Chapter 55:
Putting Down Roots

The Draconians originally had six months to clear out of Polaris, but after Samael was found guilty of blackmailing not just Hexmark Folkman, but several other council members, Draco lost their seat at court, and they were given two months to pack up and leave Alfbern Hall.

Meanwhile, the Chevalskys and Faina stayed with the Soters at Alveare. Now that Ursa was freed, the company decided to abandon the circus front and would continue their resistance work from Polaris.

Melodious had sought out a residence down the street from Alfbern Hall. Cicada toured the neighboring forests for appropriate tree houses. And Pyro had already put down a security deposit on a townhouse not far from Alveare where he would room with Skelter. The property was right on the canal, only a hair above water level.

"I don't see what everyone's making such a fuss about," Pyro would argue. "Have you seen what Samael's administration did to the housing market?"

But it was no secret that Pyro had settled down in Karkinos to be near Sonata. Sadly, not everyone was enthusiastic about the revelation of their relationship.

One evening after supper, Pasha happened to be strolling along the walk above the gardens when a commotion sounded from below. Pasha ground to a halt and peered over the railing. There beneath the shadow of a stairwell, Staccato was standing off to the side while Sonata and Javaid hissed back and forth.

"Papa, why are you being so ridiculous? I love Pyro, and he loves me!"

"What is it with all you mermaids and two-leggeds? Can't you just settle down with a nice merman?"

"Can you hear yourself right now? You sound like an absolute pescatarian! And how can you say such a thing in front of Staccato when he loved and married your sister? You're utterly impossible!" With a trembling lip, she turned and ran off through the olive trees.

Javaid shook his head apologetically. "Forgive me, Staccato, that was rude and insensitive of me."

Staccato shrugged and gave a weak smile. "I know you didn't mean anything by it. You're apprehensive is all. I understand Pyro is a bit of a rough diamond."

"A bit? Staccato, don't you remember? No sooner was the boy

emancipated from his parents than his name began popping up in headlines everywhere! Public drunkenness, incriminating situations with women—"

"Javaid, that was a long time ago. He was a boy then. Those days are far behind him, believe me."

"And this girl, Faina? I overheard his mother talking, is she really his lovechild?"

Staccato threw back his head and roared with laughter. "No, no. Absolutely not. I'm afraid the strain between Queen Bravery and her son has caused her to jump to conclusions. No, Faina is not Pyro's child."

Javaid pinched the bridge of his nose and released a heavy sigh. "Well, I suppose that's a relief."

Staccato patted his shoulder. "Cheer up, Javaid. You know the old saying, if a mermaid can't turn a bad egg around there's no hope for him."

"That's what Atergatis said about Evangeline the day she married Bruin."

Staccato's mouth twisted with a frown. "Forgive me, I didn't know. I understand your concern. Sonata can be very like Evangeline at times."

Javaid frowned as he looked out over the sea. "She has inherited her gift of compassion, there's no mistaking that."

"But Pyro is not like Bruin. I should know. He may be brash and tactless at times, but he's surprisingly selfless. Like Sonata, he seems to enjoy taking care of the people he loves. He's protective, courageous, and that's why he and Sonata have tried to hide their relationship for so many years. After working for the Saighdeoir, Pyro is afraid someone might try to hurt Sonata to get at him."

"Is that why he broke her heart so many times? She may not have shared her secrets with me, Staccato, but I can feel when my daughter is hurting, even when she is miles away."

Staccato nodded. "Your powers of empathy have always been strong. Yes, Pyro and Sonata were on and off for a while, and that is why. He wasn't trying to hurt her, he wanted to keep her out of danger. Just like I did with Lydia."

They remained silent for a long time. Staccato collapsed to a seat on the bench.

"You might as well try to get used to it. I don't see either of them backing off of this."

Javaid sighed. "Perhaps you are right, my old friend. I just don't want a repeat of my sister."

Staccato looked the King squarely in the eye. "Javaid, Evangeline was my wife, the love of my life, and the mother of my child. Sonata is very dear to me. I would never encourage a relationship that wasn't in her best interest. If I suspected for one second she was in any danger of reliving Evangeline's struggle, or that she was being mistreated in any way, I would fight to protect her with just as much tenacity as you would."

Javaid bowed his head and took a seat next to Staccato.

"I know you would. I don't believe I've ever properly thanked you for watching over her in our absence. Because of you, my brother, not only is Sonata alive but she is thriving."

Staccato shrugged. "I was happy to have someone to watch over. When the Land Lock was placed, Lydia had given birth to Katya, and to be honest I was struggling. She was married, had two lovely children, a boy and a girl, and I couldn't be a part of her joy. But Sonata, well, it's like you said, she has a gift for compassion."

Javaid smiled as he rose to his feet. "Well, you're all back together again now."

Staccato frowned. "In a way."

***

The following morning, Pasha made his way to the open air sunroom with his coffee. As he passed under the archway, he saw that Staccato was sitting with his back turned in the chair at the center of the room. Pages fluttered as he scanned through a series of notes in his lap, all the while cheerfully humming what Pasha now knew was the Lydian mode. Pasha smiled. Not wanting to disturb him, he settled quietly in the corner without a word.

Sloshing water echoed down the hallway as Katya came swimming up the passage, struggling to keep her chin lifted above the water. Evidently she was carrying something too precious to get wet, for her arm was raised over her head. Without stopping to clean the puddles she'd made, she scrambled into the sunroom.

Pasha expected her to come running to him, but to his surprise she headed straight for Staccato.

"Staccato! I have something for you!"

Staccato looked up from his notebook, startled. Removing his glasses, he set aside his work and leaned forward on his elbows with a smile.

"Good morning, Katya."

Katya pigeon-toed her feet and held out a little envelope addressed to the miraculous.

Staccato raised his eyebrows. "What's this?"

"It's the twenty-third."

He stared at her, baffled. Katya covered her mouth and giggled. "It's your birthday!"

Staccato raised his eyebrows and smirked. "So it is! I didn't even think about it."

"I made this for you."

Staccato blinked in surprise. He smiled. "How thoughtful, Katya."

She waved him on, jumping up and down. "Open it, silly!"

Staccato laughed softly as he opened the envelope, and unsheathed a small sheet of watercolor paper that Katya had painted with a lovely yellow hibiscus. Pasha inched forward and smiled to himself.

"How beautiful!" Staccato was beaming. "Did you paint this yourself?"

Katya stared at the ground with a sheepish nod.

"You're very talented, just like your mother. Thank you, darling. That was very sweet of you." He reached forward to tuck her braid behind her ear. "Your hair looks pretty. Who did it?"

Katya glanced back at Pasha in the corner. He flashed her a warning.

Katya rocked back on her heels. "Mama," she lied.

"Ah, I see." Staccato bent his head and dropped his voice down low. "Are you sure it wasn't Pasha?"

Katya put a hand over her mouth. "He told me not to tell anyone."

Staccato snickered. "Well, I'll let you in on a little secret, I used to braid your mother's hair all the time."

"Not Aunt Poppy?"

Staccato shook his head. "Not usually. So it may very well be that Pasha inherited that skill from me."

Katya nodded her head as though it were all very serious. "He has your nose."

"I believe his is a little shorter."

"You both get the same look on your face when you're angry."

"Really? And what look is that?"

Katya made a show of lowering her eyebrows in a very condescending manner and wrinkled the end of her nose. Pasha covered a snort behind his hand while Staccato laughed aloud.

"Very good! I think you have it down to an art."

She reached out towards his face to run a finger over his eyelid.

"Mama has the shape of your eyes."

He squeezed her hand. "She does."

Katya cocked her head and furrowed her brow in a most worried manner.

"But what part of me looks like you?"

Staccato pressed his lips together and examined her hands.

"Hmm … Let's see." He squinted an eye at her and beckoned for her to come closer. He tilted her head down and moved aside a curl to look behind her ear.

"Ah, there it is!"

Katya flipped her head up. "What? What is it?"

Staccato turned his head to point to a freckle behind his ear. "Same one."

Katya tittered and hopped up and down. Suddenly she froze and stared him in the eye with great sincerity.

"I won't tell anyone, I promise!"

Staccato nodded. "I know you won't, darling."

"But I can tell Mama, right?"

"Of course, you can."

"Perfect! I'm gonna tell her right now!" Katya stunned Staccato by kissing him once on the cheek, and dove back into the hallway where she disappeared below the water. Pasha shook his head and laughed.

"Brace yourself."

Staccato gave a jump. He hadn't noticed Pasha was in the room.

"Once she's decided to attach herself to you there's no getting rid of her." Pasha got up from the chair and stretched.

Staccato smiled at the puddle Katya had left behind. "She's very sweet."

"Oh, yeah, very sweet, very affectionate. It gets annoying whenever you're trying to stay mad at her. She always knows how to butter you up."

"Your mother was that way. Her mother was that way too." He reached for his coffee and, seeing that he had left it on the sideboard, stretched out his staff and summoned it into his hand.

"May I ask you a question?" said Pasha, taking the seat across from him.

"Ask away."

"If you don't need a staff to wield your powers, why do you carry one?"

Staccato waved a hand. "Oh, that? It's a funny story, really. Turns out I need it to control my powers. Rather a nuisance."

Pasha flexed his eyebrows, impressed. "What do you mean exactly by control?"

Staccato shrugged. "If emotions are running high, things tend to fly away, or break, or tremor … sometimes lightning forms."

"You can call down lightning?"

Staccato held up a hand. "Very, very rarely. It's not a regular thing, and it's definitely not common amongst most miraculous. I've only done it twice. The first time it happened I was six years old, and my brother thought it would be funny to trap me in a game pit and leave me there. I was stuck for two hours. By the time my mother found me I was so mad I was beside myself. I didn't mean to do it. Honestly to this day I still don't know how I did it, but next thing I knew there was a flash of light and my brother was lying stunned on the ground."

Pasha snorted, and Staccato smiled behind his mug. "I know I shouldn't be laughing, but he was alright." He propped his elbow on the arm of the chair and stared off at the bay. "I didn't get my staff until after your mother was born. I should have done it years ago. Evangeline was always telling me she wondered if a staff would help me control myself."

A light dawned in Pasha's eyes. It was Evangeline's hair inside the mourning token. The sudden revelation summoned the memory of her ghost hovering over the end of the dock, light rippling through her golden waves. Clearing his throat, he summoned the courage to ask Staccato something that had been plaguing him for quite some time.

"Staccato, I know everyone was trying to keep my mother's paternity a secret, but it seems strange that Evangeline didn't acknowledge you when her ghost appeared in Cetus. If we took her time away from you, I'm really sorry."

A glint of joy flickered in Staccato's eyes as he shook his head. "She did acknowledge me, Pasha."

Pasha glanced upwards, replaying the scene in his head, trying to figure out what moment Staccato was referring to. "I don't understand."

Staccato set his cup down on the table. "Evangeline's spirit visited me in private."

"But … if that's the case, why did she disappear before?"

"Evangeline didn't appear to me the same way she appeared to you. I'm a miraculous. I have all sorts of important encounters through dreams. That isn't to say I haven't dreamt of Evangeline before. As a matter of fact,

I frequently dream of Evangeline, as vividly as I've ever dreamt of anything. So in a way, I've never really lost touch with her. Not completely anyway."

Before he could offer more explanation, Pyro burst through the door, almost slipping on the trail of water Katya had left behind.

"I take it a little mermaid is running around here somewhere?"

Staccato snickered and took another sip of his coffee. "Katya."

Pyro yawned and stretched his arms over his head. "Doesn't surprise me." He patted Staccato on the shoulder. "Happy birthday, by the way."

Staccato nodded his thanks as Pyro collapsed to a seat on the sofa and unfolded a newspaper.

"Feeling old yet?"

"Considering Katya had to remind me it was today, I should say so. What with Sonata's being only the day after, I should have remembered."

Their attention turned to the entry as Lydia's and Katya's tails appeared above the water. Katya would've ran straight back into the sunroom had Lydia not stopped her by pulling on her braid.

"Not so fast, little fish. We don't want someone slipping in your puddles."

When they emerged from the hall, Lydia bent over Staccato and kissed him on the head.

"Happy birthday, Papa."

Staccato said nothing but reached up and pressed Lydia's cheek affectionately to his.

In a flash of blinding light, Cicada flew in like a swift sunrise, Skelter trailing idly behind her.

"Alright, who went into the library and hid all the law books?"

As Skelter passed, he nudged her in the side and tossed his head towards Pyro who was ducking behind his newspaper. Cicada's yellow glow turned hot pink, and she tore her head straight through the front page.

"I know it was you, Pyro! That's why you were in the library last night!"

Pyro rolled his eyes and wrenched his paper off of Cicada's head.

"Can you blame me for wanting to be spared your obnoxious spouting once you had devoured them all?"

Cicada balled her fists. "Pasha made me his advisor! I have to study!"

Pyro groaned as he turned his attention to Pasha. "I thought you were going to offer her representation on the Ecliptic Council."

Pasha shrugged. "She wanted to be closer to the resistance, and we'd miss her if she had to be in Libra all the time. Besides, I think Cici will be an excellent advisor."

Pyro jammed an accusatory finger in Skelter's direction. "And you! I thought we were partners in crime! Since when are you the tattletale? That's Staccato's job!"

Staccato turned to look over his shoulder and stuck out his tongue.

"Boys, behave," warned Lydia.

With a beautifully mastered expression of pure righteousness, Skelter's hands fluttered sanctimoniously, spelling out something akin to, "Since you mentor Faina, and Sonata has Pasha, Staccato told me to look after Cicada."

"Oh, Staccato told you, did he?" Pyro sputtered. "Well, excuse me!"

At the sound of Pyro's voice, Sonata fished her head around the archway. "Pyro Anomaly, you better not be bullying Staccato on his birthday." She swept into the room to kiss Staccato's cheek.

"How come he gets a kiss before me?" whined Pyro.

Sonata reached out and combed her fingers affectionately through Pyro's hair.

"It's his birthday, silly."

"I see. In that case, can I be the first one to kiss you tomorrow?"

Sonata giggled and pecked Pyro's lips. "You always are."

Outside there was a tremendous splash, the gasp of a maid, and something like the sound of a platter rolling across the tile like a penny.

"Well," chuckled Pasha. "Faina is up."

Sure enough, Faina came skidding into the room immediately after.

"Good morning, everybody!" She gave the back of Pyro's newspaper a hard flick, and bounded towards Pasha. "Any mail for me this morning?"

Pasha shook his head. "Not that I know of. You still waiting to hear back from those auditions?"

With the announcement that Draco would no longer be presiding over Ursa, two famous theatrical producers known as Digby and Johnson had been looking to reopen their old theater in Polaris. According to Sonata, the Polaris National Opera House had once been the epitome of high-class performing arts. In the spirit of things, they had decided to hold open auditions for their musical production of *Meet Me Under the Stars*, and Faina had leapt at the chance to attend.

She sighed and hung her head low. "Yeah. I should have heard from them by now."

Slowly, Pyro slid an envelope from his pocket and held it high over his head.

"You wouldn't happen to mean this old thing, would you? Postman said it got lost in the mail. It's addressed to 'The Maniacal Beastie at Alveare.'"

Faina snatched the envelope out of his hands. "It was addressed to you then?"

Staccato threw back his head and laughed. "Touché, Faina!"

Pyro tousled her hair. "Yeah, yeah, she's catching up to me."

Faina ripped apart the envelope, desperate to claw her way to the letter inside. Cicada hovered over her shoulder as she read. Everyone fell silent. Faina was the stillest Pasha had ever seen her. Then all at once she leapt to her feet screaming. Melodious, who was just entering the room, stumbled backwards against the doorway. In an attempt to get her to speak clearly, Pasha grabbed Faina by the shoulders.

"Did you get it?"

Faina nodded her head and squealed. "I got the lead, Pasha! I got the lead!"

Pasha threw his hands in the air. "You did it!"

"I did it!"

Grabbing her around the waist, Pasha swung Faina in a circle. Lydia smiled and lifted an eyebrow.

"I didn't hear you two the first time. Did she get it?"

Pasha dipped Faina backwards. "She got it, Ma!"

Lydia rose from her seat. "Oh, that's wonderful, darling! I'm so proud of you!"

As she folded her arms around them she placed a finger on each of their necks, and their emotional high subdued to a pleasant contentment. Pyro waggled his eyebrows.

"We've got to stop letting them have coffee so early in the morning."

Pasha and Faina settled back into the armchair together, quietly satisfied. At last, Pyro set aside his shredded newspaper.

"Well, Staccato, I think you've finally made it out of the papers."

Staccato heaved a sigh of relief. "All scandals die eventually."

"Did you ever find out where Samael found that diary?"

"I can only assume it was misplaced when we were packing up for the Other. Evangeline was never very organized. She cleaned by hiding things in whatever place was available." He chuckled. "I once found an entire set of jacks in my sock drawer. She must've stashed it somewhere inside her studio, which of course was raided after the Land Lock. Javaid believes the C.O.N. was looking for information about the mirror, and that's how the diary came into Samael's possession. I must admit I was surprised. I thought I had it locked away with our wedding pictures. Apparently, I was wrong."

Everyone stared at him in silence.

"What? What are you all looking at me for?"

Faina was the first to speak. "You have pictures?"

"Yes." His eyes darted around the circle when it finally struck him. "Oh, uh, would you like to see them?" He seemed a little unsure of himself.

"Yes!" they cried out in unison.

Staccato gave a start of surprise. "Oh, um, well, I'll just go get them then. …" He stumbled to his feet and headed down the passage. Pyro threw up his hands.

"Geez, mate! After keeping your secrets all these years we deserve to see this mystery marriage!"

Chapter 56:
Pasha's Coronation

Pasha's eyes swelled as he stepped back from the mirror to take himself in. His eyes trickled over the hunter green uniform.

"I feel like a prince."

His mother adjusted the silver epaulets at his shoulders. "Well, you look like a king."

Embroidered chains of platinum thread wove between the silver buttons of his waistcoat, looking as though they had traced a new constellation on his chest. Each stud was engraved with the national motto in lithe, flowery script—"E Tenebris in Lucem:" light out of darkness—and encircled a four-pointed star.

Two opal discs the size of sand dollars fastened a cloak of rich navy blue velvet to his shoulders. Pasha turned to admire it again in the looking glass. All the sparkling asterisms of the midnight sky had been stitched into the fabric with threads of light spun by esperites from Kochab. The same process had been repeated around the border of the mantle in a pattern of clamshells and stardust.

It had taken several weeks to remember all the meanings of the various decorations and medals which littered his uniform. There was an opal ring, a nautilus, an olive branch, and much more. But his favorite was a silver pin in the shape of Ursa Major and Ursa Minor attached at the collar, a sapphire sitting in place of each star.

His mother and sister matched him in flowing dresses of green chiffon. Silver sashes were draped across their shoulders and they each wore emerald coronets.

Lydia encircled her arms around Pasha's shoulders. "Your father would be proud."

Pasha smiled and laid his cheek lovingly against his mother's. There was a knock at the door, and the butler dipped his head in.

"It's time."

They followed him towards the flood of pounding drums. Rapturous music poured through the open doors. An astronomical number of mermaids had gathered in the watery horizon, many waving twin banners, one for Ursa with two silver bears embroidered against evergreen silk, and one for Karkinos with a white crab pinching a honeycomb between its claws. They serenaded at the top of their voices in wild, celestial choruses.

The mild heat of the sun nurtured the fragrance of the fresh grass until it rose up around them in a summery perfume. A mosaic of people flanked the streets, many of them Fay. Everyone cheered and bashed tambourines with mossy streamers. Women wore flower crowns knitted with iris and snowdrop. Men pinned silver roses to green lapels. Children carried tinsel stars they had crafted at school and waved them back and forth.

Stationed near the front of the crowd were the Coulter brothers, merrier than Pasha could ever have pictured them. They each gave a wave, and Pasha smiled.

At the bottom of the stairs, Harpagos waited, clothed in sidereal splendor. Seashells had been braided into his smoky tail and mane, and flowers circled his ears. As the crowd cheered, Pasha mounted his steed. A young mermaid blew on her conch, and liveried attendants helped his mother and sister onto their own pegasi.

Birds sang as the family paraded beneath the June sunshine to a stage at the edge of the sea. Sonata stood beneath a cascade of water fountaining from her father's trident. Pearls dripped along her forehead from a massive white crown fanning over her curls. A bay scallop pinned her blue chiton at the shoulder. Two Karkonian footmen in shell-encrusted armor stood by her side.

Pasha and his family dismounted and took their places on the platform. Below the stage, Pasha's friends were lined up in the front row, all sporting their finest green attire. Pasha quickly picked out Faina brandishing a wand of streamers and bells over her head. She smiled so brightly she could have been laughing. He could not help but think that a girl had never looked so good in freckles. To him they might as well have been diamonds.

Pasha kowtowed before Sonata on one knee, as a white shell was passed from hand to hand. She tilted his head back. Salt water rinsed from the crest of his forehead, past the tip of his nose, and bled between his lips.

In traditional mermaid blessing, Sonata bent down to kiss Pasha's brow. Light caught in his eyes as she lifted the crown into the air. Stars rose up on a single point around the perimeter. Light mined from the seven auroras were embedded at the center in geometric prisms of color. As Sonata fitted the coronet to his head, the intricate cords of metal felt cool against his skin.

A trident was placed in Sonata's hand, and, standing tall, she tapped each of Pasha's shoulders.

"Pavlo Ruslanovitch Chevalsky, I hereby crown you sovereign King of Ursa! May your seas be kind and your shells never be broken. You may rise."

Pasha obeyed and turned to face the crowd. With pride and elegance, Sonata lifted her trident high above her head.

"Long live the King!"

A felicitous throb undulated throughout the crowd as bells shook and Fay sang out.

"Long live the King!"

Chapter 57:
A Home

Staccato was scheduled to move into his own house the day after Pasha's coronation. As far as he knew, it was down the street from Alfbern Hall. Having been nomadic for the better part of ten years, Staccato had asked Sonata to search through the available properties and choose whichever residence she thought suitable.

He had never bothered to look at the property Sonata had chosen. Her judgement was sound. So he was quite surprised when they pulled up in front of the gates of Alfbern Hall.

"Sonata, why are we stopping here?"

Sonata shrugged. "Didn't I tell you? Lydia is coming with us. She hasn't seen the house yet either."

This seemed like a reasonable answer, and yet he could tell Sonata was up to something. She was never a good liar. The guard waved the motorcar through. Staccato shut his eyes and laid his head back. The car slowed and the engine shut off. Someone opened his door. Confused, Staccato opened his eyes. Pasha stood there holding the door open.

"Well, are you finally ready to settle?"

Staccato stared at him, baffled. As Pasha stepped aside, he found himself gazing upon a small, Victorian-style house with a white porch. Surrounding the wrought iron fence was a hedge of cabbage roses. Sonata let out a giggle.

"Surprise!"

Staccato wrenched around to look out the opposite window. They were a stone's throw from the palace. He faced Pasha again. Lydia came forward and helped him up by the arm.

"Well, Papa, aren't you coming?"

Staccato took a step back. "I don't understand."

Pasha elbowed Staccato in the ribs. "You told Sonata to pick out the most suitable property."

Katya took him by the hand and swung it back and forth. "And what's more suitable than right next door to your family?"

Lydia smiled and placed her hands on her hips. "Would you like me to explain it to you? You live here."

Staccato put a hand over his mouth. He didn't know whether he was going to laugh or cry, but he certainly didn't want to cry with everyone staring at him. Lydia put her hand in his and led him towards the front door.

"Come, Papa, you're finally home!"

The Glassblower

The Glassblower
Epilogue
Laudine's heels clicked softly on the checkered floor as she wandered the dark shadows of the sitting room in Apophis Manor. She was not unaccustomed to dark interiors, indeed she relished in dim, lightless spaces, which, in her opinion, were glamorous, and worldly. She considered those with darker preferences to be of a more sophisticated, enlightened persuasion. And yet there was a heaviness to the shade in the room not present in her own gloomy abode. At times it was rather difficult to see.

What's more, there was a strange emptiness that seemed incongruous with the ostentatious, almost fusty decor. With the sheer amount of gilded vases, fluffy roses, and brass figures it should have felt as though the very walls were closing in on her. And yet she simply could not shake the feeling of being adrift in a black sea, no moon, and no lamp to light her boat. Pure nothingness.

She retrieved a handkerchief from her pocket and, reaching under her veil, dabbed at her eyes. Grief over Edom seemed the only logical explanation.

"My dear woman…" a soft, melodic voice materialized behind her.

Startled, Laudine gasped and turned. The black shadows appeared to melt and pool onto the floor. Laudine blinked. It wasn't the shadows that were moving but a black, silken robe dragging across the tile smoothly and soundlessly. Her eyes traveled the length of the body, until she found herself looking upon the handsome, sympathetic face of Cobra Samael. He took her hand and kissed it.

"Allow me to offer my deepest condolences."

She clumsily placed one foot behind the other and, hesitating twice, bent into an awkward curtsy.

"It is an honor to meet you, Your—" Laudine fumbled for the correct title. "Your Majesty."

Her eyes met the Cobra's with caution. A placid smile touched his lips. Laudine felt her skin prickle. His features were so comely, so perfectly formed. It seemed impossible not to grow flustered under the gaze of his kind, innocent, blue eyes. There was a pureness about him that could only be likened to an angel.

"Your husband was a favored servant of mine." With a long sweep of his arm, he gestured for her to sit in one of the large, velvet armchairs. Laudine obliged. As she sank into the sumptuous cushions, an overwhelming perfume of dried roses seemed to seep from the fibers.

Samael took the seat across from her, folding his long, delicate hands beneath his perfect chin.

"Tell me, what is it I can do for Cottonmouth's lovely widow?"

Laudine swallowed and swept a lock of hair behind her ear. "Well, you see, Your Majesty, that's just it. I have no plans to be my husband's widow." She shook her head. The words had sounded poetic in her mind, but she now felt foolish.

Samael's long eyelashes drew down in a slow blink. The corners of his well-defined lips turned upwards as he snickered softly.

"My dear Mrs. Cottonmouth, why do you hesitate so? You needn't be anxious. I know precisely why you are here." His eyes floated towards the neckline of her dress where her wedding band now rested at the end of a golden chain. "You wish to resurrect your husband."

Laudine fingered the wedding band. "I've managed to trap his soul inside my wedding ring—"

"However, that's not enough," Samael finished for her. "To bring back Edom would require a ceremony of like-minded beings … and of course, the body."

"I'm afraid I could not transport him on my own."

Samael twisted a strand of his silky, chestnut hair around his finger.

"Naturally." His gaze travelled to her calves, prompting Laudine to feel somewhat exposed. She coughed and tucked her legs closer to the chair.

"Mrs. Cottonmouth," Samael continued, "as much as I hate to burden you under such lamentable circumstances, our best solution to dealing with grief often requires casting aside the black mantle, and rising to our feet once more."

Laudine released a heavy sigh. She was afraid he might say something like this.

"You mean helping others, or lending my hand to some charitable cause in order to distract myself from my grief."

Samael's features came alive with amused astonishment.

"What?" He slapped the arm of his chair and, throwing back his head let out a hearty laugh. "Of course not! I was speaking of revenge."

Laudine twisted her black, leather gloves in her lap. "O—oh. You were?"

His fangs seemed to glimmer as he bit at his thumbnail and chuckled. "Yes, of course, my dear woman. You see, your enemy is my enemy.

This same pack of brats responsible for killing your husband are also responsible for taking away my land, removing my country's representation from the Ecliptic Council, and denying my people fresh blood." He leaned forward. "But you, Madame, you and your faithful husband came so close to liberating me of their nuisance. Just as I came so close to barring that boy from the throne." He steepled his fingers together. "It has come to my attention that perhaps if you and I put our heads together we may be able to finish the job once and for all." He stopped and stroked his beard. "I suppose what I'm trying to say is this: if you help me get rid of that blasted boy and his little band of rebels, I will send my servants to fetch the remains of your husband, and organize a ceremony to return his soul to his body."

Laudine let out a cry and clasped her hands over her mouth. "Your Majesty, do you really mean it?"

Samael dragged his head up and down. "Every word."

Without thinking, Laudine cast herself down at his feet. "I will, Your Majesty! I promise to do as you say! Consider me your most faithful servant! You have my word!"

He placed his hand on her head. "Then it is done."

"Oh, thank you! Thank you, Your Majesty! You have no idea how much this means to me!"

Samael took her gently by the wrists and hoisted her to her feet.

"Perhaps I have more of an idea than you think." He ran the tips of his nails across her left cheek and under her chin, lifting her face towards him.

Laudine could not help but feel mortified as he peeled back the veil, exposing the blush his touch had summoned to her cheeks.

"It does my heart good to see the color returned to your complexion."

Laudine observed that the size of his fangs were just large enough to push his lips subtly forward, so that there was a slight pucker to them. She cast her eyes downward, ashamed to have noticed such a thing.

Her mouth went slack as Samael removed her hat and, reaching behind her head, unpinned her abundant hair. The waves tumbled down her back, brushing her spine and shoulders.

He lifted an eyebrow. "You want so much, and yet I sense hesitation in your heart."

Laudine took a step back, wringing her hands. "I—I'm afraid I don't know what you mean, Your Majesty."

Samael knit his eyebrows and smiled weakly. His expression was nothing short of compassionate, paternal even.

"Aren't you a disciple of Primal Instinct?"

Laudine ducked her chin. "Well, yes. I mean, I suppose so."

Samael smirked and shook his head as though Laudine were a small child, a little girl whom he loved and cherished.

"It's only natural you should lack some understanding, what with your isolated living situation out there in the Other." He placed his arm around her and drew her to the gilded mirror hanging on the wall. "The concept of denial, the word 'no' is a tool invented by the Fay as a means for controlling the less privileged in society, those born without magic. But Primal Instinct teaches us to listen to our bodies and put the desires of our heart above all else. Tell me, why would we deny ourselves any good thing?"

Laudine stared back at the mirror and watched her own large, round eyes blink childishly back at her.

"Because maybe what we think is good for us at the time is actually bad?"

"By who's authority? Hmm? Who would know better than you?" He paused and tilted his head thoughtfully to one side. "Allow me to put it this way."

She felt the palms of his hands creep up her arms. His fingers slipped beneath the material of her sweater and slowly pulled it from her shoulders.

"Whatever feels good, whatever makes you happy, whatever guarantees your success is a good thing. Your heart will tell you when something is good, you need only listen." He lowered his lips to her ear. "This is the cause your husband believed in. This is what he died for, Laudine: the freedom to indulge."

Laudine hardly even noticed that he had called her by her first name, and not "Mrs. Cottonmouth."

"I see who you truly are, my dear. I see you, the beauty of your soul, and I know you. You were born into a Puritanical society, a world of restriction, and oppression." He raked his fingers through her hair, and laid his cheek against hers. "Don't let them cage you, my darling. You're better than them. You move boldly forward while everyone else remains stuck in the past. Laudine challenges convention! Laudine refuses to be shackled! You know the truth now. Listen to your heart. What is it you want?"

Laudine stared blankly at the glass for a moment or two.

"I want to be liberated. I want power."

Samael took hold of her chin and turned her head towards him.

"Then allow me to empower you."

The End

Dying to know what happens next? Here's a preview of The Star Catcher to hold you over until Pasha's next adventure!

December 1917

The Proposition

It was clear as Staccato stood before the Warden that she was aware of his surprise at finding her so young. He fidgeted with his hands, something he was not accustomed to doing. It was not the best way to begin things. There was nothing in her expression to suggest his presence inspired any sort of reaction beyond a vague sense of annoyance. But then why should she recognize this strange man with the shaved head and short, scruffy goatee? He'd retired from government service fifteen years ago, and this young woman was barely twenty-five, not much younger than his daughter.

"I'm here to see Mr. Anomaly," he explained in his smooth, grandiose voice.

The Warden's eyes glazed over. "And you are?"

"Sir Staccato Nimbus. Friend of the family."

She crossed her arms and leaned back in her chair. Her eyes rested upon his staff with pernicious hatred. Such attitudes towards Fay were not uncommon these days in Capricorn, but it was still rude.

Staccato sighed and retrieved the note from his pocket.

"The Head of Security said to give this to you when arrived."

The Warden snatched the note from his hands and scanned over the writing with impatient eyes. Staccato raised an elegant eyebrow. Twenty years ago, the Warden's behavior would've been met with severe repercussions, but that was before Sultana Charmion came to power, when her sister ruled the kingdom.

When the Warden finished reading the note, she crumpled the paper in her fist and glared at Staccato with new significance. By now she had probably figured out Staccato was here to arrange for Pyro's release, and unlike Pyro's parents or King Thayer, he was quite capable of pulling it off. Staccato rested one hand upon the head of his staff and the other on his wrist. He threw back his shoulders, showcasing his full height. The Warden was unimpressed.

"You'll need to hand over your staff."

Staccato could have laughed aloud, but of course to do so would've made matters worse. As he turned in his staff, he wondered if it wasn't a blessing the Warden was so young and knew nothing about him. She clearly wasn't aware that he didn't need his staff to wield his powers. She made him sign a piece of a paper on a clipboard, and lead him towards the heavy steel doors with the caution tape.

A sign read "Warning: High Risk Prisoners."

Staccato knew as he passed over the threshold that the cells would be overcrowded with Fay rebels from Aquila and Delphinus, but he wasn't prepared for the inmates' horrible living conditions. Capricorn always found loopholes in the international law, but Staccato didn't fully realize the extent until he looked into the faces of the emaciated prisoners rotting in their beds. Of the countless seraphs all had their wings in vices, even though there was nowhere to fly to. Mermaids sat in tanks hardly bigger than an aquarium. The most any sylph had was a bucket's worth of soil on a stone floor.

There was no telling what they had done to Pyro. Staccato knew from the papers that Pyro had grown up to be an incredibly athletic young man in top physical condition. But whenever he thought of Pyro it was hard to imagine him as anything but a fiery-haired little boy of nine or ten. He hadn't seen Pyro in person since his parents sent him off to boarding school in the Pan.

Staccato followed the Warden around the corner. When his eyes registered what lay at the end of the hall, he let out an audible gasp.

"You've been keeping him inside a water tank?" He could not mask his outrage. "How is he still alive?"

"We monitor his vitals and take him out before any permanent damage is done."

But Staccato was hardly listening. "That's a violation of international law! Capricorn could be expelled from the Ecliptic Council for keeping such a monstrosity!"

The Warden pursed her lips. "Technically we're not breaking any rules. The water is sterile, the temperature is regulated, and as I stated before we're not allowed to confine him any longer than what's safe."

Clearly aggravated, she picked up her pace, making Staccato work to keep up with her. When they reached the door of Pyro's cell, Staccato could fully appreciate what the boy had been made to suffer. His head leaned back against the side of the tank in sleep. His chest rose and fell rapidly. He struggled to breathe. A muzzle covered his face below his nose, and he was now sporting a beard.

The Warden unlocked the door and ushered Staccato inside. It would have been easy to mistake Pyro for his brother with how thin he had grown. The thought was quite disturbing when one considered how differently the two boys had been built. Arson had taken after their mother, tall and statuesque. As for Pyro, despite being muscular and fit, he was always short and stocky. Now the bones in his chest were visible.

Staccato jumped as the Warden banged on the glass. Pyro screwed his eyebrows together and awoke with a start. He met the Warden's eyes begrudgingly.

"You have a visitor." She crossed to the back and ascended a small set of stairs leading to the tank.

Pyro eyed Staccato with foggy scrutiny. Considering Staccato and Pyro were both spies employed by King Thayer, he had expected Pyro to recognize him. But the unfamiliarity in his countenance did not fade away.

The Warden unbuckled Pyro's muzzle and deposited it on a hook beside the machine. Pyro groaned and tried to sit up straight.

"Can I have some water?"

Staccato was surprised at the lack of cheek in his voice. The Warden eyed him over.

"That depends, are you going to spit it at me?"

That was more like it. Pyro's eyes were dull. "Are you gonna punch me if I do?"

"Yes."

Pyro yawned then coughed and shook his head. "Then no. I'll save that for later."

The Warden went to the sink, filled up a glass of water, and much to Staccato's astonishment actually fed it to him. When Pyro finished, he threw back his head in a fit of hacking.

The Warden tapped her foot. "What do you say?"

Pyro wrinkled his nose. "Thanks, Nettie."

The Warden looked as though she might smash the glass over his head. Pyro rolled his eyes.

"Thank you, Ms. Green."

The Warden descended the stairs and pulled out a chair for Staccato.

"If he tries anything funny just press that button on the wall and the guards will come and assist you."

She left the door unlocked behind her and retreated into her office. Staccato sat down. He and Pyro stared at each other in silence as they listened for the noise of her clinking footsteps to die away. Finally, Pyro blinked.

"Who are you?"

"Staccato Nimbus."

"Never heard of you." He closed his eyes and leaned his head back again.

Staccato kept his voice steady, baring in mind that Pyro had been inside this tank nearly every day for the past two months.

"You don't remember me?"

"Should I?" He turned his shoulders and winced. Exasperated, he opened his eyes again and sat up. "Look, did my parents send you or something?"

Staccato nodded his head. "They did."

For some reason the knowledge of this reality annoyed Pyro. "I suppose it was too inconvenient for them to show up themselves."

"Capricorn wouldn't permit them to enter the country."

Staccato could tell Pyro was making an effort to maintain his scowl. His muscles softened a measure or two.

"Well, why are you here? I don't know you. It's not like you can bust me out of here or anything."

"Actually I can."

Pyro's eyes widened. Staccato leaned forward with his elbows on his knees.

"It just so happens that I have a proposition for you. To be honest, I'm surprised you aren't more familiar with me. Not because I knew you as a child, but because you and I happen to work for the same person."

"Are you Thayer's valet or something?"

Pyro was going out of his way to be rude now, and Staccato wasn't sure how much longer he could tolerate it.

"I do undercover work."

But Pyro wasn't listening. "Wait a second, Staccato Nimbus . . . I remember you!" He threw back his head and laughed. "Oh, they used to talk about you all the time in the Saighdeoir!"

Staccato sat tall and straightened his cravat.

"You're the chap who knocked up the queen!"

Staccato's hands dropped. A great power surged beneath the skin of his palms. He instinctively reached for his staff, forgetting he'd left it at the front desk. Pyro continued his guffawing.

"She'd been hauling your ashes how long? Three months? And ol' Bruin still thought the baby was his!" He could hardly contain himself.

Staccato flew at Pyro, knocking over his chair in the process. Pyro's skull banged against the back of the tank. Staccato never had to lift a finger.

"Here's a history lesson for you," Staccato hissed. "I happen to be the most powerful miraculous in history, one of only three who don't need a staff to a wield their powers. In fact, it only makes me weak. I've been fighting the C.O.N. since before you had the motor skills to wipe your nose. I've served the second most powerful kingdom in Voiler under two different monarchs, and held a seat on the Ecliptic Council. I've been knighted in three different countries. I was awarded a Scarlet Scale when I was ten for rescuing Queen Calliope from a fury. King Javaid, whom I am on a first name basis with, made me godfather to his daughter. Suffice to say, Mr. Anomaly, I am an important person. Important enough to kill you and have it swept under the carpet."

He flattened his hand against the glass and willed the water to claw at Pyro's throat. He lowered his voice further still.

"If you ever speak disrespectfully of my wife again, if any foul remark falls out of that stupid, inebriated mouth of yours I will see to it that you have a federal warrant in every country that matters! And the moment they arrest you I will be there to execute you myself!"

Pyro looked as though he were just short of a panic attack as he nodded his head up and down, craning away from the ghostly waves. Staccato removed his hand from the glass. The water fell tame.

"I'm sorry." Pyro took a deep breath, or at least he tried. "S—sorry. I—I been here so long I've forgotten my manners."

Staccato reached out his hand and summoned the chair right side up again.

"According to the papers—and your parents—you forgot them a long time ago."

"Look, Mr. Nimbus. I mean Sir Mr. Nimbus! Should I call you Sir Mr. Nimbus? You said you can get me out of here, right?"

Staccato made himself sound uninterested. "I can, however there's a catch. Are you familiar with the the Cirque De Faye?"

Pyro arched his neck. "Way back in history, when the Fay were still nomadic they put on performances for ordinary folk using their powers and blah, blah, blah. I wasn't half bad at history."

"As you're probably aware, the art form has made quite a comeback in the past decade."

Pyro understood. He bowed his head and groaned. "Oh no, don't tell me Thayer's got you manning that whole undercover circus thing? I told him it was a silly idea!"

"It's panned out far better than I anticipated."

Pyro leaned forward. "How does it work exactly?"

Staccato shrugged. "There are several uses. Traveling undercover enables a group of highly trained professional spies to travel places without looking suspicious. We can hunt down ophidians in the Other without drawing much attention. Best of all, we're frequently hired by well-to-do ophidians and C.O.N. members who like to dabble in Fay arts for the publicity."

They both snickered. Perhaps Pyro really was sorry for offending him. Besides, they had much more in common than one might have anticipated.

"So what do you do?" Pyro inquired. "What's your act?"

Staccato drew back, frowning with dignity. A flicker of fear flashed through Pyro's eyes, no doubt afraid he had insulted him once more.

"I'm the manager! I do not perform."

Pyro appeared genuinely surprised. "Well, why not? I mean, you are the most powerful miraculous in history, aren't you? I'll bet you can do all sorts of amazing things."

Staccato tossed his head to one side. "Well, I do provide illusions for the scenery and . . . well, at this point half the performers are hallucinations. There aren't many of us. Which brings me to my next point. If you agree to come and work for me as a performer I'll bail you out of here."

Pyro's head fell forward as he laughed aloud. "Me? A spangly circus performer?"

"You are a gymnast, aren't you?"

Pyro's face fell. "Well . . . yeah, but—"

"And a powerful igneous."

Pyro glanced from one side of the room to the other. "Yes, but—"

"I'm afraid you've got two choices: spangly circus performer, or half-starved prisoner. Which is it going to be?"

Pyro looked down at the water. Staccato crossed his arms.

"I should inform you that if you decide to come and work for me, a certain code of conduct is expected of you. You see, not only would your parents like your freedom but they'd like to see you straighten out as well. There will be no drinking, at least until you've proven you're responsible enough to handle alcohol. There will be no late night partying. No brothels. Foul language is prohibited."

Pyro lifted an eyebrow. "Blazes, do I have to attend Sunday School as well?"

Staccato slipped him a wry smile. "That won't be necessary. Our strongman is a former reverend."

Pyro smirked. "Sounds like a pretty square deal so far. Alright, Mr. Nimbus. I'll come work for you under one condition."

Staccato looked Pyro over, taking note of the overgrown beard, the bruised veins, the open blisters, and scoffed. "You have a condition?"

"Hear me out, it's only one, a small one . . . I think. See that fella in the cell behind you?"

Staccato looked over his shoulder at the underfed prisoner lying dismally on his cot. He was a young man, maybe even younger than Pyro—who was only twenty-five.

"Yes, I see him."

"He comes too."

Staccato stretched his eyebrows. "You want me to bail two high security prisoners out of Kilgoree?"

If Pyro could've crossed his arms he would've. "It's either both of us or neither of us."

Staccato turned and eyed the prisoner. Only a baby could have been less harmless looking. His brown arms and legs were long and thin. Any lean muscle had eroded away with starvation. He had a broad mouth with a natural smile and thick hair that curled like an expensive china doll's.

Staccato got the feeling from looking at him that if it weren't for his present circumstances he would've been very lively. His eyes scanned up and down the long passage of chained innocents. Freeing a prisoner in Algedi wasn't the same as freeing a prisoner in a place like Pisces, or Taurus.

Staccato stroked his beard. "What's he in for?"

"He tried to strangle Senator Sobek."

Staccato was so startled he almost knocked over his chair a second time. "He what?!"

Pyro lowered his eyebrows. "Do you have any idea the sheer amount of deaths Sobek is responsible for? It's a shame Skelter's bullet didn't kill him!"

Staccato rubbed his temples. "I'm not disapproving!" He sighed impatiently, then stole another glance at the prisoner called Skelter who was now drawing a butterfly with his finger in the grime on the wall. He was almost cartoonish.

"Him? He broke into Vega Hall and physically assaulted Sobek?"

Pyro was grinning as though they were discussing a character like Robin Hood or Sinbad.

"Turns out he's an amazing acrobat! That's how he was able to close to Sobek in the first place. He even slipped through the bars when the Warden was withholding my meals."

Staccato cringed. "She withheld your meals?"

"Yeah, she does that sometimes. But Skelter fed me. He doesn't deserve to be here! I mean, nobody does really, but look at him! How long do you think a fella like him can last in a place like this?"

Staccato cradled his head in his hands. "It's not that simple. Skelter tried to assassinate a government official. Wars have been started over such instances! Great Northern Star! The whole of the Other has been fighting for the past four years after an archduke was gunned down by radicals!"

Pyro glowered at Staccato with a hard, stubborn stare. "Oi, if you're as important as you say you are, Mr. Knighted-In-Three-Countries, you can bust my friend out of Kilgoree for trying to assassinate a murderer, not an archduke, but a man who wiped out an entire kingdom of innocents."

For illustrations and other bonus content check out Morgan True Blum's Instagram page at morgan_true_blum_author_artist